Cobra Woman vs. the Prairie Wolves in the Vortex of the Valley of Darkness

By Michael C. Healy

Netherstoned Press

Cobra Woman vs. the Prairie Wolves in the Vortex of the Valley of Darkness

Cover and book design by Megan Schiller

Netherstoned Press
netherstonedpress.com

ISBN: 979-8-218-65392-7

Dedicated to my three wonderful children, Scott, Megan, and Caitlin

Chapter 1

———

The 1932 Dodge my grandfather had left me was getting noisy as a tractor, sputtering, and coughing like an old woman, its six cylinders straining at the grade. It was a black sedan with wooden spokes and whitewall tires, and body rot along the left back panel. With over 500 miles more to L.A., it was beginning to make me real nervous. Marco had said I wouldn't make it to the county line in this heap. Fooled him. Still, it was shaky and the July heat wasn't helping. I fired up a smoke and opened the window letting the warm desert air swirl around my arm.

I was pressing along Highway 50, a lonely stretch of two-lane blacktop that would eventually take me across the great Sierra Nevada Mountain Range. I had been on the road for two and a half days, sleeping in the car, eating at truck stops, and washing up in skanky gas station bathrooms. With each mile I felt a strange mixture of excitement and fear deep in my gut as I came closer to my new life. My finances amounted to $320 in small bills, money I had saved over the past six months from odd jobs back home, working at Marco's café on the road outside of town, the WOLF Theater, and the Kendall Mortuary. Royce Kendall, the owner, was my father, an ex major from World War I who, these days, feared communists were everywhere. After all it was 1955 and the red scare was pervasive across the land, and Royce thought Senator Joseph McCarthy was a saint. I'm Charles Alvin Kendall, but most folks call me Tuckie. It's a nickname I've had since I was six. Royce hated it and wouldn't allow it to be used in the house.

I figured once I got to L.A., Hollywood to be exact, and got my $500 prize money I'd be in good shape, at least for a while until they started paying me to write my movie. Every now and then I would check the letter, addressed to me, to remind me that I had to be at Starburst/Mead Productions before 5 p.m. on Friday or forfeit my prize. It was now Wednesday, late afternoon, which only added to my anxiety.

I peered ahead over the dashboard, squinting into the golden dusk sun. The narrow ribbon of black top stretched out across the seemingly endless high desert country as far as the eye could see, diminishing into the far horizon. Heat waves rose up along the desert floor, dancing like shimmering wisps of corn silk among the scrub and tumbleweed. According to my roadmap I would be crossing over the Utah-Nevada border soon. In fact, any minute now. Suddenly the radio, which had been putting out static while going through a dead zone, picked up a local radio station. Hank Williams was singing "Hey Good Lookin," which made me think of Jenny. It was one of her favorite songs. I felt real down about Jenny, about not saying goodbye or telling her I was going out west to start my career. I did tell her about winning the contest I had entered when we were sitting on her front porch a few nights back.

"That's...very nice," she had said. "With your prize money we could maybe...you know..."

I tried to tell her then that I was leaving, but the words wouldn't come. We never really talked about marriage. I supposed it was just one of those things silently assumed. We didn't have to talk about it. Royce once said to me Marriage just happens...like road-kill.

Marco, meanwhile, encouraged me to find myself. "You're 30 years old," he had said to me while working behind the counter of his café. "When you gonna settle down and figure out what your life is going to be, think about the future, and marry that girl? What's her name...Jenifer."
When I told him I was going out to California he just shook his head and said I was crazy.

For most, Jenny Gifford, whom I'd known since high school, was seen as withdrawn, not very social, an outsider like me. Admittedly she was introverted and real shy, except with me. But getting to know her was hard. She looked like the all American girl next door who wore flowery gingham dresses and little makeup. She was not a Vogue beauty, but attractive nevertheless with long straw-colored hair, a creamy complexion, and a sumptuous, inviting figure. But she was very religious, knelt down and prayed every evening with her mother, led by Mr. Gifford, who was also president of the town's bank. One night, down by the lake several years ago, we were making out pretty hard and I tried to feel her up. We were in the back seat of the Dodge. At first she let me and then I started to go further when she suddenly drew away from me and said that God was watching us and would punish us if we did things before we got married. Just then we were hit with a sudden burst of light from the sheriff's car which had pulled up alongside us. Deputy Saunders leaned out the window. Jenny tried to scrunch down.

"Getting a little, Tuckie?" He said laughing. "I seen you Jenny Gifford. Your daddy know what you're doin'? Better get out of here before the boogeyman gets you."

He then drove off. Jenny was devastated with embarrassment.

There was a rumor that Jenny had had a breakdown once, before she and her family moved from Chicago to the prairie lands. She was now 29 and these days she worked at her father's bank. In that capacity she had a desk in back where all she had to deal with was numbers.

Back in May, I happened to pick up a copy of one of them movie magazines in the town's only drugstore. It was called "Silver Screen Play." I found an ad about the contest in the back pages. It called for submitting a story, no more than ten pages, to Starburst/Meade Productions in Hollywood, California. The entry fee was 25 dollars. All entries would become the property of Starburst/Meade Productions. Since I practically lived in the WOLF Theater I figured I knew movies. I had an old portable Underwood in my room at home and so with two fingers pounded out a story in two weeks. I figured it wouldn't amount to much, but submitted it anyway.

The plot was based on a newspaper story I had read a couple of years back about four men who attacked a woman and her husband while camping in the desert on their honeymoon. The husband was murdered and the wife raped and left for dead. I combined that story with a tale that Marco had told me when I was still in grade school about a mythological half-breed Indian called Moon Dancer who could be hired to avenge a wrong. The young woman recovers and hires the half breed to help her track down the four men. He thinks she just wants to turn them over to the authorities. But she is driven by a primal force to seek revenge rather than justice. Meanwhile, the four men turn out to be upstanding citizens in their community who were on a weekend hunting trip that somehow went out of control when they encountered the couple.

Around early July I found the letter from Starburst/Meade Productions on the kitchen table. I figured Zona, my mother's younger sister who was living with Royce and me had left it there after sorting through the mail. When I opened it, I was flabbergasted to see that I had actually won the contest out of a thousand entries. The letter was signed by Bonnie Robertson, Chief Story Editor. But there was something even more thrilling. On the bottom of the letter was a note, hand-written, in ink which said, "Your story is excellent. It shows real talent and I think we will produce it. You should come out to Hollywood and work with us on a screenplay." It was signed Frank Meade, President of Starburst/Meade Productions.

I would have left home earlier to give myself more time on the road, but Adele's funeral was a few days ago. Adele was my mother. Eighteen years ago, 1937, she supposedly ran off with an itinerant house painter named Jimmy Oliver. I was 12 years old at the time. Here's what happened. One afternoon I took a shortcut home from a matinee on a narrow path through a cornfield. It was a cloudless sweaty day. Half way along I stumbled onto a boy and girl doing it, in a small clearing, hidden by a wall of cornstalks. They didn't see me and I didn't get a good look at them, only a portion of the white flesh of their bodies gleaming in the afternoon sun. I was fascinated and scared at the same time. I figured it was one of the girls that used to hang around MARCO's and a boyfriend. A few days later I was on my way home from a movie starring my hero the Wichita Kid when I suddenly found I was being followed by Tony Billings and his little gang who called themselves the Prairie Wolves. They were the town bullies.

I fired up a smoke I'd found on the floor in the WOLF theater, trying to look older and sophisticated. It was real rank. Tony and his boys surrounded me and started laughing.

"Fucking weird dickhead kid," Tony said. "Smoking like he knows what it's about."

"Hey, Tuckie," one of the other boys said. "How come you always wearing them stupid bow ties?"

I tossed the smoke and tried to make a run for it, but was quickly blocked.

"You yellow, Tuckie?" Tony said, his eyes looking mean as he stared, unblinking at me.

I didn't react, but I could feel myself shaking.

"I asked you a question," he said and pushed his hair back from his forehead. "Okay, which one of us you wanna fight?"

I shook my head. They were all bigger and a year or two older than me.

"What? I didn't hear you," Tony said. "I think you said me. Is that right, Tuckie wuckie?"

He reached out and ripped off my bow tie.

"Damn, that's an improvement already." Laughter all around. "You got any money?"

I shook my head. Tony looked at his friends, shrugged and started to take off his shirt. He was stocky and muscular and I figured he'd kill me.

"I know one thing you might like," I blurted out and then told them the story of the boy and girl in the cornfield. I'd seen them twice now. This got their attention. I told them I could lead them to the spot.

"Bull," Tony said.

"I'll show you," I said.

"Ain't you a little young to be liking that kind of thing?" Tony said, laughing. "You ain't getting hard yet are you?"

I could feel myself turn red as a tomato and shook my head. He and his gang conferred and then agreed to let me show them but warned me it had better be worth it. Of course I didn't know if they'd be there. But I figured I could make my escape into the jungle of cornstalks. They'd never find me. Still, I silently prayed the couple would be there.

As I led Tony and his Prairie Wolves along the narrow path through the cornfield I felt, at least for a moment, a sense of power, as if the Wichita Kid, hero of the plains, had taken over. The hours spent in the dark refuge of the WOLF theater had imbedded his image so deep in my being that even today Wichita lurked somewhere in my head. When we came to the spot, which I had marked by tying a blue handkerchief to a cornstalk I told Tony that this was where we turned off the path. That the small clearing where I had seen the couple was about twenty or twenty five feet in.

"You better not be messin' with us," Tony said.

I gave the sign to be quiet, then listened for any sound. Nothing. We got down on all fours and began crawling toward the clearing through the tall stalks. As we got closer I thought I heard a girl's voice talking in hushed tones. Then silence. A few moments later an afternoon breeze whipped through the field and carried with it the sound of a girl moaning. We were now close to the edge of the clearing. I heard Tony say in a loud whisper something to the others. I didn't know what was happening. Tony stood up and counted to three, then rushed ahead of me to the clearing and spread apart the cornstalks to take a peak. The girl screamed. The boy swore. I moved up behind him and saw that it was a grown man and woman, both naked from the waist down, scrambling to get their clothes. The others began bombarding the couple with corn husks. For less than a heartbeat the woman turned back, as if to see who the intruders were and then ran, disappearing behind the man into the thick cover of the cornfield. But in that instant our eyes locked and it was like my blood had suddenly been drained out of me.

"Wow," Tony said. "They were doing it, fucking like bunnies."

"Who were they?" One of the other boys asked.

"Don't know," Tony said. "I didn't get a good look at their faces, if you know what I mean."

"What about you, Tuckie?" Tony said. "You see 'em?"

I shook my head and left feeling a little sick. As I made my way back to the path I could hear them laughing, as if to celebrate a momentous event.

When I got home, Royce slapped me across the ear for being late. That night I stayed in my room, missing dinner. I mostly lay still on my bed staring at the ceiling. When it was almost midnight Adele came into my room, knelt down by the bed and began stroking my forehead. I did not look at her.

"I hope someday you'll understand, sweet pea," she whispered.

I shut my eyes. She leaned over and kissed me lightly on my forehead.

"Mamma loves you," Adele continued. "I ...I have to leave. I can't live with your father any longer. Charles," she said, and I knew she was crying. "I'm going away with Jim. He's a good man and I love him. We're going out to California, to Los Angeles to get a new start. Maybe when we're settled I'll send for you. Would you like that?"

I hate you," I said without looking at her.

So, Adele, one bag in hand, quietly slipped away in those early morning hours. I got up and looked out the window and could just make her out walking down the path to the road, her figure silhouetted in the moonlight. And then she was gone.

Adele never got further than down the road apiece. Her remains were found in a shallow grave all these years later by a couple walking in a field just off the road with a dog. It was the dog that discovered the burial site. The strange thing was, I'd gotten a postcard once signed by Adele from Los Angeles.

Rain was coming down hard during the funeral. This was unusual for dog days in the prairie lands, but not unexpected. It had been overcast all morning with heavy dark clouds moving in from the south by late afternoon. Why did it always rain at burials? Well, it was always that way in the movies anyway. There was a zest in the smell of the wet earth that blunted the otherwise sultry summer air. As I gazed down at the enlarged picture of Adele on top of the coffin, I was struck by how full of life her large eyes were, staring back at me. The picture was taken when she was in her 20s. Some thought she looked just like Paulette Goddard. I wondered if she would have left if I hadn't seen her that day in the cornfield. A real creepy feeling came over me at the thought. Zona, who was standing next to me reached over with her right hand as if to push me back a little.

"You'll fall in you get any closer to the edge," she said.

Zona had been adopted by Adele's parents when she was an adolescent after her parents died in an auto accident. She was looked upon as Adele's younger sister and my aunt. Zona, a high school teacher, was 34, not much older than me. Not long after Adele had gone, she got caught up in some scandal with one of her students, was apparently dismissed and so came and essentially took Adele's place, helping run the house and keeping Royce company, a life of servitude, if you ask me.

After the funeral, people were invited to the house for refreshments and cocktails. Marco showed up with Vera Fouts, a former waitress of his who had once worked with Adele in the café. She was a thin women with mousey brown hair and a mass of freckles covering her face. She hugged me.

"So sorry about your mother, Charles," Vera said. "Adele was such a beautiful woman and here we thought she was out in California all these years. I told her not to…" She stopped and wiped a tear away from her eye, then smiled and held me at arms length. "And look at you. How you've grown. You must be over six feet. Who'd ever thought!"

Marco Bogdana, who was more like a father to me than Royce, hugged me hard. He taught me how to fish, and fry cook. Adele had worked for him for years as a waitress since her teens.

"Do they know what happened to her?" He said.

I shook my head.

"Sheriff Connors said that it looked like she had been murdered, beaten to death with a blunt instrument, according to the county medical examiner." I shrugged. "But he added too many years have gone by to make any final determination. He said they will investigate and keep a file open."

"There was that house painter she was...well she never told me his name," Vera said.

I shrugged.

"Where's Jenny?" Marco asked.

"She had to work," I said.

"On Saturday?" Vera said.

"She works in her father's bank and sometimes has to go in on Saturdays to oversee the week's receipts and reconcile the books."

Suddenly Royce was upon us carrying a drink, his girth pressing his stained white shirt out between his suspenders.

"I'm surprised to see you here, Marco," Royce said in a hostile tone.

"Hello, Royce," Vera injected in a high, friendly voice.

Royce ignored her and kept a hard gaze on Marco with tiny slits for eyes.

"I came to pay my respects and condolences," Marco said.

"Well, now that you have, you can leave," Royce said. "I don't want you in my house. Not now, not ever. And as for Adele...well she made her goddamned bed, didn't she."

"Marco's my guest," I said.

After giving Royce an equally hard stare, Marco turned and left. Vera shook her head and followed. That evening, Zona joined me on the front porch. The rain had settled down to a drizzle. We both smoked and watched the last vestiges of a purple sun sinking below the horizon.

13

"He means well," Zona said.

"He's a son of a bitch," I said. "He still thinks I'm 12."

"You know I think time stood still for him when Adele left," she said.

"How do you stand it?" I asked.

Zona took a drag on her smoke and pondered the question.

"Guess I don't have too many options," she said. "I know he seems gruff some times, but there is another side to him."

"Really," I said. "I've never seen it."

Later after dinner I told Zona and a drunk and belligerent Royce that I was leaving for L.A. the next morning to start my career. Royce just said good riddance and that I could go and join all those fellow travelers out there in that heathen land. He also said I would be out of his will and then stumbled his way upstairs for the night. Zona gave me a hug and wished me well. Soon there was a knock at the door. It was Sheriff Connors and Deputy Saunders. The Sheriff wanted to know if we knew the name of the itinerant painter Adele was supposed to have left with. We answered no. The Sheriff and his deputy left, assuring us again that even though it was a cold case they would keep it open. After they left, Zona gave me a kiss on the cheek and retired. I watched television for a while, then went up to my room, packed my ancient leather bag and put it next to my door with the Underwood. Then I took one last thing I had hidden under the bottom drawer of my dresser – the 44 gun grandfather had left me along with the Dodge. It was inside a cloth bag. I put it in the suitcase and would later hide it in the car. The Wichita Kid also used a 44 in all of his movies which made having it even more special.

As I drifted off, I realized I was the only one who knew the whole name of the man Adele went to meet that night so many years ago – Jimmy Oliver. That's because Adele never told anyone else except me. The one thing I remembered about him was that he had a purplish scar on his forehead just above his nose like the mark of Cain.

Chapter 2

―――――

Just as I passed the sign that said "Welcome to Nevada" a new strange noise broke through the din of the motor. It was coming up through the floorboards. Then something snapped and the car was rolling free. My heart sank. It looked like there was nothing but desert as far as the eye could see and the faint outline of mountains in the far distance west.

The car had enough momentum to make it to the peak of an incline. From there it continued free down along an easy grade for about a half mile, all the while dragging whatever part it was that had died. I put the stick in neutral, turned off the engine and sat back. Shit!

Then an amazing thing happened. The high brush along the south side of Highway 50 suddenly gave way to reveal a kind of desert oasis. Fact is, it was a broken down relic of a place. It consisted of a gas station with one pump and a dilapidated log cabin with a crooked sign over the door that said: "Lucky Bob's Roost and Sanitary Café." Still, it looked like an oasis to me.

At first I didn't see anybody around. The place had that dusty deserted ghost town look about it. I jumped out as the car slowed down, turned the wheel a hard left and pushed to get the car off the road and halfway onto the gravel drive of the gas station before it stopped. Sweat poured down my face as I gulped for breath. I shut my eyes against a warm breeze which suddenly came up and pondered my situation.

When I opened them and looked around I saw the girl. She was sitting by herself on the ground near some brush by the road, looking more like an apparition than a real person. Torn jeans at the knees, stained blue shirt and dusty boots. She couldn't have been more than 15 or 16, I thought. But from where I was standing it was hard to tell. A wide brimmed floppy hat cocked to one side threw a shadow across her face. And large pink-framed sunglasses covered her eyes. Still I could see she had a doll-like face surrounded by gobs of tomato red hair which seemed to explode out from under her hat. I watched her for a moment as she worked a cigarette along the corner of her mouth. There was something sad and downtrodden about her.

"What the hell you looking at, cowboy?" She yelled and gave me the finger.

I didn't react, instead turned back to the Dodge. While trying to push the car further into the drive a dark leathery-faced man who looked to be in his 50s appeared from the door of the gas station hut and approached. He was wearing a black and white checkered shirt hanging out over jeans and an oily looking Stetson.

"What's the trouble?" He said.

I pointed underneath the car.

"I think something broke," I said.

The man pushed his hat back, got down on all fours and looked under the car. He stood back up and dusted himself off.

"Well?" I said.

"Shit. You got yourself a problem," he said. "Looks like the universal joint popped, maybe chewed up a bit. Your drive shaft is dragging."

"How long will it take to fix?" I said.

"I ain't no mechanic but I reckon it could take a couple of weeks, maybe more depending on where parts are."

I shut my eyes and took a deep breath.

"I don't have...I've gotta be in L.A. in two days."

The man shook his head.

"This buggy's pretty old," he said. "Might have to send away for parts. Course there might be something in Ely. That's 80 miles up the road."

16

I slumped against the car feeling the day's last rays of heat wash over my face.

"While you're thinkin' on it let's push her over to the side and out of the way," he said. "You're blockin' traffic here."

"What traffic?" I said. "I haven't seen another car along this stretch in over an hour."

The girl was looking at me now. She seemed to be smirking. After we pushed the Dodge out of the way I saw a big black Harley Davidson motorcycle parked out in front of the café.

"That yours?" I asked the man, thinking that's what Star Dancer would ride.

"Nope. Belongs to a fellah inside."

The sun was now sinking behind the mountains. I glanced over at the girl one more time. She was lighting another cigarette. I went into the café. Inside it looked like something left over from the 1800s, maybe originally built by trappers or settlers. Two slot machines stood in one corner and a large ancient mirror reflected the entire room from behind the bar. An Indian woman, who looked to be in her early 40s was sweeping the floor in one corner. The only other customer in the place was a young man sitting at a table near the front. He sat staring at the beer in front of him and tapped his finger on the table as if impatient about something. He had on a black T-shirt with the sleeves rolled up to his shoulders. Tattoos covered his arms. I figured he must be the owner of the motorcycle.

I was standing in front of the bar, still kind of dazed about the Dodge when a gruff voice brought me to.

"What's it gonna be?"

I whirled around to face a tall, lean man about 65 years old with a full white beard and a shock of white hair.

"Something cold," I said. "A Coke."

The man pulled a Coca Cola bottle out of a refrigerator behind the bar, pulled the cap off and put it in front of me.

"Where's the phone?" I said.

The man laughed.

17

"Nearest phone's 80 miles up the road apiece, in Ely."

"You don't have a phone?" I said.

"Like I said, Ely," the man said. "No phone hereabouts. Never needed one."

I took a gulp of the Coke and closed my eyes for a moment, watching my new career disintegrate, captive in this god-forsaken place time had forgotten. I told the man behind the bar I had to be in L.A. in two days.

"I'll tell you Mister, we just don't worry much about time around here. Lot better that way. So, what's the problem?"

I explained about my car and what the man outside said.

"The Yaqui? Gus. He works for me. He's a good man but he doesn't know jack shit about cars. But he's my wife's brother so he works for the station. That's my wife over there sweeping up." The woman looked up and smiled at me. "I'll take a look at it," the man behind the bar went on.

"When?" I said.

The man scratched his head and gave me a faint impatient look.

"Maybe tomorrow," he said.

"I can't wait that long," I said.

"It's gonna be dark soon," he said. "Tomorrow. Maybe even before late afternoon. In the morning I'm supposed to go and look at a vein of Mercury Gus found in the hills the other day."

"Jesus," I said to myself and sighed. "When does the next bus come through?"

The man looked at his watch then shook his head. He turned around and looked at a calendar he had tacked on the wall under the mirror.

"Next Tuesday," he said.

I finished my Coke. I tried to imagine going into the offices of Starburst/Meade Productions after the deadline and explain how I had been stuck in some desert rat hole with no escape. What would the Wichita Kid do? The man must have seen the anguish in my face.

"One thing's sure, Mister," the man behind the counter said, "you ain't goin' anywhere tonight less you can hitch a ride out on the road from a trucker or such but I wouldn't count on it. Besides, you're goin' in the wrong direction if you're heading for L.A. on 50 out here."

"What? That can't be."

"What's your name?"

"Charles," I said. "But I'm called Tuckie."

"Tuckie eh. Alright, Tuckie. I'm Wally. Lucky Bob was my father. He built this place in 1857. I was born not more than eight miles from here in a little community called Baker. Lived here all my life, so I guess I know the terrain. Right?"

I nodded.

"You should have turned south at Spanish Fork on 15 down to Route 66 and then west. Your best bet now is to head for Vegas from Ely and then L.A."

Wally disappeared into the back. Just then the girl with the red hair came in, the screen door slamming behind her. She looked around, then went over and stood over the table where the young man with the motorcycle was sitting. She took off her sunglasses and stood there staring down at him. Even from where I was sitting on a stool at the bar I could see her eyes were hard. I watched in the mirror. The young man stiffened. The girl said in a loud voice that she was tired of sitting outside waiting for him to make up his mind what he was going to do.

"We gonna hang around this crap house all night or get on the road or what?" she said. The young man didn't say anything. He took a swig of his beer and looked over my way as if the girl wasn't even there.

"Fuck, this is lame, man," the girl said.

The Indian woman stopped sweeping and looked over at them, clearly a little shocked at the girl's language. She then resumed her work. I was fascinated by this scene and planned to jot something down in my notebook later. Over the years I had become a spy of people's actions and general behavior which filled several notebooks. A lot of it came from listening to folks who came into MARCO'S. When Jenny returned from

19

college she became a coconspirator, telling me with gleeful relish about juicy gossip she overheard, some in the bank, and recounted some conversations overheard between her parents about folks they believed to be sinners.

After a moment of just standing there being ignored, the girl reached down and snatched the beer bottle out of the man's hand.

"What the shit you think you're doing, fucking skanky chick," he sneered. "Give me my beer back."

The girl took a swig from the bottle and walked around the table.

"We going to San Francisco or not?" She said. "It's almost dark."

"Give me the goddamned beer you little cunt."

She held the beer up high out of reach and danced several feet away from the table, daring him to make a move. He stared at her and ran his hand through his hair, his face taking on a mean expression. He stood up.

"I told you we ain't going to no goddamned San Francisco," he said through clenched teeth. "Ya hear? Got that through your head? We're going down to Albuquerque. I told you that, so stop messing with me. Now give me that beer before I smash your face with it."

"You and who else, asshole!," she screamed.

The young man violently threw the chair half way across the room. He glared at the girl, then motioned for her to come to him with his index finger.

"You don't bring that beer over to me by the time I count to three, I'm going to mess you up good. Right here and now!"

"Oh you got me scared, creep. Start counting."

He quickly counted to three and lunged at the girl, grabbing hold of the beer bottle. As he wrestled it out of her hand what was left drained out onto both of them and the floor. He pushed the girl up against the wall, pushing his elbow into her throat. Her hat fell off. The man pulled back his hand with the beer bottle and was about to smash her in the face. I jumped off the bar stool and was aiming to jump in when Wally's voice boomed from behind.

"Stop right there, son," he said. "You ain't hittin' that little girl with that beer bottle in my place."

"This is my ole lady," the man said. "I'm gonna give her what she's got coming. You hear, old man? So don't give me any shit."

"I see," Wally said. "Well, here's my ole lady and she says it's time for you to be on your way."

The young man turned back to see that Wally had produced a revolver from behind the bar and was pointing it right at him. This was like a movie, I thought, as my adrenalin ratcheted up.

"I'm a crack shot," Wally added.

At that moment the one called Gus appeared in the doorway and stood there with folded arms. The girl's boyfriend stood still for what seemed like an interminable moment. The place was quiet. It was like, what do they call it, a tableau. I was certain the boyfriend was trying to decide whether or not Wally was bluffing. But something in the old man's voice suggested that he would not hesitate to blow the kid's head off if it came down to it.

"David, you better do like the man says," the girl said.

The boyfriend released the girl. She stepped away, rubbing her throat and catching her breath.

"Fuck it. I'm heading for New Mexico," he said to the girl. "You coming or not?"

The girl just stood there.

"Screw you, you little bitch," he said "Good riddance."

He dropped the beer bottle on the floor, turned, and strode out of Lucky Bob's Sanitary Café past Gus who stood aside. The girl ran to the door as the motorcycle roared out onto the highway. "You bastard," she screamed after him, but the sound of the bike had already faded into the night. With one final act of defiance she threw up her arm and gave the finger to the dust of her now departed boyfriend. The girl then came back in and sat back down at the table and lit a cigarette. She could be heard talking to herself under her breath. I turned back to finish my Coke. Wal-

21

ly, who had gone back into the kitchen returned with a bowl of chili and a large spoon which he put in front of me.

"I didn't order this," I said.

"On the house," Wally said. "Best in the west."

I nodded my thanks and took a spoonful. Wally was watching me. It was good, but then suddenly the heat rose in my mouth and throat to white hot, tears filled my eyes. "Jesus!" I screamed and washed down the last few drops of my Coke to put out the fire. "What the hell's in that?" Wally began chuckling.

"Good, eh?" he said. "Did I mention we like our chili spicy in these parts?"

I ordered a beer and nursed it for a while. Gus and Wally's wife disappeared into the back somewhere. The girl went over to the Juke Box in the corner and played Bill Haley and his Comets' "Rock Around The Clock."

She began dancing wildly to the music in the middle of the floor and stopped when she spotted me watching her in the mirror.

"What're you lookin' at cowboy?" The girl said and laughed. She motioned for me to come and join her. I didn't move. There was something about her I found fascinating and scary at the same time. Maybe, I thought, it was the tough, hard-knocks worldliness she came on with that was in diametric contrast with her obvious beauty and look of innocence. I decided she was a little older than I had first thought, more like nineteen or twenty.

"Come on cowboy," she said, "let's do it."

"I'm not a good dancer," I said.

She didn't pursue it. It was as if she had now fallen into a deep space in which she was the only person in the world as she moved about the floor, eyes closed, arms swinging.

"She's a live one, ain't she?" Wally said.

Around 10 o'clock Wally announced that he was shutting the place down for the night.

"It's motel time," he said.

"Are there any motels around here?" I said.

"Nope."

I had been sitting there for four hours now, drinking coffee and jotting down descriptions of the girl and her boyfriend in my notebook. The girl had left long before. I figured she went out on the highway and hitched a ride with someone. Wally had turned all the lights off. It was pitch black outside. A light balmy breeze came in from the west carrying with it the smell of sage. The sky, black and peppered with its sparkling jewels looked clear and mysterious, much like back home.

I climbed into the Dodge and stretched out across the front seat when I heard something.

Chapter 3

———

I was not alone. Something or someone was in here. The Dodge's dome light did not work so I couldn't see anything. I jumped back outside. My first thought was that an animal had somehow gotten into the car. After a few moments I cautiously got back in, leaving the door open for whatever it was to be able to escape. I got my flashlight out of the glove compartment. It didn't work. I lit a match and held it over the back of the front seat. There, stretched out on the back seat, facing away, was the girl. She was sound asleep. Her hat covered her face, but the hair was the giveaway.

"Jesus," I said under my breath. I stood still, wondering what I should do. I was about to wake her and kick her out. But then I thought there probably weren't too many places around to sleep. I stretched out on the front seat and for a time lay awake wondering how I was going to make it to L.A. before the deadline. Eventually I drifted off.

The next thing I knew it was morning. The sun was harsh, beating down on my face through the windshield. I pushed myself upright and rubbed the sleep from my eyes. Two days growth of beard felt like sandpaper along my face. It took me a moment to remember the girl. I turned and looked over the seat. She was still there, only she had changed her position and was now facing front. Her eyes were open, staring blankly at the back of the front seat, as if she were lost in some waking dream. She shifted her eyes up to catch me staring down at her.

"Who the hell are you?" she said, her voice deep and throaty with residual sleep.

"This is my car," I said.

The girl sat up and rubbed her eyes.

"Shit. I'm gone, asshole," she said. "But first I got to go pee and then get some coffee."

I just watched as she reached over and opened the door.

"What's your name?" I said, as she stepped out.

"Fuck off, cowboy," she said and was out of the car.

I watched after her as she made her way unsteadily back to Lucky Bob's Sanitary Café. Gus, who was standing in the door of the gas station, coffee mug in one hand and a cigarette in the other, also watched her. As she passed him he put his mug down and tipped his hat. She ignored him and went on into the café. I grabbed a paper bag which had my razor, soap and toothbrush and started for the café. Gus nodded at me.

"There's an outhouse in back and a sink outside," he said.

I stopped and asked Gus when he thought Wally was going to look at the car. Gus shrugged. Just then Wally's voice came booming from around the side of the gas station office.

"Good morning," he said cheerfully and winked at me. "Guess we better have a look at that car of yours. What is it?

"It's a 1932 Dodge."

"Where'd you get it?"

"My grandfather left it to me," I said.

Wally nodded and took out a bandana from his pocket and wiped his brow.

"There's fresh coffee inside. It'll be a bit fore I get started. I got to get some tools together."

I went around back to the outhouse. The girl was standing there next to it. She was naked except for a pair of black panties with holes in them. She was using paper towels to give herself a wipe-down bath from a bucket of water. Her skin was creamy with a few freckles on the back of her shoulders. Her wet skin shined in the morning sun. I watched her for

26

a moment and could tell she sensed I was there. Without looking at me she said, "Getting a charge, cowboy?" She climbed back into her jeans and put her T-shirt on, gave a backward glanced at me and went into the café through the back door.

The sink was next to the outhouse on the outside wall of the café. There was a tarnished broken mirror hanging over the sink. The water, which was barely a trickle, was cool. I brushed my teeth, shaved off the two days of stubble and went inside. The smell of freshly brewed coffee filled the place. The girl was sitting at a table near the front, sipping coffee, smoking and thumbing absently through an old magazine that must have been lying about. She looked sullen and lost. A trucker came in and ordered some eggs. He caught the girl's attention for a moment.

I sat at the bar. Wally's wife, the Indian woman, put a cup of coffee down in front of me with cream and a small container of sugar. A moment later she added a plate of warm biscuits with a piece of butter and some plum jam. They were the best biscuits I ever had, which was saying something because Adele made great biscuits too. I washed the biscuits down with coffee. A short time later I went back outside. Wally had jacked the car up and was underneath on his back. He soon pushed himself out and announced that the front universal joint was definitely a goner. I felt sick. Wally stood staring at the old Dodge for a time and then said he thought maybe he could "jerry-rig" something.

"What does that mean?" I said.

Wally looked at Gus.

"Man's got to get to L.A. for some important business," he said. "Maybe we can fix it up enough to get him there."

Gus sipped his coffee and nodded.

"If anyone can do it, you can, boss," he said.

"Then again, maybe not," Wally said and turned to me. "Why don't you get lost for a while! Go get some breakfast. My wife makes a mean Heuevos Rancheros.

"What's that?"

"Go," Wally said. "Ask her to make Heuevos Rancheros for you."

"Okay but how much will it cost to fix the car?"

Wally shook his head and looked at Gus. Gus shrugged, looked at me and shook his head. It was obviously the wrong question to ask. Wally started to walk away, telling me he had other things to do out back where he had a junk yard. I apologized and begged him to see what he could do with the Dodge. I could almost feel tears welling up in my eyes. Wally stopped and I could see he was thinking it over. He turned and came back to the car. I didn't utter another word and went into the café. I ordered what Wally had told me. While waiting I noticed the girl was gone. I asked Wally's wife. She told me the girl had left, caught a ride with the trucker heading west.

"She's a wild one," Wally's wife said.

After the Mexican breakfast I rummaged through some old newspapers lying around to kill time. I went outside and sat in the shade on the porch of the café and smoked. At around two o'clock Wally summoned me over. I watched as he took the Dodge for a short drive around the parking apron in front of the station. It made some strange noises I didn't recognize, but it was working and I suddenly felt the great weight of the last 20 hours lifted. Wally charged me $20.00 for the work and told me to take it easy on the road and I might make it to L.A. But I should have the car fixed for real when I got there.

"Nothing holding it together but spit and chewing tobacco," he said. "Remember, when you get to Ely turn south on U.S. 6 and head for Vegas. From there it's a straight run into L.A."

I thanked Wally, got in the car and eased out onto 50 heading west, very slowly at first. After about ten miles I settled on a cruising speed of 45 miles an hour and hit Ely by 4:15. I was hungry and stopped to get myself a hamburger and soda to go at the bowling alley downtown. When I came out I thought I spotted the girl. She had her back to me, but the gobs of red hair and hat gave her away. I moved around to the right so I could get a better look. She was talking to a man on the street who kept shaking his head and trying to get away from her. He finally jogged across

28

the street. She cursed him and gave him the finger, then turned and spotted me.

She made a face which I figured was her version of recognition. I did not react. Instead I crossed the street and got into to my car. Just as I turned the ignition the door flew open on the passenger side and in hopped the girl, closing the door behind her.

"What're you doing?" I said.

She was looking straight ahead.

"Can I have a bite of your hamburger? I'm really hungry, man. That asshole back there on the street wouldn't give me any money."

I thought it odd that I had to deal with her profile. I handed her the hamburger. Continuing to look straight ahead she wolfed it down until it was gone.

"What the hell are you doing?" I said. "I thought you were only going to take a bite."

She wiped her mouth with the back of her hand.

I took a swallow from my soda. The girl reached over and took it out of my hand, finished it and tossed the empty bottle into the back seat.

"You going to San Francisco, cowboy?" She said.

For a long moment I just sat there thinking I should have locked the car door.

"No. I'm going to L.A."

She sighed and settled back in the seat. Finally she turned to face me, removed her pink sunglasses and smiled. She had very large blue eyes. I have to admit her smile was like an unexpected gift, suddenly very warm and seductive.

"Why don't we go to San Francisco," she said. "We could have fun there, you know. People don't bug you there. I have friends that would put us up. What do you say? What's in L.A. anyway? I've been there. Nothing. Smog, that's what. How about going to San Francisco?"

I shook my head.

"I have to go to L.A."

"What for, cowboy?" She said, trying to be coquettish.

"You really want to know?" I said.

"What is it, a big secret or something? You a spy or cop? What the fuck?"

I fired up a smoke and gave one to the girl, then gave her the short version of the whole thing about the contest and my new career and eventually marrying the girl back home.

The girl looked incredulous. She took a long hard pull on the cigarette, blew out the smoke and then laughed.

"Well ain't that a sweet story," she said. "I mean it's sooo American."

She asked to borrow money from me because her boyfriend left with all her money.

"My mama didn't raise me to be a beggar," she said. "She'd skin me alive she ever saw me panhandling like I was doing before."

I looked at my watch and put the car into gear, keeping my foot on the clutch.

"Where's your mom now?"

"Dead. She was drunk and got run over by a truck in Virginia," she said.

"Oh, sorry," I said. "You going to hop out now?"

"What about some money for a poor orphan girl?"

I explained my financial circumstances. I waited for her to get out but she didn't move.

"Shit," she said, sounding very annoyed. "Just drop me off at the juncture."

I pulled out and headed for U.S. 6.

"What's your name, cowboy?" She said.

"Charles. Back home folks call me Tuckie. What are you called?"

"Silky," she said.

"Never heard a name like that before," I said. "Family name?"

Silky was silent for a moment. Then she said, "Forget my name. I gave it to myself. And what kind of a stupid name is Tuckie?

I explained that a three year old girl back home called me that when I was six. It stuck.

"Real cute," she said with a big hint of sarcasm. "You ever smoke dope?"

I shook my head.

"It makes you feel real good. I know where we can score some in San Francisco."

I ignored her. At that point Silky came up with a story about how she had had a baby when she was 15 and had to drop out of school to take care of it and how the father, the son of a family that was friends with her family, beat her up when he found out she was pregnant. Soon after, he disappeared for a couple of years. One day he showed up and took her baby, a beautiful little girl. She heard he was living with a woman in San Francisco and she had to go and rescue her baby. By the end of the story she was crying, or if not, doing a very good job of acting. I couldn't tell.

After a long silence, as we got closer to the juncture, she stopped crying and smiled at me as if she was finished with one story and ready to go on to the next.

"I'll give you a great blowjob if you take me to San Francisco," she said.

I chuckled. This girl who calls herself Silky is like a vixen, I thought and then wondered if that was the right term.

"I'm going to L.A." I said, pushing a tone of finality.

"Bastard," she said under her breath.

She did not get out of the car when we reached the juncture of highways.

Chapter 4

———

Silky fell asleep sometime before Barstow. Up to that point the conversation had been sparse. When Silky did say something it usually came out in staccato-like bursts, the words tumbling over each other as they came charging out of her. She had a whiskey voice which contrasted with her youth and looks.

Sometime later we stopped for coffee. Back in the car I watched Silky as she slept, her face turned toward me resting against the seat, her hat pushed way back. After finishing my coffee I impulsively grabbed my pencil and notebook from the glove compartment and jotted down remembrances about our encounters so far, and attempted a description of her. It was twilight and getting harder to see the details of her face. I leaned closer to her and noticed she also had a sprinkling of tiny freckles across the bridge of her nose and cheeks. Suddenly those great blue eyes of Silky's snapped opened.

"What in the damn hell are you doing, buster?" she said. "Trying to kiss me?"

"Sorry," I said. "I was just taking some notes."

She pushed herself up.

"Yeah, bullshit!" She said. "If you wanna get laid, just say so. Be a man. Don't go creeping around when a girl's asleep."

I pushed the notebook at her. Without looking at it she tossed it onto the back seat.

"Forget it," she said. "Where are we?"

"I don't know," I said. "Couple of hours or more out of L.A."

Silky went back to sleep. The heat coming through the Mojave Desert along Interstate 15 had been oppressive. Thankfully as night approached it got cooler. When I reached the outskirts of Los Angeles, passing the county line the countryside looked very much like the farm country I'd left more than 2000 miles ago. That changed soon enough as I hit downtown and got on the Hollywood Freeway.

I got off at the Vermont Avenue Exit on the eastern edge of Hollywood. We stopped at a small café on Santa Monica Boulevard, ordered cheeseburgers, fries and two coffees. We sat in the only empty booth left in the place. It was next to the front window which looked out at the dark neighborhood. While waiting for our order Silky stretched out on the Naugahyde booth seat, letting her legs dangle over the edge into the aisle. I was feeling a little embarrassed as if she were an uncontrollable adolescent in my charge.

"Couldn't you sit up straight," I said.

She shot back up.

"What're you my old man or something?" She said in a loud voice. "You're not my father, asshole. And you wouldn't want to be because he's the biggest slime ever walked the earth."

The food arrived. The waitress looked at Silky askance as she walked back toward the kitchen. Silky gave the waitress the evil eye and then began to devour her cheeseburger.

"Let's get a motel," Silky said when she was halfway through her burger. "I need to sleep in a goddamned bed, you know. I haven't slept in one for over a week now. My ole man, that creep David back there in Nevada, he would never spring for one. Cheap cocksucker!"

A middle aged couple in the next booth right behind Silky spun their heads around. Their expressions left no doubt that they wanted to see what kind of a young woman would use such language. I heard the woman mumble that the redheaded girl must be some kind of lowlife prostitute. Silky overheard the remark, laughed and turned to the couple over the back of her booth seat.

"Sex, drugs and grabbing life by the balls, lady," she said. "That's what it's all about."

Silky then howled with laughter. The woman turned away. Silky looked at me. By this time I had slid down in my seat as far as I could.

"What's the matter with you?" She said.

"Let's get out of here," I said.

"You going to stiff me on getting a room, too?" She said. "At least David had a motorcycle. So, am I supposed to sleep on the fucking street or what?"

As the couple in the next booth got up to leave, the woman turned to Silky and said, "Your mother should wash your mouth out with soap young lady, and your hair while she's at it." They started walking out. Silky flipped the woman the finger.

"Go get yourself laid, twat face," she yelled after her.

The woman's companion was already out the door while she stopped halfway down the aisle and glared back at Silky. For a moment I thought she was going to come back and slug her.

"You know you have the face of an angel," the woman said, shaking her head. "So, why such ugliness?" Beat. "God help the world if you're an example of our youth."

By this time everyone in the café had tuned in. Silky just grinned. The woman turned on her heels and left. I was certain we were about to get kicked out as I noticed the waitress looking our way and shaking her head in dismay over the scene

"How can people be so lame?" Silky said, giggling, and munching on a French-fry.

I stood up.

"You liked taunting that woman, didn't. you," I said.

Silky stopped giggling.

"That woman is a cow just like my ole lady was fore that car hit her. Damn. So don't give me any shit."

Silky went out to the car. When I paid the check the waitress at the cash register leaned over and said in a low voice: "Your girlfriend's a piece of work."

I got some coffee to go and got into the car. Silky was humming to herself and finishing up the remaining fries that she had wrapped in a paper napkin.

"Don't you have any friends in Los Angeles you could stay with?" I said.

"No," she said tersely. "Not in this horseshit town. Lend me some money. I'll go find a place."

I put the coffee down, fired up a smoke and told her I wasn't giving her any money.

"That's really boring," she said.

After I'd taken a couple of drags she reached over and took the cigarette out of my mouth and finished it. For some reason I didn't mind. It was like my act of charity. I looked at my watch. It was almost eleven o'clock.

"Where's your dad?" I said trying to make conversation, and remembering her description of her father.

"Dead. Got run over by a car in Virginia."

I chuckled, finished my coffee and pulled out onto the Santa Monica heading west. After a few minutes Silky screamed that we just passed a motel with a neon sign out front that said "Vacancy." I didn't slow down.

"Forget it," Silky said. "Hey, I got an idea. Let's go out to Venice Beach. I heard there's always action out there and lots of freaks. Shit, you'll fit right in, man."

Santa Monica Boulevard was all but deserted in that part of town, just a few scattered souls wandering about or hanging out on street corners.

"I'm getting tired," I said. "I'll drop you off somewhere."

"I could've hitched a ride to Frisco," she said. "But instead I thought what the hell, I would keep you company and this is my thanks, getting dumped in the gutter?"

"It's just that I have this girl back home and…"

"Jesus Christ," Silky screamed. "I won't rape you, Tuckie baby. If you want to get rid of me, give me some money."

My body was beginning to ache from the hours of driving. But I wasn't sure I could sleep with all the coffee I'd downed. As for Silky I decided she was crazy.

"I don't have much money," I said.

Silky threw her head back against the seat and pulled her hat down over her brow.

"Let's see, what was that again you're going to do, outer space scientist, oh I remember, screen writer. Screen writer, my ass. Right? I mean what a crock! Give me twenty and I'll give you a blow job. Right now, here in the car. I'll bet even a hayseed like you would enjoy that, eh? Best in the west."

"What?"

"Come on, twenty bucks," she said, sounding exasperated. "Okay, fifteen and that's rock bottom."

I pulled the car over to the curb and looked over at this young woman sitting in my car.

"Why'd you do that?" She said.

"You really are disgusting," I said. "Now get out."

"What are you a fag?" She said. "I'm not going anywhere."

I opened my door and started to get out with the idea of going around and yank her onto the sidewalk. She reached out and grabbed my hand.

"Hey," she said. "Be cool. I didn't mean to be a total turnoff. It's just the way I am sometimes, you know. Please. I don't want to be alone."

I looked at her for a moment. This was a new side of Silky. I closed the door and started driving again.

"So, are we going to get a room or what?" She said.

I shrugged and then sighed.

"Okay," I said.

Chapter 5

———

The Knights Inn Motel was just a half mile down the road, just off Santa Monica Boulevard. It was a seedy two story beige building that was in bad need of a paint job. It had a single, sad-looking palm tree in front and very little else in the way of landscaping. Only one other car occupied the parking lot. It was at the far end from where we were. Next to the Vacancy sign was a second sign that said: "Free TV."

I pulled in and parked the car a ways from the office and told Silky to stay in the car.

"I'm going to tell them we're Mister and Missus…er Jones. No, that sounds phony. I know, Riggs. Mister and Missus Riggs. Yeah, that has a better ring to it. Newly weds, like in the movies."

"What're you kidding me?" Silky said. "We're gonna shack up, not rob a bank. I mean who cares? This joint probably rents to the local hookers by the quarter hour."

I got out and went into the office. After ringing the bell on the counter several times the night clerk finally appeared from a doorway in back, blurry-eyed and cranky. He was a tall, string bean of a man wearing a dirty T-shirt over pajama bottoms. Strands of his thinning dark hair were scattered in every direction back from a high forehead. There was a smell of cheap wine about him. He watched me as I signed the guest card. I volunteered we were newlyweds from the Midwest. The clerk just grunted and looked at me expressionless.

"How many nights?" He said.

"Just one night," I said.

"That will be $12.50 and no pets. Check out time is noon. If you decide to spend a second night you get a dollar discount."

After I paid him with a ten and a five he gave me change and the key.

"Room 203, the bridal suite," he said without irony. "TV might be a bit fuzzy on some channels."

Back outside I motioned to Silky. She was sitting on the fender of the car, smoking. Inside room 203 was one sagging double bed with a brown stained spread. Years of stale cigarette residue permeated the place along with a faint smell of urine. Flowery wall paper was peeling off the walls. And one dim naked light bulb that hung from the ceiling was the room's only illumination. The TV, which sat on a stand in the corner opposite the door, looked like a relic. Silky immediately squatted down and began fiddling with the knobs. A test pattern came on. "Fucker," Silky said to herself as she turned the channel selector. Snow came on the screen with each click. She turned the TV off, stood up and began to pace the room, cursing the Knight's Inn.

I went back to the car and got my suitcase, which was coming apart in one corner. Silky was in the shower when I got back to the room. I decided to check on my money which I'd kept in the suitcase under a false bottom. It was all tens and twenties held together by a paper clip. I put it in a small paper bag I'd found in a waste basket by the night table and started to put it back in my suitcase, but on an impulse changed my mind and hid the money under the bed's box spring.

I sat on the edge of the bed, then leaned back and shut my eyes and imagined myself being interviewed on TV about my movie writing career. I was drifting further and further into this fantasy when I heard a voice in the background and felt drops of water punching me in the face. I opened my eyes. Silky was standing over me, stark naked, drying her hair with a towel. At first I instinctively averted my eyes. But I then found myself staring at her as she walked around. Her body was very smooth and creamy like her face. Other than her freckles it was as if the sun had never touched it. She was perfectly proportioned; her breasts were full, but not overly developed, a lot like Jenny's. When Silky finished drying off her hair she turned and caught me gazing at her and grinned and flashed her eyes.

"You think I have a good body?" She said.

I nodded.

"My daddy thought so too," she said.

"Huh?" I said.

"Since I was about 13 my daddy made me have sex with him, made me suck him off all the time. The funny thing is, I liked it. Mom had been killed and I was the woman of the house. Cool, eh."

I didn't say anything, primarily because I wasn't sure whether to believe her or not. But there was something in her tone that made me think she was telling it right.

I fired a smoke, took a drag and blew the smoke out toward her. She turned the TV back on and after several dead channels found "The Tonight Show" with Steve Allen. It was kind of a zany program, I thought. Zona always stayed up and watched. Silky went back into the bathroom and came back out, the towel now wrapped around her. She held up her pair of black panties.

"Clean," she pronounced. "My daddy always told me that if I do nothing else in this life, I should always start the day with freshly washed underwear. It's the only thing he ever told me that made sense. Got to hang them."

She went back into the bathroom. When she returned she was dressed in her torn jeans and T-shirt and said she wanted to go out and party somewhere.

"Don't you have any other clothes?" I said.

She rolled her eyes.

"You see me with a suitcase or knapsack? My other clothes ran off with David and his motorcycle."

I nodded.

"Let's go to the place by Venice Beach I was talking about before," she said. "Let's go there."

I told her I was too tired and thought I would stay at the motel and sleep.

"Forget that, cowboy," Silky said. ""Let's celebrate your first night in L.A. Okay. I want to do this for you. You need to get rid of your small town baggage and let 'er rip. You know what I mean?"

I put my head in my hands and shut my eyes.

"Fine," she said. "Give me the keys to your car. I'll go on my own."

I opened my eyes and looked up at her.

"You're not taking the car," I said. "We're lucky it made it this far."

Silky paced the floor in front of the TV. She stopped and watched Steve Allen for a few minutes.

"I wonder how much he makes doing that show," she said aloud to herself.

She turned off the TV and looked at me.

"How're you gonna know anything to write about you don't go out and do it, do life," Silky said.

I shrugged.

"How far is the ocean from here?" I said. "I wouldn't mind seeing the ocean. I've never seen it before except in movies."

"I don't know," she said. "Can't be far. Just keep going west until we run out of road."

"What's this place you're talking about?" I said.

Silky asked me for a cigarette. After she lit it and took a drag she said that it was a kind of club she'd heard about called: The Dog's Leg or something like that. You can drink and dance there. I think they have a band."

I rubbed my eyes, then went into the bathroom, took a quick shower, shaved, put my jeans back on and came back out bare-chested. I felt better.

Silky, who had put on her pink framed sunglasses, looked me up and down.

"You look much stronger than I thought," she said.

"Was that true about your baby being kidnapped by a boyfriend and taken to San Francisco?"

Silky finished her cigarette.

"What do you think?" She said. "Come on, can we get our asses in gear."

I put on a wrinkled white shirt from my suitcase, over a T-shirt and tucked into my jeans. As an afterthought I added a red bow tie, one that I wore back home from time to time. It kind of made me feel like I was dressed up. Silky snickered but didn't comment. It was a little cool out so I put on my windbreaker.

I was nervous about the Dodge. But somehow it managed to keep going, albeit making some strange sounds. We headed for Venice Beach, which was farther than I thought it would be. It took forty minutes and I had to get some gas. A half hour later just driving around we couldn't find a place called the Dog's Leg. I drove back to Hollywood without seeing the ocean. We finally landed at a place called Ye Coach & Horses on Sunset Boulevard. I agreed to go in with Silky just to have a look. It was dark inside. Even at that hour, which was now 1:30 a.m. the place was packed with the shadowy figures of men and women moving about. The din of conversations and laughter created a sound just below a steady roar, punctuated by the clinking of glasses. It was not a huge place, but not small either. For all intent and purposes it was a Bar and it smelled of alcohol and sweat.

A jukebox was playing Old Black Magic by Frank Sinatra. As my eyes became accustomed to the low light, I could make out People dancing, some with drinks in their hands as they moved about the small dance area. "This is cool," Silky yelled in my ear. A moment later she was dancing with some guy who looked like a slightly larger version of her motorcycle boyfriend. Some people left a table and I quickly grabbed it and sat down. A cocktail waitress rushed over and asked for my order, telling me it was last call for drinks. I ordered a beer. Silky came and plopped herself down, out of breath. We were soon joined by the guy she had been dancing with. He brought his own chair and put a beer in front of her. He leaned over and said something in Silky's ear.

"Cool," she said, laughing.

She took a swig of beer, wiped her mouth and introduced her dance partner to me as her new friend. His name was Rodrigo.

"Rodrigo's an actor," Silky said proudly

"An actor," I repeated. ""You been in anything I might have seen?"

While looking at Silky he said he did mostly stunt work and bit parts so far.

"Silky tells me she's a fugitive, like an outlaw chick," Rodrigo said. "So what's your thing, man?"

"Huh?' I practically shouted.

"What do you do? What's your handle, man? What'd she say your name is?"

"Chuck," I said.

Silky lit a cigarette and took a quick swallow from her beer.

"He's called Tuckie," she said. "He's a writer."

"Right," Rodrigo said, sounding vaguely interested and leaned in closer. "What kind of shit do you write, man?"

It was clear to me this guy was a bit drunk and a little aggressive.

"I know this guy who writes," Rodrigo went on. "He writes these hot porno flicks, some juicy shit, you know. Not much on plot, but lots of action. I was in one once. Made seven hundred bucks. Let me tell you man it ain't easy."

"All you got to do is keep it up," Silky interjected. "I dig porno flicks. There's something honest about them. They don't pretend to be anything but what they are."

Rodrigo nodded.

"I like the way this chick thinks," he said to me and then leaned in close to Silky and kissed her on the cheek. "You want to be in one. I can arrange it."

"Maybe," she said and giggled.

Rodrigo turned to me.

"She's a freak, man. Know what I mean?"

I nodded absently and wondered what Jenny was doing at that moment. Fast asleep of course. I tried to picture her in a nightgown, her head on her pillow, her blond hair splayed out. Silky suddenly said, "What the…" and stopped giggling. A strange expression came over her face as she looked toward the back of the room. I followed her gaze to see what it was that caught her attention. There was a very short, squat man with a large head and a bulbous red nose, as near as could be told in the low light. The man looked like he was suffering from a disfiguring disease. At that moment he was attempting to dance with an attractive Amazon of a woman, who, at about six feet in height, was almost twice his size. She had on a very short orange skirt that was now hiked up around the top of her hips, and spiked heels. Her body moved in every direction to some nameless Rhythm & Blues number. They were the only ones dancing.

"Jesus Christ!" Silky yelled, spilling part of her beer on the table.

"What?" Rodrigo said and turned around to see what she was looking at.

"You see him?" She said "The man dancing with the monster woman in the pink panties."

Rodrigo shook his head.

'You mean that ugly little potato bug over there?" Rodrigo said, laughing. "That's Henry or Herman something or other. They call him Fat Eyes. He hangs out here once in a while. Someone said he's a big talent agent."

I moved over slightly to get a better look. I could now see his face even better than before, and understood the nick name. His eyes bulged out of their sockets like a frog. I figured he maybe had a thyroid condition.

"I think he's beautiful," Silky said. "I want to dance with him."

Silky took off her pink glasses, pushed herself up from the table and unsteadily made her way toward the small dance space where she tried to cut in. The woman in the orange skirt tried to steer the little man away from Silky who pursued them relentlessly.

"What do you want, honey?" the big woman said. "Move out of the way before I kick your skinny ass."

Silky didn't say anything, just continued to try and get between. After a moment of maneuvering Silky pushed her hat back and rushed the bigger woman as if she were going to tackle her. The one called Fat Eyes released his dance partner and stepped back, looking both amused and bewildered. He was probably wondering who this mad little chick was. Silky was given a hard push by the larger woman. She fell backward and landed on the floor face up. The crowed began yelling at her to get up and kick ass. Someone helped her to her feet. Both Rodrigo and I stood up to watch. Silky then put her head down and charged the larger woman, her head slamming into the woman's stomach. Both of them went sprawling across the floor. The bartender yelled at them to knock it off or he'd throw them both out.

The larger woman got to her feet first only to discover she was soaking wet along her rear end and back from a puddle of beer on the floor.

"Sonofabitch!" She screamed and made her way through the crowed back to the women's bathroom.

Silky grabbed her hat which had fallen off and got to her feet. There were whoops and hollers and clapping from the crowed as she started back to the table. She turned her head back for a moment and caught Fat Eyes grinning at her.

"Go fuck yourself," she said to him and then danced the rest of the way to her seat and ordered another beer. I was surprised that she was not asked for her ID.

"You are one crazy chick," Rodrigo said.

The bartender, a large burly man came from around the bar and hovered over Silky like some kind of hulking predator.

"Alright, girlie, you're eighty sixed," he said. "Out of here. Now."

Silky looked up at him with a wide eyed confusion.

"Moi?" She said in a phony French accent. "I do not speak the English so good. What does your American expression mean? What ees it again, Sixty Nine?"

"Real cute, sister," The bartender said.

Rodrigo said: "She didn't mean anything, Marty. Just having some fun, liven the place up a bit. You know."

"Screw him," Silky said.

The bartender looked at Rodrigo and shook his head, then looked at Silky.

"You heard what I said, young lady. Out."

Silky shrugged and got to her feet. The bartender stepped back and watched.

"How old are you anyway?" He said. "Jesus, probably not even 21. Don't come back here."

Silky smiled.

"Come on," she said to no one in particular. "Screw this roach joint. Let's go find some action somewhere."

The Bartender went back behind the bar. Rodrigo stood up and said he knew where there was a party.

"It's at a friend of mine's in West Hollywood. Not far from here."

I looked at my watch. It was almost two.

"I should go back to the motel," I said.

Silky was already out the door with Rodrigo just behind her. I followed. Outside Silky suddenly came over and put her arms around me, pulling me closer to her. Her T-shirt smelled a little ripe. She pushed her sunglasses up to her forehead. Her eyes danced with energy.

"Listen, cowboy," she said her mouth moist against my ear. "I need you to stay with me here, you know." Her voice took on a low sultry warmth like Lauren Bacall in To Have and Have Not. "I'll be cool, I promise." She looked over at Rodrigo who was leaning against the building, smoking. "I don't want you to leave me alone with this guy. We'll go to the party. Just for a while. Okay?"

"Hey over there," Rodrigo said. "Anybody got wheels?"

"Yeah," Silky said. "We do."

"I've got to claim my prize tomorrow by 5:00 o'clock."

Silky kissed me.

"That's a century from now, cowboy," she said.

The three of us walked to the Dodge which was parked a half a block away. Rodrigo stopped short and stared at it as I walked around to get into the drivers side.

"Wow," he said. "What is it?"

Silky sat up front with me. Rodrigo sat in the back seat. I checked Rodrigo in the rear view mirror. I suddenly had a real strange feeling come over me, like a foreboding.

Chapter 6

——————

We must have wandered around West Hollywood for close to an hour looking for this mythical party. It was an excruciating hour for me. I was getting real antsy. At this point I just wanted to get away from these people, but didn't know how to do it. I didn't want to leave Silky and Rodrigo stranded. They were depending on me.

It was now almost 2:30 in the morning. Finally Rodrigo thought we had found the right place. There were some people milling about in front of this house which was somewhere between Santa Monica and Fountain, west of Fairfax. I parked the car. We got out and went into the house and discovered we'd crashed an early morning wake for someone's great aunt.

"Shit," Rodrigo said as we got back into the car. "Someone asked which side of the family I was on."

"What'd you tell them?" Silky said.

"The side looking for a party," Rodrigo said, laughing "Who the hell holds a wake at this time in the morning? It's insane, man."

I said I heard someone say it had been going on since late in the afternoon the day before.

As we pulled away Silky leaned out the window and screamed at the top of her voice: "May the old girl rest in peace, motherfuckers!"

Rodrigo thought we should drive down another block on Kilkea Drive. He was certain it was on this street. But there was no sign of any activity in the next block. I continued driving, one, then two more blocks.

Just when the prospects of a party were looking pretty bleak we stumbled onto the right place in the third block, almost by accident. We started to pass when we spotted two men and a girl standing out front of a dark house sharing a bottle of something. We stopped and Rodrigo asked what was happening. One of the men pointed toward the back. I parked the car a half a block down and we walked back.

The party was actually in a house behind a house. A narrow gravel path along side of the front house led back to the party house. There were people strewn outside on the house's sagging porch. The front door was wide open. With Rodrigo leading the way, Silky and I entered. It was a small place, maybe one bedroom. But the living room was large with a listing wooden floor as if the foundation was giving up on one end. It was jammed with hot sweating bodies, some making an effort to move with the music which was coming from a stereo built into a bookcase against the wall. Others were stretched out on what little furniture there was or sitting on the floor. There was an acrid smell drifting through the room that I didn't recognize.

"Everyone here is stoned, man," Silky said as we made our way though the tangle.

She and Rodrigo disappeared. I sat down on the floor and leaned against a couch. Someone handed me a beer. I looked up to see that it was coming from a very pretty young woman in a yellow blouse and flowery cotton skirt. She was standing there holding two beers. I took the one she was holding down to me.

"Thanks," I said.

She eased herself down next to me, pulling her legs under her. Neither of us said anything for a while, just sat there sipping our beers, listening to the music and watching a sea of legs in motion. She asked me if I had a cigarette. I gave her one and we both fired up.

"So who are?" She said, slurring her words after taking a drag. "I haven't seen you around before."

I told her I was called Tuckie.

"I'm Fran," She said, then smiled. "No, that's not true. I just made that up. Why'd I do that? Shit, I'm really messed up." She looked at me. "I mean everyone's got to have some other name, right. We're more than just one person, aren't we? So, why not have more than one name? One name for each person we are or think we are. Isn't that a good idea?"

I nodded, not really sure of what she was talking about.

"I mean, is Tuckie your real name?" She said.

"Not exactly," I said. "My real name is Charles."

"See what I mean," she said excitedly. "You have another name too. That's good. My name is really Margo. That's my real name. No last names please." She leaned in closer to me. "Tuckie, that's a cute name and you are very cute to go with it, you know. But I've got to tell you, you don't look like you fit into this crowed. You just get out of the army or something?"

I shook my head.

"I just got out of prison," I said in a matter of fact way, though I wasn't sure why I said it.

Margo's eyes got wide.

"What were you in prison for?"

I looked around the room as if to see if anyone else could hear, as if it was possible above the noise of the crowd.

"Kind of a murder," I said. "Just a small one. Nothing too big."

Margo stared at me incredulously. Then she laughed and shook her head.

"You're putting me on," she said. "I get it."

I took a swallow of my beer.

"You're not a cop are you?" She said.

"Nope."

"Good," she said. "Want to smoke a joint?"

"Marijuana? I said. "I…no, I have to leave soon. I'm going to write for the movies."

Margo finished her beer, took another drag on her cigarette and looked at me with suspicion. Her eyes narrowed, as if trying to determine whether maybe I was a few degrees off plumb. She slumped over for a moment, as if to get her bearings and then brought her head back up.

"Movies?" She said. "I have an uncle in the movie business. Uncle Maurice. Moe."

"That right," I said.

Margo, who was barely getting the words out now told me her uncle Moe was actually in the finance and distribution end of the business. Mostly B horror flicks for the drive-in circuit.

"I hear he does okay," she said. "Moe's always been kind of mysterious, my dad says. My dad says he thinks he has underworld friends, if you know what I mean. Ooops, I'm talking too much. I know uncle Moe owns a large pawn shop as one of his businesses. I'm closer to him than my folks. He always slips me a fifty or a hundred whenever he sees me."

"What do you do?" I said.

"I work in a women's clothing boutique on LaCienega. It's called Bright Lights."

I leaned back against the couch and tried to fight off an overwhelming need to sleep. Someone or something caught Margo's eye. With great effort she pushed herself up.

"You ever hear of a man named Jimmy Oliver?" I said.

"No," she said. "Who's he?"

I shrugged. She then waved to someone on the other side of the crowed toward the front and stumbled her way in that direction. Margo stopped, turned, came back and looked down at me.

"Maybe I'll see you sometime," she said and gave a little wave before being swallowed up by the mesh of swaying bodies on the floor in front of me.

After a couple of minutes I got to my feet, wondering what had happened to Silky and Rodrigo. There was no sign of them in the front room. I checked inside my windbreaker pocket to make sure I hadn't lost my car keys and wallet. After trying a couple of doors, one of which was a bathroom where a couple was stretched out in the bathtub, I entered a bedroom. It was dark. I flipped on the light. Silky was on the floor, naked from the waist down as near as I could tell. Rodrigo was on top of her, his pants down around his ankles,

"Shut the goddamned light," Rodrigo said.

"Who's that?" Silky said. "Get out."

I turned the light out.

"It's me," I said.

"What the hell do you want?" Silky said. "Can't you see we're busy here?"

"Yeah," Rodrigo said. "Beat it!"

Silky giggled.

"Maybe he wants to watch us, see how it's done," she said.

I was instantly reminded of that time in the cornfield all those years ago, Adele and Jimmy Oliver, their naked flesh glistening in the afternoon sun. A strange feeling came over me.

"I want to go back to the motel," I said. "I'm real tired. I've got to get some sleep."

"Just crash on the bed here," Silky said. "It'll be okay. We'll wake you later."

"Can we knock off the bullshit," Rodrigo said.

I took off my windbreaker and dropped it at the foot of the bed and collapsed on the raw mattress, no bed clothes. As I drifted off I was aware of Silky grunting and making loud breathy noises in rhythm with the sound of slapping bodies and wondering what I was doing there.

Chapter 7

———

T he blow to my rib cage was enough to catapult me from a hazy dream about Jenny to a harsh consciousness. Jenny with a sad face melded into morning light seeping through my cracked eyelids. Everything was hazy for a moment. Where was I? I opened my eyes as wide as I could, which was not much just as another blow glanced off my side. My ribs felt like they'd caved in.

"What the...I shouted as I realized someone was kicking me and yelling something. I looked up and could make out a shadowy figure standing over me next to the bed. The shape was that of a short stocky person in an olive drab tank top shirt and a large gut that hung over his belt like a sack of potatoes. Whoever it was, was saying something in a high pitched, screechy voice which made my ears ring. I thought it might be a woman because the hair was long, almost shoulder length, which in an era of butch haircuts and pompadours struck me as odd if it were a man.

Woman or not I came out of my sleep with a vengeance in the form of a wild round house punch that clipped my attacker somewhere around the right temple. The attacker was knocked backward, and my body almost followed off the bed. I fell back on the bed and shut my eyes, just a few more minutes sleep was all I wanted.

"Sonofabitch!" The person screamed. "Get your ass out of my bed, goddamn it. Now!"

I raised myself up on my elbows and squinted at the person before me. I was aware from peripheral vision that someone else was also in the room standing behind the attacker back near the bedroom door. I could see now that my attacker was a man. He was standing back, his face contorted in anger. The person behind him was a young woman wearing only panties and bra. At first I thought it was Silky. But when I finally focused past the man I could see this woman had dark hair and a slightly darker complexion. She was leaning against the wall peering at me as if I were some strange curiosity, smoking and sipping something from an oversized mug.

"Who is he, Jack?" The woman said, flicking her cigarette ashes on the floor.

The man called Jack spun around to look at her.

"Beats the hell out of me," he said. "And how about finding a fucking ashtray! Place looks enough like a goddamned garbage dump without you adding to it." He looked the woman up and down, as if noticing for the first time that she had little on. "I thought you were changing."

"I'm taking a small break," she said. "You mind?"

"Grungy cunt," The man said out of the side of his mouth.

The woman laughed. Jack turned back to the business at hand – me. I pushed myself up and swung my legs over the side of the bed.

"I come home and find the place a total wreck and this asshole on my bed like it's some fucking flop house."

The woman giggled.

"He looks like an alien," she said. "Kind of goofy, don't you think."

Sunlight flooded the room through open blinds on a large window on the far side. I looked at my watch. It was almost 3:00 and my heart must have lurched. I scrambled off the bed.

"I've got to get out of here," I said. "I've got to be somewhere."

Jack and the woman exchanged glances.

"Really?" Jack said. "Where do you have to be?"

I took a deep breath and explained that I was starting my career as a movie writer today and I have to be at Starburst/Meade Productions before 5:00 this afternoon.

The woman almost choked on her coffee and began coughing. When she'd recovered she said: "I think this guy's out there in orbit somewhere!"

Jack scratched his head. I started looking for my shoes which I had taken off before crashing. They were half under the bed frame. I started putting them on when Jack moved in close, wedging me against the bed.

"He's starting his movie writing career today," Jack repeated, rubbing the side of his head where I'd clipped him. There was a growing menace in his tone.

I got my shoes on, grabbed my windbreaker and stood up, towering over Jack.

"You going to get out of my way?" I said.

"How come he couldn't have started his career yesterday," the woman said. "Or maybe the day before. That might have been a good day. Damn."

I pushed passed Jack, who grabbed my sleeve and pulled a small hunting knife out of his back pocket with no sheath, the blade gleaming in a shaft of morning sun. He pointed it at me threateningly.

"Not so fast," he said. "Put your career on hold for a few minutes, okay. This is Maggie and you know my name. So, who are you and what are you doing here?"

I told them my name was Tuckie and that I had just arrived in L.A. last night and came here to a party with some friends.

"Where are these friends of yours?" Jack said.

I looked around.

"I don't know," I said. "They must be around here."

"Do you remember their names?" Jack said.

"A girl named Silky; has lots of red hair," I said. "And a guy named Rodrigo. Said he was an Actor. About my height with thick shaggy hair. He's the one knew about the party."

"Did he have a last name?"

I shook my head and eyed the knife, wondering if I could be quick enough to take it away from him.

"Didn't give it," I said. "You must have seen them?"

Jack came up and put his arm around my shoulder as if we were long time buddies, holding the knife close to my neck with the other hand.

"It's a mystery about your friends," he said, looking perplexed. "But there is someone, or something here we have to deal with, don't we."

He let go of my shoulder. Even though it was getting warm I put on my windbreaker, primarily to signal that I was about to leave, knife or no knife. He then put the knife in his belt.

"What're you talking about?" I said.

Jack found a pack of cigarettes on a dresser and lit up. The woman-Maggie adjusted her bra which had been slipping a little. She was not unattractive. Nice figure, soft brown eyes and dark brown hair, cut short. She noticed me eyeing her and grinned.

"I'd better get some clothes on," she said and dashed into a bathroom.

"I don't know about your friends, Lucky," Jack said. "But I do know we have got a problem here that I think you know about. A real serious problem! And I'm going to need you to groove in on it with me."

"Names, Tuckie," I said. "And I don't know what you mean."

"Tuckie. It's like this, Tuckie. There's a dead woman in the living room behind the couch."

Maggie came out of the bathroom. She had on a black and white checkered shirt tucked into a pair of black shorts.

"A what?" I said.

"Don't you hear," Jack said. "A body. The body of some chick. She's out there in the living room and before long she'll be stinking up the place." Jack extended his arm in the direction of the living room. "Behind the couch, man. So you're saying you don't know about it. "

"It's a joke, right?" I said.

"You can go see for yourself," Jack said. "But here's the thing. It has to be a secret for now. I want you to help me dump the body somewhere. I can't afford to have some stiff hanging around here."

I just looked at Jack in disbelief. This could not be happening.

"I have to use the bathroom," I said.

I went in, peed, threw cold water in my face, with my finger and a dab of tooth paste I found on the sink, brushed my teeth. The tarnished mirror above the sink did not flatter me one bit. I thought I looked like something the cat dragged in. I rubbed the stubble of growth on my face and looked for a razor. None to be found. My pink bow tie was still on. I straightened it and went back out. Jack and Maggie were waiting.

"If there's really a body out there why don't you call the police?" I said.

Jack looked at Maggie who shrugged and then back to me.

"Here's the story, Lucky…Tuckie. I don't want the police snooping around here. Gives the neighborhood a bad name. Now, let me give you the story as I see it. I'm away. Some friend of mine who is staying here for me has a party. I come home and the place is a wreck, my friend who is not really a close friend is nowhere to be found. The only person here is you and the body of a woman. Getting the picture?"

I just stared at Jack, still not quite comprehending what he was saying, or where all this was going. I was sure this whole thing was a practical joke and Silky and Rodrigo would appear any minute laughing hysterically. I folded my arms and looked down into the puffy face of Jack who's narrow eyes were unblinking on me, as if challenging me.

"Okay," I said." And thought this is unreal. "I've seen this movie. And it wasn't all that good."

"I think we're entering a cosmic realm," Jack said.

Maggie smiled at me.

"He's not bad looking for a space cadet," she said.

"Let's see this body," I said.

Jack crocked his finger at me.

59

"Why don't you come out to the front room and see for yourself. Then you and I have work to do."

Jack noticed me looking at my watch. It was 3:20 and my heart was beginning to race.

"Don't be looking at your watch, man. For all I know you're the one that snuffed her."

"Snuffed her?"

"Yeah, killed her,' Maggie said.

I then asked for a pencil. Maggie found one on the floor and they watched me while I wrote the date on a piece of scrap paper I found in my pants.

"What was that word again?"

"What word?" Jack said, rolled his eyes and started for the front room.

"Snuffed," Maggie said and followed Jack.

"Right," I said and jotted it down and stuffed the paper in my pocket along with the pencil. "I have to go now. If there's a dead body out there, which I doubt, I don't know anything about it."

"Maybe you did it and maybe you didn't," Jack said, once we were in the front room. "Frankly, I don't give a rat's ass."

For an instant I shut my eyes and considered that maybe this was a dream and I was really back home in my own bed and would wake up soon. I could even smell the aroma of freshly brewed coffee wafting up from the kitchen where Zona was doing her duty for Royce.

"Here's the thing," Jack said, snapping me out of my little reverie. "See if you can picture this scenario. I call the Fuzz. That's cops to you in case you want to write it down. They arrive, sirens blasting. Like an action flick. They take over the scene. There are questions. Lots of questions. Where a body is concerned there are questions. The point is, I don't have time for this shit and it sounds to me, Tuckie wuckie, you don't either. Am I right, or what?"

I took a deep breath and for a moment felt a little nauseated. The place looked like there'd been an explosion. Furniture was overturned. A bookcase with the stereo had been knocked over. And the room reeked of puke, beer, cigarettes and just a hint of back alley piss. All kinds of trash had been strewn from one end of the room to the other, including a few broken bottles.

"Where's your roommate?" I said. "Maybe he knows something."

"It's a she and she's flown the coup as they say," Jack said. Probably down in Mexico by now."

I looked at my watch again.

"I have to go," I said. "You can't keep me here."

"Right,' Jack said. "Got to go and crank up the old career by...when was that...5:00 o'clock latest?"

I ignored the comment and felt in the right pocket of my windbreaker for the car keys. They weren't there. Feeling a sudden rush of panic I ran back into the bedroom, got down on all fours and began hunting around the floor and under the bed. Not there. I pulled my wallet out from my other jacket pocket. I sank down on the bed. My money was gone. I looked up to see Jack standing in the doorway watching.

"Someone take you?"

I jumped off the bed and bolted from the bedroom, past Jack, through the front room, and out the door along the narrow path next to the front house to the street. I was vaguely aware of Jack chasing after me yelling something unintelligible. Halfway to the next block, my body was heaving and my sanity diminishing. The empty spot where the Dodge had been parked zoomed out at me. Maybe, I thought, Silky and Rodrigo borrowed the car to go get some breakfast and would be back for me. But I knew deep down I was kidding myself. They had robbed me. "Goddamn they robbed me," I said aloud.

Back inside the house Maggie was picking things up. They had put the bookcase back up and Jack was trying to see if the stereo was still working. It wasn't.

"So," I said, "where's this body?"

Jack nodded toward the couch. It was the same couch I had been leaning against that morning, a big lumpy thing, faded green, tattered along the sides. I slowly made my way over. Jack and Maggie stopped what they were doing to watch me. I moved around to the back of the couch. There on the bare floor wedged in between the wall and the couch was the body of a young woman.

"Jesus," was all I could get out.

Chapter 8

_____

I knelt down to get a better look. Maybe she was alive, I thought. It's easy to make a mistake and assume someone is dead when they're not. I learned that as part of my work at Royce's mortuary. A body was brought in once that had been declared dead and suddenly started breathing. It was very weird.

In this case there was not much doubt. I pulled a piece of cotton out of a hole in the couch and held it under her nose. Then I felt her face which was cold and her skin a bluish hue. It was then that I realized she was the same young woman who gave me the beer and talked with me just after getting there. What was her name? I remembered it started with an M...Margaret...Margo. Yes, it was her. I recognized her clothes, a yellow peasant blouse and flowery skirt.

Jack and Maggie came over and hovered above me as I reached back down and shut her eyes. There was something very creepy about a dead person whose eyes were wide open. It was like they were staring into your soul from some far off place, silently recording your thoughts and feelings. When I was a child, Royce actually brought the body of a man home to store in our front hallway over night. He was in a box covered by a sheet. When Adele and Royce had turned in for the night I snuck downstairs and peaked under the sheet. I had never seen a dead person before that. The man's eyes were open and it even looked like he was smiling at me. I had nightmares about it for at least a week.

"She's dead," I said without looking up.

"Real good observation Sherlock," Jack said, and nervously lit a smoke.

"She was pretty," Maggie said, "can't have been more than twenty two or three."

I got to my feet and looked at Jack and Maggie who were continuing to clean up the trash.

"How can you calmly go around picking up the junk around the room when you've got a dead girl lying here?"

"Won't make any difference to her," Jack said. "It's getting hot and she's going to be ripe before too long. We've got to get her out of here."

Jack was getting red-faced. He reached up, grabbed his long hair and yanked it off the crown of his head revealing an absolutely hairless scalp, covered with beads of sweat. It was then that I noticed he had no eyebrows. I just stared at him.

He noticed me looking at him.

"I had scarlet fever when I was a kid," he said.

I nodded.

"Who was she?" I said without acknowledging that I had actually talked to her and knew her first name.

Jack shrugged.

"Never laid eyes on her before."

"Me neither," Maggie said. "There's no blood or anything."

"Yeah,' Jack said. "Just some chick that happened in here for a party and probably got heavy into something. A lot of 'em like that."

Jack draped an arm around my shoulder. "Say, man, you got wheels?"

I moved away from him.

"My car's gone," I said. "My friends, Silky and Rodrigo, must have borrowed it. They're not really my friends."

"I'll say," Jack said. "Like I said, you got taken, man."

Shit! I suddenly remembered I'd hidden the gun grandfather had left me in a compartment in the back of the car.

"I've got my car," Maggie said.

"That piece of shit?" Jack said. "Probably couldn't make it two blocks, much less where we need to go."

"Screw you, Jack," Maggie said. "Take it or leave it."

Jack nodded.

"Just kidding," he said. "Let's hope we don't get stopped."

Maggie said she would go get her car and back up along the driveway as far as she could.

"What about the people in the front house?" She said.

Jack said they weren't around. Maggie then went out. I began pacing nervously and kept glancing at my watch, as if hoping it would help time to stand still, like a watched pot won't boil. I glanced down at the body again and wondered if maybe I should wait here in case Silky and Rodrigo bring my car back. That notion left me as soon as it arrived. Jack was right. I'd been taken.

"Maybe she had a purse," I said. "We could at least find out who she was."

Jack shook his head and lit a cigarette and put his wig back on.

"I looked," he said. "Couldn't find anything. Fuck that anyway. I don't want to know who she was or where she came from. I just want that stiff out of here."

Jack went into the bedroom and soon returned with a double sized brown blanket. He draped it over the body. But that didn't work. He then spread the blanket on the floor in the middle of the room. As I watched this operation, I froze, wanting as little to do with this scene as possible.

"Just grab her ankles and help me lift her onto the blanket," Jack said.

"I still think the police should be called," I said.

Jack gave me a hard look.

"You've got to be somewhere soon, right? Shut up and help me get her into the car. We'll find a spot up off of Mulholland Drive and dump her and then drop you off."

I nodded solemnly. It was like a movie had just become life and I was an actor in the middle of it. It was all very strange since I had not been in Los Angeles one full day yet. While I did not like being dragged into this situation I figured Jack was right about being detained for some time by police investigators. Anyway, it was just switching places for Margo. No real harm in that.

Maggie soon appeared at the open front door. Jack took one end of the blanket and I took the other. We carried the dead girl out of the house. It was a struggle to keep the body from rolling out of the blanket which it almost did at one point along the path. A neighbor from down the street walked by and looked our way for a moment, then kept going. We squeezed the body into the trunk of Maggie's car, a 1949 Ford. Most of the bottom half of the car was primed gray, with the right fender missing. The top was a pale yellow. On the way up to Sunset our worst fear was realized. We were followed and then stopped by a motorcycle cop. All of our hearts were racing and we held our breaths while he walked around the car. The officer then leaned into the window and told Maggie her license plate was hanging sideways by one bolt and that she should get it fixed. He gave us the once over and went on his way.

Jack told Maggie to take Laurel Canyon up to Mulholland Drive. I learned that it was the top of the Hills that divided Hollywood and the San Fernando Valley. It looked like country up there. Maggie drove west for about a mile and pulled over onto a dirt turnout. The hillside below was covered with tall weeds and scattered trees.

"This is perfect," Jack said.

We got out of the car, looked around to make sure nobody could see us and pulled the body out of the trunk. Maggie walked up the road a ways and back and signaled it was still clear. We carried the body to the edge, and let the girl roll out of the blanket down the hill. I watched as the body stopped about 20 feet below. I suddenly thought of Adele and wondered what she had thought or said the moment before her death. Maybe Jimmy Oliver could answer that question. Jack folded up the blanket and put it back in the trunk of Maggie's car. He told Maggie to drop him off at a place called Schwab's Drugstore down on Sunset Boulevard at the bottom of the hill.

The day had turned muggy. Rain was predicted for late afternoon according to a rapid fire disc jokey on Maggie's car radio. It was hard to believe, given the current hot sunny day that it was at that moment. But then the whole day was hard to believe, so far like a very bad dream. The thing is, I could not have imagined what lay ahead.

It was just a little after four when Maggie took me back to the Knights Inn Motel. The day clerk let me in and stood just outside the door while I looked around. My suitcase was gone. A shaving kit Zona had given me for my 18th birthday was still in the bathroom with my razor. I found the paper bag with the rest of my money still under the box spring. It now occurred to me that I had left a copy of my ten page manuscript "The Prairie Wolves" in the car with the gun. At least I kept the Starburst/Mead letter on me.

I told Maggie who was also waiting by the door that I was going to take a quick shower.

"Oh no you don't, Mister," the Day Clerk said, "not unless you want to pay for another night, which I should charge you for anyway since you didn't check out by noon. I told your friends when they showed up to take a shower they'd have to pay. They said okay but then ran out. "

"They say where they were going by any chance?" I said.

The clerk shook his head.

"Not likely," he said. "They seemed in a big hurry. I did hear that freak of a girl say something about San Francisco."

Maggie drove me to Starburst/Meade Productions, telling me she was heading to the beach to meet a friend after dropping me off. I learned a little about Maggie along the way. She told me she was raised up in Washington State along the Olympic Peninsula. Her mother and father were still there, but she rarely saw them.

"They're always preaching to me that I should get married, settle down and have children. That's their idea of living the American Dream."

Maggie said she'd been living in L.A. for about a year and a half, trying to make ends meet. Her desire was to get into photography. I figured she was about 25 or 26 years old. Maggie had the kind of angular looks that grew on you.

It took a little while to find Starburst/Meade Productions which was on Olive Drive just off Santa Monica in West Hollywood. We drove by it a few times before figuring it out. The letter head only had a P.O. Box for an address. Earlier I had gone into Schwab's with Jake and checked a phone directory. Starburst/Meade was listed with an address. But, there was no address or sign in front of the building that was located where the address should have been. It looked like an old warehouse, gray paint peeling off the front walls, and a sagging wooden entry. There were no windows in front, only a single red door.

"Don't look like much," Maggie noted as I got out of her car. "Must be a real low budget operation. Maybe I'll come back and see how you made out. And maybe I won't."

I just waived and checked my watch. It was 4:53, time to start my career. As I made my way to the entrance I was suddenly overcome by a strong sinking feeling in the pit of my stomach. I turned around to see that Maggie was watching after me. She then drove off. I figured that was the last I would see of her. Just as well, I thought. On the other hand I secretly hoped she might actually return and be waiting for me when I finished my business here. Of course this might take some time, I thought.

It occurred to me that I was not thinking beyond this initial meeting with the Starburst/Meade folks who were going to make my story into a movie.

Inside the entrance alcove the door was open. I went in to find a small empty room. It might have been a reception area at one time. It was full of dust and cobwebs. An old oak desk was the only furniture. There was light that came from an opaque glass door, which seemed to be the boundary line between where I was and whatever lay beyond.

"This cannot be the right place," I said aloud.

I just stood there for a minute then started to leave when I heard a sound coming from the other side of the opaque glass door. It was music, very faint. A woman's voice angrily rang out, telling someone to keep the

noise down. The music became fainter. I knocked on the door and waited. No one came. I stood very still with my hand on the door handle for a
time feeling nervous. After several moments I opened the door and found
myself in a mammoth room with an open ceiling, exposed beams, pipes
and wires running every which way. The floor looked like a giant checker
board of black and white linoleum squares.

About 15 steps in to my right sat a very large woman at a gray metal
desk thumbing through a pile of papers in front of her. She was wearing
one of those fat dresses called a Mumu and chewing on a cigar. Her hair
was gray and cut very short, which made her face and head look huge.
She did not notice me standing there. At the back of the room a young
Asian woman was at a desk sorting through envelopes from a pyramid of
mail on the floor next to her chair.

I cleared my throat.

"Looks real busy here," I said.

The big woman jerked her head up, put on a pair of horn-rimmed
glasses and peered up at me, at first with a blank expression and then with
a scowl.

"Who the hell are you?" She said, her voice reminding me of a large
truck without a muffler.

"Hi," I said. "I'm Tuckie...Charles Kendall."

"Who?"

I repeated my name and noted that most folks back home called me
Tuckie.

"Is this Starburst/Meade Productions?" I asked.

I noticed the Asian woman had stopped what she was doing and
looked up with interest.

"What do you want?" The big woman said. "This business is closed
to the public. How'd you get in here?"

I gestured with my hand toward the front.

"Door was open, ma'am," I said.

The woman stood up. She was not as tall as I had thought, but I
figured she must weigh at least 250 to 300 pounds.

69

"This is not a drugstore or whatever it is you're looking for," the woman said in a loud voice, turned toward the back and yelled at the Asian woman for forgetting to lock the "goddamned door."

"I'm looking for Starburst/Meade Productions," I said. "Is this it?"

The woman moved closer to me and took the cigar out of her mouth.

"Depends on who wants to know," she said. "You a process server, trying to give me some hick routine with that little twang of yours, or an actor?"

"I'm here to write movies," I said. "I won your screen story contest and I came out here to get my prize money and work making my story into a movie."

The woman stared at me. She looked incredulous.

"Come again?" She asked.

I reached into the inside pocket of my windbreaker and handed her the now slightly crumpled and stained congratulatory letter. I handed her the signed release too. She scanned both pieces of paper and looked up.

"You were supposed to mail this form back," she said. "These don't mean shit now. You're late, so you're disqualified. Capiche? Comprende? Now, get out of here."

I glanced at my watch. It was 4:59 and a couple of seconds.

"It's not five o'clock yet," I said and explained how I'd come over 2000 miles to start my career and that my car had been stolen.

"Tough titty," The woman said.

She wadded up the letter and release into a ball and tossed it at her waste basket. It missed and skidded along the floor passed her desk. Glaring at me now she scrunched up her bloated face, tiny black eyes squinted out from deep within folds of pink flesh.

"You going to get out of here or do I have to call the police?" She said.

"Where's the woman who signed the letter?" I said. "Bonnie Robertson, Chief Editor."

The woman spit on the floor in front of me and then looked up at the ceiling as if calling on the heavens to come to her aide. After this gyration she once again peered at me.

"Chief cocksucker is what she was," the woman said.

I just stared at her.

"Pardon me," the woman said, now smirking. "She's no longer with the company. Departed quite suddenly if you know what I mean."

I repeated that my car had been stolen and I had no place to stay and needed my prize money.

"Sorry," the woman said. "Your life is not my problem, so just go out the way you came in."

The woman grabbed me by the arm and started to guide me out but was interrupted by the Asian woman who had come up behind her now and whispered something in her ear. She eyed me out of the corner of her eye and smiled while she was talking to the older woman. Then she started out toward the front door.

"Bring some French fries with that burger," the woman said. "I'll pay you when you get back."

I pulled away from the woman's grip and went back and retrieved the balled up letter and release off the floor. When I stood back up the woman was practically on top of me.

"Who runs this place?" I said. "Who's the boss?"

The woman didn't answer. I started to leave, but stopped for a moment to look at a couple of faded old movie posters on the wall. One was for "Vixens From Outer Space" staring Tyrone Willets, and Hillary Fox. The other poster was for a movie called "Tijuana Love Thing" starring Virgie Lowe. Both had been produced by Frank Meade.

"Frank Meade," I said aloud. "He wrote the note on the bottom of the letter. I guess I'll go to the police if I don't get my prize money."

The woman's attitude changed.

"Mr. Meade is the boss," she said. "Why don't you come back and talk to him. He'll be here in an hour or so."

I nodded and went back out onto the street suddenly feeling very hungry.

Chapter 9

———

I looked up and down Olive Drive to see if Maggie had come back. It was ridiculous, of course, to think that she would. She didn't know me, so why would she. And yet I was wishing she had come back. I felt a strange connection with her which I couldn't figure.

The sky was darkening now. I felt a couple of drops of rain slide down my face. Since I had a little time I decided to find some place to eat. Just around the corner off Santa Monica was a place called Barney's Beanery. Inside was like looking through a kaleidoscope, reds, greens, yellows, blues, in strange patterns wherever my eyes landed. The walls were covered with old fashioned pub mirrors advertising various beers, photos of movie stars past and present were tacked up behind the bar, along with displays of sports memorabilia. There was also a room with pool tables. Marco's eyes would pop out in this place, I thought.

I took a booth near the front and ordered a grilled ham and cheese sandwich, and coffee. The waitress brought the coffee first. I took a sip, fired up a smoke and thought about my encounter with the woman at Starburst/Meade. Then my mind wandered back to the last thing Royce said to me in the kitchen the morning I left. "I'm changing my will and leaving everything to Zona," he said, as if that were my punishment for leaving. He said I shouldn't bother to come back. I didn't care about the will, but I was startled at how vehement the old man's anger toward me was. Even for Royce it seemed over played. So, Zona's servitude would pay off, I mused.

A soft rain was beginning to come down. A picture of Margo's body on the hillside getting wet sprang up in my head and a deep sense of loneliness came over me. It left me with an urge to tell someone she was there. I was looking out the window when I was aware of someone sitting down in the booth opposite me. It was the Asian woman from Starburst/Meade, setting her hamburger down in front of her. The Asian woman smiled and winked at me as she took a bite. I did not smile back.

"Hey," she said.

I stared at her.

"I was going to head back but I guess I'll wait until the rain passes," she said. "I like the rain. You?"

I nodded.

"What do you want?" I said.

"What?"

"Why did you come over here and sit down uninvited?" I said.

The Asian woman's mouth dropped open.

"Jesus," she said. "I was just trying to be friendly. Why are you angry with me? Never mind. Forget it."

She leaned forward as if to stand up, stopped and said: "I'm Sherry Woo" and stuck out her hand. I did not take it. She pursed her lips and sat back down.

"Where are you from?" She said after a few moments of awkward silence. "Apparently you weren't taught any manners."

I took a sip of my coffee and a pulled on my cigarette. The waitress brought my sandwich. I put out my cigarette and immediately ate half of the sandwich, washing it down with the rest of the coffee.

"I'm not angry at you," I said, finally. "It's just that…"

"What's your name?" She said.

I told her my full name and then added what folks back home call me. She then asked me why I'd come out to Los Angeles. I told her about starting my career.

"You're career, eh?" She said. "Boy, are you funny."

She wanted to know what made me think I could write for movies. I tried to flatten the winkles out of the letter as much as possible and put it in front of her. She read it and shook her head.

"You know about the contest?" I said.

Her mouth was full as she finished the last of her hamburger, sipped some water and sucked her teeth. She looked out the window. The rain was coming down hard. She turned back to me.

"That's one of my jobs around there," she said. "I open the entries and do the first reading. These days I probably do the only reading. You know we get anywhere from 1500 to 2000 entries with each contest. At $25 bucks a pop it adds up, pays the rent."

"What?" I said. "How many contests do you hold?"

"Four to five a year," she said. "Going through the entries gets pretty tedious, but sometimes a funny one comes in and I get a laugh. I mean some of the entries are so lame..."

She looked down at my letter again and wrinkled her brow.

"I see it's signed by Bonny Robertson," she said. "But this is very odd."

"What do you mean?"

I reached across the table and took the letter back.

"Since I've worked at Starburst/Meade Productions, I've never known Frank Meade to write a personal note like that. In fact he never even looks at the entries. He doesn't give a shit as long as..."

I leaned forward to hear the rest of what she had to say.

"Never mind," she said. "I have to get back."

She caught the waitress's attention and asked if the cheeseburger-to-go was ready. The waitress yelled back that it would be a couple more minutes. Sherry Woo looked at her watch and then back to me.

"Don't mind Jocelyn," she said.

I gave her a puzzled look.

"The woman you talked to back at the office," she said. "Jocelyn. She likes to act tough and shock people. I think sometimes it's the only pleasure she gets out of life. When I first started she tried to bully me. I don't think she liked it that Mr. Meade hired me directly without going through her. We're okay now."

"What did you whisper to her?"

Sherry Woo looked taken aback.

"When you were leaving, you stopped and whispered something to her."

She grinned and ducked her head. I could see her face turning red.

"I shouldn't be telling you this but well, I told her I thought you were kind of cute and if she was a little friendlier she might get lucky."

I didn't react.

"Just a joke," Sherry Woo said.

She went on to explain that Jocelyn and Mr. Meade went way back, had an affair. Also that she was once an Earl Carroll girl, and eventually a starlet. Her stage name was Josie Powers. Her real name is Jocelyn Bukowski. "Anyway, she worked in a couple of B movies Meade made at Republic years ago before he became an independent producer. Later she signed on as his assistant and all around go-for. You know, go for this go for that, etc."

"Who's Earl Carroll?"

Sherry Woo ordered coffee and lit a cigarette. I joined her.

"Not important except that Jocelyn was once a beautiful glamour girl. I know, hard to believe now that she looks like two-ton Annie. Anyway, Meade pretty much let Jocelyn run the place while he spent his time wheeling and dealing. When Bonnie Robertson waltzed in one day she acted like she expected to be Queen Bee. She had once been an important story editor, worked for all the majors at one time or another, but the booze caught up with her, according to the story and she fell on hard times. Bonnie immediately demanded that Jocelyn not smoke those awful cigars while she was on the premises. She had this high pitched affected voice that drove Jocelyn up the wall. Jocelyn told me she was certain Bonnie was only there because of a couple of one night stands with Mr. Meade. "Whenever Bonnie was in hearing range, Jocelyn would mock her or imitate her voice, ending with – tut, tut, my dear are we going to make a fucking movie or what?".

As she finished reciting this bit of history Sherry Woo began laughing uncontrollably and shaking her head in dismay at whatever image the telling conjured up for her.

"I mean Christ, I've only been at Starburst/Meade for about a year now and that scene she made was worth everything I've had to put up with."

"Like what?"

Sherry Woo sighed.

"Low pay, no pay at times, yelling and screaming matches, lying to creditors, you name it. But it was the only job I could get in this business when I got out of film school, Theatre Arts at UCLA."

"What happened to Bonnie Robertson?" I asked.

Sherry Woo, tears running down her face shrugged, sipped her coffee and took a drag on her cigarette.

"It was weird. One day Bonnie started talking to herself in a loud voice and began screaming at the top of her lungs that she knew there was a conspiracy against her, that there were covert operatives after her. She kicked over the waste basket next to her desk, then turned over her desk, walked out the door and never came back. She was drunk."

"So what happened to your car?" Sherry Woo said. "I overheard part of what you told Jocelyn."

I was barely listening. The crunched up man I'd seen the night before dancing with the Amazon woman at the bar on Sunset Boulevard had come in and taken a table. What was he called – Fat Eyes? There were four other people with him, two men and two women. One of the women, a platinum blonde, was clearly with Fat Eyes, not the same woman he had been dancing with. This woman looked like a model, tall and slender. The other woman, also attractive was a brunette.

"You know him?" Sherry asked.

"No," I said and then explained. "They call him Fat Eyes."

"Strange looking creature," Sherry Woo said. "Not a dwarf, he's a little larger. I've seen him around. He's supposed to be some kind of high powered agent."

The Blonde, who was very pretty, was rubbing the back of Fat Eyes' neck. His round bulbous face seemed to sink into a blissful state.

It stopped raining. The waitress came over and put a paper bag down in front of Sherry.

"Well, it's been nice talking you, Tuckie," Sherry said. "Maybe I'll see you around."

She reached over and fingered my bow tie.

"Do you always wear a bow tie?" She said. "I mean, this is the west. Unless the party is formal dudes out here don't normally wear them. It's all a matter of image, all about acting out who you want to be. Just a tip."

She grabbed the paper bag and hurried out.

I reached up and felt my tie, and then took it off. I looked over at the table where Fat Eyes was sitting. The two men, who looked very tan and dressed in T-shirts and jeans had gotten up and were now in a game of pool. I did overhear the taller one say he hadn't worked in a month, that the last role he had was in "Flesh Eaters from Planet Six." The other one said the only way he had been able to sit through that turkey was "stoned out of his gourd." The taller one laughed.

It was getting late. I paid my bill and headed back to Starburst/ Mead.

Chapter 10

J ocelyn almost filled the doorway, successfully barring it. She told me that Mr. Meade was out negotiating an important deal and would not be available. I should come back at another time, she said. I asked when, but all I got was the outer door slammed in my face. I considered this a slight setback to beginning my career as a movie writer.

I stood on the sidewalk out front, staring at the Starburst/Meade building for a few minutes. It was not exactly what I imagined a movie company would look like. I walked the half block down to Santa Monica and spotted a bus stop on the other side of the street. Even though the sun had come back out, the bench was still a little damp from the rain. I was feeling weary and didn't care as I sat down. I could feel the cool dampness seeping through my pants. Evening was fast approaching now and I had to think about finding a cheap place to stay. My money would not last long.

The hues along the hazy western sky changed to an incredibly luminous orange and purple. It reminded me a little of the sunsets back home except there was no smog to filter the twilight. Again, I wondered about the girl and if anybody had discovered her body yet.

"Beautiful, isn't it?" A throaty voice next to me said, breaking into my thoughts.

I turned to see who owned the voice. It was a grizzled black man who looked to be in his 70s sitting on the bench. He had on a tattered brown jacket thrown over his shoulders, an old broad brimmed hat pushed down over his forehead. The hat was covered with badges, buttons, and patches, suggesting it had been to many wondrous places.

"What?" I said.

"The sunset," he said. "It's like God is telling us all is right with the universe, even if it's not."

"Where does the bus go that comes by here?" I said.

"All the way to downtown, where City Hall is," he said.

"Thanks."

"You look like a nice young man," he said.

I just looked at him and moved a couple of inches further down the bench. He didn't seem to notice. Instead he began to tell me about himself, how he fought in the "Great War" — World War One — that he'd fought against the Germans in an all Negro unit because they didn't allow them to fight alongside the white units. He proudly noted that the Germans referred to him and his comrades in the 93rd Combat Division as "Hell Fighters." He said the French gave him a medal, the Croix de Guerre, which he pointed to on the lapel of his jacket. It was a tarnished cross hanging from a faded green cloth with red stripes. The man concluded his story by saying that life had not been good to him after serving his country.

This was fascinating, I thought, and took the little notebook out of my windbreaker and began jotting down some of what he was saying.

"What are you writing, young man?" He asked. "You writing about me? Here, take this down. The Veterans Administration ought to be investigated by the Congress of these United States. Wanna see something?"

The man pulled up his pant leg to reveal a badly disfigured calf and knee.

"Sure," he said. "I was wounded, but this wasn't cuza no wound; those butchers at the VA hospital done this to me, man. I can't work and I got no home."

I stopped taking notes and stood up. The man reached out to me, touching the sleeve of my jacket.

"How old you think I am, son?"

I shrugged.

"I'm only 56," he said and tears welled up in his eyes. "Can you help me out, son? Can you give an old vet a little something? I'm hungry. I'll get some soup with whatever you give me."

I stared at the man, trying to decide if his story was true, and then pulled a one dollar bill out of my pocket at the same time calculating how much I had left. The man eyed it and shook his head.

"Can you do a little better than that, son?" He said. "I'm thinking of heading north."

I pulled out a five dollar bill and was pondering whether or not to give it up. The man spotted it and his eyes lit up. Before I could stuff it back in my pocket he reached up and snatched it out of my hand.

"Bless you, son. Bless you."

A horn honked. I looked over to see Maggie screeching up to the curb in her Ford, tires burning, black smoke pouring out of the back. I was never so glad to see someone before and jumped in.

"What's happening?" Maggie said as we pulled away back into the traffic lane.

"Nothing."

"How much you give that guy?

"I felt sorry for him, gave him five bucks," I said, "actually six."

"Not bad," she laughed. "On a good day he probably pulls down a hundred, maybe more. We should all do so well."

"He was crying," I said.

"He's good," she said. "I've seen him working the streets before. He pretty much owns that bench."

"The man showed me his war medal," I said.

Maggie nodded.

"Maybe he got it for real, maybe he found it at some antique shop or war surplus store," she said. "It doesn't matter."

Maggie maneuvered the car into the flow of east-bound traffic. She told me she'd gone to the beach, met some friends, smoked some weed and generally had a good day. She had been on her way back to her place when she spotted me at the bus stop.

We were silent for several blocks.

"I almost didn't stop," Maggie said, as if wanting to say something to break the quiet." But I was curious. How'd it go with collecting your prize and starting your career?"

We were passing La Brea Avenue. Traffic was heavy, cars jockeying for position, horns honking, drivers screaming at each other out their windows.

"Real good," I said. "Great."

Maggie just looked over at me and grinned.

"Let's celebrate. I have some wine at my place."

Maggie turned left on Vine and headed up toward Hollywood Boulevard. When we reached Hollywood and Vine I yelled stop and jumped out of the car. Maggie stopped even though she had the signal. A car behind her began honking madly. I just stood there under the sign looking like a kid who'd just been to the newly opened Disneyland. I jumped back in the car.

"What the hell's the matter with you?" Maggie said.

"I've been hearing about this place most of my life. I just wanted to stand on Hollywood and Vine."

"It's getting pretty trashy, you ask me," Maggie said.

She drove up past Franklin into the hills, making a few turns in a scramble of streets, and pulled up to a large old house, a relic from a bygone era. It looked kind of like a gothic castle complete with moat which was dry and filled with tall weeds and ivy. It was almost dark now and hard to take in the house's entirety. I could tell it was three stories with great windows facing west, reflecting the last sliver of light from the pacific horizon.

After crossing the moat on a rickety wooden bridge, Maggie drove slowly up the driveway to a kind of juncture. The left leg merged onto a circular driveway that passed the main entrance to the house. We took the right leg which wrapped around the down slope side and parked. I got out and let my eyes sweep over the milky way of lights below, twinkling like jewels on black velvet. A soft breeze whispered through the nearby bushes and trees along the edge of the property. The air was filled with the fragrance of Night Blooming Jasmine. Maggie gingerly got out and slowly closed the car door.

"What is this place?" I said.

"Shhhh!," Maggie said. "Not so loud. It's my pad. I have a room here."

I then slammed my door shut.

"Jesus," she whispered.

"What's the matter?"

"Never mind," she said. "Come on in."

I followed Maggie along a dirt and gravel path I could barely see around to the other side of the house and then up the hillside a short distance to a door. Maggie got a key out from under a nearby rock and opened it. She turned on a table lamp just inside and closed the door behind me. I looked around the room. It was small with a low ceiling of cracked plaster and open beams. In one corner there was a sagging double bed mattress on the floor, piled with large pillows. In the opposite corner was a hot plate sitting on a wooden packing crate. Near the door was a wicker chair.

"What's that smell?" I said

"Incense."

I asked where the bathroom was. She pointed to a curtain. Behind it I found a small alcove with a toilet, small basin and a makeshift shower. I peed and checked myself in the mirror above the basin. My hair was getting shaggy and I had two days growth of beard. I borrowed Maggie's razor, since my shaving kit was in her car, and shaved using soap for lather. She also let me use her shower. It felt good. When I came out the light had been turned off and there were just some candles burning. They gave off an eerie glow.

Maggie was sitting on the floor. She had put a record on her phonograph called Mister Sandman and was smoking something that overpowered the incense and filled the room with an acrid smell. I figured it was marijuana.

"The Chordetts," she said. "Want to get high?"

She held what was left of the rolled cigarette up to me. I shook my head. Maggie shrugged and finished it off. I eased myself down near her and fired my own smoke. Maggie looked sullen in the flickering light of the candles. It then occurred to me that I should call Jenny, knowing it would not be an easy conversation.

"Do you have a phone?" I said.

"No," Maggie said.

She opened a can of beer she pulled out of a small refrigerator that also served as a night stand for the lamp. It had been painted black. She tossed me an unopened can. I was caught off guard and just managed to intercept it before it hit my head.

"You're something else," she said, laughed and tossed me the opener. "They must have beer back where you come from."

"Oh yeah, lots of beer," I said. "I'm no stranger to beer. Tell you the truth I even know a couple of kids back home that have smoked weed. I never have though."

I took a sip of beer.

"You should try it," Maggie said. "It'll get your head straight."

"I have to think about what I'm going to do now," I said, more to myself than to Maggie.

She began to giggle.

"Oh, you mean your career as a fucking writer of movies," she said. "You better think about just surviving. Out here that's what life's about, you know."

Again we were silent for a time. Maggie put on another record, this one was soft jazz, noting it was Stan Getz on sax. She stretched out. I continued sipping my beer and finishing off my smoke. Suddenly there was the sound of muffled ringing.

"What's that?" I said.

"The phone," Maggie said.

She crawled the short distance across the room to a pile of clothing next to the bed. She pushed the clothes away piece by piece. The phone continued to ring with some urgency.

"I thought you said you didn't have a phone."

"I lied," she said as the phone was revealed on the fifth ring. "Maggie's Hot Tamales," she said into the phone. "Maggie's out." She rolled her eyes. "Oh, hi. Nothing. No I don't feel like doing anything. No, I said. Jack, forget it. I'm not your chick, so knock off the bullshit. Okay? Cool. See ya." She hung up. "Asshole!"

"What'd he want?"

"Wants to get laid," Maggie said. "He can stay home and jack off as far as I'm concerned."

"I thought maybe he was your boyfriend," I said.

Maggie crawled up on the mattress and lay on her back staring at the ceiling.

"We made it a couple of times," she said. "That's it."

She told me that she had been thinking about the girl we dumped in the hills.

"Death is such a strange and mysterious thing, you know," Maggie said. "Someone somewhere must be worried about her."

"Yeah," was all I could think of to say.

"What's done is done," she said.

There was something alluring about Maggie and at the same time being with her felt like being on the edge of a cliff with a shear drop to oblivion. She motioned for me to join her on the mattress. I hesitated. But then I remembered something Silky had said to me when we were crossing the desert. She had wanted me to take a side road, stop and run naked in the warm sand. I told her she was crazy and kept going. She then had said to me that I should be more spontaneous, that I was wound a little too tight. Oddly enough I was impressed with that and even jotted it down.

I climbed on the mattress next to Maggie. She did something that kind of shocked me. She pushed her shorts down around her thighs, reached into the crotch of her panties and pulled out a small plastic bag. After pulling her shorts back up she opened the bag and pulled out another marijuana cigarette. She looked over at me and laughed.

"Got to hide it somewhere," she said.

She lit it, took a drag and offered it to me. This time I took it. She showed me how to smoke it and force the smoke into the brain. I felt light headed and soon very giggly.

"Wow," she said. "Pure gold. You, Tuckie have now busted your cherry."

The phone rang again. Maggie let it ring a few times and then got off the mattress and answered it. I could see a sour expression come over her face as she listened.

"Tonight?" She said. "Okay. Sure. No I don't mind. See you."

She replaced the receiver and looked pensive.

"I have to take care of some business," she said. "You stay here. I'll be back after awhile."

"Where do you have to go?"

"Out," she said flatly.

"Oh," I said.

"I have to go upstairs and meet with my landlord. We have this..um...business arrangement."

I looked at her blankly. Maggie stood up, went into her bathroom. When she pushed the curtain aside and came back out I barely recognized her. She'd combed her hair which now had a sheen to it, put on pale pink lipstick and changed into a clean blue blouse and full skirt. It was a complete transformation. She now had an almost girl-next-door look.

"Who owns this place?" I asked.

"Grover Marcuse," she said. "He's older, an artist. I model for him sometimes and he gives me this place rent free. He's working on a painting of a women working in a brothel. I'm no judge, but I think his work is good."

"While you're gone may I use the phone?"

"Help yourself," she said.

I told her it would be long distance, but I'd get the time and pay her. Maggie nodded. After she'd left, I lay back down on the mattress, still feeling the effects of the grass. I must have drifted off. I was beginning to dream when I heard a noise in the room. I opened my eyes to see the black shape of a figure sitting in the wicker chair on the other side of the room. Only two candles were still burning. My eyes tried to penetrate the darkness. It wasn't Maggie, that much I knew. Whoever it was, was smoking.

"Who's there?" I said.

Chapter 11

———

"Hey, man," came a familiar high pitched voice out of the dark from across the room. "How you doin, man? How's that career of yours going?"

I pushed myself up to a sitting position and leaned back against the wall trying to adjust my vision, aware that there was muffled music coming from somewhere in the house.

"Jack?" I said.

"Yeah," he said.

"What're you doing here?"

He stood up and weaved his way into the glow of the candle on the coffee table.

"I'm stoned, man." He said. "Wow, what a buzzed day, what a fucking buzzed day."

I looked at my watch. It was 9:30 which meant it was 11:30 back home. I swung my feet off the mattress, stood up and grabbed the phone. Luckily it had a long extension cord. I told Jack I had to make a phone call and would be a few minutes. He waived me off. I went into bathroom and gave the operator the number. It rang several times. A sleepy male voice answered.

"Hi, Mr. Gifford," I said, keeping my voice low.

"Who the hell is this?"

"It's Charles…Tuckie, Mr. Gifford. Can I talk to Jenny?"

"Tuckie?" He said angrily. "Do you know what time it is?"

I lied and told him I had forgotten the time difference. There was a click and Jenny came on the extension phone which was in the hallway downstairs. I figured she may have been watching TV. When she heard my voice she told her father it was okay and she would take it. Mr. Gifford grumbled, stayed on the line for another couple of moments and then hung up.

"Where are you?" Jenny asked.

"I'm in California...Los Angeles."

"I called your dad and he wouldn't talk to me," Jenny said, now sounding tearful. "Your aunt told me you'd just up and left. Why'd you do that without telling me? It's like you were all conspiring against me."

I fired up a smoke, thinking that a strange thing to say.

"What? No, no," I said. "I don't know why I didn't tell you. I tried to tell you but...the words wouldn't come."

I then explained the whole story to her about my career and all and that some day I would be back. She told me she loved me and would wait for me but urged me to come home soon. I promised to keep in touch. I hung up. I could hear jack behind the curtain clapping.

"That was real sweet, man,' he said. "So what the hell are you doing here anyway? That's the real question."

I pushed the curtain aside and came out, turned on the lamp and sat back on the mattress. I could see Jack clearly now, back sitting in the whicker chair. He had on a new wig, this one very curly and blonde. It made him look like an aging Little Orphan Annie with a pot belly. We stared at each other for a long moment.

"Do you think anyone has found the girl yet?" I said.

"What girl?" Jack snapped back. "I don't know anything about any lost girl."

"The girl whose body we took up to the hills," I said. "That girl."

Jack got up, went over to the refrigerator and grabbed the last beer. He found the opener which he then threw across the room after using it. He looked at me, his eyes looking inflamed.

"Don't know what you're talking about, hayseed, so why don't we just forget about it and move on down the road, so to speak. Know what I mean?"

I ran my hand through my hair and finished what was left of my smoke.

"How come you're here in my chick's place?" Jack went on. "That's the question of the moment."

I told him I thought Maggie probably felt sorry for me, deciding not to challenge whether or not Maggie was his girlfriend. I didn't care. Jack stood up and began wandering around looking through Maggie's things.

"Yeah, a heart of gold that chick." Jack said then pointed to his temple. "She's got it up here. Yeah, went to Stanford, made the dean's list, graduated cum laude or whatever the fuck that is. Shit, man I barely got out of goddamn grammar school. So where is she?"

I told him she had to go see her landlord about some business and wouldn't be back for awhile. Jack stopped pacing around and looked at me, then began laughing. He knelt down on the floor and doubled over, holding his midsection as his laughter turned into a harsh cough. When the coughing stopped he got back up.

"What's so funny about that?" I said.

"Business, my ass," Jack said. "Crazy assed chick! I'll show you something that will make those farm-boy eyes of yours bug out of your head. Let's go check it out."

"Where?"

Jack pointed toward the ceiling.

"We'll go sneak up on them," Jack said "It's a scene, believe me."

I hesitated.

"Don't worry about it," Jack said. "Come on I'll show you."

Outside I followed Jack down the hill on a gravel path along the back side of the house to a low window. He tried to open it. It stuck for a moment then gave and went up. Jack climbed in. I crawled in after him. It was pitch-black inside and smelled dank mixed with the faint sweet aroma of soap. We stood in the dark. Jack mumbled a curse to himself about not

91

bringing a flashlight. He lit a match which provided just enough illumination to make out that we were in a laundry room. Jack was giggling like a child getting into mischief as he made his way to a narrow stairway at the other end of the room. The match went out. He lit another one. I followed him up a narrow flight of stairs feeling an odd mixture of excitement and dread.

At the top of the stairs we went through a door and crossed a hallway into another room and up more stairs to another door where Jack motioned for me to crouch down. I did. Jack opened the door a crack. Bits of light zipped through the dark at instant broken intervals. I could hear the music better now. It sounded like opera. When I peered over Jack's shoulder I could see that the door led to a balcony that over-looked a very large open room. Even in the low light below I could see a few scattered pieces of furniture and a bench next to the right wall with a single lamp on it. A few feet from the bench was a table with tubes of paint and various size brushes. Giant half-finished canvases leaned against the other wall. The most astonishing thing was a giant ball of tiny mirrors hanging down from the ceiling going round and round flashing particles of light everywhere. The flashing light reflecting off the mirrored ball was a spotlight placed high on the opposite wall.

"Look at that those lights, man," Jack said. "It's fucking wild."

I moved closer to get a better view.

"Where's Maggie?" I said.

"Look," Jack said. "There's Marcuse, Maggie's landlord."

I could make out a tall, thin white-haired man who looked to be in his mid 50s. He was naked. His body looked luminous and very pale as if it had never been out in the sun.

"Maggie said he's an artist," I said. "Why's he naked?"

"He's a fucking freak," Jack said. "A rich freak. Town's full of them."

I moved back into the shadows.

"I don't think we should be here," I said. "It's like spying,"

Jack giggled. I moved back in close again, flat on the floor and peered down between the posts of the balustrade. Grover Marcuse was moving slowly around in time with the music, almost as if he were in a ballet. He held a sketch pad and scribbled furiously as he moved. When he was next to the table he picked up a bottle of wine and put it to his mouth. Wine dribbled down his chin. He set the bottle back down, wiped his chin with the back of his hand and continued moving around. Jack nudged me and said he thought Marcuse was playing the role of the mad artist, like Van Gough or someone like that. I'd never heard of Van Gough.

Maggie appeared. She'd come through a curtain onto a platform at the far end of the room and began moving to the music. The fractured light from the Strobe, as Jack called it, made her motion look like a flickering silent movie or like one of those mechanical men you sometimes see perform on the street. I saw one once on the television news back home. Maggie was also naked except for a shear piece of pink cloth she waved around in front of her. She looked like a professional dancer. I was mesmerized by the primal – I think that's the word – nature of the scene. It was hard to connect her with the chain-smoking, hard talking young woman I met that morning at Jack's place.

Grover Marcuse drank more wine and was stumbling around.

"Fucker's drunk, man," Jack yelled out and started clapping.

Marcuse spun around and peered up toward the balcony. Jack stood up and started jumping up and down, and hooting. I scooted back into the shadows.

"Great show, Maggie!" Jack yelled. "Why don't you finish the act and make it with this old asshole on the floor so we can watch and rate your performance!"

Jack was laughing so hard now he almost went head first off the balcony. I reached out and grabbed him by the shirt tail.

"Isn't that what all this artsy shit is about? You make it with this horny old bastard and the rent is free. Goddamn right! Hell of a deal."

"Who's that?" Grover Marcuse demanded, as he grabbed a robe from a nearby chair behind the table. "Who's up there? I'm calling the police."

For a long excruciating moment Maggie just stood there, seemingly oblivious to her nakedness, the scarf or whatever it was casually draped over her shoulder, the fragments of light washing over her like millions of tiny fireflies. She raised her hand to her brow and looked up where Jack was hanging over the balcony railing, light pulsating against his face, and me standing back a foot to his right. Grover Marcuse walked over and turned off the stereo system. He looked up again, clearly shaken by our presence.

"Why don't you two douche bags get the hell out of here!" Maggie screamed.

She turned to Marcuse.

"Don't call the cops, Grover. Please. They'll leave. And I am so sorry."

I grabbed Jack, who was still laughing manically now and pulled him away from the railing.

"She thinks she's Mata Hari," he said as we stumbled out and back up the hill with me holding him up.

Jack jerked away and disappeared into the night down toward the driveway and bridge. I yelled after him but there was no response. I went back into Maggie's wondering if I should stick around or not. Maggie returned about a half hour later. When she saw me sitting on the floor smoking she said nothing. Instead she went to a small dresser just outside her bathroom and pulled out a bottle of red wine from under some clothes. "Still here, eh?" She said to the bottle as if it were an old friend. She took a swig of the wine and then looked at me with unfriendly eyes. I figured that was my cue. I stood up and walked to the door.

"You don't have to go," she said.

I stood there looking at her.

"I wouldn't blame you if you wanted me to get out," I said.

She sighed.

"I'm going to kill that fucking Jack Wallace the next time I see him which I hope is never."

I came back and sat down on the floor next to Maggie. She handed me the wine bottle. I took a swallow and put it down and fired up a smoke.

"What do you know, anyway," she said without looking at me. "I have an arrangement here, understand? Sometimes I model, sometimes I perform, sometimes I...I do other things for Grover. It's easy work and it pays the rent and sometimes a little more. I make no apologies. So, I don't need any bullshit from assholes like Jack or you."

She looked at me now.

"Got it! I could have gotten my ass kicked out. Grover didn't say anything but I could tell he was plenty pissed."

She took another gulp of wine and suddenly she broke out laughing.

"Jesus, what a scene," she said. "It was like something out of a Fellini movie."

Maggie put on some music. We didn't talk for awhile. Later she opened a can of "chili con carne" which she dumped into a small pot and put on the hotplate. After we'd eaten, Maggie asked me to tell her more about my story, "Prairie Wolves." I gave her a brief synopsis.

"Sound's like corny exploitation shit," she said, her voice trailing off.

"It's based on a true story I read in a newspaper back home," I said. "I have to go back to Starburst/Meade Productions tomorrow."

Maggie didn't say anything. I looked over at her. She was sound asleep, her head flopped over the edge of her mattress. I picked her up and stretched her out and covered her with a blanket. The candles had burned themselves out. I turned off the lamp and lay down on the floor with a thin blanket over me. As I drifted off, the image of the dead girl sprawled on the side of the hill left me with a strange sense of loss as if she had meant something to me. And then another image surfaced as the curtain came down, Adele, as I had remembered her, her lifeless form lying cold in a shallow grave, dirt and branches being thrown on top of her by an unseen hand.

Chapter 12

———

Morning broke clear and warm. Maggie made coffee. She put fresh grounds from a Hills Brothers can into an old fashioned coffee pot with boiling water. "Cowboy coffee," she remarked as I sat there on the floor furrowing my brow. I spit the grounds out into a saucer as I sipped from an enameled tin cup. Otherwise it tasted good, strong. Maggie turned her radio on to a country western station. Between records the disc jockey announced a local show with teenage singer Molly Bee. "I've heard her," Maggie said. "She's real down home." After a few minutes came the news, mostly international. This was followed by the local news. Heading the local news was a report that the body of an unidentified woman in her 20s had been found in the Hollywood Hills off Mulholland Drive. Police were investigating. Cause of death not yet determined. Maggie and I just looked at each other.

"Shit," she said and disappeared behind the curtain into her bathroom. She reappeared about twenty minutes later. This was another Maggie. She was dressed in a clean white blouse, trim black skirt, nylon stockings and high heels. Her just-washed hair shined in the bright morning light and smelled of shampoo. She lit a cigarette, took a sip of her coffee and eyed me over the rim.

"Why are you staring?" She said.

"You look different," I said. "So far I've seen three different Maggies since yesterday."

"You're full of it," she said. "I have a job today in an office. It's a clerical job through a temp agency, so I have to look a certain way. I type, which means I can work pretty much when I want." She looked sullen for a moment. "Sometimes I feel like I'm a Chameleon."

"What's that?" I said.

"A kind of lizard," she said. "It..well it has the ability to blend in wherever it is."

"Oh."

Maggie drove me to Starburst/Meade. As I got out of her car she told me that I could stay at her place for a few days until I figured out what I was going to do. She hurriedly explained how to get back to her place and reminded me where the key was hidden.

Then, just before driving off she said, "I'm sure there's no way they can trace that girl to us."

I just stared after her, feeling my stomach churn for a moment.

Once again I found myself barred at the door by the fat woman called Jocelyn. She asked me what I wanted as if she had never seen me before. Her face was close enough that I could smell the stink of cigar on her mouth and clothing. I explained again that I was there to collect my prize money for my story, "Prairie Wolves," and start my writing career.

"Prairie Wolves?" She said. "Never heard of it."

"I want to see Mr. Meade," I said.

"He's not in," she said. "Come back another time."

"When?"

"He's a busy man," she said and slammed the door in my face.

Back out in front I sat down on the front step to wait in hopes of catching Mr. Meade. But after waiting all day with only a short break to get a cheeseburger, not a soul came or went. Not even Sherry Woo. But it was Saturday, so I figured she was probably off. As evening approached I caught a bus back to Franklyn and Vine and walked the rest of the way up the hill to Maggie's place.

On my third morning at Maggie's I read a story in the morning paper which I found in the driveway out in front: Woman Found in Hills

Identified. "The body of a young woman found in the Hollywood Hills two days ago has been identified as 23-year-old Margo Teresa Benson. She was a student at Pepperdine College. According to the coroner's office the cause of death was an apparent mix of drugs and alcohol. She was the daughter of Charlotte and Edward Benson of Brentwood. They were quoted as saying their daughter never used drugs in her life. She must have fallen in with a bad crowed. Services are to be held at Forest Lawn on Saturday at 11 a.m.

The following night Maggie and I almost made love on her mattress. Actually Maggie had initiated it. It was half hearted at best. I did not respond. She then asked me what I thought of her, did I like her? The question came at me softly in the dark as I was almost asleep. I didn't answer. She then turned over on her side and soon her breathing was heavy and regular. I stared into the darkness and thought about Jenny. Then I switched to my story. I figured I would begin working on a script. Since my original story was in my suitcase, which was probably in the Dodge, which was probably in San Francisco, I would work from memory. In the meantime I would have to find a way to make some money and more importantly find a way to see Mr. Frank Meade who was beginning to seem more like a phantom than someone who actually existed.

"What's your experience? The man behind the counter asked me. His name was Chick. He was a large black man with a large head and a great round face. He had a knowing look that said he'd seen it all. The place was called Chick's Burger Palace, basically a hole in the wall with greasy windows. The sign on the door outside said "Breakfast, Lunch and Dinner" It was morning and the place was not busy. There was one waitress wearing a pink uniform who looked about 18 years old. She was handling one half of the place and Chick the other half.

Chick was moving back and forth, almost like a dance, turning hash browns, bacon, and eggs on the grill one after the other all the while interviewing me. I sat at the counter opposite the grill. The smell of the bacon dominated. Next he put everything onto a plate and served a man down at the other end of the counter. With the frying pan in one hand

and a spatula in the other he flipped the eggs high into the air, almost to the ceiling and burst into song as he watched the eggs flip in mid-flight. On their descent he raised the pan up to meet them, brought the pan down with them at a slightly slower speed until the eggs and pan met with perfect precision. I was impressed.

"A soft landing for these babies," Chick said.

In a continuing motion, he slid the eggs onto a plate and added the remaining hash browns from the grill.

"Here," he said handing me the plate. "Take these down to those folks in the booth near the door. That order is for the man. Be careful."

I did. Chick followed me with the woman's order, a short stack that he'd apparently set aside.

Earlier I had tried to get a job at a café on Santa Monica Boulevard not far from Starburst/Meade but they weren't hiring. A waitress at that café had overheard me talking to the manager and told me about Chick's Hamburger Palace on La Brea near Melrose. Chick gave me an application which I filled out. It was a mimeographed copy of an original that had been hand-written. The heading at the top said "Chick's Fantastic Burger Palace Employment Application. Return to Personnel Department."

"It says here, in addition to working at some restaurant called MARCO's," Chick said, " you worked in a movie theater as an usher and sometime projectionist, on dead folks in a mortuary, even made some of them up, I imagine to look pretty for kin. Must have been spooky."

I explained about learning the business from my father and that the work never bothered me.

"So, how come you quit that exciting business and came out here?"

I shrugged.

"Guess, I didn't want to do that the rest of my life," I said, and looked at Chick who was expressionless as if waiting for some kind of punch line. So I said, "I really just wanted to come out here and work at Chick's Burger Palace."

He stared at me for a beat and then broke out in laughter.

"God damn," he said. "You got your wish, kid. That is, I'll give you a try. Screw up once and you're done. How old are you anyway? Long as you're over 21. You ain't exactly a kid. Never mind. One more thing. Never refer to me as the owner."

"When do I start?" I said, deciding not to ask why.

"Now," he said and tossed me an apron and a white cap.

During my training, Chick proudly told me that without question his burgers were the absolute best in the entire state of California, maybe even the U.S.A. He knew this because he traveled from one end of the state to the other, tried every hamburger in every one horse town, truck stop, as well as the big city restaurants along the way and determined that his were the best. No contest, a scientific fact.

"It's in the sauce I use along with the best fresh ground beef," he said. "The sauce is a secret recipe given to me by my mother. It's about the only thing I inherited from her after she passed. I perfected it over time. Folks love it."

I looked around.

"I don't see them fighting to get in here," I said.

"No mind. I just bought this place. First thing we've got to do is clean the joint up, scrub the grease off the windows. Look at them. You can barely see outside."

Chick told me he would pay me top dollar.

"You'll get $1.15 an hour plus tips and meals."

That night at Maggie's I celebrated my new job by guzzling a can of beer. Maggie joined me with a glass of red wine.

"What about your famous movie writing career?" She asked.

I opened another beer and fired up a smoke.

"My career?" I said. "My career is…is on course. Yes it is. Don't worry."

"I'm not worried," Maggie said, sounding mildly irritated at the suggestion. Her voice deepened. "Frankly my dear I don't give a rat's ass."

"Very good," I said and clapped. "Clark Gable could not have done it better."

Maggie shook her head, pulled a cigarette out of a pack she had on the coffee table, leaned over and pressed the end to my lit cigarette. There was something very intimate about it. She took a deep drag and tried to blow smoke rings.

"You're really into this movie horseshit thing aren't you," she said.

I took a deep breath and shut my eyes for a moment as old movie images flashed behind my eyes. I took a swig of beer and wiped my mouth off.

"For every thought you ever thought," I began, "every emotion you've ever felt, every dream you've ever dreamed, it's all in a movie somewhere. Did you know that? It's all there on the big screen in a dark theatre, or some vault where they store old movies. It's like being able to live in another world for a time, or like finding an oasis with cold water in the middle of a blazing desert. And a lot of what you see on that screen stays with you, becomes a part of you. Like the Wichita Kid. I think he's inside of me, holding the reins, yelling faster at me. Someday I hope to meet the Wichita Kid."

Maggie pulled on her cigarette and stared at me.

"Who the hell is the Wichita Kid?"

I just grinned at her.

"I kind of like you, Tuckie, but if you want to know the truth I'm not sure you're running on a full tank of gas."

I lay flat on the floor and stared at the ceiling, which had a network of cracks like a giant spider web.

"Sometimes," I said, "I feel like I'm on a mission or something. Maybe I am."

"What do you mean?" Maggie said.

"To bring my movie back home," I said absently. "But I...I have another reason for being out here."

"What's that?"

"There's this man I want to find. His name is Jimmy Oliver. He ran off with my mother when I was 12 years old. He came out here to Los

102

Angeles as far as I know. But my mother never got any farther than a few miles from our house. Or maybe she did and came back. "

Maggie suddenly looked very interested.

"I don't understand," she said.

I explained that she had been murdered and buried, and how her remains had recently been discovered after all these years.

"Wow," Maggie said. "And if you find this guy? What then?"

I shrugged and rolled over on my side to face Maggie.

"I don't know," I said. "The really strange thing is I got a postcard from her not long after she left. It came from out here."

Maggie stood up and put two tiny steaks she'd bought into a small electric broiler that had been hidden under some clothes. After a few minutes smoke began pouring out of it. She opened a window, then came back, hiked up her skirt and sat down cross-legged on a lime green pillow. The smell of meat cooking reminded me of Marco's on a Saturday night when just about everything on the menu was barbecued. Maggie held the bottle of wine to her lips and took a couple of swallows. She handed the bottle to me. I took a sip and handed it back.

"You must have hated this Jimmy Oliver for taking your mother away at the time," she said.

I shook my head.

"I blamed my father. He would drink and abuse her. She was much younger than him and wanted a new life I guess. I was real angry at first. I wanted them to take me with them."

After we had our steaks, which were slightly charred, Maggie began talking about her own life. She had come down from Seattle Washington to find herself. Her father was an engineer at Boeing Aircraft and her mother a teacher at a local high school. After a while she put on a Joni James recording, Purple Shades, and danced sensuously, still holding the wine bottle.

"In a way, I envy you," she said. "You have a dream about doing something, writing movies. I don't know how realistic that is, but it's a crazy force in you, driving you."

Maggie was beginning to slur her words. I figured she was getting drunk. She stopped dancing and stretched out on the floor and finished the bottle. She appeared to be contemplating me thorough half closed eyes.

"Tuckie, why don't you come over here with Maggie? Maggie wants to see you."

I didn't move.

"Okay," she said. "Guess I'll have to come over there."

"Why?" I said and then felt stupid.

Maggie crawled over to me, kissed me half on my face and half on my mouth. She turned over onto her back and rested her head on my lap. Her arms reached up and pulled me down so that our mouths barely touched. It felt awkward.

"Relax," Maggie whispered. "It's okay. Don't talk."

I could smell the wine on her breath, a sweet fruity smell.

"I...I guess I'm not sure what' we're doing," I said.

Her eyes were full of laughter.

"I feel like making love with you, No, having sex with you," she said. "You don't have to say you love me or any crap like that. Don't question it. Just go for the ride, okay."

I took a deep breath and nodded.

"Mmm. Good," Maggie purred from deep in her throat.

She kissed me, her tongue working its way into my mouth, at the same time taking my hand and pushing her skirt up and placing it on the inside of her thigh. She then moved her hips so that my hand grazed the warm wet middle of her panties. I was consumed by the softness and heat of her body. Both of us were beginning to breathe heavier now. She wiggled out of her clothes, undid my pants and pulled them off along with my shorts. I instinctively made a fumbled attempt to cover myself but gave up. Maggie then slowly bent down kissing my belly, lingered for a moment and then took me into her mouth, sucked for a few moments before raising up again and pulling me down on top of her. I lasted for a long time before exploding in her. Afterward, sitting naked, smoking and sipping more wine from a new bottle Maggie laughingly told me it was an impressive performance for a farm boy.

"In fact, if word got out you might find yourself in demand," she said.

I shrugged, feeling a little embarrassed.

"Must have been the beer and wine," I said and found myself grinning at her, even feeling affectionate toward her.

"What if we made a little Tuckie?" she said.

"What?" I said.

"Don't panic," she laughed. "I can't have children. No uterus. I had a hysterectomy a couple of years ago. Cancer. It was discovered when I got out of Stanford."

I just stared at Maggie blankly, not sure what to say. Maggie nodded her head slightly, her eyes closed. I thought she might be going to sleep. Suddenly her head snapped up and she looked at me, squinting in the dim light.

"I met this man once who might be able help you. He's a very strange looking man, very small. I met him at a party Grover Marcuse took me to. Grover knows him. At one point I thought he was trying to make it with me. I might have gone for it too. There was something really powerful about him. He gave me his card. Grover told me that he was an agent, at one time one of the most powerful talent reps in this town. He knows people.

"What's his name?"

"It's an odd name," Maggie said and closed her eyes as if trying to picture him. She opened them again. "Herman. Herman Zeppelin. But he's called some other name."

"Fat Eyes?" I said.

"Yeah," Maggie said. "How did you know?"

I recounted two sightings of the man. She thought that was weird, but maybe a sign. Before we went to sleep I told Maggie that I was going to go to the funeral of the girl from Jack's place.

"How do you get to Forest Lawn?"

Maggie's eyes popped open and she stared at me in astonishment. She lit another cigarette and accused me of being an escapee from a nut house somewhere.

"Why do you want to go to the chick's funeral? It's insane."

"I know," I said.

"You'll stick out in that crowed," Maggie said. "And those clothes you've been wearing are getting pretty ripe. What's more the Fuzz will probably be there."

"Fuzz?"

"Cops," she said. "I mean it is the craziest, stupidest thing."

"Yeah," I said. "I know."

Chapter 13

The morning of Margo Benson's funeral, I awoke feeling strangely excited. I wasn't sure what it was that was drawing me, only that I had to go. It was like a dream where you could feel that there was something ahead of you that you had to get to, but was veiled in a sort of fog that prevented you from seeing what it was. Yet you feel somehow it is important. It wasn't until I got there that it came to me.

A few days before, I called Jenny while on a break at Chick's Burger Palace. I used a phone in back. Jenny was still at the bank. She said she had been worried about me since she hadn't heard from me in a week. She told me that Zona called a couple of times to see if I had called her again. It was particularly troubling because Royce had received a call from the Los Angeles County Sheriff's office about my car. That it had been found abandoned. It was impounded and towed to a storage yard waiting to be claimed. The Sheriff's office said there was no police report on it being stolen and wondered what the story was. Royce was going to hang up on them but Zona took the phone and got the information which she passed along to Jenny who gave it to me.

"When are you coming home?" She said, her voice taking on a plaintive tone.

"I don't know," I said. "My career hasn't quite started yet."

After work, which was about 2:30 because I was working the breakfast and lunch crowds, I took a series of busses to get to the storage yard in East Los Angeles. The place was huge, several acres at least. It was like looking at a sea of rusted car hulks, stacks of rubber tires, and mountains scrap metal. The office, which was nothing more than a shack was just inside the entrance. A heavy set man with three days growth of beard wearing a straw hat greeted me. The nameplate on his desk said Butch Sunlove.

"If you want the car it will cost $75 for towing and storage." Butch said.

"Where did they find it?"

He looked at the paperwork on his desk.

"It says here Boyle Heights," he said.

I told him I would like to look at the car first to be sure it was mine. Butch went outside and pointed down one row.

"All the way to the end," he said. "You can look but do not take anything from the car, even if it's yours."

I found the old Dodge at the very end of the row. It looked like it had been in an accident, one side scraped. Underneath one end of the drive shaft was on the ground. I figured the universal joint had finally given up. Inside, on the floor in the back, the Suitcase was still there. I looked around to make sure no one was coming and then pulled the back seat forward, reached in behind the spare tire and was barely able to get my fingers on the small cloth pouch with my grandfather's gun. It had been wedged in pretty tight. I shoved it into my belt and covered it with my shirt. I did another check around. The manager was talking to someone just outside the office. I grabbed the suitcase and crouched down. Using the next row over for cover I made my way to the entrance and out onto the street. I had to run to catch a passing city bus at the corner. Just as I got on the bus I looked back to see Butch run out shaking his fist at me.

My outline for The Prairie Wolves was still inside the suitcase and my clothes. I found a book at the public library which gave me some idea of how to format a script, describe action and camera angles. I scribbled in longhand on white lined paper to develop a script, sitting on Maggie's floor using the coffee table as a desk. Between my efforts to dream up characters and plot points I drank coffee and smoked. Getting started had not been easy. But now I felt some momentum. Day after day, page after page, a script was beginning to form. Maggie typed the pages for me and even did some editing. She seemed to enjoy doing it.

I went into Maggie's bathroom, shaved, showered and put on a dark gray suit I found at the Salvation Army for $7.00 and a white shirt for fifty cents. It was a very tight fit but I figured a suit would be more appropriate for Margo Benson's funeral. The finishing touch was my red clip-on bow tie. Perfect.

When I came out from behind the curtain Maggie was standing there in a terry cloth robe. She looked at me and her mouth literally dropped open, the cigarette she'd just lit dangling form one corner of her lower lip. She took the cigarette in hand and burst into hysterical laughter.

"What's so funny?" I said, feeling a little annoyed as I worked to press down on my cowlick.

"That suit," she said. "It looks like a 1930s depression special."

"It was all I could find that fit," I said.

Maggie bent over laughing even harder now.

"I've got news for you," she said, tears running down her cheeks. "You look like a refugee just off the goddamned boat."

I paid no mind, and put on a pair of sunglasses and smiled broadly. Maggie got out her old box camera and took a picture of me. I asked if I could borrow her car but she offered to take me to Forest Lawn after further commentary about the stupidity of going. She dressed, putting on a thin blouse, no bra, and washed out denim pedal pushers with a hole in one knee.

"You're going like that?" I said.

Maggie glared at me.

"What are you, my mother?" She shot back. "You want a ride or not?"

The drive to Forest Lawn took about 20 minutes. Maggie parked her car just outside the entrance and said she'd wait. I walked from there. There were no policemen in sight. The service was going to be at the Church on the Hill according to the most recent notice in the newspaper.

I stopped a man on the path and got directions. I couldn't believe how big and well groomed the place was. Back home cemeteries were more like weed infested stone gardens.

I entered the Church. It smelled sweet. An usher directed me to sign the guest book which lay open on a stand in the vestibule. I hesitated at first, but noticed the usher's gaze boring in on me, probably taking in my suit as well. I signed Charles Kendall and put down Maggie's address. The family would likely send me a thank you note.

Soft organ music filled the main chapel. I stood by the door as mourners filed past, some stopping to appreciate the various floral arrangements. Everyone looked spit shined. I began nodding at arrivals as if I were there in some official capacity, acknowledging their grief. However one couple gave me the fish eye, clearly not impressed with my Salvation Army suit.

It was a well-heeled crowd, no doubt about that. There were lots of lavish jewels displayed on skin burnished by the California sun. These people must spend most of their time sitting around swimming pools, I thought. Everyone looked properly solemn, speaking in hushed voices as they greeted each other. "She was such a beautiful girl," I heard one woman say to a friend she was hugging that she apparently hadn't seen in some time. "How could such a thing happen?"

Just inside the chapel I stood and looked closely at the face of every man who entered. I was trying to identify a particular face, but I had no idea what the face looked like. It was a long shot but I thought maybe Frank Meade would show up, that he would know some of these people.

The bronzed faces continued to move passed me. They were many and varied, young and old, beautiful and important looking. Lots of potential uncle types. When it looked like the family filled the front rows on both sides of the aisle I strode up and pretended as if I were looking for someone, trying to spot a likely uncle type who could be in the movie business. There were three faces that looked promising. Suddenly I felt self conscious. Everyone was looking at me. I turned and walked up to the open casket and peered in. There was Margo Benson, hands folded across

110

her chest. She looked beautiful. They'd put her in a simple blue dress. Accessories were a white beaded necklace, matching earrings and a blue bow in her hair. I was appalled at the amount of make-up they'd used. Her lips were unnaturally red, all wrong for her coloring.

I felt a tap on my shoulder and turned around to face an usher giving me the onceover.

"Could you take a seat, please," he said. "The service is about to begin."

The service was conducted by a minister who said he was a long time friend of the family. In his eulogy he spoke of Margo's beauty, her gentle spirit and how she had somehow allowed evil to enter her young life and take control in a way that ultimately led her into the darkness. I wondered if I was a conspirator in that place of darkness. After the minister finished a young man in a black suit got up and introduced himself as Margo's brother Johnny. He talked about how close they were and then his voice cracked and he wept. Silence followed and it was as if no one knew what to do next. The minister started for the podium but was interrupted by a commotion that had erupted near the front. A stocky man in a black and white checkered sport coat and yellow and black polka dot tie stood up. The woman next to him tugged at his arm. She could be heard saying, "Please don't." Both were obviously agitated. The man jerked his arm away from the woman's grip and went to the podium.

He cleared his throat and scanned the more than 200 people attending. Even from where I was sitting I could see the muscles in his square jaw rippling with anger. Who ever this guy was, he was cut from a different cloth than the rest. Next he put his hands on each side of the podium, gripping the edges tightly and leaned into the microphone. I noticed that he had rings on several fingers and a pinky ring on his left hand. He glanced at family members and scowled.

"They didn't want me to speak," he said in a low whiskey voice. "But I'm Margo's uncle Maurice – Moe - and I'm angry and I got something I wanna say."

So, that's uncle Moe, I said to myself. All I could remember was Margo had said, though it had been hard to hear above the noise of the party, that she had an uncle who had something to do with movies, and his name was Moe.

"Now I don't know about whether she let the devil take over her life or not, or even what that means exactly. What I do know is she was taken from us, taken from us by others who took advantage of her innocence and introduced her to drugs, you know. So, what I'm saying is, I want the scum who did this to my niece to pay. They're out there somewhere. They'll be found. She was a good girl."

A hushed murmur rippled through the chapel. Mourners looked at each other quizzically. I felt there was a sense of uneasiness and embarrassment with the family at the uncle's words and his bullish demeanor. There was even something a little scary about him. On the other hand I was real happy that he came forward to speak.

Uncle Maurice took a handkerchief out of his breast pocket and dabbed at beads of sweat on his large brow and nose. "That's all I got to say," He said and returned to the pew.

The minister invited anyone who cared to say a few words about Margo to come up. Several people spoke. When the last person finished the minister was about to close the service when I jumped up from where I was sitting, which was close to the front and jogged to the podium. The minister eyed me with shock and suspicion as he stepped aside. I stood there for what seemed like an eternity as it came to me that I had no idea what I wanted to say. I tried to recall speeches from old movies during moments like this but none came to mind. People were beginning to cough and fidget.

I nervously fiddled with my tie and cleared my throat a couple of times. I looked around the room and saw Maggie peaking out from behind a pillar at the back. The sight of her got me to start talking.

"Frankly, I don't believe God had any plan to take Margo from us so soon. If he did, then it was a foolish plan without any point to it. No, Margo loved life. She loved people. She loved animals. She loved nature.

Even bugs were creatures with rights to her way of thinking. So, what kind of plan would take such a person away?"

I was now feeling the momentum of what I was saying, the words rushing out of my mouth, carrying me along. I looked out into the mass of faces for some hint of reaction. Nothing. Only stone cold eyes staring back at me like zombies, as if I were some sort of apparition. I went on, "What I think is, Margo put her trust in the wrong people who used her up and threw her away like garbage. Garbage! Evil people, Communists, drug users who must be weeded out so that others like Margo will not fall into the same trap. Yeah!"

I nodded and returned to my seat, all eyes following me. The minister announced a gathering at the family home. Pallbearers carried the casket down the aisle and out to a waiting hearse. A few minutes later as people were leaving Maggie reached out and grabbed me just outside.

"Are you out of your cotton picking mind?" She said, gritting her teeth. "What the hell are you doing?"

I looked around. Mourners were heading to the gravesite. I heard snatches of conversation as folks began moving in a column up a path. One man talked about how his stocks were doing, another man was impatient to get to a golf game, and a woman noted to a friend that an afternoon swim at the club sounded good along with a martini.

I spotted Margo's father in the crowd. He had on a black suit and tie, and looked to be in his early 50s.

"Stay here," I said. "I'll be right back."

As he started heading for a waiting black limo I strode up and extended my hand. He looked bewildered as if he wasn't quite sure what to do. He finally stuck his hand out and we shook. "Hi," I said. "I'm Charles Kendall. I'm sorry we had to meet under these circumstances…But I was wondering, do you know if Mr. Meade came her today?"

"Meade?"

"Frank Meade, the movie producer," I said

Mr. Benson shook his head.

"I'm afraid I don't know the man."

"Oh," I said. "I just thought...well someone said he might be here... So..."

"I didn't get your name," Dr. Benson said.

"Charles Kendall," I said.

"Where did you know my daughter from?" He said.

I smiled and looked around to see if I could spot uncle Maurice. No sign of him.

"Oh, just around." I said. "You know."

"I see," Dr. Benson said. "Those were... err...very interesting remarks you made. Communists?"

Mrs. Benson approached, nodded at me and guided her husband to the waiting limo. As they were walking a way I heard her ask her husband who that strange young man was. He just shook his head.

It was getting hot and I was beginning to sweat under my shirt. I began to head back to the gate. Maggie was standing alone on the side of the drive just inside the gate, smoking. As I headed in her direction I saw uncle Maurice standing by himself on the grass lighting a cigar. I veered off the path and pretended to walk by him casually.

"Hi," I called out. "Nice day."

Uncle Maurice pushed his sunglasses up to his brow and scrutinized me then returned his glasses and looked out across the vast expanse of green. His broad craggy face was pockmarked and reminded me of a scary movie character. I approached, told him my name and stuck my hand out. He didn't take it.

"You're Margo's uncle Maurice, right? I liked what you said inside the chapel."

Without looking at me he said kind of absently: "All these people come here and pretend to mourn. But they don't really give a fuck about Margo. It's more like the social occasion of the season."

He looked at me again as if seeing me for the first time.

"Do I know you?"

"No, sir," I said. "Your niece mentioned you. She was very fond of you."

114

Uncle Maurice pulled on his cigar and flicked some ashes.

"Really?" He said, his eyes rising to my face as he pocketed his matches. "Where exactly did you know her from? It wasn't school. You look older."

I shook my head.

"Around different places," I said.

"Uh, huh. Well, I'd like to get hold of the vermin that dumped her in the hills. I'd string that son of a bitch, or those sons of bitches up by their heals."

I smiled weakly and looked away, then back to uncle Maurice and nodded my agreement.

"What do you do?" He said.

"I'm writing a movie," I said.

I could see Maggie out of the corner of my eye gesturing impatiently for me to get out of there.

"That right...What's your name again?"

I told him.

"Charles, you and every other fucking asshole in this town are writing a movie. I think my gardener's even writing a goddamned script or something."

"What do you do, Maurice?" I said.

Uncle Maurice gave me a very hard look.

"What the hell business is that of yours?

"Margo told me you're connected to the movie business, Maurice."

Uncle Maurice raised his glasses again so that I could see that he was glaring at me.

"First of all, no one calls me Maurice. It's Moe. Second, I don't talk to punks in moth-eaten suits about my business. Especially punks on the make."

I moved around to Moe's left out of the glare of the sun, not sure what he meant by "on the make."

"I was just wondering if you know the producer I'm working with on this movie I'm writing? His name is Frank Meade, Starburst/Meade Productions."

Moe laughed and then began coughing and took the cigar out of his mouth.

"That asshole," Moe said. "Biggest scam artist ever walked the streets of this kookville town. I wouldn't give him the sweat off my pecker in Death Valley in July." Moe stopped for a beat. "He was pretty good once. Some of his films actually made money in the old days. But he's washed up, hasn't done shit in years. Good luck!"

"Oh," was about all I could get out for a moment. Then I said: "Moe, I'd like to talk to you about my movie."

"I don't talk business at funerals," Moe said. "What'd you say your name was?"

I repeated my name and added that most folks call me Tuckie. Moe frowned, then reached into his wallet and handed me his business card.

"Tuckie?" Don't sound like a grownup's name. "You got chutzpa though, I'll say that. You wanna see me, call. And by the way, my niece hated bugs."

Moe turned and walked away.

Later, on the way back to her place, Maggie said she thought my speech was weird, and the uncle's remarks sent shivers up her spine.

"He's a pretty sleazy looking character," Maggie added. "I'd stay away from him."

Chapter 14

———

She came into Chick's Hamburger Palace. It was about a month after Margo Benson's funeral. I was working late, moving fast hustling burger's behind the counter. I looked toward the other end to see her climb onto a stool and thumb through the hand-written menu. At first I couldn't place her, only that her profile looked familiar. She had a scrubbed look. I thought maybe it was an actress I'd seen. A few moments later I went down to get a closer look and stared at her, almost full faced. It finally hit me that it was the Asian woman from Starburst/Meade. Sherry something? It was her hair that made her look different. She had cut it short. I started to say hello but was distracted by other customers at the counter shouting orders, three cheeseburgers and one without. I jotted down the order, put it on the order cylinder and spun it into the kitchen.

Chick had been right about his recipe for hamburgers. In no time his place had developed a following. Customers came from all over. A trucker came in one day and said he'd heard about Chick's Hamburger Palace while driving through Bakersfield a few days before. Chick had to hire a dishwasher and two more full time waitresses to keep up with the demand. Without question it was his secret sauce that brought people in. It had a hickory flavor to it. Chick was very secretive about how it was made. He barked at me when I asked about it once, and told me not to be sticking my nose where it didn't belong. But then he grinned and put his thick arm around my shoulder. Both the grill behind the counter and the kitchen were busy.

"Look at them folks scarf down my burgers," he said. "And not one of them saw an advertisement. Just one person telling another, best advertisement in the world."

Chick also decided to buy imported green coffee beans and roast them himself. This was also a hit with customers even though he charged an extra nickel.

I remembered the woman's name was Sherry Woo. She ordered a cheeseburger and a coke. I served it to her. She looked up at me but didn't recognize me. It may have been the white apron, cap to contain my longish hair, and a mustache I'd been cultivating. She began reading the Hollywood Reporter while munching on her first bite from the burger.

"How do you like it?" I said.

"Fantastic," she said, her mouth still full.

I stood there watching her, wondering if I should tell her who I was. I was feeling embarrassed that my movie writing career was stalled and here I was working as a hamburger jockey. Despite the stone wall I'd run up against with Starburst/Meade I was pleased with my progress writing the script for the Prairie Wolves. It was almost completed.

Sherry Woo had stopped eating and was staring at me.

"Why do you look familiar?" She said. "Do I know you from somewhere?"

While I was serving a man who had sat down next to her I said out of the side of my mouth that I had met her at Starburst/Meade. She looked puzzled for a moment then her face lit up.

"Oh," she said. "You're the guy who claimed to have won one of the writing contests we hold. I remember you now. You look different."

"I wondered if you were going to recognize me," I said.

"Add a cup of coffee to that order," the man sitting next to Sherry Woo said.

I poured the man a cup of coffee and went back to Sherry Woo.

"You look different," she said. "So how long have you been working here?"

"A few weeks, actually a month," I said. "You still at Starburst/ Meade?"

She nodded with a sigh.

"Still there," she said and gave a short laugh. "It's like being in an elevator stuck between the first and second floor."

Chick called to me to get some more pre-cut potatoes from the back room. I told Sherry to stick around, that I'd be right back. I wanted to talk to her. But when I returned a few minutes later she was gone. Chick told me the Chinese girl had paid and left. I ran outside to see if I could catch her, but no sign of her.

After work I went to Starburst/Meade. It took two buses to get there. After pounding on the door it opened a crack. Jocelyn Bukowski stuck her head out.

"What do you want?" She said.

It was clear she did not recognize me. I told her I was looking for Sherry Woo, that I was an old friend and was supposed to meet her there at Starburst/Meade. Jocelyn told me she wasn't there, probably at her writing class. I pretended that I forgot and that was really where I was actually suppose to meet her but I couldn't remember where it was. Jocelyn was incredulous, then rolled her eyes skyward. She started to close the door on me. I put my foot in the way. She told me the class was being held in an old pink bungalow on North Orange Grove Avenue a few doors from Romaine.

"Some geezer has-been writer teaches the class," Jocelyn said and slammed the door behind me as I left.

I caught an east bound bus on Santa Monica to Fairfax Avenue. From there it was a few minutes walk. There were mostly apartments on North Orange Grove. I found the pink house in the middle of the block. It was a small stucco house with a front lawn that was near death with large patches of brown, sprinkled with creeping weeds. The front door was ajar. I walked in and stood in the small vestibule for a moment. It smelled musty and dank. I went into a room on my left which was a small front room with a fireplace. Muffled voices were coming from an adjoining room closed off by double doors. I walked over and put my ear to one of the doors. A man with a thick foreign accent, maybe Russian or something like that was talking. I went back to the hallway and found my way to the kitchen. There was a swinging door at the end. I pushed it open a crack and peaked into what looked like the dining room. I counted nine students sitting at a long oak table. With the exception of Sherry Woo and a few others, most of them looked middle age and older. At the head of the table, lecturing, was a white-haired man who looked to be in his 70s. I pushed open the door and crouched down and took an empty seat against the wall. No one noticed me.

The old man was talking about story ideas that begin with seeds that you plant and let grow naturally. "They can't be forced," he said. "Give them nourishment, give them love. Be patient. If the seeds are good they will grow into ideas, and in turn beget ideas, situations, plots, characters. They will flourish like flowers in a meadow." He waived his arms apparently at the imaginary flowers in the meadow.

I fired up a smoke. The old man looked across the room at me and shook his head.

"Please, no smoking in here," he said. "Are you a student? I don't remember you."

I put my cigarette out and said I was a friend of Sherry Woo's. Sherry spun around and stared at me. The old man suggested they finish up the session.

"Characters must drive the bus," he said. "They must have a kind of map that will take them down the road so to speak to the obligatory scene and ultimate denouement. "Boy wants girl. Boy gets girl. Boy looses Girl. Boy gets girl back." The old man grinned, obviously pleased with himself.

He took a drink of water from a glass on the table in front of him and cleared his throat.

"In real life it is the same," he said. "I mean, are people hanging around this earth to carry out some grand scheme, players on a grand stage, or are they simply making it up as they go along?

So students, that is the question you must ask yourselves as you begin your journey. See you all next week."

Outside on the sidewalk, Sherry Woo demanded to know what I was doing there. I told her I was there to see her, to talk to her.

"What about?" She snapped. "And be quick. I'm going to a movie with a couple of the girls."

"I need your help," I said. "Get me in to see Mr. Meade so I can talk to him about my story. You're his production assistant."

Sherry Woo snorted a laugh. "That's just another word for flunky." She said.

I fired up a smoke. We started walking toward La Brea.

"Listen," she went on, "you don't get it. It's all bullshit. Starburst/ Meade doesn't produce anything and hasn't in years. The only money the company makes comes from the contests. At twenty five dollars an entry it adds up. I mean, multiply that by a thousand entries. We hold a contest at least every other month.

I tried to comprehend what she was telling me. Sherry took on a sympathetic expression.

"Frankly, you are never going to collect the prize," she said. "It's very rare for anyone to actually win the contest. If you read the fine print it says Starburst has the right not to pick a winner."

"Yeah, but I won according to the letter with a hand-written note at the bottom?"

Sherry shrugged.

"That is strange," she said.

I told Sherry Woo that I didn't really care about the prize money now, that I just wanted to see a movie made from my story, also that I'd written a screenplay. When we reached Fairfax she turned to me and borrowed a cigarette.

"Look," she said. "If you ask me, Frank Meade will never make another movie. I mean he hasn't made one in years. He does keep saying though he is waiting for just the right story or script to come along. But truth is he's blown out."

"I've got to see Meade face to face," I said."That's all I want."

Two women from the class who were behind us caught up and told Sherry Woo they should get going if they're going to get to the movie on time.

"Bring your friend," one of them said.

Sherry made a face then shrugged.

"You want to come with us?"

I had no where else to go. Maggie told me earlier that she would be busy with her landlord that evening.

"Sure," I said. "What's the movie?"

"The Bicycle Thief," Sherry said. "It's Italian."

"Never heard of it," I said.

We all piled into Sherry's car which was a Chevy convertible that had been a present from her parents when she graduated from UCLA. She drove like a maniac.

Chapter 15

———

After the movie, the three women and I went to a bar. It was a dark dingy joint not far from the theatre and smelled of rot-gut alcohol and stale tobacco. There was a pinball game toward the back where a couple of drunks were making bets. The Jukebox was playing Frank Sinatra singing, Old Black Magic. The women ordered wine. I ordered a beer. We sat in a booth staring silently at our drinks for a time as if we'd all been stunned by some morbid event. It was strange. Sherry then lifted her glass and said, "Wow, here's to Italian realists and their ability to find gut wrenching drama in day to day life in post war Italy."

"Yeah," the younger of the two women said. "It was really sad."

"I'd give my left tit to be involved in a film like that some day," Sherry said and turned to me. "What did you think, Tuckie?"

I took a swig of my beer and wiped my mouth with the back of my hand and nodded. In a way I was a little like the kids in the movie, street waifs trying to survive, in my case in a foreign land. Of course the foreign land I was in was a land of palm trees, lush houses, swimming pools, traffic, and smog.

"Yeah, I liked the Bicycle Thief," I said. "I mean it was good and all, but I like Westerns like Singing Guns and the Wichita Kid. But I liked it. Yep."

The woman all looked at each other and giggled.

"The Wichita Kid?" Sherry said. "What's that?"

"Fastest gun in the west," I said. "He always got the bad guys in the end."

Before long, Sherry Woo had downed three tall glasses of wine which she topped off with a shot of tequila. It was obvious she was feeling no pain. She began gushing about something she called cinema verite and said she hoped to work in a real studio some day.

"It used to be you had to be born into this business and preferably as a boy child," she blurted out with a certain rancor and slapped the palm of her hand down on the table. The glasses on the table bounced. Other customers were looking at us. "It hasn't changed much," she went on," but someday it will. I got myself a little movie camera, a 16 millimeter Bolex. Second hand. I keep it at the office."

"What are you going to do with it?" The older woman said.

Sherry, looking a little blurry eyed shrugged.

"Make my own goddamn movie," she said. "Yeah, then some day my children, if I have any, will be born into the 16 millimeter feature film world. That'll show the bastards." She was now laughing so hard she almost fell under the table. "Maybe I'll make Blue Movies. There's money in that stuff you know."

"What's a blue movie?" I said.

The girls laughed in unison.

"Pornographic," Sherry said. "Boys and girls getting it on for real."

Nat King Cole was singing Nature Boy. There was another lull in the conversation. I finally steered the conversation with Sherry back to the contest. I asked if there were files on all the winners.

"Oh, sure," Sherry said. "We have to keep records in case someone decides to investigate or do an audit, particularly the IRS."

"So," I started…

She just looked at me quizzically.

"Maybe there's something in the file," I said. "I mean about my entry, and prove my claim."

At first it was as if she wasn't listening. She began ranting again about women being discriminated against in the production end of the

124

movie business. For a long moment she looked sullen. Then she looked at me and broke into a wide grin.

"Screw it," she said. "Let's go look."

"When?" I said.

"Now," she said "I have the keys to the joint."

She suddenly produced a set of keys and dangled them in front of me, and beamed with a sense of triumph.

Fifteen minutes later Sherry parked in a small area in the back of the building hidden on the other side of an old pickup truck. It was a miracle we got there, given that she kept crossing over into the path of oncoming traffic along Santa Monica Boulevard. We entered through a metal door at the top of a short flight of wooden stairs, passed through a storage area, through another door and down some steps to the main room. A night light burned on a credenza behind Jocelyn Bukowski's desk. Sherry put her handbag down turned on a small lamp and told me to stay out of the way while she looked through the files. She soon began pulling out drawers like a mad woman from the tall metal file cabinets that were lined up against the wall. She giggled drunkenly like a child delighted in being naughty. She stopped.

"When was that again?"

I told her when I entered and the date of the letter. Ten minutes later she found a file that had in it the story outline I had entered.

"Charles A. Kendall," she said absently. "Story - The Prairie Wolves."

"That's it!" I said and rushed over and peered over her shoulder.

Sherry began reading the synopsis of my story.

"Not terrible," she said. "Actually it's pretty good. I think it has something, the woman as victim and then avenger with the help of...Star Dancer? Yeah, I like it."

"You mean it?"

Sherry nodded.

"Too bad it will never happen," she said as she continued to flip through the file. "Here's the letter they sent you." She read it silently. "Oh, a little mystery here. This is not the same letter you showed me."

"Huh?" I said and fired up a smoke.

"It's just the standard 'better luck next time' letter. Nothing about winning the contest. It's signed by Bonnie Robertson."

I took the letter out of her hands and put on some reading glasses I had for low light situations. Now I felt like I'd been kicked in the gut.

"This can't be," I said. "Something's wrong."

I pulled the folded up letter I had gotten out of my jacket pocket to compare them. It was also signed by Bonnie Robertson. Sherry looked and said the signatures were definitely the same. The note on the bottom was even a bigger mystery. Sherry handed the letter back to me and put the file away.

"Actually," she said. "You could have written the greatest outline for a screenplay ever and it would have gone nowhere accept into the ashcan. When I first got a job here I was told I could be a production assistant on Frank Meade's next film. But I soon realized that the only thing they did here these days was hold that contest."

I sank into a nearby chair and imagined folks back home having a good laugh, Royce spewing his gospel about the evils of communist infiltration, Jenny happy to see me back, Mr. Zickwolfe standing in front of his theater shaking his head sadly. I spent many hours living deep in the dark refuge of what was the creaky, cavernous WOLF Theater. Its bleached clapboard construction made it look more like a giant barn. In the early part of the century it had been a general store. About the time movies first had sound, Henry and Cora Zickwolf purchased it and converted it into a theater. They had come to our small town on the prairie lands from Chicago. Even during the depression it became the town's main attraction and somehow operated in the black for many years, mainly with the help of popcorn. Before I left to come to L.A. Mr. Zickwolf, who was ill, wished me good luck and looked forward to running my movie at the WOLF.

Sherry Woo said something that brought me out of myself. I put out my cigarette and looked up.

"It's just all very weird," she said.

"Where's this Bonnie Robertson?" I said.

Sherry borrowed a smoke from me and lit up.

"She was a pain, always putting on airs, complained about smoking in here while she smoked like a chimney, and nipped at a bottle of Scotch she kept in the bottom drawer of her desk. It was clear her real job here was to service Frank Meade."

"What does that mean?" I said. "You mean…"

"Boy, you are just off the turnip truck," Sherry giggled. "Lunch time story conferences were in the back room, which was usually locked. This one time it wasn't. Jocelyn and I went back to get coffee and didn't think to knock. There they were – Meade sitting on a box with Miss Prim and Proper on her knees in front of him and she wasn't exactly praying. Jocelyn and I quickly backed out. But Frank saw us. You know what he did? He winked. Later as he was leaving he said in a loud voice, "That was one hell of a story conference." Bonnie Robertson who was back at her desk was stone faced."

"What finally happened to her?"

Sherry told me that Bonnie Robertson went nuts, accused them of talking about her behind her back and plotting against her. Sherry said Jocelyn worked hard to make her think that too.

"Bonnie was paranoid to begin with so it didn't take much to drive her over the edge," Sherry said. "She began acting stranger and stranger, carrying on long conversations with herself in a loud voice as if the imaginary people she was talking to were hard of hearing. Then one day which I will never forget, she came totally unglued. She came in, marched to her desk, sat down, then stood up and began shouting obscenities to her imaginary enemies, flipped over her desk and kicked her wastebasket half way across the room. We just stared goggle-eyed, wondering if she had a weapon. It was scary. She then went into the bathroom and stayed there for two hours. We were afraid to go look, thinking maybe she was dead.

She came out calmly picked up her purse and walked out. We never saw her again."

"Man," was about all I said.

"Bonnie used to be a well-respected story editor at some of the major studios," Sherry added.

"I'd sure like to talk to her," I said.

"What good would that do?"

I shrugged.

We sat in canvas director's chairs facing a large couch in the middle of the room. There was a coffee table with some trade magazines stacked on top between the couch and the chairs. Sherry found a bottle of tequila in the bottom drawer. She poured two small glasses. We talked about movies. Actually she did most of the talking, going on about foreign films from Italy and Sweden. "I saw a film in Italy last summer called La Strada," Sherry said. "It was amazing. Anthony Quinn was in it. But it was the girl, Giulietta Masina who was magical. And it was all in her face, her expressions. She hardly said a word. Magical cinema."

"Never heard of it," I said.

"It hasn't been released in the U.S. yet," she said.

I was thinking about finding Bonnie Robertson. She must be around somewhere. I decided to start looking for her. It was now past midnight. Sherry suddenly jumped up and said she heard a noise coming from the back.

"I didn't hear anything," I said.

Sherry shushed me, putting her fingers to her lips. I heard it this time, footsteps, somebody bumping into something. We turned off the lamp so that the room was dark except the night light on Jocelyn's credenza. Then we crouched down behind Sherry's desk and listened.

"Someone's there," Sherry whispered.

Chapter 16

———

It was the craziest thing what happened next, like right out of Hollywood Confidential. We kept hearing the noise coming from the mezzanine where we had entered earlier. Two sets of footsteps on loose
floor boards, the sound of someone stumbling. Muffled voices could now
be heard. Sherry glanced at her watch which glowed in the dark.

"This is weird," she whispered.

"Robbers?"

Sherry shook her head.

"Who the hell would want to burgle this place? Could be some of
Frank Meade's cronies who sometimes come here to party. But, Jesus not
at this hour."

A male voice could be heard, louder now. Another voice, this time
clearly a woman's was heard giggling. We could hear whoever it was coming down the steps into the back room. The woman was saying oh no, oh
no, then laughed and whooped. "This really your place?" She said.

"Oh, my god," Sherry said. "It must be Frank."

"Really," I said. "I wonder if I could talk to him?"

Sherry nudged me hard with her elbow.

"Are you crazy!" she said. "Frank's a real bastard under the best of
circumstances. There's only one reason for him to show up here at this
hour with a woman and that's to give her one of his special auditions with
no trail."

"Huh?" I said. "What does that mean?"

"It means he comes here because his wife would string him up by his balls if she caught him playing around. She's the one with the money. And he claims she has had him followed in the past."

"His wife's rich?" I said.

"I heard she's an heiress to a potato chip fortune and in real estate," Sherry said.

I shifted my legs under me. I started to say something else but Sherry quickly put her hand over my mouth as we huddled close together on the floor hidden behind a partition by her desk. I could smell the sweetness of wine with the heat of her breath on my neck. When I first met Sherry at Barney's that first day I showed up at Starburst/Meade, I did not really like her. I thought there was something arrogant about her, that she was stuck-up. Or maybe it was the way she clipped her words, kind of staccato like. Staccato, that's a word I learned when I was studying that book about how to write a screenplay. Tonight though, I thought, I'd seen another side to her, a funny and mischievous side I found more attractive. We both had a love of movies, though different kinds.

Hiding in the dark waiting for something to happen, I began to think about my just-completed draft script for The Prairie Wolves. I envisioned the story this way: a young couple on their honeymoon camp near a lake in some unknown part of the country. Earlier that evening they stop at a hunting lodge and bar for a beer. Four men who are on a hunting trip are also there drinking. A jukebox is playing. One of the men grabs the young wife to dance, but she rejects him and pushes him away. The just-married couple soon leave the lodge and go on to their campsite. Their blissful state is interrupted when the same four men come upon them and draw them into a malicious game. As the evening wears on, the campfire going, the couple begin to get more and more nervous, and then frightened as the men continue to drink and display their guns. The husband accuses the men of following them and tells them to leave. They refuse and begin saying nasty things to the wife in front of her husband who feels helpless. When one of the men grabs his wife, kisses her and tries to grope her, the husband intervenes. He is beaten to death in front of his horrified wife. She tries to run and is caught, raped and beaten by three of the four men and left for dead. The fourth man had tried to stop his friends.

The next morning she is found by passing hikers and taken to the hospital. When she recuperates she is a totally different person than the innocent wife of that terrible night. The local sheriff investigates, but tends to treat her as if she had been the cause, possibly leading the men on and brought the attack on her husband and herself. In any case, they have no leads. The people at the lodge had never seen them before and no witnesses. Two years later and still no arrests. The young widowed bride goes back to the scene and finds a wallet half buried in some brush. It contains an ID of one of the attackers. She then contacts someone she has heard of who is a professional avenger, a mysterious half-breed Indian called Star Dancer. He is almost a mythical character who makes turquoise smoke as a ritual, rides a motorcycle and is said to have assassinated many a bad buy, though authorities could never prove it. The young widow finds him living in a remote cabin in the southwest. He is now an old man with long white flowing hair and flaming eyes. At first he refuses to help her, saying he is retired. But something in her story brings out the rage in him and he agrees to one last job. He will help her seek out her quarry, four men who turn out to have regular jobs with families and in some cases, pillars of their community who go to church on Sundays.

Before I could finish my thought the door to the back room flew open slamming against the wall. All we could see was the glare of a moving flashlight beam which suddenly appeared out of the dark, like a white hot disembodied eye. A deep male voice behind the light said, "This way doll. Watch your step, baby."

Sherry whispered to me that it was Frank.

"Okay, Mr. Meade," the female voice said behind him. "I can't see a thing. Can we turn on a light?"

A couple of moments later Frank Meade switched on a standing lamp. It was by the couch which was about 20 feet from where Sherry Woo and I were hiding. We raised our heads up over the partition to take a peak. I wanted to see what Frank Meade looked like. Instead we saw only the woman. She was standing next to the couch looking around as if trying to figure out where she was and what lay in the darkness beyond the circle of light from the lamp. She turned her head and looked in our direction. We instantly ducked.

The woman then eased herself down onto the couch and crossed her legs. She was an attractive blonde with a roundish face, a little on the plump side. Her eyes though were heavy with mascara, making them look like black pits, particularly contrasting with her very white skin. Frank Meade had disappeared. Sherry whispered that he might have gone over to a wet bar to make some drinks. Some time passed with no sign of Meade.

"How old do you think she is?" Sherry asked.

I shrugged.

"Maybe 19 or 20," I said.

We took another peek. The young woman took off her jacket and draped it across the back of the couch. She patted the back of her hair and looked around again.

"Where did you go, Mr. Meade?" She called out with a nervous laugh.

There was no answer. She began whistling to herself, then picked up a magazine off the coffee table and began thumbing through it. I adjusted my leg again and made a slight noise. The young woman looked over our way again. "That you, Mr. Meade?" She tossed the magazine back on the table and drew her legs up under her. "This is getting creepy. Maybe I should leave."

At that moment, strange music, soft and rhythmic began drifting out of the darkness on the other side of the room. Frank Meade suddenly appeared like a ghost, stepping into the light. I had to bite my tongue from reacting to what we saw. Sherry gasped and clamped her hand over her mouth. The blonde jumped off the couch and screamed and then just stood there and stared, her mouth agape. "What a freak!" Sherry whispered.

A strange screeching voice came out of the darkness, "Frank Fucks Frogs."

"What was that?" The blonde said, looking even more startled.

"That's my friend Gertrude," he said, "She's a very naughty Mynah bird."

Frank Meade stood stark naked in front of her, his upper body painted white with red and black markings on his face and arms. His paunch jiggled as he moved. He looked like one of those African tribesmen you see in National Geographic magazines getting ready for war or some ritual. A fat black wig crowned his head. In one hand he held a bottle of whiskey and in the other, two glasses. About all I could tell was that he was a stocky man of medium height with a heavy face. His one outstanding feature was his voice. It was low, confident and suggested power.

"Isn't he too much?" Sherry whispered, her mouth on my ear. "What a scene!"

The blonde, seemingly in shock sat back down. Frank Meade handed her a glass and poured some whiskey. He sat down beside her, poured his own glass and motioned for a toast. They both took sips.

"To you, doll, staring in my next movie," he said. "You'll knock 'em dead."

"I'm not sure I like this, Mr. Meade," she said. "I mean...well what are you doing?"

She started to get up from the couch. Frank yanked her back down.

"You know doll, when I saw you in that bar tonight I knew you were it. The new "It" girl, like Clara Bow. So, let's drink to that."

"Who's that, Mr. Meade? Who's Clara Bow?

The blonde seemed to forget how bizarre this was, or was trying to distract him.

"You know, doll, I've been making movies for a long, long time and in all my years I've never seen a face the camera would love as much as yours. Know what I mean?"

The blonde adjusted her skirt, pushing it down tight over her knees.

"You really think so?" She asked. "I guess I know what you mean."

Frank Meade told her she had to go with it, make it work for her. He then leaned in close to her and traced her mouth with his finger. "You have a beautiful mouth," he said. "Beautiful."

"Oh, thank you," she said and you could tell the girl was frightened.

Sherry Woo whispered to me at that moment that she had a great idea. She crawled back to her desk. Frank Meade was now leaning back against the couch, his body sliding into a slouch, legs stretched out in front of him. He had a fresh drink in his hand and began fondling himself with his free hand. Sherry Woo returned with her small movie camera. She had wrapped it in a sweater she said to muffle the sound of the motor. She said she also turned on a sound recorder.

"What are you doing?" I said.

"What do you think! I'm going to record this little scene for posterity? This could be my ticket, yours too, into something."

Sherry positioned the camera, which had three lenses, one telephoto, one wide angle and one normal.

Meanwhile the blonde sat woodenly next to him staring straight ahead of her, obviously trying to ignore Frank's nakedness and the semi erection he was working on. She listened silently as he rambled on for a time about the movie business, how it had been his life's work and now it was run by bean counters, sucking the blood out of his art.

"I really should go, Mr. Meade," was about all the blonde could get out. "I mean it's getting late and you were going to show me one of your films and..."

"Going now?" Frank said. "Is that right?!" A malevolent edge had entered his tone. "Show you one of my films?"

"Well, that's what you said at the bar. My girlfriends said I shouldn't go with you, but, well I thought you were, you know...okay."

"Shut the fuck up!" Frank said. "Ever done any acting, doll?"

She shook her head.

"Actually I was in a high school play, but I only had two lines."

Frank laughed and finished his drink.

"Shit, some of the biggest stars in this town didn't even have that going for them before they hit it."

"Do you know any big stars, Mr. Meade?" The blonde said.

"Knock off the Mr. Meade crap," he said and let his hand slide up under her skirt to about mid thigh. "Show me your twat, honey, your pussy. I want to see it."

Sherry nudged me. The blonde pushed his hand back a little. He then reached up and cupped her right breast. She finished her drink.

"So, do you know any big stars, Mr err...Frank?"

He moved his hand to her other breast and squeezed.

"I know them all, doll, big, small, medium-sized. And most of them ain't worth shit."

The blonde made a feeble attempt to move away.

"So, who do you know, Frank?"

Frank rolled his eyes heavenward.

"Forget this bullshit and do something for ole Frank," he said. You're a friend now and friends do things for friends, you know. I hope you'll be a good friend. Are you going to be a good friend?"

The blonde swallowed hard and nodded almost imperceptibly.

"I want to see that mouth of yours working and good things come out," he said. "Now you want to be in movies?"

"I guess so," she said. "Beats teaching elementary school."

Sherry reloaded the camera.

"I got about three minutes worth so far," she whispered. "I hope there's enough light. It's high speed film so...guess we'll see. I'm going for broke now."

She crawled like a commando along the floor around the partition to a closer position. The blonde suddenly stood and looked in our direction, squinting her eyes as if to penetrate the darkness that hid us.

"Did you hear something?" She said.

"Come back here, doll," Frank Meade said, pulling her back down on the couch.

"I...I thought I heard something," she said.

He tugged at her to move closer to him, then took her left hand, kissed her palm and placed it on his penis.

"A little help," he said and closed his eyes. "That's all I ask."

She took her hand away. Frank opened his eyes.

"Why'd you stop?" He said and yanked her hand back to his crotch.

The blonde left it there for a minute.

"I think I want to go," she said. "Really."

She continued rubbing him for a time but apparently nothing was happening.

"God damn it!" Frank Meade said to his penis. "Stand up there like a man you sonofabitch!" Frank grabbed the blonde by the back of her head and pushed her down until her mouth was on him. She resisted at first but then relaxed and continued.

"Good, real good," Frank said in a low voice and leaned back moaning. "You're the best, doll. I'm going to put you in my next movie. You've got what it takes."

I could just make out Sherry. She looked back at me and it looked like she gave me a thumbs-up sign.

Now I'd never heard of a Mynah bird before, but on that occasion it got in the last word.

"This place stinks," Gertrude croaked from the darkness.

Chapter 17

———

A couple of days later, when I got back to Maggie's after my shift, there was a man there waiting to talk to me. He was big, thick with gigantic beefy hands which stuck out from a sport jacket that looked a little to small for him. His pink shirt was open at the collar. There was something official looking about him. He was sitting on an apple crate that had been reinforced with a piece of plywood across the top. Maggie had painted it purple and green. It served as a catch-all for her books and magazines. Maggie sat on her bed chain smoking. She looked nervous. Her tank top was soaked in spots with sweat. The man appeared to be taking notes in a small note pad on whatever it was they were talking about. It was early evening and it was warm. The strange man looked to be in his early forties. He had a round florid face and tiny brown eyes. His butch haircut accentuated a large head.

As I entered, the man looked up, then stood. He had to bend over slightly because of the low ceiling. I looked questioningly at Maggie and then at the stranger who had his hand extended out to me. At full height he had to be six four or five.

"Hi," the man said with a warm smile. "Name's Mark."

"This is Mr. Horgan," Maggie said, her lips quivering as she obviously labored to get his name out. "He's a detective. Wants to talk to us about someone named Margo Benson."

I took his hand.

"I'm Charles Kendall," I said. "Most folks call me Tuckie. Kind of a nickname."

Mark Horgan reached into his inside pocket and produced a wallet, opened it for me to see. There was a badge and an official looking identification card.

"Actually," he said, "I'm a private detective. I used to be with the LAPD, but that was a few years back. I keep up my contacts in the department though. Never know when they will come in handy," he added, making it sound like a soft but veiled threat.

He handed me his card. I nodded.

"So what can we do for you Mark?" I said.

The detective eased himself back down onto the apple crate which looked like it might give way at any moment. He smiled at me showing small uneven teeth, then at Maggie, as if to reassure us that all was well.

"The thing of it is, I've been retained by Margo Benson's family to look into her death. And by the way, they wanted me to let anyone I talked to know up front who I was working for so there would be no confusion."

"That was over a month ago," I said.

"I know. But the sheriff's office handled the investigation because her body was found in an unincorporated area of the hills. It was determined that she overdosed on drugs and well you probably know that. For them — the sheriff's office — due to various reasons including budget constraints and no foul play indicated, it ended there. Case closed. However, there are of course lots of unanswered questions. My point is, the family has hired me to follow up, mostly I think to ease their own minds of whether or not they could have, you know, done anything differently as a family that might have prevented this tragedy. It's hard to say what they hope to get. And then there's the question of the body. Who dumped it in the hills? You see what I mean. Anyway, I don't want to take up too much of your time, Miss Langston and Mr. Kendall err...Tuckie. May I call you Tuckie?"

I nodded. He looked at each of us and again smiled as if he were there to sell Bibles. He sighed and looked at his watch.

"This won't take long," he said. "I will be taking notes just so you understand. But again, this is not a criminal investigation. More like a fact finding mission. My questions will be strictly routine."

I went over and grabbed my own notebook and a pencil out of my suitcase. I then sat down on the floor and scribbled the date and a little heading: Interview with Detective Mark Horgan. This did not go unnoticed.

"May I ask why you're taking notes, Tuckie?"

I explained to him that I was a writer and that I liked to take notes on conversations, that they might come in handy some day. Mark Horgan nodded.

"I see," he said. "First of all, how close of a friend were you to Margo Benson, Tuckie? Would you say very close, casual, or barely knew her?"

"Casual," I said. "Guess I'd have to say casual."

Mark Horgan made a note. He looked up.

"How often did you see her?"

I shrugged.

"Not…not too often."

"Any particular place?" The detective said.

"You know, just around," I said and looked over at Maggie who lit another cigarette.

Mark pursed his lips thoughtfully for a moment.

"Just around," he repeated aloud and again jotted something in his notebook.

"Uh huh," I said.

Maggie nodded as if in agreement and tried to blow a smoke ring.

"You must have felt something strong for her as a friend," Mark Horgan continued. "I mean you took the time to go to her funeral. That's how I happen to be here. You signed the guest register. Also you spoke and some of the guests apparently thought your remarks very strange, even goofy if I may say so." Mark gave a short laugh and shook his head, as if he were trying to conjure a picture of that scene. "But you don't strike me that way. Anyway, no one seemed to know who you were…you see my point. I must tell you I think you knew Margo much better than you're letting on. You want to tell me about it."

He gave me that warm, friendly smile again. I made a note about his suspicions in my note book.

"Nothing to tell, Mark." I said.

Maggie shifted her position on the bed, pulling her legs up under her. She tried another smoke ring and this time was a little more successful, the smoke forming the shape of an elongated ring.

"Damn," she said. "Almost had it perfect."

"It takes practice," Mark Horgan said.

Maggie forced a smile.

"I'm curious," she said. "How could you have found…Mr. Kendall…Tuckie here just from signing the guest-book.? I mean you really must be a good detective."

"Yes, well there's a place for an address so that the family can send thank-you notes."

"Oh, sure, I get it," Maggie said and looked over at me, her smile turned to a grimace. "Did you get your thank you note, Tuck?"

The sarcasm was not lost on me and probably not on the big detective either. But he did not react, just stared blankly into space for a moment. He cleared his throat.

"So, Tuckie when was the last time you saw Margo Benson?"

I scratched my head.

"Gosh, Mark," I said. "I don't really remember. Maybe at a party or something like that."

Mark jotted a note.

"Do you remember where the party was?"

"No, sir," I said. "Just a party. You know, parties just happen."

Maggie blew an almost perfect smoke ring. She clapped her hands excitedly.

"Look at that," she said. "Now that's respectable."

The big detective glanced over and grinned.

"I'd say it is," he said, and turned back to me. "I know about parties. Got a couple of kids. The older one, he's twenty, always going to some damn party. The teenager, well he's in another orbit somewhere. In the scene, as he puts it." Mark Horgan laughed. "They live with their mother. Mind if I ask you what you do? I mean my sense is you're a little older than the bunch Margo Benson ran around with."

"As I told you, I'm a writer," I said.

"What do you write?"

"Movies. I'm a movie writer."

"I love movies," Mark said. "Have you written any movies I might have seen?"

I fired up a smoke.

"Well…I haven't actually had anything produced yet. I'm just sort of trying to get my career moving down the road, if you know what I mean."

"Sure," Mark said. "Well, good luck. I know you're not from around here, so how did you meet Margo Benson? Do you remember when that might have been?"

I shook my head and took a drag on my smoke and looked over at Maggie. She looked sullen.

"A year ago, two years ago?" Mark said. "When? Come on, give me something. It won't mean anything to you, but it will help me do my job."

I tried to look like I was digging deep into my memory.

"Let's see, it's 1955. Might have been a year ago. I just don't re-member. Sorry, Mark. I'd really like to help."

The big detective sighed, stood up as if to go, stretched and sat back down on the apple crate. He was now looking at me with a much different face, a hardened face. Before going on he reached down into a large leather satchel he had sitting on the floor next to him, pulled out a can of beer with an opener, punched a hole on top and took a long swig. He shut his eyes momentarily as if savoring the taste, then opened them, squinting at me.

"Bullshit!" He said, and looked down at his notes, flipped through some pages with his free hand and then looked up again. "It couldn't have been too long ago, Tuckie because you haven't been out here on the coast that long, in fact just a few months."

Mark's eyes looked even smaller as he peered at me through the tiny rolls of flesh that framed them. I wondered how he could possibly know that about me. I looked at Maggie who gave a tiny shrug of her shoulders. This was not going well I thought.

"Oh, yeah, well it seems like it's been longer," I said.

"Way too long if you ask me," Maggie muttered.

There followed a long silence as Mark continued to consult his notes. The moments seemed to get heavier and heavier.

"You see, Tuckie, I know about that old heap of a car of yours being stolen and impounded and that you were spotted taking something out of your car at the storage yard. I know about your family, your father, Royce Kendall, not a pleasant man and your Aunt Zona. I even know about your girlfriend Jenny Gifford. I talked to Jenny. She sounds very nice, very concerned about you. Says she doesn't hear from you much. Is that right?"

Mark took another swig of his beer and set it down on the floor. I just stared at him in amazement.

"Mark, you are good," I said. "Isn't he good, Maggie," I said. "You should be in movies. You are a definite type. I mean I know a good type when I see one."

Mark grinned and wiped his mouth with the back of his hand.

"You think so?" He said.

I held up my hands and made a frame with my fingers, peering through it at Mark.

"Yeah," I said. "You've got something. You really do. I wouldn't kid about a thing like that."

The big detective nodded.

"So where did you meet Margo Benson? And no bullshit."

"Sorry, Mark. I honestly don't remember."

Mark nodded and put away his notebook. He picked up the beer, finished it and tossed the empty can into a waste basket across the room.

"Okay, I think that's it for now." He said

Mark Horgan stayed for another twenty minutes, told some jokes and then motioned for me to follow him outside. Standing on the path about fifteen feet from Maggie's door, Mark stopped and his friendly face suddenly became menacing. He grabbed me by my windbreaker and pulled me close to him.

"I'll be back you lying fucking asshole," he said.

He released me and trundled on down the path to his car. I watched after him until he disappeared and then went back inside. Maggie had gotten off the bed and was now standing by her kitchenette drinking wine.

"What did he say to you out there?" she said.

"Nothing. Just...just thanked me for my help. Seemed like a nice fella."

Maggie looked extremely agitated.

"Nice fella...yeah like a smiling rattlesnake. Oh, but loved his jokes. Maybe he'll come back and tells us some more. Wouldn't that be nice?"

Maggie lit another cigarette and plopped back on her bed.

"You smoke a lot," I said.

"Don't tell me about smoking you stupid son of a bitch!" she screamed, jumped up and stomped her feet like a child that wasn't getting its way. "I can't believe you gave them my address. You wrote it down in their fucking guest book? Her face took on sickly smile. "So the family could send you a goddamned thank you note for your fine performance at their daughter's service. How touching! Jesus, I don't believe it."

I went over and sat on the apple crate and watched Maggie. She had suddenly begun talking about her life and how her parents hated her because she was a bum in their eyes, particularly after spending so much on her education and jail was not where she wanted to be because it would give them a perverse satisfaction and that would be a drag. The words tumbled out of her like baggage and trash out of a crammed closet. For several moments she was out of control. I made notes. Maggie stopped ranting, wiped tears from her eyes and fixed her gaze on me.

"What are you doing?" She screamed again. "What the god damn hell are you doing? You are one cold motherfucker, you know that. You're just so detached from it all, maybe from life. I don't think there's a person in there."

"Where?"

She was now pacing the floor.

"What do you mean, where?" She said, pointing at me. "There, inside you, inside your head, man."

"I was just making a note," I said.

Maggie bent down and flicked the ashes from her cigarette into a small bowl on the coffee table. Some of the ashes missed and floated to the floor. She watched them float down. "There's my life, just a tiny heap of ashes on the floor."

"I thought the detective was okay," I offered, deciding not to say anything about his threat.

Maggie threw up her hands.

"I don't know if you're naïve or just stupid," Tuck. "You don't know shit. Nothing but a goddamned hayseed who blows into town and thinks he's going to begin his career. What kind of shit have you been smoking anyway?"

I took a deep breath and screwed up my face into a tight knot of flesh.

"Do you want me to leave?"

Maggie was crying.

"Don't know," she said. "I should throw your ass out of here, only it might make things worse. That detective might come back and think something is up if you're not still here. That grinning hyena would have me and who the hell knows where you'd be. Screw that."

"We didn't do anything. I mean, not really," I said.

"I wonder if he knows about Jack?" Maggie said aloud to herself. "I should probably call him and let him know what's happening, except I don't want to talk to him. Screw it. You call him."

I did something that was totally foreign to me. It was simply impulse. I stood up, walked over to Maggie and put my arms around her and pulled her close to me, hugging her firmly. I'd seen it countless times in the movies. Still I was embarrassed. But Maggie put her head on my shoulder and held on to me as if she was afraid she might fall into some dark place and disappear forever. She continued to softly cry.

In the morning after a hot shower and coffee I told Maggie I was going to go to a pawn shop. It was on Vermont and I wanted to borrow her car.

"Why are you going to a pawn shop?"

"I just want to see this guy about investing in my movie," I said.

Maggie looked incredulous. Luckily she didn't need the car until much later.

"It needs gas," she said.

Chapter 18

———

It was late morning when I got going. I parked Maggie's car and had to walk a block. Margo Benson's Uncle Maurice's place was a large two-story cinder block building the color of putty. It was on the east side of Vermont just south of Sunset Boulevard. This was not what I figured. My image of pawn shops came from the movies, small cluttered rooms with cages. They were always run by craggy middle aged men with bony elbows who wore green eyeshades. I imagined these shops smelled like old typewriter ribbons. Uncle Moe's pawn shop took up half a block and had a green awning over the entrance. The bars on the building's one window made it look kind of like a prison. I had called a few days before from Chick's to try and make an appointment, but his secretary all but hung up on me. She refused to put me through to Moe.

Inside, it was brightly lit and thick beige carpeting gave the place a soft, almost elegant feel. Far from old typewriter ribbons the place smelled fresh and crisp, the air even slightly perfumed. It looked like a department store. Hoards of customers were scattered from one end to the other browsing and checking out various items. I saw two well dressed clerks behind a long counter negotiating with walk-ins about the worth of items to be pawned.

"May I help you?"

It was the voice of a woman coming from behind me. I spun around to face a slender, bespectacled woman I figured to be in her forties. She was wearing dark slacks and a plain gray blouse. Her hair was bobbed in back. It made her look real tidy like a schoolmarm, a very attractive schoolmarm. Now I only mention all of this because of what I learned about her later.

"I'm just kind of looking around," I said.

"Anything in particular you're interested in?" The woman said.

"No...well I'm thinking of getting a camera for a friend of mine," I said. "She likes picture taking."

The woman clerk explained that the camera section was at the other end of the building and that they had lots of cameras to choose from.

"Come this way."

I reluctantly followed the woman as she led the way through a maze of display cases which had everything from watches to silverware to musical instruments. On the way I tried to keep an eye out for Uncle Moe.

"Is this a Christmas gift?" The woman asked. "Christmas is just around the corner, you know."

"Christmas? Right."

The next thing I knew we were standing in front of a large glass display case containing all kinds of cameras, all shapes and sizes. Some of them looked ancient, and some brand new.

"Which are the good ones?" I asked.

"They're all good," the woman said laughing.

She pointed to a row of cameras in one of the cases, opened it up and pulled out one camera and handed it to me.

"It's a Nikon, 35 millimeter and comes with three lenses, a 50 millimeter, a 28 millimeter, and a 300 millimeter, eight-to-one zoom. It's a steal at $800. And we'll throw in a light meter."

I examined the camera, nodded and handed it back to her.

"Maybe something in a lower price range," the woman said. "This camera is really for professionals."

She gave me a big smile showing even, white teeth. I suddenly thought there was something familiar about her. It was very odd, I thought, since there was no way I could ever have run into her before... unless.

148

"What is it?" The woman said. "You have this funny look on your face, like you've seen a ghost."

I continued to stare.

"You ever been in Chick's Hamburger Palace on La Brea?"

The woman shook her head.

"Why do you ask?"

"I don't know," I said. "Just that you seem kind of familiar, I mean it's like I've seen you before."

The woman shrugged.

"I don't know," she said. "I am an actress. I don't get much work these days. Maybe you saw me on television, mostly in bit parts or in one of my old movies. I've actually been in lots of them over the years when I was younger, mostly B westerns and one vampire movie. I work here between jobs and because it's steady."

"Were you ever in one of the Wichita Kid movies?" I said.

The woman laughed.

"Oh, my god, I was in three of them. I always played the daughter of some besieged rancher. That was so many years ago. I was very young and considered pretty in those days. We used to shoot those old horse operas in six days. Bill Coughlin who played the Kid took it pretty seriously, always wore a cowboy hat in public and even put long horns on the hood of his convertible Cadillac so folks would know who he was when he drove around town. I thought maybe he was blurring his movie character with his real life, if you know what I mean."

I momentarily saw myself sitting in the back row of the WOLF Theater and seeing this woman now standing in front of me on the screen. It gave me a delicious sensation.

"Whatever happened to him?" I said.

"Bill? Oh he retired long ago and now lives in a nursing home. He's getting up there you know, like all of us."

"Wow," I said. "I'd sure like to meet him."

The woman shook her head sadly.

"I could arrange that, but I think maybe you should think of him as the Kid," she said. "He's non-compos-mentis, his mind is completely gone."

"Oh," I said, feeling let down. "What's your name?"

"Iris. Iris Madigan."

I took out my little notebook and jotted down her name. Just then I spotted Uncle Moe coming hurriedly through the front door, a cigar dangling out of the corner of his mouth. He was carrying a large box which he had cradled in both arms. After setting the box down on the long counter he leaned on it to catch his breath. After a moment he called out to one of the clerks to take the package up to his office.

"Be careful!" He yelled as a young man swooped up the box and started for the stairs. "It's some stuff I picked up at an estate sale this morning."

A few heads turned to see who was doing all the yelling.

"That's Maurice Miller," Iris Madigan said. "He's the boss."

Uncle Maurice — Moe — looked around. I thought he looked like he was counting customers in his head. He stopped scanning the room when his eyes fell on me. I waived, excused myself and walked over to Maurice, my hand outstretched.

"Hey, Moe," I said. "How about this…running into you. I was going to call you. Gosh, what a coincidence. I mean this place is great, you know, great."

Moe did not take my hand. He took the cigar out of his mouth and looked me up and down as if I were some bum from the street. I had put on the same suit I'd worn to the service for Margo, including the bow tie which was a little crooked.

"Who the hell are you?" He said.

"It's me, Moe. Tuckie Kendall."

"I don't know you," he said.

"That's okay, Moe," I said. "My hair's gotten a little shaggy, longer than when you last saw me."

"And when was that?"

"At Margo's funeral," I said.

He looked at me and nodded like it was coming back to him now.

"Let's cut the crap, kid," he said. "You did call. My girl told me someone with a funny name called. So, it was you."

I held up the palms of my hands.

"You got me, Moe," I said.

"What was your name again?"

"Tuckie. Tuckie Kendall."

"What do you want? You like my place, eh. It's a class operation. I'll give you a deal on anything in the place. Just tell me what you want."

I looked around and then back to Moe.

"Well, I wanted to talk to you about what we talked about before. You know after Margo's funeral?"

Moe looked puzzled, checked his watch, which I figured was meant as a message he didn't have time to waste on me. He began walking toward the other end of the store. I followed. I told him about my movie script and reminded him that he had told me he, along with some friends, sometimes finance movies. And that he had said to come and see him.

"So, here I am," I said.

Moe was distracted. He was looking beyond me at a statue which was sitting on the floor by the wall. He yelled at one of the clerks to move it to a spot near the entrance.

"Christ," he muttered. "Have to tell these people when to take a piss. Nobody thinks for themselves. He turned back to me. "What were you talking about?"

I repeated everything I had said.

Moe continued on up the stairs to the second floor and then down a hallway and into a large cluttered office. He moved around the desk and slipped down into a red leather swivel chair. I just stood there. The phone rang and Moe picked it up. He pulled the cigar out of his mouth.

"Yeah," he said sharply. "Get that cock-sucking load out of that warehouse before three o'clock or it may be too late. You know what I mean? Right! Do it!"

He hung up, made two quick calls and motioned for me to take a seat. When he had finished he turned and looked at me, raising his very thick eyebrows slightly.

"Say, kid, I don't have a lot of time. Get to the point. What is it you want?"

I stood up and began pacing the floor, back and forth in front of Moe's desk trying to look like someone who knows something. I pulled out a cigarette.

"Okay if I smoke?"

Moe nodded, but clearly getting impatient. I fired up a smoke and took a drag.

"Moe, "I began slowly, "it's simple. I have written this script for a movie, for which I won first prize in a movie writing contest and I'm offering you the opportunity to put together the financing for it."

"Just like that, eh," Moe said. "You write some cockamamie movie script like a million other hacks in this town and you want me to put up the money for it. Are you fucking crazy? You got chutzpa, kid, I'll give you that. Now get out of here before I have to call a security guard."

"What's utzpa?"

"Get out!" Moe said.

"You said you sometimes invest in movies," I said.

Moe rolled his eyes and flicked the ashes from his cigar.

"And who's going to produce this movie of yours?"

I took another drag on my cigarette, trying hard to look smooth.

"Frank Meade of Starburst/Meade Productions," I said.

Moe leaned way back in his chair and grinned.

"Frank Fucking Meade. Oh yeah it comes back to me now. Meade hasn't made a film in years. I grant you he once had a good track record. Those bottom feeder flicks of his always made money, particularly in the southwest drive-in circuit. He's a crazy son of a bitch but he had the touch. Mostly horror and science fiction shit. Last I heard he was on the sauce pretty good and that he has a gambling addiction. What makes you think he'd want to produce your script?"

"Well, my script won his national movie writing contest."

Moe laughed hysterically, his face turning red as a beet, his arms waving madly. After a moment he calmed down and then as if addressing some invisible person said, "I have to admit, I made a bundle off a couple of his flicks."

He refocused on me.

"Three D is the thing now. Creature from the Black Lagoon did well, I hear. How much do you think this little gem of yours is going to cost?"

I just stared at Moe and shook my head.

"I don't know," I said.

"Jesus, what the hell do you know? Look, kid, I figure this is some kind of exploitation job we're talking about here or you wouldn't be fucking around with Frank Meade. If Meade buys it and is willing to produce it, provided he's fucking sober and he can bring it in for say a hundred grand or less, I might consider trying to find some money."

I could feel my heart pounding, my blood coursing through my veins at a hundred and twenty miles an hour.

"You won't be sorry, Moe." I said.

"Right. Well, I don't think you're going to get Meade on board so I'm not going to worry about it."

"I'll call you," I said.

Moe waived his cigar at me.

"You do that."

As I walked down the hall toward the stairs I could hear Moe's gravely voice again laughing hysterically.

Outside the sun was a shock. I put on a pair of sunglasses. I then changed my mind and went back inside and found Iris Madigan and bought a used Leica camera with a leather case for Maggie. Miss Madigan said it was on sale and had a very good lens. She put them in a paper bag for me. I thought the camera would please Maggie, maybe even cheer her up a bit. I could tell she was struggling with something. I didn't know what the cause was and the fact was, I didn't care. I couldn't afford to care. If I'd learned anything during my time there it was to take no detours. The Prairie Wolves was all that mattered. The gift of the camera was really to smooth the growing tension between Maggie and Me.

I walked up to Sunset Boulevard and found a pay phone. I called Sherry Woo.

"I can't talk now," she whispered. "Jocelyn is hovering nearby. She's like a rhino today, snorting and moving around like she's going to charge at any moment."

"When can we meet?" I said.

"I don't know," Sherry said. "Actually tonight."

"Okay, but I'm working late."

"I'll pick you up at Chick's. I got the film developed. We'll be able to look at it. I can't wait to see how it came out."

Next, I called Jenny. She'd still be at the bank. I put in all the change I had left for three minutes time. She picked up the phone on the second ring.

"Hello, this is Miss Gifford. How can I be of service?"

I didn't say anything. I wasn't sure what I wanted to say.

"Hello?" Jenny said. "Is anyone there...Tuckie? Is that You?"

"Hi, Jen," I stammered.

"How come I haven't heard from you? Where are you living? Why can't I call you? When are you going to give up that stupid movie idea and come home where you belong? I saw Zona yesterday. She says they never hear from you. It's like they've swallowed you up out there."

"I've been real busy," I said.

"Are you at least coming home for Christmas? I think your father misses you. He'd probably never admit it, but it sounds like that when I talk to Zona."

I automatically shrugged as if she could see me.

"I don't know," I said. "I think I'm on the verge of something happening."

"Maybe I'll come out there," Jenny said. "I have some time coming to me."

154

"No," I yelled into the phone. "Don't come out here." Operator said time was up.

"Why'd that detective call me?" She said hurriedly.

"I have to go. Bye."

I hit the glass on the booth with my fist and then began walking aimlessly along Sunset Boulevard before I realized I was going the wrong way. Then something strange happened. When I turned around to head back to the car I happened to catch sight of a young woman climbing into a black sedan. There was something familiar about her. She had black hair piled up on top of her head and wore heavy makeup, high heels and a skirt. As she settled into the front seat and the car pulled away I got a much closer look. Even with the completely different look there was no question about it, it was Silky.

I dropped off Maggie's car and took the bus to work.

Chapter 19

———

Sherry Woo was waiting for me in her car out front of Chick's. It was ten o'clock, pretty much a black night with no trace of a moon and few stars. The air was brisk and felt amazingly fresh against my face. It was a welcome relief after a long sweaty night behind the counter where the air was permeated with the heavy smell of frying onions mixed with the acrid smell of cigarettes. Chick had turned me into a short-order cook so it was practically non-stop from the time my shift started. The place had been packed and it seemed like everyone smoked, including myself when on break.

In one hand, I carried the bag with the camera and in the other, I balanced a small box with two Styrofoam cups of coffee. Inside the car I handed one to Sherry. She nodded, thanked me and lifted the lid to let the steam out, then took a sip and pushed the top back on, scrunching up her face. "Hot." She handed the cup back to me, put the car in gear and rolled south a half a block on LaBrea to Melrose, turned right and headed west. Traffic was light. I handed Sherry back her coffee which she sipped with one hand on the wheel.

"What's in the bag?" She said, glancing over at me.

"Nothing, just an old camera I got for a friend," I said. "So where're we going?"

"A friend of mine's place," Sherry said. "She has a sixteen millimeter projector."

"How'd the film come out?" I said.

"I guess we'll see," Sherry said. "I just picked it up this evening. The guy who souped it told me he checked a couple of frames and said it looked like something was there. He added an optical sound track from the tape recording.

It only took ten minutes to get to Sherry's friend's place. It was a pinkish apartment building on Harper and Willoughby. Palm trees lined the front flagstone path that lead to a high-arched entrance. You had to be buzzed in, but luckily the iron security gate was ajar. We went into a courtyard that had a small swimming pool in the center surrounded by three levels of apartments. Sherry's friend lived in apartment 2-B on the second level. We had to knock several times before her friend, a young woman named Claire, opened the door. She quickly explained, apologetically, she'd been watching something on television in the bedroom and didn't hear us.

After introductions, Claire announced that she had to go for a late night guitar lesson and told Sherry where the projector was stashed. She said it had been her father's, that she'd never used it but was sure it worked. Before leaving she asked that we not smoke inside. Sherry helped herself to some wine Claire had left on the counter that divided her tiny kitchen from the living room. I found some medical books on the coffee table where Sherry set up the projector. Sherry spotted me looking through them and told me Claire was a registered nurse. After threading in the film, she pointed the projector at a blank white wall behind the couch. Sherry then took a gulp of wine. I told her how I had run the projectors at my hometown theater and once let one reel run out before the next one was to start. She just nodded as she double checked to make sure the film was on the sprockets, clearly caught up in the anticipation of what we were about to see. We turned off most of the lights.

"Show time," she said and flipped on the switch. "Screw it, I need a cigarette."

As a series of numbers flashed on the wall, Sherry lit a cigarette and fanned the smoke with her hand as if that would make any trace of smoking disappear. The film went dark. We could not make out any images,

158

only shadowy fragments of movement. There were voices. The woman was saying she should go. Frank Meade was saying something and then the woman said something, barely audible over the sound of the projector. Sherry turned the volume up. Suddenly as if someone had switched on a harsh light the images appeared. There was Frank with his heavy Jell-O-like painted body. He was sitting on the couch next to the blonde, his erection very visible. The film jumped and was slightly out of focus for a moment and the voices were out of sync with their lip movements. The film cut to a new angle when Sherry changed her position and got in close. Overall the film was about eight minutes long.

"Shit," Sherry said laughing, "It's like a mini porno."

"Why do you think he painted himself up that way?" I said.

"I don't know," Sherry said as she rewound the film. "I mean, let's face it, he's a candidate for a straight jacket." She looked pensive for a couple of moments. "Wait a minute, he did make a movie once about this lost tribe of head hunters deep in the jungles of South America. It was down the Amazon. Tribesmen kidnapped a white woman and performed some sexual ritual with her. The young men of the tribe would paint themselves up, kind of like the way Frank did. In the movie it was a symbol of their power."

"Weird," I said.

"Frank's wife would go ape shit if she ever saw this little vignette. I think we should show it to Frank and..."

"No," I said. "Not just yet. Make some copies."

I suddenly felt very confident, very sure of myself as if I'd had an instant transformation. And in a way it was true. For the first time since coming to Los Angeles I was finding a way to take control of events, of my career. Finding a source of power, that was it. The question was how best to use it, how to use this piece of film. I was trying to formulate an idea.

Sherry was taken aback for a moment at my abruptness, took another sip of wine, and nodded.

"Sure," she said. "We can make copies."

"Good," I said.

"So, what are you thinking?" She said.

I looked up at the ceiling and shook my head.

"I'll let you know," I said. "Right now I'm wondering where Bonnie Robertson is. I want to find her and talk to her."

"What?" Sherry said. "Why?"

"I want to find out about the letter," I said.

"Sherry finished off the wine, then went to Clair's refrigerator and found a can of malt liquor, opened it, and walked back around the counter into the living area with her head tilted back, guzzling it. Some of the beer dribbled down along the sides of her mouth which she wiped away with the back of her hand. She finished it off, plunked the can down on the counter and confronted me.

"Bonnie Robertson?" She said. "Screw Bonnie Robertson! What does it matter?"

I took a deep breath and fired up a smoke.

"I want to talk to her about the letter," I repeated.

Sherry looked incredulous.

"What is this stupid obsession you have about that dumb letter?"

I felt a sudden flash of anger, my jaw muscles felt like they tightened.

"I have my reasons, okay," I shot back.

Sherry threw up her hands.

"You going to help me or not?" I said.

"That letter you got is no longer relevant," Sherry said. "Not rel-e-vant. Get it? Don't matter no how." She laughed and shook her head. "Let's take this film to Frank Meade and see if we can't make him squirm and maybe make a goddamned movie."

I went and opened the front door and blew smoke out, then came back and faced Sherry.

"That's what I aim to do. Make a movie. But, I would like to talk to Bonnie Robertson about the letter anyway. Somebody wrote that note after reading my story submission and must have liked what I wrote. So, it's kind of like someone validated what I did. Nobody's ever validated anything I did before back home. Not really."

Sherry just looked at me.

"Validated? Fancy word for a hayseed."

"Will you help me go look for Bonnie Robertson?"

"Right," Sherry said. "It's pathetic. I get the privilege of chauffeuring your ass around so you can get the Good Housekeeping Seal of approval. What a crock!" She rolled her eyes. "I guess we can start with the phone book. Who knows, she might actually be listed."

There were several Robertson's listed. There was no Bonnie, but Sherry found a B Robertson who lived on Silver Lake Boulevard. Sherry made the call. The B turned out to be Bill. However, Bill told Sherry that Bonnie was a cousin of his and he thought she lived in an apartment down near Crenshaw, near Culver City. He hadn't seen her in a long time but had heard she might be having some personal problems.

"What kind of problems?" Sherry said.

A long silence followed.

"Are you a friend of hers?" Bill Robertson said.

Sherry explained that she had worked with Bonnie and needed to get in touch with her about a project she had been working on.

"Oh," Bill said. "Anyway, my sister tells me Bonnie hasn't been too well lately. She talks to her. Maybe you could look her up, whoever you are. Bonnie used to go to church every Sunday. Are you from the church?"

Sherry looked at me and stifled a giggle.

"Right," she said into the phone. "I'm from the church."

She put her hand over the phone and said this guy sounds goofy.

"She doesn't go to church anymore," Bill said. "I don't know you, but you...you sound alright, from the church and all. I'll see if I can find Bonnie's number for you." He came back a few minutes later and gave Sherry a phone number, noting that it was an old number. He then asked if she had seen Bonnie in church.

"Not really," Sherry said, thanked Bill and hung up and immediately dialed the number. It rang ten times and Sherry was about to hang up when someone finally answered. But there was no greeting or voice on the other end.

"Hello," Sherry said. "Anyone there?"

Both of us listened. Silence except for the faint sound of labored breathing, and music in the background. Sherry said hello again a couple of times. Still no answer. She looked at me and shrugged. "Strange," she said. "Bonnie is that you?"

"Who's this?" It was a raspy voice, the words sounding like they were spoken under water.

Sherry looked at me and nodded. I continued to keep my ear to the phone.

"Bonnie, this is Sherry Woo."

"Sherry who?"

"From Starburst/Meade," Sherry said. "Remember me?"

A long beat.

"Oh, yeah," the voice said. "You're that chink chick who wants to get into the business."

Sherry put her hand over the phone.

"She sounds really bombed. Still want to see her?"

I nodded. Sherry took her hand away from the phone just as Bonnie Robertson asked if anyone was there. Sherry asked if it would be okay to come over and see her.

"What the hell for?" Bonnie said. "You want to get into my pants or something?"

Sherry snapped her head back and blew air in a silent whistle.

"I have someone with me who needs to talk to you. It's really important to him. We'll explain when we get there."

"He's not a cop is he?" I heard Bonnie say.

"No," Sherry said. "He's…he's a writer."

"Fuck, that's worse."

"Worse," Bonnie said.

Bonnie said she didn't give a shit and spewed out her address which turned out to be close to the Venice Beach Boardwalk. After hanging up

162

Sherry complained that it was a fairly long drive. I said I didn't mind. Sherry muttered: "fuck all," under her breath.

Chapter 20

It took forty minutes to get to Venice and find Bonnie Robertson's place. It was one of those large, old, three-story, wood-frame houses built in the early 1900s. Sherry thought it was what they called a Craftsman's House. It looked like it had what was left of the original paint job, most of which had peeled away exposing raw gray wood. Based on the mail boxes at the entrance it appeared to be a triplex, made up of three flats. Bonnie Robertson lived in the top flat, three flights up creaky musty stairs. A dog barked as we passed the second level. At the top was a dimly lit landing. There, we were greeted with the faint smell of urine.

After several hard knocks, Bonnie Robertson opened the door about four inches where it was stopped by a chain. She peered out at us, squinting with suspicious eyes.

"If you're selling something, I don't want any," she said.

"It's me, Bonnie, Sherry Woo. I just talked to you on the phone."

Bonnie Robertson continued to peer at us and then finally unchained the door and let us in. Her flat was darkish with only one small lamp burning near an arm chair. Once inside I could see that Bonnie had the remnants of a once attractive woman. She looked to be in her forties, maybe older. Her face was a little puffy, and her brown hair was streaked with a few strands of gray. It was a tired looking face featuring blood-shot eyes. Bonnie adjusted her stained silk kimono which was loosely wrapped around her. She looked us up and down then gestured for us to come all the way in. We sat down on her couch. She offered drinks. Sherry shook her head. I accepted a drink which was straight bourbon over some ice. I took one swallow and let out a soft whistle and glanced around. The floor was covered with old newspapers, magazines, books and beer cans. A cat box near the door to the kitchen looked like it had not been emptied in a month. A typewriter with paper in it was on an antique roll-top desk in the corner. A small television on a Formica table against the wall was turned on to a test pattern. Bonnie turned it off, grabbed a drink she had apparently been working on and took a chair opposite the couch.

"Looks like you're working on something," Sherry said.

Bonnie began coughing and bent over for a few moments. She recovered, took a sip from her drink, lit a cigarette and nodded.

"Some freelance work until I land a job at one of the studios. I'm talking to Warner Brothers about some possibilities."

"They say you're a real pro as a script doctor and editor."

Bonnie took a drag on her smoke and scoffed.

"Yeah, makes you wonder why I got mixed up with that prick Frank Meade. So, what's your friend here want?"

I stood, a little wobbly from the drink and took out the folded up letter and handed it to Bonnie. She put her drink down and took it, then took a pair of glasses out of a pocket in the kimono and put them on.

"What's this?" She said as she opened it and looked it over. "So?"

"Did you sign it?"

Bonnie looked down at the letter again and shrugged.

"Looks like my signature," she said, then laughed. "Oh yeah, I remember this. I was pissed at Frank and decided someone should finally win, so I guess it happened to be you. I may have been drunk, come to think of it." Bonne mused over the letter for a moment. "You know, I might have actually liked your entry."

"What about the hand-written note?"

Bonnie made a face. She tilted the letter and read the note, her lips silently forming each word. She looked up.

"It's signed Frank Meade," I said. "Like a personal note."

Bonnie hunched her shoulders and shook her head. She returned the glasses.

"I don't know, but I can't believe Frank would write a note like that or any note. It's hard to tell about handwriting. Doesn't look like his signature. In fact he never saw the letter. No, someone else must have written it."

"It wasn't you?" I said.

"Jesus, no," she said and picked her drink back up. "Who cares anyway? What the hell does it matter?"

"That's what I've been saying," Sherry said.

I took the letter out of her free hand, folded it back up and stuck it in my pocket.

"That note is pretty much why I came out here," I said. "I... thought someone believed in me, someone who didn't know me but who liked what I submitted in the contest. It was kind of like telling me who I am. You know. That's it. That's what it means. I'm not sure I really knew that until this very moment." I put my head in my hands. "I have to see my story made into a movie. That's what I have to do."

Both women stared at me as if I were in a freak show. The room fell silent as Sherry and Bonnie both lit cigarettes and seemed to ponder the moment.

"You're real messed up aren't you," Bonnie said and finished her drink. She turned to Sherry. "I mean I thought I was messed up, but your friend here is...goddamned delusional." She looked at me. "Listen, you'd better forget all this bullshit with the note. I don't remember what you wrote but the whole thing with Starburst/Meade is a scam anyway. No one wins. Frank Meade is a bum. And that's about it."

Bonnie pushed herself up, her kimono hanging loose and open to reveal her naked underneath. She did not bother to close it as she kicked some newspapers on the floor out of the way and poured herself another drink. She closed her kimono and went and sat back down.

"I've had enough of this crap," she said. "Get out. I don't want to talk anymore. Okay?"

Sherry and I looked at each other and shrugged. We got up and walked out the door which Bonnie slammed behind us. We stood on the landing for a moment. Just as we started down the stairs, we could hear Bonnie sobbing behind the door. We said nothing, but it was clear we could feel her anguish all the way down the flight of stairs.

Sherry dropped me off a few blocks down the hill from Maggie's. I did not want her to know exactly where I was staying. She told me she would catch up with me at Chick's when the copies of the film were ready. Walking up the hill I was still feeling little pain from the drink. I guess I wasn't used to the hard stuff. I thought about that little speech I made at Bonnie Robertson's and felt a tinge of embarrassment at all that stuff I said, sort of like letting a stranger know a secret part of yourself that you never intended to let escape. At that moment I wanted to sit down on a curb and scream.

It was after one in the morning when I walked in the door. Maggie was waiting for me. She was standing by the curtain to the bathroom. I could tell she was slightly drunk.

"Where the hell have you been?" She demanded like some fish wife.

"What?" I said, startled.

"I had something important to tell you and I drove down to Chick's thinking I'd surprise you and pick you up. I got there just in time to see you drive off with some woman. Is she a girlfriend?

I was sobering up fast now. I'd never seen Maggie so enraged.

"No," I said. "She works for Starburst/Meade. She's trying to help me."

Maggie threw a glass at me which glanced off my shoulder.

"Bullshit!" She screamed. "So where did you go? You screwing her?"

"No," I said. "What's it to you?"

"Liar! Fuck you, fuck you, fuck you, Charles Kendall. You've become nothing but a phony user of people just to get your stupid career as you call it out of the starting gate. You're not that innocent hick I took in months ago. That's for sure. Fuck You!"

168

I just stood there, staring, as Maggie sank down onto the floor and curled up in a fetal position and began weeping into her drink. For a moment I thought of the last sounds of Bonnie Robertson. I went over and hesitantly sat down on the floor. She didn't look at me.

"I don't get you," I said.

"And you never will, you goddamned hick," Maggie said.

"I thought you just said…"

"Never mind!" Maggie snapped and wiped the tears away from her cheeks. "What's in the bag?"

I reached over and put it down in front of her.

"It was for Christmas," I said.

Maggie looked at me and slowly took up the bag, opened it and pulled out the camera. She stared at it and then more tears began flooding her eyes.

"What did you want to tell me?" I said.

She wiped her eyes and looked through the viewfinder.

"Wow, a Leica," she said. "It's really a good camera."

"Good," I said. "I wasn't sure."

She sniffed, pulled out a cigarette, lit it and took a deep drag, eyeing me now through the smoke. After a moment she crawled over and put her head on my shoulder.

"I got Grover to put a lunch together for you with that agent," Maggie said. "The one I told you about. He's supposed to be very powerful."

"Fat Eyes?" I said.

Chapter 21

————

I nervously scanned the restaurant every few seconds looking for the man who was going to join us, the man who it was said could kick-start my career. He was late and I was anxious, certain that the lunch meeting was going to be a complete bust or the agent would be a no-show. I mean, all kinds of images were going through my head, one of which was that crazy Silky trying to dance with Fat Eyes at that bar the first night in town. I checked my watch. It was almost an hour past the meeting time. Grover Marcuse and Maggie were quietly nursing drinks and reviewing the menu. The Restaurant was in Beverly Hills. It was pretty fancy. Grover had said on the way over that it was owned by a man claiming to be a Russian Prince or something, but that everyone knew he was a pretender which only enhanced his popularity.

Fat Eyes finally appeared. He pushed his way through the front entrance where a crowd of customers were waiting to be seated. He had on oversized sunglasses and was being followed by a blonde woman twice his size. It was the same one I had seen him with at Barney's Beanery. The maitre d' rushed up to welcome him. After some handshaking and a few words exchanged, the maitre d' pointed in the direction of our table. I wore my tattered suit from the Salvation Army, complete with my red bow tie. Maggie, her hair pulled back, wore a simple cotton dress and high heels which gave her a completely different look than the other looks I'd seen. I had not realized how attractive she could be.

As Fat Eyes approached I pushed back my hair which had gotten lighter in the California sun, leaned back and shut my eyes. It was a brief moment in which I drew sustenance from long admired images buried deep behind my eyes, a lone figure in the distance, silhouetted against the horizon, sitting astride a horse that rears up on its hind legs, the Wichita Kid. The image morphed into a man on a motorcycle, the motorcycle rearing up on its back wheel, Star Dancer with blazing eyes, ready to meet danger head on. As I sat there in that restaurant I could almost smell the fumes from that motorcycle. Without realizing it I was making a revving noise, like a motor stuck in my throat.

"Tuckie," I heard Maggie say and then she shook my arm. "You look like you're off somewhere else, day dreaming."

Herman "Fat Eyes" Zeppelin was moving through the restaurant like a diminutive king, negotiating a path around tables. All eyes seemed to be on this ugly, cadaverous-looking little man as he led the long legged blonde toward them. People stopped eating to watch him pass by. I figured more as a curiosity than anything else.

Maggie whispered something to Grover just as Fat Eyes and the Blonde reached our table. They giggled. Then there were quick introductions. The Blonde, whose name was Bambi, was first to sit down next to me. Fat Eyes sat next to her. He took out a cigarette holder stuck in a cigarette. Bambi fumbled in her purse and came up with a lighter. I was startled at how high and shrill Fat Eyes' voice was.

"How are you, Mr. Zeppelin?" Maggie said.

Fat Eyes took off his sunglasses, held his cigarette holder and peered at Maggie.

"Do I know you?" He said. "Are you an actress? You look like an actress I used to know."

Maggie smiled and shook her head.

"No sir. We met at a party and talked for a long time. It was a year ago."

Fat Eyes nodded.

"I go to a lot of parties. What did we talk about?"

Maggie shrugged and took a sip of her wine.

"Mostly you talked, Mr. Zeppelin."

"Sounds about right," Bambi cracked out of the side of her mouth.

"Mostly about philosophy," Maggie said.

"Ah, yes," Fat Eyes said, "must have been my philosophy period. I was going to invent a philosophy machine with a coin operated box on top. Put in a quarter and out would pop a philosophy on any subject." He looked at Grover. "Clever don't you think, Grover?"

"Philosophy my ass," Bambi interjected and nudged Fat Eyes. "I'm starved. We gonna order or flap our lips all day?"

Fat Eyes looked at her without expression.

"Some patience, please," he said. "How about a drink?"

"A drink?" Bambi shrieked. "It's the middle of the goddamned day."

Nearby customers at other tables turned their heads. The waiter rushed up to see what the matter was. Fat Eyes ordered two Dubonnets on the rocks with lemon twists and a plate of Oysters Rockefeller. Bambi relented and approved the order with a toothy grin. Fat eyes turned to Grover Marcuse.

"So good to see you, Grover," he said. "How are things?"

Grover nodded.

"Couldn't be better," he said.

Fat Eyes turned to Maggie then let his eyes pass her and me to Bambi.

"I've known Grover here since he was a young man. Hell, since I was a young man. I was a struggling actor in those days. Had a few parts. Hard to imagine me as an actor? But parts were limited for a man of my stature. Grover's father, Jonathan was actually a star in silent films, mostly epics, the kind that De Mille made. Wonderful face, wonderful dark eyes, very Latin looking. A god, a true matinee' idol! Made the ladies swoon." He turned and winked knowingly at Grover who was nervously clutching his glass, apparently anticipating what was coming. "Even though he fathered Grover here, Jonathan didn't really have much use for the ladies as it turned out. He did go through the motions of marriage and carried out the pretense of a happily married family man rather well." Fat Eyes leaned into Grover, his bulging eyes looking mischievous. "But, he liked boys, young nubile boys. Am I right Grover?"

Grover looked away as if he did not hear Fat Eyes.

"Sorry, Grover," Fat Eyes went on, "I didn't mean to embarrass you. After all, how important is one's sexual persuasion in the context of the universe. Still, even I was horrified by such a revelation, as I'm sure you were when you were old enough to understand."

Dead silence followed. The waiter returned with drinks. Bambi grabbed hers and downed half of it in one gulp. Fat Eyes delicately sipped his, one pinky extended. I noticed that he had long graceful fingers which seemed at odds with the stubbiness of the rest of him.

"I love Dubonnet in the afternoons," Fat Eyes declared. "Grover, dear, are you still painting or whatever it is you do in that old relic of a house of yours?" He turned to Maggie. "It's the one thing his father left him."

Gover Marcuse nodded.

"He's very good," Maggie said to Fat Eyes.

"Really?" Fat Eyes said. "He used to be awful as I remember." He looked at Bambi. "No sign of any talent whatsoever." Back to Grover he said, "I suppose in time you've learned some technique."

I glanced at Grover who was now sweating profusely. He took out a handkerchief and wiped his brow. Fat Eyes giggled as if he'd just remembered a private joke.

"Grover used to paint large bugs with spindly legs, and...certain parts of the female anatomy," Fat Eyes continued.

Bambi looked bored.

"That Right?" She said. "Can we order some food goddammit. What the hell are we doing here anyway?"

She lit a cigarette.

"Grover," Fat Eyes said. "Why don't you have a showing! I have a friend who's opening a gallery on La Cienega. I'm sure he'd be delighted to look at your work. You're not getting any younger you know."

"I...I don't know if I'm ready," Grover said. He looked real uncomfortable.

"What parts?" Bambi said.

"What my dear?" Fat Eyes said.

"I said, what parts?" Bambi said. "What parts of a woman's body does he like to paint?"

Fat Eyes laughed which sounded more like a woman screaming for help in a dark alley.

"Oh my, got your attention," he said. "Why, do you want to offer some parts for modeling?"

Bambi took a drag on her cigarette and blew the smoke into Fat Eyes ears.

"I've done some modeling," Bambi said. "My picture has been in magazines."

Fat eyes laughed again, his bulging eyes dancing.

"Pornographic magazines don't count, my dear," he said.

Maggie looked away and bit her lip, I figured to keep from loosing it altogether.

"Forget it, Herman," Bambi said. "I don't think you take me very seriously."

Fat Eyes looked around at us grinning and then leaned in close to Bambi.

"That's not true, baby," Fat Eyes said. "I take you very seriously, particularly when you go south if you know what I mean. Very seriously! It's a source of power. Nations have been built on such power, and great stars have been launched with such power."

"Oh, shut-up, Fat Eyes, you little shit," Bambi said and giggled.

Fat Eyes turned crimson and went into a rage. He snatched Bambi by the hair and yanked her head back.

"You never use that name," he said in a shrill menacing tone.

We all cringed. I clenched my fists under the table and was about to let one fly across the table at the agent when Maggie, sensing danger, reached down and gripped my wrist, shaking her head. Tears rolled down Bambi's cheeks which she quickly tried to wipe away.

We ordered lunch and ate in silence. Afterward, we sipped coffee.

"Well, Grover, what is this fucking lunch all about, ah?" Fat Eyes said. "It's your dime. What do you want?"

Grover cleared his throat.

"It's not me, Herman," he said. "This young man here, Charles Kendall, has come here from middle America to begin his career as a movie writer. We thought…well maybe you could offer your wisdom, advise so to speak."

Fat Eyes removed his sunglasses and stared at me with grim resolution. I returned his gaze, trying hard not to blink, challenging him with my eyes. I noticed for the first time that he had a tiny tick just below his left eye.

"So, who are you, Charles Kendall and what are you about?"

The bluntness of the question kind of threw me for a second. One thing I knew — I figured I had to make my answer count for something. I had to project confidence, nothing murky or shadowy. In that moment I was the Wichita Kid and Star Dancer rolled into one.

"I'm movies," I said flatly. "Movies and action." I ratcheted my voice down a notch. "I believe in movies, I believe they're vital to the world we live in, they are America. That's what I'm about."

Maggie kicked me under the table and whispered that I sounded strident, even hostile.

"I see," Fat Eyes said. "Let's see, you are movies, movies and action. Is that what you're saying to me?"

"I guess so," I said.

Fat Eyes leaned back in his chair and shook his head.

"Whatever the fuck all that means," he said and looked over at Grover. "Is this fellow carrying a full load?"

Grover didn't respond. I threw up my hand as if in a classroom.

"Mr. Zeppelin…Herman, I think you should talk to me," I said, still keeping an edge to my voice. "I want my script to be made into a movie."

"You have a script?"

I nodded.

"He wrote it," Maggie said. "It's very good. I typed it for him."

Fat Eyes stuck another cigarette in his cigarette holder and lit it. Maggie also lit a cigarette. Bambi looked bored and began to fidget.

"Tell me about your script," Fat Eyes said.

I spent the next forty-five minutes explaining the story and then showed him the letter signed by Bonnie Robertson with the handwritten note at the bottom. Fat Eyes seemed singularly unimpressed. He noted that he knew Miss Robertson to be a washed up lush. He also noted that the note at the bottom was certainly not Frank Meade's style.

"My advice to you, Kendall," Fat Eyes said, "is to forget this letter, go home and pick back up whatever life you had."

I gritted my teeth.

"I'm going to see my script made into a movie."

Fat Eyes sighed, took a deep drag on his cigarette and rolled his eyes. "What do you want of me?"

"I...I want a meeting with Frank Meade."

"Frank Meade is a looser," Fat Eyes said, "hasn't made a movie in years and is usually half in the bag, probably be in jail if it wasn't for that rich bitch wife of his." He shook his head looking exasperated. "So, why should I help you?"

I shrugged.

I told him I didn't know and asked what he would want. He turned to Bambi and asked her what she thought he wanted. She was still sulking and did not answer. He turned back to me.

"What do you call your script?"

"The Prairie Wolves," I said.

Fat Eyes asked me if I had a copy of the script. I reached down under the table and brought up a thick manila envelope and handed it to Fat Eyes. It contained a mimeographed copy. Sherry Woo had told me to protect myself and mail a sealed copy to myself which would show a postmark. I did.

"I'll look it over," he said. "If it amounts to anything, I'll be in touch through Grover. If you don't hear from me, that will be the end of it as far as I'm concerned. But if I decide it's worth pursuing I'll represent you for a piece of the action."

I just looked at him, not sure what that meant.

"I'll want some money up front out of any financing and points in the back end."

I nodded. I'd learned about points from Sherry.

"Good," Fat Eyes said.

Maggie stood up and pulled the camera I'd given her out of her bag.

"Before everyone leaves, I'd like to take a picture of the group," she said.

Maggie adjusted the F-stop and snapped off four shots. Fat Eyes held up his hand.

"I don't want to see myself on the cover of some national tabloid – looking like some skid row pimp lunching in Beverly Hills."

We all laughed. Fat Eyes and Bambi stood to go. He turned to me and shook his head.

"Scratch the purple glasses and bow tie," he said.

Chapter 22

We watched after Fat Eyes and Bambi as they made their way through the thinning lunch crowd and disappear out the entrance.

"What a pair," Maggie said. "I kind of felt sorry for Bambi."

Grover looked sullen.

"I hope he likes my script," I said.

Grover snapped out of it and looked at me, shaking his head.

"Frankly I doubt he'll read it or we'll ever hear from him again. Maggie thought he might be helpful, but I never really believed it. I think he's just going through the motions. He doesn't have the juice he used to have."

"He certainly was being an asshole about your work," Maggie said.

"No matter," Grover said.

Maggie took a picture of Grover and I and then one of me with my purple glasses and bow tie.

"He'll probably give your script to Bambi," Maggie quipped. "She'll squeeze it between her legs and if she gets off on it, it'll mean it has promise."

Grover smiled at the image. He paid the check and left saying only that he had to be somewhere and was already late. After he'd gone Maggie scolded me for not thanking Grover for setting up the meeting and paying for lunch.

"Sorry," I said. "I guess I was...thinking."

Maggie decided to take one last picture to capture the opulence of the restaurant. It had an old world look, like pictures I'd seen in LIFE Magazine of grand places in Europe. Looking through the viewfinder she suddenly stopped and gave a short yelp. She motioned for me to come and look. I did. At first I wasn't sure what she was talking about.

"What?" I said.

"To your left," Maggie said.

I moved the camera left until I saw what she was excited about. Across the room leaning against the bar with eyes on us was the bulky figure of Mark Horgan. He had a drink in one hand and his notebook in the other.

"Jesus," I muttered. "What's he doing here?"

"I'd forgotten about him," Maggie said. "It's been over a month now since we've seen his fat face."

Mark Horgan waived and smiled as if suddenly recognizing old friends and began heading our way. Maggie said "Oh no." A moment later he was on us, hand outstretched.

"What a coincidence running into you two," he said "I mean god, I just happen to come in to get a bite to eat and a drink and well, here you are. I almost didn't recognized you, Tuckie, with those purples shades and bow tie. Your hair's longer too. Anyway, isn't that something?"

"Really," Maggie said. "Doesn't seem like your kind of place."

Still grinning, Mark said, "You'd be surprised."

Maggie lifted her camera and pointed it at the detective.

"You don't mind do you," she said. "Never know what you're going to get out of a camera."

Mark Horgan went into a pose.

"If it turns out good maybe I'll buy it off you. I'm going to be singing in a new opera production at a theater in Pasadena and they might need a publicity shot." He turned to a profile for another shot. "Happy 1956."

Both Maggie and I must have looked startled which Mark seemed to enjoy.

"You sing?" Maggie said slowly putting down her camera.

"Most of my life," he said. "I trained for the opera. Detective work is how I make a living. But Opera is my real love. I grew up listening to Caruso and once I shook hands with Mario Lanza."

"Wow, opera," I said, "never would have thought. You still working on the Margo Benson thing?"

Mark sat down at our table and set his drink down in front of him. He told us he had a family emergency in Colorado where his younger brother had been in a terrible car accident. He said the doctors didn't think his brother was going to pull through, but he did. He finished by saying he was still working on the case.

"Have you found out anything more since we saw you?" I said.

Mark took a sip of his drink and looked at Maggie and me with a sly grin.

"I found someone who said she'd gone to some party in West Hollywood the night before the body was most likely dumped. She saw Margo at this party, but doesn't remember where it was."

"Who's that?" Maggie said.

"I can't really talk about it except to my clients," Mark said.

I nodded.

"Oh, sure," I said. "Say, Mark, how would you like to be in my movie? That is, when they make it. You'd be perfect for one of the parts."

Mark laughed.

"Is there a part in it for an opera singer?"

"There could be," I said.

Mark picked up his notebook, finished his drink and looked at me.

"Actually," he said, "I have a couple more questions."

Maggie excused herself to go to the lady's room.

"I don't think she likes me," Mark said looking after Maggie.

"So what do you want to know?" I said and fired up a smoke, primarily to give my hand something to do.

The big detective began thumbing through his notebook, humming to himself until he came to a specific page and stopped. I began to feel butterflies crashing into each other in my gut as I waited.

"Here we are," Mark said and looked up smiling warmly at me. "You said, at least my notes indicate you said that you had known Margo Benson from around. Very general. You see my problem? So, I was just hoping that now that you've had time to think about it, you could be more specific about when you first met her. Anything, a place, a time. This would be very helpful and I probably wouldn't have to bother you again."

I shrugged.

"Gosh, Mark, I just don't remember. It's real hard to remember specific places where you meet people."

"Think about it some more. Take your time, see if anything comes to mind."

We sat silent for several long moments. I shut my eyes as I pretended to reach back into the recesses of my memory. I gave Mark a disappointed look.

"You say she went to a party?" I said.

Mark nodded.

"I guess I can tell you that her friend is asking around to see who in her crowd might know where the party was that night."

I saw Maggie poke her head out of the ladies room and then disappear back inside. Mark picked up his notebook and handed me his card.

"I don't remember if I gave you my card before or not. If you think of anything I'd appreciate a call. If I'm not there leave a message with my mother. I live with her since my divorce. She acts as my secretary."

Mark started to leave and then turned back.

"Frankly, Tuckie I don't think you're going to think of any of those so called places where you met Margo."

"You never know," I said.

"No I don't think so," he said. "You see I don't think any such places exist. I don't think you really knew Margo Benson at all. Just a theory of course. I'm not sure why you showed up at her memorial service, but I don't think it had much to do with Margo. You take care now. Oh, and if they do get around to making your movie and there's a part in it for me, let me know. I just might be interested."

Mark left. Later in the car, heading east on Sunset Boulevard, Maggie tried to light a cigarette with one hand while guiding the steering wheel with her elbow. The old Ford nearly veered into oncoming traffic, narrowly missing a pickup truck.

"Watch it!" I yelled.

"Don't tell me how to drive!" She screamed back. "So what did that bastard private cock want now?"

"He wanted to know all about you," I said. "Told me I should stay my distance from you. Said you were trouble."

Maggie puffed away on her cigarette and for a moment looked askance at me. I turned and looked out the passenger window to hide the grin that had crept across my mouth.

"You bullshitting me or what?" She said.

I turned back with a straight face and began laughing.

"Asshole," Maggie muttered.

"He lives with his mother," I said.

"Really, a big boy like that?" She said. "So, what did he want?"

I told her about how he wanted to know where I had met Margo Benson and when and all that. Maggie tried to blow a smoke-ring at me at the next stop signal.

"Guy bugs me," she said.

"Opera singer?" I said. "Little weird."

Maggie laughed.

"That's what my friends say about you," she said.

"Oh, yeah," I said. "What friends?"

"I have friends you don't even know about," She snapped back at me.

"You mean like Grover Marcuse?" I said.

She seemed to muse over my mention of Grover. When the signal changed she peeled rubber throwing me back against the seat.

"Grover went out of his way to help you with Herman Zeppelin. He didn't have to do that. And then he had to take that shit about his painting and then his father. It was mean. I felt for Grover. You could see he was hurt."

I nodded.

"Did you have to do anything special for him to get him to do it?"

Maggie pulled over to the curb and hit the brakes. She glared at me.

"Sometimes you really make me sick, Tuckie. You just don't know anything about people."

I didn't say anything, just stared ahead as we pulled back into traffic.

"Right," Maggie went on. "Don't react. You never react to anything. You know that. No matter what I say or do, you don't react. All you care about is your stupid fucking movie."

I remained stoic.

"See what I mean?" Maggie said, who appeared to be on a roll. "Nothing. Put something in and nothing comes out, like a broken vending machine, and the money's gone. Is that how you protect yourself? I think it's how you don't face things. You just clam up and that's it. Can't get in. Knock, knock. No one home."

We were silent for a time. But the tension was pretty thick.

"I wonder if Fat Eyes will read my script?" I said.

"Jesus," Maggie said.

I looked at my watch and told Maggie I had to go to work. She dropped me off at Highland and I took a bus down to Melrose and walked over to La Brea. Along the way I had a sudden impulse to call Jenny. I found a phone booth and called her at the bank, figuring she'd stay late to do paper work. She answered the phone and I told her about my meeting with Herman Zeppelin. She tried to sound excited but made it clear she wanted me to come home soon. Six months had gone by and my career still hadn't started.

"I miss you terribly, Tuckie," Jenny said sounding very plaintive. "I miss doing certain things with you...you know what I mean."

"Me too," I said.

184

I was afraid to ask her if she'd read the copy of The Prairie Wolves I'd sent her. She volunteered that she had spent several weeks staring at my script. Finally, she said she picked it up and read it.

"It's very violent," Jenny said. "I mean it's very good...but..."

She told me that she was surprised because it was not a side of me that she had ever seen before or had any inkling that such thoughts and ideas were going on inside my head.

"It's just a story," I said.

She said she knew and repeated her reaction. We hung up. I walked the remaining blocks to Chick's Hamburger Palace.

Chapter 23

————

I pushed myself up out of bed after a restless night, knowing that in a few short hours I would finally see the producer himself. The appointment with Frank Meade was set. I dreamed about the meeting. As sleep drained from my brain I recalled that we talked, but that there was no sound, like a silent movie without captions. I saw myself talking, my mouth moving. Then I was overcome by a foreboding. Other people began appearing, none of whom I recognized until a face in the distance came closer and finally into focus, the face of a woman, the face of Adele bending over me, smiling, saying goodbye as she had done almost 18 years before. I could almost smell her perfume.

The sense of foreboding left me and was replaced by a sense of optimism. Not sure why, except that I was looking forward to the meeting after all the time had gone by since first coming to Los Angeles. And the morning had broken bright and clear. I made coffee, added cream and sugar and drank it out of a tin cup. Maggie, still in bed, moaned softly. It was already warm and in her sleep she had pushed the covers down over her bare back and across the crack of her behind. She had been running hot and cold lately and I was thinking of moving out, finding a room somewhere. Maggie had been my savior, true, but she was also an enigma, her anger flaring sometimes at the littlest thing. It was distracting.

Later while riding on the bus the weather made a sharp left turn as dark clouds rolled in from the north-west. It was like a dark shroud had suddenly been draped over the city. My earlier optimism slipped away and again I was infused with this feeling of being on the edge of an abyss, staring down into darkness below. I was carrying a cheap leather briefcase I'd bought second hand for two dollars. Inside was a copy of my script, The Prairie Wolves. Also inside the briefcase my ace weapon, if I needed it, a copy of Sherry Woo's little "blue" movie as she called it.

As the bus moved along Santa Monica I stared at the passing life on the streets, motionless figures in doorways, on bus stops, business men in fine dark suits who looked important moving along with a sense of purpose into and out of office doorways. For a split moment I wondered what they all did and what their lives were like. What did they do at night? And then I wondered about the old black man I'd met sitting at the bus stop that first day I showed up at Starburst/Meade. Where was he now? Strange that I would have such thoughts. I remember as a kid back home I once asked Marco if he liked his life. He said that it was a stupid question, then said, "For me life is now in this restaurant. For you life is down the road a piece and you'll always be trying to catch up with it, kid." I didn't really know what that meant. Later that night in my bed I figured that was an odd question to be asking an adult. It had just come out of my mouth with little thought behind it.

I must have been moving my lips because a woman sitting next to me on the bus who had been knitting, stopped and stared at me as if I were a nut case. "I'm a movie writer," I whispered to her. She twitched and went back to knitting. A light rain was now beginning to fall.

Jocelyn Bukowski met me at the door. She looked me up and down quizzically and said to wait. She went back to her desk and checked her appointment book. She came back and ushered me in without any sign of recognition, and guided me to the couch, the same couch where a naked Frank Meade had sex with the blonde school teacher. My appointment was for two o'clock. I was right on time and settled in for my wait. By three thirty there was no sign yet of Frank Meade. Jocelyn was on the phone constantly and I wondered if he had tried to call to say he'd be delayed. Or had she forgotten to tell him about the appointment in the first place?

It was raining hard now, with thunder in the distance. The lights went out for a few minutes, leaving the place in almost total darkness. Jocelyn screamed that it was the end of the world. I could hear Sherry giggling. After the lights came on Jocelyn came over fondling her cigar and stood over me, a behemoth of a figure. I set my briefcase down on the floor, leaned back and fired up a smoke, ignoring her presence.

"You look familiar," she said. Mister...mister...I know I've seen you before."

"Kendall," I said.

"Right, Kendall," she said. "You a magazine writer going to do a feature on Mr. Meade?"

I just looked up at her and shook my head.

"Well then, what are you, an actor or what?"

"No," I said without further explanation.

She made a face and walked away. But soon she was back to confront me, once again hovering over me looking determined.

"So, what do you do?" She said.

"Nothing."

"Nothing," she repeated. "You one of those rich rock 'n roll people who want to invest in movies? You got that look." She grinned, showing yellowish chipped teeth. "Well, you can't go wrong with Starburst/Meade Productions. We've produced some of the biggest grossing exploitation block busters in the history of this industry. King Kong wanted to be in one of our movies but we turned him down, we try to stay away from type-casting."

She plopped down on the couch and peered at me. I was wearing my purple sunglasses, and there was no question I needed a haircut, all of which made me realize why she was having such a hard time recognizing me. Also, it had been some time since she last saw me.

"That was a joke, what I said before, you know about King Kong," she said. "Okay, you want to tell me what you're appointment with Mr. Meade is about? You see I'm Mr. Meade's personal...executive assistant and he forgot to tell me what this was about."

"No," I said without looking at her.

I picked up a LIFE magazine with a picture of Shirley Jones on the cover riding a carousal horse.

"What?" Jocelyn said. I could tell she was taken aback by my tone.

"You heard me," I said, as I pretended to take interest in one of the photo layouts. "It's highly confidential."

Jocelyn stood up fuming, her large face flush, her eyes narrowing into slits. She muttered, "sonofabitch." Finally, she went back to her desk and tried to look busy shuffling through papers.

Fat Eyes had set up the meeting with Frank Meade after more than two months had passed since the get together in the restaurant. He told me he thought my script had promise. But when I asked what he thought of certain scenes he brushed the question aside and said that there was a character in the story named Amber Jane.

"A perfect part for Bambi," Fat Eyes said. "Don't you think. If I'm going to help you, you must consider Bambi and her considerable talents for the part of Amber Jane."

"Oh, absolutely," I said.

He went on to say that he was skeptical that Starburst/Meade could get the financing to make a film and that his piss-ant contests for the self-deluded was about all the business he had.

"His wife Pamela has all the money," he had added. "Inherited a fortune and made another fortune in real estate."

He went on to say that Pamela was a very savvy, tough business woman. I shouldn't count on her as an investor. She's tight-fisted and she keeps Frank on a short leash.

"One more thing," Fat Eyes said, "Bambi thinks you need more sex in the script, more tits and ass. Shower scenes are good, screwing scenes are definitely good, running naked in the woods like a nymph is the best for maximum titillation. That's my Bambi. From here on you're on your own. I had to use a little deception."

He did not explain.

It was another half hour before Frank Meade showed up. Even though the rain had subsided, he looked wet. He wore a leather jacket over a black shirt stuffed into baggy pants. When he saw me he immediately went over to Jocelyn and asked her in a loud voice who the "fuck head" was, nodding in my direction. Jocelyn reminded him that I had been sent over by Herman Zeppelin. "I think he might be a reporter for a magazine or newspaper and wants to do an interview," Jocelyn said.

"Oh, yeah," Frank said. "I forgot this asshole was coming over here today. Last thing I need is to sit here and bullshit with some reporter. Fat Eyes said he writes feature stories and profiles. Guess it can't hurt."

Frank Meade walked over and stood in front of me. I stood and extended my hand. I was about three inches taller than Mr. Meade. He looked up at me as if taking my measure but did not take my hand. He then sat down in a chair opposite the couch and lit a cigarette. I eased myself back down on the couch.

"So Herman Zeppelin sent you," he said. "You one of his protégés?"

"He's an acquaintance," I said.

Frank made a face and blew smoke in my direction. He yelled at Jocelyn to bring some coffee. Jocelyn yelled at Sherry to bring us coffee.

"Acquaintance, my ass," Frank said. "Fat Eyes doesn't lean on someone like me just for an acquaintance. So, he's either in love with that boyish face of yours or wants something else which means he thinks you're going to help him get it. Well forget that. Ain't gonna happen."

I shrugged.

"You know why they call him Fat eyes?" Frank said.

"No, sir," I said.

"Because he's a greedy, evil little cocksucker, that's why." Frank said, nodding his head as if agreeing with himself. "And his eyes bug out. You think I should be associating with someone like that? Fuck him and the horse he rode in on."

He stood and began pacing around, stopped and looked down at me.

"What'd you say your name was?"

"Charles Kendall," I said. "Most folks call me Tuckie."

"What's with the purple shades and bow tie?"

I removed the sunglasses and smiled.

"You got suspicious eyes," he said. "Something about them…hmm. Listen, I'm only talking to you because I owe Fat Eyes a favor. When I came back from the war in 45 he helped me get a job at Republic schlepping anything that needed to be moved. No union card required. I did everything. I had one rule. I never said no to anyone no matter what. That's how I got my start.

That's when films were made by artists with a vision, they told stories." He raised his eyes as if to the heavens looking for a sign. "As for the future of Starburst/Meade Productions, all we need is a great script. They don't grow on trees. That's where the heart and soul of this business is."

Frank Meade wiped spittle that had gathered at the corner of his mouth with the back of his hand, but hardly missing a beat as he rambled on.

"But then the ghouls started arriving from some dark place, by the car loads, bean counters, bottom line assholes who don't have a clue about anything except the last dollar coming in. Put that in your story!"

He stopped and looked down at me. I glanced over at Sherry who brought coffee and was shaking her head. Jocelyn Bukowski was staring at me and she looked like she'd seen a ghost.

"Where's your notebook?" Frank said. "Why aren't you writing this shit down?"

He didn't wait for an answer, instead went over to his bar and poured himself a drink.

"So," he said, returning, "I forgot what Fat Eyes told me. You write for Box Office, Variety, Time…what?"

I shook my head.

"I don't know what Mr. Zeppelin told you but I'm a screen writer," I said.

He looked at me through his glass.

"You're not here to do a feature story on me for a magazine?"

"No sir," I said. "I'm here to talk to you about my movie script, The Prairie Wolves." I reached into the briefcase and pulled out the manuscript and put it on the coffee table. "I won your screen story contest. I want my script to be made into a movie."

Frank Meade looked over at Jocelyn as if this were her fault. She shook her head and shrugged. I pulled a photo copy of the folded letter I had made out of my pocket and held it out to him. He seemed to be in shock and it took him a moment to take it and look at it.

"This is over six months past the deadline," he said.

I explained that I had gotten there before the deadline last year and was turned away by his assistant, indicating Jocelyn with a nod of my head.

He finished his drink and went back to the bar for a refill, came back and looked at the letter again. "Fucking Bonnie Robertson," He muttered and turned to me. "What do you want?"

"Did you write that note on the bottom?"

Frank Meade looked at the note, took a deep breath and shook his head.

"No!"

He crumbled up the letter and tossed it toward a waist basket near the bar. It missed and rolled along the floor.

"I came all the way out here from back home, more than two thousand miles because of that note. It inspired me to want to start my career as a writer of movies."

Frank Mead threw up his hands and looked back over at Jocelyn who was puffing on a cigar.

"This guy's a nut case," he said, turned back to me and screamed, "Time to get your ass out of here. I've done my little bit for Fat Eyes. He knew I wouldn't see you if he'd told me you were a would-be screen writer. So that's it. Beat it!"

I just sat there and stared at Frank Meade like he'd just killed my dog, if I had a dog.

"What's the matter with you?" he said. "Why aren't you out of here already?"

He reached down and grabbed my arm to try and pull me up. I jerked away and stood up. Now I was looking down at him. He looked dissipated, out of shape and barely alive behind the eyes. I could feel my anger getting stronger and seeking a counter attack but at the same time wanting to bring Frank Meade back to life again.

"I guess I had you wrong, Mr. Meade," I said calmly. "I was told that when it came to making low budget action films you were the best, the master. I've seen your films. They had something. So when I won your screen story contest I thought how lucky, because if Starburst/Meade makes a move from my story, it will be done real well. That's what I thought, Mr. Meade.

"Get the fuck out of here!" He said. "Jocelyn, call the cops!"

"Will you read my script?" I said. "It's on the coffee table."

"I got scripts coming out my ass," Frank Meade said. "I don't need any more god damned scripts. Now get out! The cops are on the way."

"My script is different," I said. "Mr. Zeppelin said it was good. And I don't care about the five hundred in prize money I was suppose to get."

Frank looked over at Jocelyn.

"Where are those cops?"

"On the way, boss," she said.

"There's one more thing," I said.

I reached into the briefcase again and this time pulled out the small round tin canister and placed it on the coffee table alongside my script. "Here's a short film you should see. It's only a few minutes. Sixteen millimeter."

"What?"

"I think you'll want to see this film," I said. "You're staring in it."

Frank reached down and picked up the can.

"What the hell you talking about?"

"You should watch it in privacy," I said.

"What's the joke?"

"I don't think Pamela will think it's a joke," I said.

Frank looked at me with a contorted expression. If nothing else, I had his attention.

"Pamela, my wife Pamela? What the fuck?"

I picked up my briefcase and the letter from the floor and started for the door passing a bewildered looking Frank.

"Watch the film," I said. "Read the script, The Prairie Wolves. I'll call you this time tomorrow."

Before reaching the front entrance I turned my head back and caught Sherry Woo grinning.

Chapter 24

I was late for work. Chick stood behind the counter shaking his head as I rushed in. I quickly went in back and exchanged my windbreaker, which was still damp from the rain, for a freshly cleaned white jacket. The jacket had the monogram, CHP in deep purple so as not to be confused with the California Highway Patrol insignia. Chick had followed me back.

"Tuck," he snapped. "This is the third time you've been late this week. What gives, man?"

I apologized and explained about having to wait for Frank Meade. He knew I was trying to get my career as a movie writer started, but I figured he did not really think much of it, that it was all bullshit to him and that the real world was right there in the Hamburger Palace.

"Waiting for some flaked out producer, which is what this guy sounds like, doesn't cut it with me," Chick said. "Janet, the new girl had to leave on some emergency which means we only had one waitress, and I had to take care of the kitchen and counter by myself. Quality is sure to suffer."

I screwed up my face and nodded.

"Okay, let's get to work. We got folks waiting out there."

"It won't happen again," I said.

"Good," Chick said. "I got two ways to go with you. I can fire you, which I was considering. Or, I can make you manager of my new place

I'm planning to open out on Ventura Boulevard near Studio City. I have to be able to depend on you."

"You're opening another place?"

"There's more. I had an offer to sell my recipe for the hamburger sauce by the bottle. A big company will bottle it and market it to all the major food chains and give me a royalty. Course they won't put my black face on the bottle, but who cares, man."

"Wow, that's fantastic," I said.

At around 8:30 Sherry Woo came in, sat at the counter and ordered a cup of coffee. It was several minutes of filling orders before I could stop and talk.

"What a weird scene that was," she said, leaning across the counter as if afraid of being overheard. "Frank Meade exploded after you left, ranted and raved for ten minutes about how someone called Fat Eyes had scammed him. Jocelyn and I pretended we didn't notice. Anyway, I didn't know you'd seen any of Frank's films."

"I saw one at our hometown theater called Amazon Mud Monsters," I said. "I didn't realize it was one of his until I saw a poster advertising it on the wall at Starburst."

Sherry laughed.

"Missed that one," she said. "So you gave him the footage. That ought to give him something to go nuts about."

I looked over to see if Chick was watching.

"You know this is getting to be a high stakes game," Sherry said. "I mean, it is blackmail, kind of, and we're partners in that."

"I'm supposed to call him back tomorrow," I said.

"You know what I want, don't you," Sherry said. "I want to be involved in production. Maybe we should go have a drink and talk about it after you get off work."

"Not tonight," I said. "But you can drop me off."

Maggie, wearing a long blue work shirt over bare legs padded out of the bathroom, a cigarette dangling out of the corner of her mouth, a glass of red wine in her right hand. I sat on the floor reading a copy of Daily

Variety. She came around the coffee table and sank down onto the floor and folded her legs under her. She blew smoke at me. I looked up and could tell something was bothering her.

"What?" I said.

"I think I saw that creepy detective again today," she said.

"Mark Horgan? Where?"

"This afternoon when I came out of where I was working. I had a typing job at an office on Cherokee. He was in his car across the street with his head way down low, a hat over his forehead so that you could only see his beady eyes peering out."

"You sure?"

"I'm sure it was him," she said. "He scares me."

I fired up a smoke.

"Damn. I wonder what he's up to now?" I said.

Maggie turned on the radio to a Top Forty station. On came Mr. Sandman by the Chordettes. She sipped her wine and asked how it went with my meeting. I told her I thought Frank Meade was spooky, but that I gave him my script. I tossed the Variety aside, stood up and paced around, pulling drags on my cigarette and wondering if he had watched the film yet. What if he just laughed at it? The question then was, should we go ahead and send it to Frank's wife? I was suddenly feeling real jumpy.

"What's the matter with you?" Maggie said.

"I'm going for a walk," I said. "You want to come?"

"No," Maggie said. "I have to go pay the rent – so to speak."

I guess I gave her a disapproving look, which was not lost on her. I then went into the makeshift bathroom and checked myself in the mirror. My hair was getting pretty shaggy, and some stubble of beard was showing. I decided not to change. I was wearing a black T-shirt, faded jeans, a torn world war II surplus flight jacket and secondhand cowboy boots. After throwing some water in my face I came back out and started for the door.

"I saw you give me that preachy look," she said. "It's just posing. Nothing else and what do you care anyway?"

"Say hello to Grover for me," I said.

I walked down to Hollywood Boulevard and headed west. When I got to Highland I decided to find a pay phone and call Jenny. It was almost ten which meant it was almost midnight back home. Maybe Jenny would be up late watching television, I thought. I needed to call. I went into the Hollywood Roosevelt Hotel, got change from a cashier, who gave me a suspicious look, and found a phone booth in the lobby. It rang only once as if Jenny had anticipated my call. As always, the first words out of her mouth were, "When are you coming home?"

"I don't know," I said. "Things are starting to happen."

"I don't understand what it is you're doing out there all this time. I don't know where you live or if you have friends out there. Do you have any friends?"

I explained that I had met some folks.

"You haven't met any girls out there have you?" She said, sounding real plaintive. "Nothing like that I mean."

I was distracted by something I saw at the other end of the lobby. A group of four men and two women near the entrance to the bar had caught my eye. It was one of the women. Something about her was familiar, even in no more than the blink of an eye. She had turned away the moment I'd glimpsed her. The woman had long black hair which framed her face and accentuated the creamy white of her skin. As members of the group shifted positions I got a full bodied look. She had on a long black low-cut evening dress that attempted to project elegance. The men wore dark suits with what looked like name tags pinned to their lapels. The other woman was blonde. All were drinking and laughing.

"Tuckie, are you there?" I heard Jenny say.

"I have to go," I said and hung up.

I wished now I hadn't called. It was always the same conversation, always the same underlying panic in Jen's voice.

When I turned back the group was gone. I hurried into the Cinegrill and spotted the men at the end of the bar. The bartender was just refreshing their drinks. The blonde was sitting on a stool at the curve of the bar nursing a tall drink, ignoring the men. But the other woman was no where to be seen. I moved closer to the group until I was only a few feet away. One of the men looked up and noticed me standing there watching them. He gave me an unfriendly look and nudged the man next to him. "I think that scrounge over there is interested in us for some reason," I heard him say. "How does a low life like that get into the hotel anyway?" His friends laughed. The blonde looked over at me and laughed too. Sensing trouble I turned away and scanned the rest of the room. I felt a tap on my shoulder and turned around to find myself face to face with the man who'd made the remarks. He had a strange crooked smile which distorted the lower part of his face. He was almost my height, but stocky and barrel-chested with a thick neck, heavy face and butch haircut. Classic jock type, I thought. He looked to be in his early forties and was clearly feeling no pain.

He took a swallow from his tumbler and then turned back and handed it to one of the other men who'd come up behind him. I started to leave. The man reached out and grabbed my arm to turn me back.

"Where do you think you're going?" He said.

"I'm looking for someone," I said "I thought I saw her with you guys."

The man chuckled.

"That right," he said. "Tell me, you one of them beat bohemian types, or a gypsy or just a bum who happened in here with respectable people who come to enjoy themselves."

I looked down at the man's name tag. It said Bill Jensen, Annual Lumber Convention.

"Actually, no Bill," I said. "I'm in the movie business."

"Movie business," he repeated. "That right. What do you do?"

"I'm...I'm a writer."

He turned back to his friends.

"He writes for the movies," Bill said in a loud shrill voice and turned back to me. "Anything I might have seen? I'm from Seattle. We have movies up there."

"Good," I said. "Glad to hear it."

He was no longer smiling.

"You being a smart ass with me or what?!" Bill demanded. His eyes were blazing.

I was feeling nervous, but I was ready for a fight if that's what was going to happen.

"Come on, Bill," one of the other men called. "Leave him alone and let's go party."

Bill yelled back to his friends to wait a minute that he wanted to take care of some business here.

"Listen," I said. "I'm not looking for trouble. I'm looking for the woman who was with your group earlier when you were in the lobby. I think it's someone I know."

Bill said he didn't know what I was talking about and called me white trash. I countered by saying it was the woman with the long dark hair that was with he and his friends.

"You're full of shit, you know that scrounge. I'm going to fucking kick your ass right here and now. He pulled back his right arm. I moved back a step and braced myself, ready to try and block the punch that was about to come my way. Suddenly out of nowhere a large meaty hand clamped around Bill's arm pulled it back behind him hard. The man yelled in pain. People milling around in the Cinegrill room were looking our way.

Mark Horgan told Bill in a quiet, powerful way that he was about to get his arm broken unless he settled down and got the hell out of there. He then let Bill go.

"Who the hell are you?" Bill said.

"I'm the man who's going to take you down hard if you continue messing with my friend here.

Bill looked at me and then back to Mark. He was shaken and seemed not sure what to do, so he just stood there.

"I think it's over, don't you" Mark said.

"What're you his body guard?" Bill said.

Mark took a deep breath and moved close to Bill.

"I'll say it one more time," Mark said, clenching his fists and bringing them up for display at chest level. "Is it over?"

Bill nodded and turned back to his friends mumbling to himself. Mark and I watched after him. As he and his friends were leaving, Bill could be overheard in a loud voice explaining to his friends that if he were sober he could have probably taken the big guy.

Chapter 25

———

Mark turned to me, a giant crescent grin snaking across his face. I was sure he thought of himself as a hero, riding in on a white horse to save the day like the Wichita Kid. Even in his drunken state you could see that the lumber man was terrified of this new hulking presence. I sighed with relief and glanced around once more to see if I could spot the mystery woman, whom I was certain was Silky. Without question it was the same woman I had seen getting into the black limousine near Moe's business. It was not the same Silky I had picked up at lonely Lucky Bob's Roost and Sanitary Café back in Nevada. This was a slightly older looking reinvented Silky of the night, but underneath lurked the same crazy red haired girl. Of that I was pretty certain. The blonde who'd been with the group was also gone.

"Can I buy you a drink?" I said to Mark.

"Thanks," Mark said. "Don't mind."

We climbed up on two empty stools at the bar and ordered two beers.

"That guy was about to give you his Sunday punch," Mark said sipping his beer directly from the bottle."

"I was getting set for it," I said.

"Showing off for his friends," Mark said. "I see a lot like that. Blowhards who slip into town for a sales convention. It's a life filled with back-slapping and bad jokes. But underneath for some there's something wrong, sadness and loneliness along with a seething hostility, maybe hovering just below the surface. It's mostly about their desperate lives." Mark shrugged. "I suppose most lives are desperate in one way or another. Not much action at home, an unhappy wife, screaming kids, maybe a latent homo. The whole package."

"You sound like some kind of psychologist," I said.

"I like to observe human behavior," he said. "You're a writer. I imagine you do the same and take notes to boot."

We both laughed. I told Mark I'd be right back. I hurried back to the lobby and looked around one more time, but there was no sign of the woman in black. Back at the bar I fired up a smoke. Mark just sat there staring at his beer looking pensive.

"You really sing opera?" I said.

"I told you I did. Don't you believe me when I say something? Opera is my life, it's in my blood. I sing baritone. You want me to sing something?"

"You mean now?"

Mark nodded his head. I looked around at the crowd.

"Some other time," I said. "So what are you doing here?"

Mark Horgan laughed again.

"Just in the neighborhood," he said. "What about you?"

I explained about coming to make a phone call and spotting this woman that looked familiar. I described the woman in detail. Mark nodded and sipped his beer but said nothing. We were silent for a time. I began thinking about Jenny and was brought up short by Mark nudging me.

"How's your movie coming along?"

"Okay," I said.

"You meet with Frank Meade yet?"

I stared at Mark in disbelief. I began to sense that his being here was of course no accident, and that he had something specific on his mind that he was slowly but surely getting to, sort of reeling out his agenda in his own good time. My grandpa, Adele's father, was like that. He'd come to visit and you knew right away he had something on his mind that took him a while to reveal. Usually it was nothing real important.

"How'd you know about Frank Meade?" I said. "I don't remember saying anything to you before about him."

Mark took out his notebook and began thumbing through the pages until he seemed to find what he was looking for.

"Let's see, Starburst/Meade Productions. Sure, I know about them. I've seen some of his movies, mostly at drive-ins. What do you call that script of yours?"

I told him and threw in a brief description of the story.

"Don't forget me if it gets produced," Mark said. "Remember you said there might be a part in it for me where I could sing. Not to change the subject, but how's that girlfriend of yours, Maggie?"

I shrugged.

"Okay," I said. "She's not really my girlfriend. I have a girl back home."

"Right," Mark said, and went through some more pages in his notebook.

"You still working for Margo Benson's family?"

Mark took a big swallow of his beer, keeping his eyes on me. He wiped his mouth with the back of his hand and let off a small belch.

"Yep," he said.

"Seems like you've been on the case for some time now," I said.

"Getting close to the end, though," he said. "But I need to talk to you about something."

Mark excused himself, went to the men's room and returned a few minutes later. He ordered another couple of beers which he paid for this time.

"Here's the thing," Mark said. "What do you really know about Maggie? Tell me about her."

I shrugged. He nodded as if to say he suspected as much.

Again he referred to his notebook. "Maggie Langston. Raised in Seattle, majored in art at Stanford, moved down here a couple of years ago and got in with some bad people, renegades, people using marijuana

207

and hard dope. You think she had anything to do with Margo Benson's death? And don't worry. It's just us talking."

"Huh?" I said, a sickening feeling creeping around in my stomach.

"I think she's involved. I'm not sure how. But that's my theory."

I just sat there trying to absorb what he was saying.

"Wait a minute," I said finally. "You really think Maggie had something to do with Margo's death?" I shook my head. "No, can't be. Anyway, I thought I read in the newspaper that the police said Margo died of a drug overdose. Why would Maggie have anything to do with that?"

Mark reached up and put a hand on my shoulder like an old buddy about to give me advice or counsel me on some matter.

"I can't tell you what I found out except that I think Maggie's involvement is a lot deeper than you know. Now that's all I can say except that she was connected to Margo through the underground."

"Underground?" I said. "What underground?"

"That's it. That's all I'm saying," the big detective said. "So, be cool and keep that to yourself." He pulled his hand back and finished his beer. "Be cool, man. Keep plugging. I think it just might happen for you, your movie I mean."

Mark pushed himself off the barstool, gave me a little waive and started to leave. He turned back.

"By the way, that woman you described. Sounds like an exotic dancer called Delilah. I saw here earlier. I've seen her at the Pink Owl Club down on Ivar. Watered down burlesque, you ask me."

I nodded but was certain we were not talking about the same person.

"See you," Mark said.

Mark disappeared into the crowd. I thought about what he had said about Maggie, remembering back to that morning I woke up in Jack's place and how stupid it was to allow myself to get involved in getting rid of Margo's body. The truth of the matter was I didn't really know anything about what might have gone on during the night after I passed out. I only knew what Jack and Maggie told me. Jesus, did Mark really have something, I wondered? And when I thought about it, Maggie always looked panicked whenever Mark showed up.

I left the hotel and began walking down Hollywood Boulevard toward Vine. When I started to pass Ivar I stopped and debated with myself about whether or not I should check out the Pink Owl Club, its neon sign flashing a half block down. I started to move on then decided it couldn't hurt to check it out. Just inside the recessed entrance there was a large poster on an easel that had eight by ten glossy photos of three dancers. There was Hedy, The Voluptuous One; Marilyn, The Tiger Woman; and Delilah, The Exotic Vamp.

I leaned in close and examined the photo of Delilah. It definitely looked like the same woman I'd seen at the hotel earlier, but still couldn't be sure it was Silky. I went in and was immediately hit with a door charge of $5.00. It was dark inside and not very crowded, maybe half the tables occupied, mostly by men and a sprinkling of women. A hard faced cocktail waitress in a tight dark skirt pointed the way to a little round table for me near the front. It had a single candle inside a glass container. There was nothing going on at that moment. I ordered a Cuba Libre, one of the few mixed drinks I knew.

"How old are you?" She said. "I need to see some ID."

I showed her my driver's license from back home. She examined it carefully with a little flashlight and handed it back with an apology noting that it was hard to tell in that light.

The Waitress brought two drinks in tall glasses, explaining that there was a two drink minimum and it was the policy of the bar to serve them both at the same time and collect the tab.

"We used to get stiffed on a lot of drinks," the waitress volunteered when she saw the shocked expression on my face. "And it comes out of our pockets."

I shrugged and paid her.

"Show starts in fifteen minutes," she said

I began nursing one of the drinks. It was sweet, and I could barely taste the rum. After a while a short fat man in a green jacket and wide green tie got up on the stage and took the microphone. The spotlight suddenly popped on and shined on the man's bald head. He looked around at the half empty place, took a handkerchief out, and wiped gathering beads of sweat from his brow.

"Good evening lady and gentlemen," he said in a shrill voice and then laughed. "Oh, sorry, is there more than one of you out there, girls?" He laughed again as he made a face reacting to the snickers form the customers. "I've worked a lot of joints but this is the first one where the acts outnumber the patrons." He paused. "Okay, the girls will be out in a minute, so have another drink, sit back and enjoy because these girls are special. Take my word for it, their mothers would be shocked to see them now. So would the nuns that used to teach them. Oh yeah these girls are right out of the convent. You can imagine how they wanted to let loose. What do they call it? Oh yeah, pent up desire, baby. So we got 'em and that's your good fortune. I mean, what the hell, that's show biz. Right?!"

"Get on with it," came and impatient male voice from the back.

The MCEE introduced the band which consisted of a base, a sax, and a drummer and noted that on special nights they had a piano player.

"What do you think this is, the Coconut Grove?" He laughed again. It was a very hollow, very lonely kind of laugh.

"Get your ass out of there," another male voice yelled from behind me.

There was a drum roll, followed by the base and sax as a pretty redhead somewhere in her thirties slithered out from behind the curtain, wearing a short skirt and pasties over her nipples. After a few moments she took the skirt off to reveal her panties. Her act took about four minutes.

"Let's hear it for Hedy," the MCEE said.

Next was Marilyn, a tall blonde who stumbled and almost took a header off the stage. She appeared to be drunk. Finally Delilah poked her head out from behind the curtain, then a bare leg, and then sashayed across the stage, coming back close to my table. She wore a short black jacket open to partially reveal her breasts, and a short sequined skirt which she kept lifting in a teasing way as she moved, revealing lithe thighs and black bikini panties.

As I watched her I was beginning to think it wasn't Silky after all. She looked a lot like Silky, same size, maybe a bit heavier than I remembered, and long shiny black hair. Darkened eyes and deep ruby red lipstick had the effect of expanding the size of her mouth. The thing was, she just looked older. At one point all three girls were on stage at once gyrating back and forth along the edge of the stage. A woman from the audience yelled for the girls to take it all off and show the customers what they had. She even volunteered to come up on stage and strip down herself. The MCEE noted that they stay within the law at the Pink Owl Club. That got a laugh.

"Weren't they something," he said. "Girls you'd like to take home to meet the folks, right. How about a nice hand!" No response. "Jesus, have a heart, you know. Okay, let's give les girls a hand," he said with a French accent. "Come on yahoos, even a single clap would be welcome. "

There were boos and polite scattered clapping.

"Wonderful," the MCEE said. "I love show business. The girls will be out in a minute and you can buy them a drink. They're sweet things."

A few minutes later both Hedy and Marilyn came out and mixed with some men at the bar. I stood up to leave when Delilah came out. I sat back down and watched. She was now wearing the same black evening gown she had on at the hotel. I watched her as she slowly made her way among the tables, smiling at customers, finally landing at a table next to mine. An older, gray haired man was sitting there alone. They exchanged a few words and then she got up, looked around and suddenly she was sitting opposite me.

"Would you like to buy me a drink?" She said. "You look like you could use some company."

I stared at her for a long moment trying to study her face in the shadowy light.

"What's the matter?" She said. "Shy? What about that drink?"

I nodded. She ordered a drink and leaned over and lit a cigarette from the candle.

"So," she said. "I'm Delilah. You a visitor or local?"

Feeling nervous I fired up a smoke, letting the smoke create a temporary wall between us. As the smoke dissipated I took a sip of my second drink.

"Kind of Both," I said.

"How'd you like the show?"

I shrugged trying hard to overlay my recollection of Silky's face onto Delilah's face."

"Oh…err great!" I said. "Real great."

She laughed.

"It's garbage. But a girl's got to make a living," she said. "Sometimes any way she can, if you get my meaning."

I nodded.

"You don't say much do you," she said and smiled at me over the rim of her glass. Even her voice seemed a little deeper.

The overhead lights came up. Delilah was looking square at me now.

"Have I seen you before?" she said.

I looked away and then back again.

"Weren't you at the Roosevelt Hotel down the street a while ago, in the lobby?" She said. "I was talking to those convention people about a party. You were looking at me. You're not that creep who's been following me all over are you?"

"No, but you're right. That was me at the hotel. "It's only accidental that I found my way in here."

"So why were you staring at me?"

"You…You remind me of someone."

"Who?" She said. "A long lost girlfriend, your mother?" She paused. "What do they call you?"

"Charles," I said.

"What do you do, Charles?"

212

I took a drag on my cigarette and blew the smoke away while keeping my eyes on her.

"I...I'm a salesman," I said. "I sell hamburgers at Chick's Hamburger Palace on La Brea."

Hedy came by the table and whispered in Delilah's ear. They both giggled. She turned back to me.

"Hamburgers, eh?" She said

Delilah leaned closer across the small table, here eyes dark from the eyeliner and eye shadow, her expression intense. I could smell the sweet fragrance of her perfume and makeup.

"Okay," she said in a low voice, just above the din of the Pink Owl. "Let's cut the bullshit. It wasn't me that wanted to take that piece of crap of a car of yours. It was that asshole Rodrigo. I haven't seen him since. I went up to San Francisco, stayed with friends for six months and came back. So, are you stalking me or what?"

I shook my head and sat back, hardly believing it was really Silky after all.

"What was that name you used, started with a T...or...?"

"Tuckie," I said.

"Yeah, Tuckie, I didn't recognize you at first, your hair's longer or something. So, you're slinging hamburgers in some grease joint and in the meantime jacking off to your fantasy about being a big movie writer? Got it. Classic shit. Yeah, I remember you were gonna start your career."

"You changed your name to Delilah?"

"It's my stage name, cowboy," she said. "Hell, you didn't think Silky was my real name did you? I didn't like the name my parents gave me, I can tell you that. Know what it was? Lucile. Can you imagine any parents in this day and age naming their kid Lucile? They must have hated me from the moment I popped out. Mom soon ran off and I lived with my pa, but as I got older I kinda became his wife. Truth be told, I didn't mind none. I was the queen of the house. Fuck!"

"You look older," I said.

She leaned in closer.

"I'm not even twenty one," she giggled. "They'd throw me out of here if they knew."

The emcee told the girls to get ready for the next show. Silky stood up, stubbed out her cigarette and said that maybe she'd see me around sometime.

Chapter 26

————

No sign of Maggie when I got back to her place. I took a shower and made some coffee even though it was close to midnight. I figured I couldn't sleep. I needed to think, wondering what Frank Meade was going to say or do once he saw the film. In the morning I would go back to see Margo Benson's uncle Moe to talk about financial backing for The Prairie Wolves. Yes, that's what I should do. For an instant my mind traveled back home and Royce. Would Royce be proud of me if I get my movie made? No. He'd probably call me a commie for associating with anyone out here.

Adele, on the other hand, would have beamed with pride and bragged to her friends about her little boy, of that I was certain. I pictured her in the kitchen, cooking turkey at Thanksgiving when I was around nine or ten and she'd let me lick the bowl of left over bits of cake mix. Her beautiful, winsome face always smiled down at me with love in her eyes. And late at night, like many nights, I would hear her cry in the upstairs bathroom which was next to my room. It was like the sound of a dying animal out on the prairie. I did not understand what made her so sad.

I brought the warm coffee cup up against my cheek and imagined that it was Adele's cheek against mine. And where was Jim Oliver? Was he still painting houses? My little reverie was interrupted by Maggie coming in looking disheveled, flushed and exhausted. She was wearing a full white peasant skirt with flower designs sewn on, a pink blouse, partially hanging out, and her hair, thick and tangled hanging down below her shoulders. It had grown these past months. She also had on a lot of make-up, unusual for her. Heavy mascara and blue eye shadow. I just sat there and stared at her. She breezed past me and flung herself down on the bed. She lit a cigarette.

"What're you staring at?" she said, her tone a little hostile, eyes looking tired.

"You look…different," I said. "In fact you look like someone else every time I see you."

Maggie made a face, as if wondering if I was on something.

"Grover was fantasizing," she said, "about a peasant girl made up to look like a whore running in a field of mustered weed."

"I don't get it," I said.

"Never mind. What'd you do on your walk?"

I told her about the incident in the hotel with the lumber guy. Maggie got up and went into the bathroom, talking to me from behind the curtain. She flushed the toilet and returned, the cigarette dangling out of the corner of her mouth. She wanted to know what I was doing in the Roosevelt Hotel in the first place. I told her I wanted some change…to get cigarettes from the machine.

"So how come this guy wanted to choose you off?" She said. "What'd you do to him?"

"He'd been drinking, wanted to show off for his friends," I said. "At least that's what Mark thought."

The minute I said it I wanted to take it back. Too late.

"What?" Maggie snapped.

Maggie's eyes went wide. She poured herself some wine and began pacing around the room.

"Let me get this straight. Mark whatever his name is, that fat-assed detective was there?"

"It was just a coincidence," I said.

Maggie began laughing hysterically. She sat down on a pillow by the coffee table.

"Coincidence, my ass," she said. "I mean how gullible can one be! Jesus."

I didn't say anything.

"I don't trust that sonofabitch," Maggie said.

I took a sip of my coffee, fired up a smoke and without looking at her said, "He doesn't trust you either."

Maggie sat up straight, her eyes squinting at me in the low light.

"What do you mean?" She said. "What'd he say about me?"

I took a deep breath, sorry I'd said anything.

"Okay, "I said after a long beat, "he thinks you had something to do with Margo Benson's death."

Maggie sprang to her feet and began pacing around.

"Jesus, I don't believe this," she said. "What did you say?"

"Nothing," I said. "What could I say? I mean I told him I didn't believe it. I told him I didn't think you knew Margo. He said he thought you did."

Maggie stubbed out her cigarette and poured herself some more wine.

"This is really bullshit," she said wheeling around to face me. "What else did he say?"

I shook my head.

"No, wait. There was one other thing. Something about you being a member of the underground and that was your connection to Margo. I didn't know what he was talking about."

"Bunch of crap," Maggie said. "I never saw her before that morning at Jack's. The man's delusional."

Then Maggie did a strange thing. It was as if she suddenly turned to a new channel. She got her Leica and began taking pictures of me, moving around me, snapping away.

"What are you doing?" I said.

"Maybe you'll be famous some day and I'll have these pictures of you when you were a fucking nobody, a stupid hick who...forget it."

217

She soon handed me the camera and instructed me to take pictures of her, at first just poses with her mugging, lifting her skirt high to show her thighs, then in various stages of undress until she was naked vamping, a shot of her sitting on the toilet, another in the shower, her face peeking out from behind the shower curtain. After the last shot she wrapped herself in a sheet and told me she had a friend with a darkroom who would make eight by ten glossy prints which she would then send to her father.

"It'll prove his worst fears bout his little girl, don't you think?" Then she said in a high pitched mimicking voice: "My mother will say something like 'oh, she must be upset about something, dear. You know how she gets.' All the time I was growing up she never had a clue about who I am."

Later, around two in the morning, a hard rain began to fall followed by thunder. I was lying on the floor on a blanket, wide awake. A single candle was burning on the coffee table. Maggie jumped at the second round of thunder. In a soft little girl voice she asked me to get on the bed and hug her. I looked over and could make out in the glow of the candle tears running down her cheeks. I just lay there for a long moment and then climbed onto the bed and put my arms around her. She nestled in like a child seeking protection. The candle burned out.

"How come you never talk about your family?" She whispered, the heat from her breath warming my ear.

"Nothing to say," I said.

"Kinda closed off aren't we, Tuck?" Maggie said. "You've been here almost a year now and I don't know who you are."

I was silent. After a while I said I wanted to try and sleep. I was finally beginning to drift off when Maggie's voice pierced the silence.

"Do you believe what Mark Horgan said about me?"

I tried to halt the shade that was dropping on my consciousness and grasp Maggie's question. But instead I continued to sink into a dream state where Jenny's face flashed behind my eyes. She looked unhappy, or maybe I just felt that she was unhappy, or maybe she was trying to get a message to me telepathically.

"I don't know," I heard myself mumble into the darkness, "maybe sometime in the future." As I sank deeper into sleep I wondered if what I said made sense.

In the morning, on her way out, Maggie told me she wanted me gone. She did not want me there any more, not one more night. I looked at her, rubbing my eyes, confused. She did not wait for a response, just slammed the door. A moment later the door opened and she stuck her head in.

"And I want your shit out of here too," she said. "Leave the key on the coffee table."

She started to leave again and again stuck her head back in. "I don't know who you are and I don't want strangers hanging around my place."

Still groggy with sleep I thought maybe I had dreamed it. But later as I brushed my teeth and shaved I knew Maggie's demand to get out was real. Her voice, shrill and tight rang in my ear. Still, I wondered what had gotten into her. On the other hand, maybe it was time to leave, I thought. There had been something edgy going on with Maggie lately, and what did she mean she didn't know who I was? I decided I would be glad to get out of there. I'd worry about where to land later.

After some coffee, I called Moe's pawn shop. A clerk told me Mr. Miller was in, but tied up at the moment. I packed all of my things in the old leather suitcase, including the script for The Prairie Wolves. Before leaving it by the door I felt the side pocket to make sure my grandfather's gun was still there. It was, inside a sock. I closed it up.

Down the hill I caught a bus to the pawn shop. Inside I saw the woman who'd waited on me before. She was across the room talking with someone. I almost didn't recognize her. She had let her hair down, instead of bobbed. It made her look younger and prettier. I pulled out my little notebook to check where I'd jotted down her name. Iris Madigan, the actress who'd once worked in films with the Wichita Kid.

She spotted me and came over, smiling. She told me Mr. Miller had just left to run an errand and then join some business associates for lunch and probably wouldn't be returning until late, if at all. I thanked her and started to leave. She suggested that I come by some time and take her to lunch.

"I'd really like to hear more about your movie," she said. "I'm still acting, you know. Mostly bit parts, but sometimes I get a featured role." She grinned and squeezed my arm. "I'd really like to get together with you about it."

"How did you know about it?" I asked.

"You must have mentioned it, or maybe Mr. Miller said something. He invests in movies. I have an apartment near here. You could come over and I could fix lunch some time."

I didn't say anything. I guess she could see I was a little nervous.

"It's just for lunch," she laughed. "I won't try to seduce you or anything."

"That'd be great.....I mean sure, okay," I said and turned to leave. I turned back. "I almost forgot. Where is Mr. Miller's lunch meeting?"

Iris Madigan stepped closer, her smile broadening.

"Well that's the thing," she said, now being very coy. "I just don't think I can remember on an empty stomach. It's still early and well, we could have that little lunch and chat now. Don't you think?"

I checked my watch. It was 11:30.

I...I really should go," I said.

Iris Madigan nodded.

"It was nice talking to you," she said. "Bye now."

She turned and started to walk away.

"You mean you won't tell me where he's going unless we have lunch?" I said.

She topped and turned around.

"I didn't say that. I just said I don't think I can remember on an empty stomach. My brain gets all fuzzy about this time until I get something to nibble on." She laughed. "Oh, come on. I won't bite and I make a respectable lunch."

About six minutes later I found myself sitting on an orange and brown couch in Iris Madigan's tiny living room. A small television set with rabbit ears sat on a table across the room.

A green shag rug covered every inch of the floor and pictures of Miss Madigan, old and new took up just about every inch of wall space. The glass coffee table in front of me had several magazines stacked up on it, LIFE, Look, Saturday Evening Post and Esquire, also copies of the Hollywood Reporter and Daily Variety. On the side table was a framed photograph of Iris on the set with the Wichita Kid. She was wearing a cowboy hat and checkered shirt. She looked very young next to the craggy Kid. I picked it up. There was an inscription at the bottom. "To Iris, with great affection, signed Billy Coughlin, AKA the Wichita Kid."

"Wow," I said aloud.

I got up and walked around. There was a glass framed cover of a LIFE magazine hanging over the mantle. It was a full head shot of Iris in 1945, her hair swept back as if being blown by a strong wind. She was beautiful. The caption read: "Rising Star Iris Madigan".

Iris returned from her small kitchen with two glasses of white wine.

"The studio and my agent got LIFE to feature me that year. I mean I'd already been working as an actress since I was eighteen." She sighed. "Time passes, you get older, and the work doesn't come along as often."

Iris handed me one of the glasses of wine. I took a sip and went back to the couch and sat down, setting the glass on the coffee table. She followed, sat down next to me and crossed her legs which brought her tight skirt up to mid-thigh. She tugged at it without much success.

"Tell me about this movie or yours," she said.

I gave her a brief synopsis and told her about winning the contest. Trying to avoid eye contact, I took another sip of wine. I could feel her eyes appraising me. After a moment she pushed herself closer to me. I could feel her body heat. She tapped me on the shoulder.

"So, do you think there's a part in it for me?"

I began to feel my body squirm. Even after a year of being in this foreign land I had not really learned the art of cool. Even with Maggie, it was real hard to truly connect. There was something inside me that wouldn't let who I am, or who I think I am get out, exposed so to speak. It was true with Jenny, too. She always said I was uncommunicative.

"I don't know," I said.

"I'll bet you could find a teeny, weensy little part for me, couldn't you?" She said and laughed. "Something with a couple of lines, even one line?"

I pursed my lips, trying to look thoughtful.

"Yeah, maybe," I said. "So, where's Moe...Mr. Miller having lunch?"

Iris reached up and began running her hand through my hair.

"You have a nice profile," she said. "But you're tight as a drum. You need to loosen up."

I nodded.

"So, where's Mr. Miller having lunch?"

"You have a one-track mind," she said, still stroking my hair and neck. "I'd be really grateful if you could do something about a part. Really very grateful if you know what I mean."

I leaned back and closed my eyes trying to decide what to do next when I felt her hand begin to caress my leg, and then move slowly up the inside of my thigh, using her fingers to propel her hand, like a spider moving to it quarry. She leaned in and kissed me, catching about half my mouth. I could feel the tip of her tongue exploring. Her hand found its target and I could feel myself getting aroused. I was about to let whatever was going to happen- happen when she suddenly took her hand away and stood up.

"Time for lunch," she said.

While I thought sex with this attractive woman would be very enjoyable, I felt oddly relieved. I told her I did not really want lunch. She told me that if this were a movie I would have taken her to bed by now.

"Right," I said.

She made a face and sighed.

"Farmer's Market," she said, sitting back and finishing her wine.

Chapter 27

———

T he afternoon warmed up. To me the city looked bright and fresh under an iced blue coral sky. Earlier a strong breeze had whipped through the basin and took with it any signs of smog. That was a new word I'd learned since coming out to the coast. There was no such thing where I came from.

It took two buses to get to the Farmers Market at Third Street and Fairfax Avenue. During the ride I thought about Iris Madigan and wondered why she fell off the cliff. I figured something must have happened along the way that she did not want to talk about. That, or the world she knew changed and left her behind. Maybe I could find a part for her in The Prairie Wolves. I would have to think about that.

Like a village unto itself, the Farmers Market was a sprawling combination of stalls selling everything from fresh produce and meats to freshly baked breads and pies all mingled with numerous restaurants. It was a phantasmagoria of color and activity mixed with the din of chattering voices, shuffling plates and clinking glasses. The place was buzzing with both tourists and locals, near as I could tell. It reminded me of the county fairs Adele took me to when I was a kid. At the fairs though, you were hit with the aroma of cotton candy and hot dogs wafting through the air, colliding with the smell of livestock in nearby pens. Just the thought of those times made me momentarily homesick.

It took me a while of wading through the maze of vendors before I finally spotted Moe. He was strutting through the crowd, a fat cigar hanging from one corner of his mouth. A straw hat shaded part of his face and the Hawaiian print shirt he wore flapped over his belly. A short lean man with dark glasses, about fifty, wearing a white shirt tucked into tan slacks greeted him. They then maneuvered their way to a nearby table where a third man with black thinning hair in a candy striped blazer waited. After Moe and the other man sat down they ordered beers. There was a fourth chair waiting to be filled by someone. For a split moment I thought fate meant it for me. But then a very small man with chalk white skin and a large head capped by a reddish brown wig appeared and took the seat. It wasn't until I saw Bambi standing off to the side like a lady in waiting that I realized it was Fat Eyes. This was too strange to be believed, I thought. I bought a draft beer and watched from a few feet away.

"Hey, Herman, how come you brought the broad?" The one in the candy striped blazer said. "She your bodyguard or what?"

They all laughed. Fat eyes snorted and shot each of the others a patient look.

"When you reach my age you always bring the broad, especially when she's young and beautiful. Know why, you jerk-offs? Because the world thinks you're either very rich or a great lover, thus extending you both credit and respect."

"So which is it?" Moe said and winked at the others.

"Both," said Fat Eyes in a matter of fact tone. He reached behind him and touched Bambi's hip. "Right, baby?"

"You're the best, Herman," she cooed as she caressed the back of his neck.

"I thought we were going to get together for poker," the man in the white shirt said, sounding annoyed. "What's she going to do, kibitz?"

Laughter all around. Moe suddenly looked in my direction as if he sensed he was being watched. I covered my face with my hand and ducked behind a women who was just standing there, apparently waiting for someone.

"Don't matter," Moe said as he moved his cigar from one side of his mouth to the other.

"We'll have some lunch and then I got a room for us at the Beverly Wilshire. Herman's blonde will dress up the room maybe keep us supplied in drinks. You bums should do so well."

They all stared at Bambi. Finally the man in the striped blazer with a scowling face got up and brought a chair over from a nearby table. Bambi thanked him and sat down. A waiter came by and they ordered. As I watched I formulated a plan for making my entrance before they all left for the hotel. I did not want to miss this chance to talk to Moe about financing my movie. With my beer in hand I walked up and stood over Moe's table. No one noticed me. I turned, walked about ten feet away and then came back. Everyone was leaning in toward Fat Eyes who was telling some story about a famous actor who was about to be slapped with a paternity suit.

"The studio told him to keep his pecker in his pants until it blew over," Moe said. Everyone laughed. Bambi who was laughing the loudest looked up and stared at me. She had a blank look on her face at first then her mouth curled up in recognition.

"Hey, I know you," she said. "You're that guy who wrote that script, right?"

"Oh, hi," I said. "I remember you. And you too, Mr. Zeppelin…err Herman."

Fat eyes turned and looked up, shielding his eyes from the sun.

"You're that friend of Grover Marcuse," he said.

I nodded.

"I was just walking by and saw you gentlemen and…"

"Cut the bullshit, kid," Moe said, taking the cigar out of his mouth and pushing his hat back.

"Find a chair and join us if you like."

"Oh, hi, Moe," I said. "I didn't see you sitting there."

Fat eyes looked at Moe.

"You know this kid?" He said.

Moe nodded.

"Kind of a funny name – Tucker…Tuckie?" Moe said.

I found a chair and squeezed it in between Fat Eyes and the man in the white shirt. All faces were now on me. I told them my name was Charles but that I was called Tuckie. All heads nodded. The man in the white shirt was Bernie, and the man in the blazer was Jack.

"This kid either has balls the size of grapefruits or he's one crazy sonofabitch!" Moe said. "I don't know which."

"What're you talking about, Moe?" Jack in the candy striped blazer said.

Moe pulled a handkerchief out of his shirt pocket and dabbed perspiration that had gathered along his forehead.

"He wants me to finance his cockamamie movie. So I'm sitting here looking at him and I think, what's he doing here? This ain't no goddamned coincidence! But hey, I admire that. That's how this town got built, hell that's how the whole country got built. Huckstering!" Moe looked at me and winked. "So, don't try to bullshit me about you just happening to be passing by."

I threw up my hands.

"You got me, Moe," I said which I followed with a nervous laugh. "You got me good."

Moe nodded.

"So, spill it," he said.

I looked at each of the faces at the table, even Bambi's. They were all looking at me, anticipation of something heavy written all over their faces. I cleared my throat and explained that I wanted Moe to finance this movie that I'd written. Everyone started laughing. Moe held up his hand to quiet them.

"Why should I do that?" Moe said. "What's in it for me?"

I shrugged.

"Money, profit, your name on the screen," I said.

Laughter all around again. Moe pulled out a fresh cigar, bit the tip, lit up, and blew smoke across the table. "Fresh from Havana," he said. For a moment the smoke permeated the air with its acrid smell. Fat eyes coughed and turned his head away, brushing the air with his hand.

"You guarantee investors a profit, kid?" Moe said. "Is that what you're saying?"

"Maybe a tax right off?" Jack said.

Fat Eyes leaned forward.

"It's a pretty good script, Moe," he interjected and turned to me. "I thought you were working with Frank Meade to produce it."

I nodded.

"Alright," Moe said, "we might have some investors right here at this table. Anybody here want to invest in a movie? Might do better than putting your money on the ponies at Hollywood Park."

Birney said, "I'm actually thinking of putting money into spaceships and shopping centers on Mars."

Jack looked thoughtful. He put up his hand.

"Tell you the truth, I might be interested if you can show me why it will make money, and also find a part in it for my wife. Get her off my back. She did a little acting once."

"Yeah, she was great in those fuck films, Jack," Birney said. "But she would have to say lines."

Everyone laughed, even Jack. I started to say something, but Moe stopped me.

"Here's what you do, kid," he said and went on to instruct me to get Frank Meade back in the saddle, put together a prospectus, which should include a budget, distribution and market potential, name actors if any, etc. "You put together a presentation and have an angel party. If we like what we hear, maybe we'll buy in. If Mead's in, tell him to call me and we'll talk. Got it?"

I nodded and stood up.

"Moe's right," Fat Eyes said. "And don't forget Bambi here."

I walked away just as the lunches were being delivered to the table. I took several deep breaths and then went back. Everyone looked up.

"My film's going to make money," I said. "You don't invest, it's your loss."

Moe banged the table with his fist, making the plates jump.

"What'd I tell you?" He said. "Kid's got chutzpah!"

Suitcase in hand I walked into the Hamburger Palace. It was early evening and the dinner crowd would soon fill the place up. Chick, who was behind the counter talking to a customer spotted me and began chuckling to himself as if he somehow knew what had happened. He shook his head and motioned for me to put my stuff in the back. Later when we'd closed down for the night I told Chick how Maggie had gotten kinda hysterical and thrown me out. He just sipped at a beer and grinned knowingly.

"Strange creatures, women," he mused. "You should have known my ex-wife. She tried to kill me."

"Really?" I said.

Chick then told me how he'd come home one night from work a few years back and how she'd kissed him sweetly. Then he followed her into the kitchen thinking she had drinks ready when suddenly she whirled around and tried to attack him with a butcher knife.

"She had this real wild look in her eyes, like an animal, and said she was going to cut off my balls and everything that went with them and feed them to our dog. I'm telling you it was scary. I mean I would never have suspected such violence out of that woman. Anyway, I got the hell out of there with a cut arm. Later I found out she thought I was fucking this woman who lived a couple of doors from us."

"Wow," was about all I could get out. After a moment I said, "Were you?"

"Was I what?" Chick said.

"Doing it with the neighbor woman?"

Chick looked shocked. He took a swallow of his beer and stood up.

"Hell yes," he said. "But what's that got to do with anything?" He chuckled. "Now, remember you can only camp out here for a couple of days 'till you find something else. I don't want no permanent tenant here. You can use that folded up cot that's out back. The TV works, but you might have to adjust the rabbit ears."

Earlier that evening Sherry Woo came in looking very nervous. She told me things had gotten very weird around Starburst/Meade. She said Frank Mead had not been seen nor heard from since I was there. That he usually checked in. And Jocelyn was so paranoid it's a wonder they haven't carted her away, Sherry said. "This morning she told me she was sure she was being followed and has started wearing disguises."

"I wonder if Frank's watched the film?" I said, more to myself than to Sherry.

"Maybe he watched it and decided to go to the police," Sherry said. "I mean it is kind of blackmail, isn't it. Pitiful as it is. And, well I'm a conspirator, so to speak."

"You really think he'd go to the police?" I said.

"He's a crazy bastard," she said. "Anything's possible. We could be in deep shit." She lit a cigarette. "What should we do?"

"Nothing," I said. "We wait. I figure he wouldn't want anyone to see that film."

It was after midnight when I stretched out on the cot in back and tried to sleep, which did not come easily. There were unidentifiable noises, possibly mice, and the pungent smell of onions. The next morning I awoke to the clanging of pots and pans coming from the kitchen. I could hear the sizzle of butter on the grill and eggs frying and the smell of freshly brewed coffee. After washing up in the dishwashing basin I went out front. A few customers had come in for Chick's early bird special. Laverne, a new waitress Chick had hired for the morning shift grinned at me.

"You sleep back there last night?" She said.

I nodded, still a little groggy, poured myself a cup of coffee and found an empty booth. Laverne offered to bring me something. I shook my head. I was lost in thought about what to do about Frank Meade when I was aware someone was sitting in the booth opposite me.

"How you doing?" Mark Horgan said smirking like he'd caught me stealing something.

"What're you doing here?" I said.

"Just in the neighborhood," he said, adding that he was back working with his voice coach and also taking some acting lesions. "I'm boning up so I'll be ready for a part in that movie of yours."

I nodded and sipped my coffee.

"Real good idea," I said.

Mark Horgan said he had to go and check in with one of his clients, a wife who hired him to follow her husband whom she believed was having an affair.

"So I follow the husband and this gorgeous dark-haired woman around for a few days and finally catch them in the act, so to speak by peaking through a motel window. Imagine my shock at what I see. The gorgeous dark haired woman turns out to be a blonde haired man in drag. The husband screamed when he realized the truth." Mark laughed. "What a scene, man."

"Wow," I said. After a short silence Mark stood up. "What about Margo Benson?"

He picked up his briefcase which he'd set on the floor, opened it and produced a large sealed envelope.

"It's all right here," he said cryptically. "I'm holding on to it for now, but don't know how long I can sit on it."

Mark slipped the envelope back in his briefcase, turned to leave and over his shoulder said, "Don't forget now. A nice little part, that's all I ask. Oh, and a chance to sing. My mother would be so proud."

He then burst into an aria as he went out the door. Everyone in the place jumped as if there'd been an explosion. A woman screamed. Laverne came over and refilled my coffee.

"Jesus," she said. "What was that?"

I shrugged.

"He's studying opera."

"Sounded like some horny prehistoric animal's last cry," Laverne cracked as she returned to behind the counter.

I watched after her and then stuck a nickel in the new juke box satellite Chick had installed on the table of each booth. I played Joni James,

"Why Don't You Believe Me?" I fired up a smoke, sipped my coffee and went back to wondering about Frank Meade.

Chapter 28

Five days gone and still no word from Frank Meade. I had set up a temporary answering service that I could check from time to time. I had hand-printed the number on the can containing the film. During the week I called Star/Burst Mead. Each time Jocelyn answered. And each time I didn't say anything, just let the silence hang in the air. I wasn't sure what I thought would happen. On the fourth call Jocelyn threatened to call the police and trace the phone. She sounded hysterical. I decided to just wait it out.

Meanwhile my dreams were getting darker and darker. I kept seeing this shadowy figure, always moving away from me down the road a piece, and me following. On one occasion I could make out Jenny sitting on a bench in the middle of nowhere, reaching out, but too far away to connect. It made me feel sad.

During my off hours I walked the streets of downtown, like a lost soul. One day I wandered aimlessly along the skid row gauntlet where scarred hands reached out from dark alcoves of abandoned buildings, scratchy voices hoping for a contribution, whispering, "A quarter, a dime or nickel, even a penny would help." I took notes. On this one day a grizzled man who had started following me from doorway to doorway yelled at me to scram, that I was an outsider. He began shadow boxing like an old punch-drunk fighter, which, in fact, he might well have been. His nose was flat and his face was a bulbous tangle of scarred flesh. I began to hurry my steps.

"Run you bastard before I beat your face!" He yelled and threw a couple of jabs in my direction. He then turned and moved south, crouching and throwing punches at the air. Now here's the strange thing. A middle aged woman with yellowish white hair was sitting on some blankets nearby on the sidewalk. She had been watching and told me to pay no mind to the shadow-boxer whom she called Jasper.

"He's touched in the head," she said. "Come closer, dear. I want to look at you and my eyes aren't so good anymore."

I hesitantly took a few steps closer to the woman until I could smell the stink of stale wine and urine. I stopped. She continued to beckon me. I took two more steps until I was only a foot away. She looked up and grinned at me, her mouth a toothless, rubbery wonder.

"Got a smoke?"

I handed her a cigarette and lit it for her. She took a deep drag and closed her eyes as if caught up in a moment of rapture. She opened her eyes, which were teary and red and a new look crossed her face, a look of anguish, even fear.

"You must go elsewhere to find what you're looking for," she said. "This is not the right place".

"What am I looking for?"

"I don't know," she said. "I know it's something or someone. When I was a girl I went to the beach. The ocean breeze and spray on my face always felt good. It was cleansing. I could think good. Go to the beach. Maybe you'll have luck." She pointed to her head. "I know these things. That's where you must go."

I laughed to myself as I walked away, thinking she was just another demented street person, living on cheap wine. Yet, there was something about her that reminded me of a fortune teller I once saw at the county fair. I must have been around nine or ten. Adele had taken me into the woman's tent, but cautioned me that it was all make-believe. The fortune teller, who claimed to be a gypsy, looked at my hand and told me I would go away some day in search of my destiny. Afterward Adele asked me what the gypsy said. I told her and she laughed and said that's what they tell everyone.

On pure impulse I boarded a west bound Red Car. It was a streetcar which went all the way to Santa Monica. I was going to get out there, but again on impulse I went on to Venice Beach, just a little over a mile south. It was hot. I walked along the boardwalk, stopped, got a cup of coffee, sat on a bench and looked out at the vastness of the pacific. The old woman was right about the ocean breeze. I closed my eyes and let the wet salt air wash over my face. It was kind of magical the way it carries you to some distant place in your head. After a moment I opened my eyes, fired up a smoke and continued on down the boardwalk when I saw her stroll by in front of me. She had on dark glasses and no makeup. Her hair was fairly short, a mousey brown under a floppy straw hat. She was wearing a green one-piece bathing suit, sandals, and a pink terry cloth towel over her shoulders. A large canvas bag hung from her other shoulder.

At first I just watched after her absently, like so many other bodies floating by. There was something vaguely familiar about her. I followed her with my eyes as she made her way down to the beach. I wasn't sure, but it looked a little like Bonnie Robertson. Once on the beach she negotiated her way among the sea of bodies, men, women, and children stretched out as far as the eye could see.

Keeping my distance I followed the woman. About halfway down the beach to the water she found a spot, put down her bag and stretched out on her towel. I moved closer, then circled around her to get a view from different angles to see if it was Bonnie Robertson. I still wasn't sure. I sat down on the sand a couple of feet away from her. After a while she must have sensed she was being watched. She turned and looked right at me, a blank expression on her face. I gave her a little wave. She did not return any sign of friendliness or recognition, but instead went back to a magazine she was reading. Now I was certain it was her.

I sat in the warm sand and pondered my next move. After a few minutes I pushed myself up and stepped to the edge of her towel and stood there, partially blocking her sun. She looked up.

"Hi," I said. "I thought that was you. It is you isn't it?"

The woman brought her hand up to shade her eyes and peered at me.

"I think you've got the wrong 'You', "she said. "Would you mind moving out of the way?"

I stepped away.

"Thank you," she said, put down the magazine and grabbed a book out of her bag.

I leaned down and read the title.

"Bonjour Tristesse?" I said, which she ignored. "You probably don't remember me."

Bonnie Robertson put her hand up again looked up at me and shook her head.

"Can't say that I do." She said.

I sat down beside her.

"Hold it buster. I don't remember inviting you to join me. This is my little space here and I want to keep it that way. Okay? So buzz off."

I did not react, just looked off toward the pounding surf.

"You're the famous script editor Bonnie Robertson aren't you," I said without looking at her. Then I turned and caught her grinning. She swiveled her head around as if to say, what kind of bullshit is this?

"You a process server?" She said. "Or did I meet you in some dive somewhere? Don't tell me I fucked you in an alley. Jesus. Forget it. What do I have to do, call a lifeguard or the cops? Beat it. Okay?"

I changed my tone to sound officious and authoritative.

"Alright, lady," I said deepening my voice and feigning a reach for my wallet. "I'm an undercover agent for the FBI. Are you Bonnie Robertson or not?"

"What?" She said laughing. "If you're an FBI agent, I'm Nancy Drew. Okay. I'm Bonnie Robertson. Who the hell are you?"

"Charles Alvin Kendall. But I'm called Tuckie."

"And what's your claim to fame, Mr. Tuckie?"

I pushed my hair back and let my eyes slide over to her.

236

"I was once the one and only son of the Wichita Kid."

She laughed so hard she began coughing.

"The Wichita Kid? You mean Wild Bill Coughlin, the actor who played the kid? My first job as a script girl was on one of his horse operas. Not a bad guy, though I think he began to believe he really was the Wichita Kid. Wherever he went he wore his cowboy outfit and his holster and gun. So, you're Coughlin's son?"

"No," I said emphatically. "Not Bill Coughlin. The Wichita Kid. Big difference."

She gave me a strange look.

"Oh sure," she said. "I...I know what you mean now."

Bonnie Robertson looked away as if trying to decide if I was a nut case. I could almost feel her thoughts as she took off her dark glasses and peered directly into my face. Her blue eyes were deeply circled and a little bloodshot.

"Okay, let's cut the crap," she said. "Have we actually met before?"

I explained about Sherry Woo and I visiting her one night. She had no recollection of any such meeting at first, but then it began to come back to her that Sherry Woo had come to her place one night some time back and that she did have a man with her.

"That was me," I said and went into more detail on the purpose of the meeting. I then told her about the old homeless woman downtown who said I should come to the beach. Bonnie just looked incredulous and said "weird."

"So you never collected your prize money," Bonnie said. "I'm not surprised, though Starburst has paid off so-called contest winners in the past. I mean to keep the operation looking legit. I worked there for a while and read a lot of shit. But, every now and then a little gem would fly across the transom. Ya Know?"

"What would happen to the gems?"

"Sometimes nothing, sometimes Starburst would pay the prize money, get a release signed and peddle it to some producer hard up for a story.

It would put a few extra bucks in the coffers. Say how old are you anyway?"

I ignored the question and showed Bonnie the original letter she had signed which was now looking worn.

"Why do I get this feeling of déjà vu?" She said. "Did you show this to me before?"

I nodded. She scanned the letter and scrunched up her face when she got to the bottom.

"That's my signature alright. But I can't tell you who wrote that note on the bottom. It wasn't Frank. His handwriting is big and sloppy. And you know it wasn't that crazy bitch Jocelyn. This handwriting is small, delicate like a woman's. The Chinese chick – Sherry Woo was only working part time then, so very doubtful."

She handed the letter back to me.

"So, what difference does it make?" She said.

"I came out here, driving more than two thousand miles in an old car my grandfather left me mainly because of that note. I would start my career. So, the note and who wrote it is important to me."

Bonnie looked at me and slowly shook her head.

"You're a case, you know that," she said. "Like a Gila Monster. They say they sink their teeth into you and won't let go until the sun goes down."

I started to get up to leave. She stopped me and told me about this woman, a temporary employee at Starburst who helped open contest entries. "She was kind of an oddball, about fifty with silver streaks in her hair which looked like a bushel basket on her head. But, I can't imagine why she would write such a note."

"Do you remember her name?"

Bonnie pondered the question for a long moment.

"Anna something." she said. "Sent over by a temp agency called Ercam. She left abruptly."

"Where did she go?"

Bonnie shrugged and lit a cigarette.

"She belonged to some mysterious 'workshop' which she was always gabbing about. Like one of those truth seeking existential bullshit deals. I was curious and let her take me to a meeting one night."

"The workshop?"

"It was run by a guy who calls himself Zoltan. One name. Everyone always did exactly what he told them to do. Kind of scary actually. He was like a dictator. He also has a TV show where he talks about the Fourth Way."

"What's that?"

"I don't know. Came from some Russian guy many years ago. You can catch his show on Sunday mornings on KTIZ. The show is called The Fourth Way with Zoltan."

I pushed myself up to a standing position, a feeling of emptiness creeping up my spine. I gave her a wave and started to walk away and then turned back. She was watching me.

"One other thing," I said. "Did you ever know an actress by the name of Iris Madigan?"

Bonnie took a deep drag on her cigarette and laughed the smoke out in a rush.

"Jesus," she said. "Where did you ever come up with that one?"

I just stared at her.

"I don't know her personally, maybe met her once or twice. But I know about her, everyone knows about her. Why do you ask?"

"She was a rising star and I was wondering what happened?" I said. "I've met her."

Bonnie shook her head and for a moment looked out to sea as if gathering her thoughts, maybe caught up in the lavishness of the late afternoon sun reflected in the waves. She took a deep breath.

"Iris was caught sleeping with the husband of a very powerful agent who had a private detective get photos of Iris and the husband in a motel in Malibu. One photo showed Iris naked on her knees giving hubby a superb blowjob, judging by the look on his face. You know what that is, don't you? They have those where you come from, right?"

I nodded feeling my face flush.

"The wife – the powerful agent – made sure the photo was well cir-culated in the industry and of course it was a prime exhibit during their divorce proceedings. Just about every bar in town also had a copy to be shown upon request. Needless to say, Iris's career went south after that. I mean, the moral of the story is, don't get caught. I should know."

Chapter 29

The next morning I got the number of Ercam Temps from information. But Ercam would not give me any information on a
woman named Anna who was sent to Starburst/Meade Productions almost a year and a half back. The woman who answered the phone
was very officious. She told me if I was not an employer seeking a temp
she could not give out any information about their employees. I told the
woman I was an employer. She hung up.

I decided that what I needed was a professional to ferret out this
Anna person. I called Mark Horgan and asked if I could hire him to
check out Ercam. At first Mark said he couldn't do it. He questioned why
I wanted to bother, and added, "It's a waste of time."

"I'll make your role bigger in The Prairie Wolves," I said. "Maybe
two songs."

Mark was silent, apparently thinking it over.

"Yeah, if it gets made," he finally said. "Alright, I'll do what I can.
And you will owe me."

Mark said he would get back to me when he had something. A few
days passed with no word. And still nothing from Frank Meade. I called
Jenny and told her my movie was on hold until financing came through.
She asked me how much would be needed I didn't know. She begged me
to forget the whole thing and come back home where I belonged. She said
she needed to have me near her. I had been gone almost a year now. Jenny
was sounding more and more off center every time I called her, like there

was this craziness or something just below the surface. It was as if every word she spoke was like lifting a heavy weight. She would also digress a lot in the middle of a thought, sometimes to something totally inconsequential like the state of the weather, or something else unrelated to anything. Jenny had always been a little strange, high strung, according to Mr. Gifford, and fragile. I'd heard, even before we started seeing each other, that she'd had a nervous breakdown in the tenth grade, but recovered after loosing a semester. There was always this sense of desperation in her voice.

One evening when not working, I waited for Sherry Woo to come out of Starburst. Just in case Jocelyn came out at the same time, I waited down the street out of sight where it would be easy to spot her. It was about 6:30 when she finally appeared. When she saw me she turned and went in the opposite direction toward Santa Monica Boulevard. I caught up with her at Barney's Beanery. She'd taken a booth near the back. We did not speak for several moments. I watched her as she played absently with a fork.

"I don't know what's happening," she said.

"What do you mean?"

"I was supposed to get my check today, but I didn't. Neither did Jocelyn. Believe it or not she actually broke down and cried. She knows more than she's saying. Frank signs our checks and no one has seen or heard from him. Bills are piling up. Even his wife hasn't heard from him for almost a week. But she did not want to call the police just yet."

"I wonder if he ever looked at the film?"

"I don't know," Sherry said. "But I don't think I should be seen with you. If Jocelyn saw us together and this business about the film comes out she would put it together. So, do me a favor and leave now and pretend you don't know me. It's better this way, at least until we know what's going on."

I looked at her long and hard, then nodded.

"I have to ask you something," I said.

"Jesus, what?"

"Do you remember a woman who worked as a temp at Starburst last year? An older woman named Anna?"

Sherry rolled her eyes.

"Yes. She tried to get me to join some group she belonged to. Why?"

"Just wondering," I said.

Before I left I jotted down my answering service number and told her to call and leave a message or come by the Hamburger Palace if she heard anything.

Outside, I stood on the curb and was momentarily overcome by a feeling of deep despair, as if everything including myself was falling into some bottomless black hole from which there was no return. Sherry was scared. I could see that. I decided at that moment it was probably time to get out, go back home, reassure Jenny and settle back into the non-threatening life I had before. Work in the mortuary. I'd have to listen to Royce rant about my failure, and enigmatic Zona quietly observing. But at least I wouldn't be in jail for extortion because that's what it was, that's what I'd committed. Wasn't it? And yet it all seemed abstract, like something in a distant land that did not really touch me.

During the next few nights, sleeping on the cot in the back of the Hamburger Palace, my mind was continually in a whirl. Lying in the dark I saw images of shadowy human figures moving across a lifeless landscape like a dead planet. These mysterious figures were without discernible faces. Yet I instinctively felt I knew these figures, knew the terrain as I watched from a distance. One of the figures stopped and waived to me. It was a woman. It was all like a waking dream which left me drained and fearful that I was forgetting something important that I must do, only couldn't quite remember what it was. I wondered if the woman was Anna, or the strange homeless woman who told me to go to the beach that day.

When I told Chick I was thinking of heading back home, all I got from this large black man who'd taken me in and befriended me was this look of disgust as if I were betraying him somehow. He walked away without saying anything. It was a Friday night. The Palace was jammed with many new customers as well as regulars. I wondered if people knew that Chick was the owner. I figured most just thought he was the cook. He told me he had to get a white friend to arrange the lease for him or it probably never would have happened. Even though Chick signed the checks I think the waitresses thought they were working for a franchise corporation.

Laverne was working the late shift. You could hear her wisecracking with the customers in her section. The other waitress, Jill, was prettier than Laverne but maintained a cool aloof air about her. She was strictly business, rarely smiled. Chick thought they counter-balanced each other. He chuckled when Laverne mocked Jill's demeanor. Jill, on the other hand, regarded Laverne a Philistine. At least that was what she whispered to me.

"Hey, I almost forgot," Jill said. "A very cute chick was in here looking for you earlier."

"She leave a name?"

Jill shook her head and went off to pick up an order.

After closing and everyone had left, Chick came up behind me while I was wiping off the counter and grunted loudly. It got my attention. He then sat on a stool after getting a beer from the refrigerator and sipped it as he watched me.

"How long you been here in the golden land now?" He said.

Without looking at Chick I shrugged and said, "Over a year now."

"A whole damn year," he said with a sneer. "Hell, what's that? Nothing! I know'd folks been here struggling for fifteen or twenty years, working parking lots, delivering mail, you name it, just to survive while looking for that break. My point is…"

"I know what your point is," I said, cutting him off.

"So what's this bullshit about giving up?" Chick said. "I thought you were going to start your career. Isn't that what you said?"

I continued to wipe the counter. Chick picked up the beer bottle and brought it down hard on the counter. The salt and pepper shakers jumped. I stopped and looked at my boss.

"Isn't that what you came for?"

I nodded.

"Now you gonna run away like some panty waste. Shit, and I thought you had something, something inside you, a kind of madness that keeps you moving down that bad road no matter what."

"My movie is dead, like my career."

"Shit, your movie ain't dead," Chick said. "You're in it right now."

"What're you talking about?"

"I'm talking about your life, man. It's a powerful movie about a young man looking for something, looking for who he is. You know what I mean? What's at the center! That's what my Nana used to say. When you figure that out, you will have discovered a great secret that will carry you to the end of the rainbow."

I tossed the rag behind the counter and looked at Chick.

"I don't know anything about that," I said. "You don't understand."

"Oh? What don't I understand?" Chick pulled a thin round stogie out of his pocket, lit it, blew the smoke at me and took a swallow from his beer. "Okay, I don't know what's going on with you, but I do know I don't want you to leave. In fact I was going to save this news until later but I'll tell you now."

I eased myself onto a stool and fired up a smoke. He told me he was opening a new place out in the valley on Ventura Boulevard. That he already had his permits, financing and a signed lease.

"I want you to manage it. If you agree I'll give you a piece of it, a small piece. It's kind of like a built-in incentive. I'll teach you what you need to know."

For a moment I just stared at Chick as if seeing him for the first time.

"Jesus," I finally got out. "That's great, Chick. Real great, but I…I don't…"

"Hey, man," he said cutting me off. "It's just the beginning. I'm going to open another one after that and start franchising. That's where the real money is, man. In the multiples, that's where it's at. You could be part of it Tuck. You think on it, man."

245

I checked my answering service. There was a message from Mark Horgan to call him. I did. A woman answered who told me she was his mother. She told me Mark was out. The next day he showed up at the Palace. I bought him a hamburger and coke. He reported that he had located the woman called Anna. She had left the temp agency and was now living and working on a farm up north called The Fourth Way. It's little more than an hours drive. Mark said the farm belonged to that guy who has the television show on Sunday mornings, Zoltan. He noted that the farm was not open to the public.

"It's like some kind of cult," Mark said. "My sources tell me there are armed guards."

"You sure this woman Anna is there?"

He nodded and pulled a black and white eight-by-ten glossy photo out of his briefcase and pushed it across the table at me. "That's her. That's Anna Asparagus. Turns out I have a friend at the agency. She pulled this for me."

I examined the photo. She was middle-aged with the remnants of a once pretty face. Her hair was very long with gray streaks. What struck you were her eyes which looked intense as they stared out from the photo, as if they could see you and read your thoughts.

"How do I get there?"

Mark shook his head.

"Frankly, I'd forget it," he said. "You probably couldn't get into the place."

"Is there a bus that goes up that way?"

Mark Horgan sighed and began finishing his coke until his straw was sucking air.

"You working Monday?"

I got up, went over and looked at the work schedule Chick posted on the wall behind the counter, then came back and shook my head.

"I'll drive you up," Mark said. "I'm actually kind of curious about this place."

Saturday night, Maggie showed up alone at the Palace. She sat at the counter and ordered a grilled cheese sandwich and coffee. Jill took the order then came over and told me it was the same chick who'd come in before looking for me. I took over the order. Maggie looked depressed, sullen. She just sat there playing with her napkin and then began absently flicking her finger at the glass of water I'd put down in front of her. I brought her sandwich and set it down. She looked up at me for the first time since coming in.

"Where're you staying?"

"Here," I said. "In the back, sleeping on a cot. At least for now."

After a beat she said I could come back to her place.

"I really want you to come back," she said. "I don't know what got into me."

Her eyes filled with tears and she looked away.

"Thanks, but I don't think so," I said. "I...I may...might be leaving soon."

"What?"

"Things aren't working out," I said.

Maggie picked up a paper napkin and wiped her eyes then reached across the counter and put her hand on mine.

"I'd really miss you," she said. "Where would you go?"

"Back home."

Chick yelled at me to take care of another customer who'd just come in. I just shrugged at Maggie and walked to the other end of the counter. I could feel her watching after me. Before I could get back to her, she paid her check and left. A few moments later I felt like an explanation was in order and ran out to the street to catch her. Maggie was nowhere in sight. That night I thought about her, pictured the two of us making out as we had a few times. I wondered if Mark's suspicions about Maggie knowing Margo Benson had been borne out. Mark had said it was all in the large brown manila envelope he had shown me, ready to be handed over to his clients.

Sunday morning I made a discovery that would turn everything upside down. Even now as I recount this story it is hard to believe the strange coincidence of it all.

I was awakened by the TV which sat on a crate next to the sack of onions. Chick was adjusting the rabbit ears and flipping the channels, some of which were only showing test patterns. I rubbed my eyes and looked at my watch. It was just before ten.

"Chick, turn it to KTLX."

"Good morning to you too," he said sarcastically. "Nothing but shit on that channel."

He found the channel and stepped back. A children's romper room was just signing off. A few commercials aired followed by a graphic. An organ was providing background music. The graphic said: ZOLTAN SPEAKS.

"This what you want?" Chick said. "I seen this guy. He's way out there in la, la land, man. But probably raking in the cash."

Chick made a face and went out front where a breakfast crowd was beginning to gather. I could already hear the sizzle of eggs on the griddle. Laverne, Jill, the fry cook, and a kid who only worked weekends were helping Chick take care of the day shift which left me free until the early evening shift. Laverne brought a cup of freshly brewed coffee back to me and a small plate with a couple of buttered biscuits.

As I sipped my coffee I was glued to the TV. There was an abrupt cut from the graphic to a sandy haired man in his 50s looking kindly into the camera. His outfit was not what I would have expected. He wore a plaid shirt with a string tie, bib overalls and sat at a plain wooden table, a coffee mug in front of him. The background looked like a wood paneled den. There was a large portrait photo of President Eisenhower hanging on the wall behind him. It was all very folksy. I reckoned it would be something more exotic.

"Good morning folks," he started, speaking with a slight drawl. "May your Sunday be a happy and productive day for you and your loved ones. This is Zoltan speaking to you this morning from the special studio we have set up here at the Fourth Way farm. For those of you tuning in for the first time, I teach and live as a humble agent of The Fourth Way, as brought to light from the ancients by philosopher and simple carpet dealer George Gurdjieff in the early part of this century. During these half hour Sunday morning sessions, I hope to take you on a journey to achieve a higher state of consciousness. I call it the 'Work' which to me means a way, a glorious path to self realization as a microcosm in the macrocosm of the universe.

At first I stared at the small screen. The voice of Zoltan was smooth and deep. But as he went on, something about him began to capture my interest way beyond any curiosity I had about this guy. It was not the words coming out of his mouth. In fact they had all but faded into the background. I found myself blinking rapidly as I tried to focus on this man who called himself Zoltan. I moved closer to the TV, then backed away and looked at each feature of his face. My stomach began to churn. One feature particularly had caught my eye. And in that instant I knew who he really was. It was real bizarre that in the great city of Los Angeles I would see his face in a 15 inch tube staring back at me, a face I had not seen in 18 years. The face had changed. It was heavier with a beard and the blonde hair thinner. But there was no mistaking that strange purple mark like a scar above his nose between his eyebrows. The man calling himself Zoltan was Jim Oliver, the man who murdered my mother.

"Please send your contributions to…"

I turned the TV off.

Mark reluctantly agreed to give me a ride up to the fourth way ranch on Monday.

Chapter 30

———

W e didn't wait until Monday. Luckily, according to Mark, he didn't have to stay with his mother as he usually did on Sundays. She was hosting a bridge game so he was free to drive me up to the Fourth Way Ranch that day. At first he said no, he'd decided against it. I said I'd pay for gas and make his role in The Prairie Wolves even bigger, two songs and a speaking part. Mark laughed and said it was like I was giving away free tickets to a mirage. I didn't get it. He said okay. He'd drive me. I didn't tell him about my grandfather's gun which I had taped to my ankle, like in the movies with the muzzle down inside of my right boot. I had bought the boots and a broad-brimmed camouflage hat second hand from a war surplus store a few days before.

I figured I would confront Jim Oliver or Zoltan as he was now called and if I had to, I'd use the gun to make him talk. Just like the movies. Since Adele's remains had been found and knowing that she had not gotten more than five miles from the house all those years ago, I had fantasized about finding and exposing him. Before we knew her fate I had always thought that some day I would go out to California and try to find her. But then there was the postcard. Who sent it? Jim Oliver to make us think she was alive and well?

"Even though this Zoltan character is on TV," Mark said as we headed north up Ventura Boulevard, which was also Highway 101. "I've heard this Fourth Way farm of his is like a fortress and very secretive. That's what I've heard anyway."

"Guess we'll see when we get there," I said and shut my eyes to try and catch up on some sleep. As I slipped off for a few minutes I wondered if Jim Oliver would remember me.

North of Thousand Oaks, we turned east on Highway 23 toward Moorpark, then north again on 118 until we got to the turn-off which was not far from Simi Valley. Occasionally Mark referred to a piece of paper he'd made a crude map on and taped to the dashboard. The land along the country road we were now on was hilly with expansive green pastures on both sides, wire fencing running along the edges. Occasionally we spotted horses and cows grazing. I rolled down the window and breathed the air, which was fresh and earthy like back home.

The day was sweltering and Mark's seven-year-old Mercury station wagon was beginning to cough and sputter. Finally it stalled on an incline as a cloud of steam rose up from under the hood. He let the car coast over onto a grassy shoulder.

"We better let it cool down," Mark said. "I brought some extra water just in case."

"How much farther is it?"

"Shouldn't be too far now," Mark said as he stepped out of the car.

We were losing time, I thought. I had to be back to work by seven. We got out of the car. Mark opened the hood. The radiator cap looked like it was going to explode. I sat on the side of the road and fired up a smoke. We waited a half hour until the engine cooled down. Mark started the engine and let it idle while he poured water from a canvas bag into the radiator. A few minutes later we were back on the road again.

It was early afternoon and the heat of the day when we arrived at the Fourth Way Farm. There was a small sign that indicated the turn off. We turned right onto a dirt drive for about a hundred feet until we came to a closed gate. A man dressed in a khaki uniform with a cowboy hat stepped out from a guard shack on the left side of the gate and came up to the window. He was about five foot seven and looked like he weighed three hundred pounds. A gold badge pinned to his shirt said: Fourth Way Security. He peered in at us, a big friendly smile on his face.

"Howdy, folks," he said. "Hot today, eh? What can I do for you?"

"This the Fourth Way Farm?" Mark said.

The guard turned and pointed to a high wooden arch just beyond the gate with the legend: FOURTH WAY stretched across it.

"You folks got some business here?"

Mark nodded.

"We came up from Los Angeles. My friend here would very much like to visit a woman here named Anna Asparagus. She's an old friend and we just wanted to say hello."

The guard took a handkerchief out of his pocket and wiped the sweat from his brow. He shook his head.

"Anna Asparagus?" He said and laughed. "I don't know if we've got anyone here by that name. Folks here only use first names and mostly made up names. But she could be here. We've got over sixty or so people here now. You have to be among the chosen each week to come to the farm. It's considered a great privilege."

"That right?" Mark said. "Real impressive. What do people do here?"

"They farm the land, tend to the animals and fix things that need fixin'. Believers also attend lectures by our great leader Zoltan. It's in the work that we find our fundamental selves, our natural core if you know what I mean, sir."

Mark looked over at me and rolled his eyes, then turned back to the guard.

"I know what you mean," Mark said. "How big is the farm?"

"Oh, about thirteen hundred acres or so," the guard said.

We showed the guard a picture of Anna Asparagus. He nodded. He said he thought he might have seen her around but didn't know her. I was getting impatient.

"Can we get going here?" I said in a loud voice.

Mark laughed.

"My friend here is very anxious to see our old friend, Anna. Hasn't seen her in years. May we go on in and visit with her?"

The guard wiped his brow again and shook his head.

"Zoltan has given strict orders, no visitors without a special appointment. There are certain days when the farm has an open house and visitors are invited to take a tour and have lunch. But this is not one of those days."

"Maybe you can make an exception for us," Mark said.

The guard pursed his lips thoughtfully for a moment, went back to the gate house and made a call. He then came back and told us he could not let us in, that Zoltan was conducting a meeting at that time and no visitors were allowed.

"Why don't you come back next Saturday?" The guard said. That's an open house day and you'd be very welcome. Good bye now. Have a safe journey back to L.A."

The guard went back to the shack and picked up a magazine. Mark backed the car out of the drive to the road. He was about to turn the car to go back to L.A.

"Hold it," I said.

Mark hit the brakes and looked at me.

"Let's go the other way. I know farms and I'll bet there's another way into this place."

"That's crazy," Mark said sounding irritated. He was sweating. "You thinking about sneaking in there? Bad idea. These people may all be fruitcakes. You trespass and you are fair game. They could shoot your ass for fouling their sacred ground or some damn thing like that."

"Let's go up the road apiece."

Mark gripped the steering wheel so hard his knuckles went white. He gritted his teeth which told me he was going to do as I asked. He turned right and we went slowly along the narrow road following the northern perimeter of the Fourth Way Farm. Eight foot high barbed wire fencing ran along the property's edge. It looked menacing, leaning out as if ready to strike any intruders with its sharp barbs. There were signs every hundred feet or so that said trespassers enter at their peril. I had second thoughts, but decided not to be scared off. I figured instead to assume the persona of the Wichita Kid.

I saw a spot along the road and told Mark to stop. He hit the brakes and again lectured me that it was stupid to sneak into the farm. But by this time I had transformed myself in my head. Charles Kendall was now a totally separate being, someone I knew who would have to stay out of the way. The Kid had a mission, to rescue the woman called Anna Asparagus who was surely being held captive by this secret society, and even more importantly, to confront the evil high priest who called himself Zoltan.

The spot was a drainage ditch that ran alongside the road and intersected with a small creek that ran through a large pipe under the road. It looked to be about a foot and a half deep under the fence, just enough to crawl under. A trickle of water ran along the creek. I got out of the car. Mark frowned at me.

"I don't get why you want to get in there so bad," he said.

"I…I have to see this woman, Anna," The Kid said. "Maybe she needs my help. Maybe she's a prisoner."

Mark looked incredulous.

"And maybe you're a full blown nut case," he said. "Don't think I haven't considered that possibility. In fact I just might include a note about this episode in my final report on the Margo Benson case. Yeah, I still got that to wrap up and you better believe your friend Maggie Langston is in my sights, right in the cross hairs, my friend."

Mark's eyes were intense, his mouth thin, tight as a drum. Then his lips slipped into a barely recognizable grin.

"You think I want to hang around here all day?" He said. "I'm heading back to the city. You're on your own."

The Kid looked away. For a moment I was myself again.

"Okay, your part in The Prairie Wolves just got bigger. Seems to me sticking around for a while is a small sacrifice to make for you career." I said.

Once again he did a slow burn, gripping the steering wheel.

"You're not only crazy, but actually kind of evil," Mark said. "Okay, I'm as crazy as you are. I'll see you here at dusk. About four hours from now. Six o'clock sharp. You'd better be here or I'm coming back with the troops."

The Wichita Kid nodded, got down on his belly and managed to squirm under the fence on his back, holding his hat on his chest. The trickle of water sent a welcome chill up his spine and left a wide wet streak from his neck to the back of his pants. The Kid splashed some water in his face. It was a welcome relief from the heat. The Kid turned over, put the hat on and crawled for about twenty feet. Masked by tall brown grass he raised up and scanned the terrain. There were a few scattered cows grazing. In the distance where the Kid figured the Fourth Way Farm center was located, a line of tall trees looked like sentinels guarding the compound. He began making his way in that direction. As the Kid got closer he could make out a water tower rising up beyond the trees.

Still some distance from the center, the Kid stumbled onto a long building that was completely hidden by tall brush and trees. It looked like one of those low slung hot houses. There were actually three such buildings. They were all locked. But there was a window in the doors. The Wichita Kid peered in one and saw rows and rows of strange looking plants. Coming from farm country he was familiar with all kinds of vegetation. But these were different. They were not marijuana plants either, which was his first thought and which he'd seen pictures of in old western magazines.

Keeping low, the Kid crossed an open field to the top of a ridge ahead. The Kid flattened out and scanned the Fourth Way Farm compound. It was about fifty yards ahead. A swarm of folks gathered in an area to his left in front of a large rambling two story house with a belfry or tower crowning the center of the roof. Most of the people were sitting on the grass facing the porch of the house as if waiting for something. It was then that the Kid noticed a security guard wearing khaki pants and shirt, dark glasses, a cowboy hat, and holstered gun hanging off his belt.

He was perched on something like a lifeguard stand you might see at a beach on the edge of the open grassy area. At the moment he was doing 360s with binoculars and sweeping toward the Kid. He quickly ducked and wondered if maybe this wasn't such a good idea to break in to the place. Too late to turn back. Besides it wasn't in the Kid's nature. He raised himself up to see what was happening.

The Security guy had climbed down from the lookout stand and was heading to the back of the house. The Kid made his move. Still staying low he crept unnoticed down to where folks had gathered. There were at least fifty or more people ranging in ages from 20 to 80, but most were somewhere in the middle. The Kid found a spot of unoccupied grass and sat down near a lone young woman with long reddish blonde hair. She was taking sips of something from an odd shaped cowhide bag with a nozzle at its neck. It had a strap which hung loosely over her shoulder. Just the sight of her drinking from it made the Kid's mouth convulse with thirst. He moved closer to her.

"What's that?"

The woman twisted around and looked at him.

"Are you talking to me?"

The Kid pointed to the raw-hide bag.

"It's a Boda Bag," she said. "It's for wine or water. On hot days I keep cold water in it. You've never seen one?"

The Kid shook his head and asked if he could have a sip of water. The woman looked at him with some uncertainty for a moment and then slowly handed him the bag with the instruction to bend his head back, holding it away from his mouth and just squeeze. He did as instructed. The water tasted exquisite, some dribbling down his chin. He wiped it away with his hand and handed the Boda Bag back to the woman who was staring at him. She looked to be in her late 20s or early 30s and had a winsome face, full expressive lips.

"Where'd you come from?" She said. "I don't remember seeing you around before."

The Kid pushed himself up to a full sitting position.

"I'm just a soldier of truth and justice," he said. "I'm called the Wichita Kid."

She laughed and shook her head in disbelief.

"Well, Mr. Wichita Kid, I'm Beth, which of course is not my real name either," she said and reached out to shake the Kid's hand. "We all give ourselves pseudonyms to represent our parallel selves. Are you here to listen to Zoltan, our great leader and teacher? He should be appearing at any moment."

"What does he teach?" The Kid said.

Beth looked puzzled.

"You're not one of us are you," she said. "I'm wondering now what you're dong here." Beth paused. "He teaches us about our place in the universe, about the body transcending to achieve a higher state of consciousness. It has its roots in Gurdjieff's philosophy of the Fourth Way."

At that moment a hush swept over the crowd. Zoltan appeared on the porch of the house. He was wearing a long flowing robe like Arabs wear. Using a microphone he motioned for everyone to stand and follow him in a series of movements which he called "finding our center". The Kid, not wanting to look conspicuous followed. Zoltan then told everyone to return to earth – sit back down.

"That was excellent," he said. "Such exercises will help you harness your inner selves where truth and power lie side by side."

"What is the Work?" A man from up front asked, clearly a shill.

"It is a resource deep within us all that must be mined like gold and silver."

Everyone clapped. Beth looked to be in rapture. The Kid tapped her on the shoulder.

"I'm looking for a woman," he said.

"We're all looking for someone...or something," Beth said in a dreamy way without looking at the Kid.

"Her name is Anna. Anna Asparagus. Do you know her?

Beth turned around to look at the Kid and laughed.

"You're joking," she said and went back to her trance.

The Kid felt a tap on his shoulder. He turned around to look up into the broad tanned, unfriendly face of the guard with the cowboy hat and gun standing over him.

Chapter 31

———

T he Kid ignored the guard and continued to look in the direction of Zoltan, who was still speaking. He felt another tap on his shoulder, only this time it was more like a hard poke.

"What?" the Kid said, trying to sound put out. "Can't you see I'm trying to listen to our great leader Zoltan."

"Stand up and come with me," the guard said as he reached down under the Kid's arm pit and tried to yank him up. The Kid made myself dead weight and was back on the ground. The guard then told the Kid he would not tell him again to stand and patted his gun threateningly.

Beth turned around and asked the guard what the problem was and why was he harassing a fellow student, namely the Wichita Kid.

"Keep out of this, Miss," he said sharply. "It's none of your business. This man is an intruder."

"I don't think you should talk to me that way," she said. "I'm very close to Zoltan. He wouldn't like it if he thought I was being abused."

The security guard looked at her for a long moment and then tipped his hat.

"Sorry, Miss," he said in a hushed voice, as they were beginning to attract attention. "But I have a job to do."

Folks were turning around to see what the commotion was. Zoltan stopped and was looking the Kid's way. The guard noticed and looked flustered. He motioned for the Kid to come with him, once again trying to pull the Kid up. This time the Kid didn't fight it and stood up. Underneath the guard's very official looking badge was a name tag that said 'Ishmael.' He spun the Kid around and started to put handcuffs on him. Beth who was still watching looked startled.

"Handcuffs? She said. "Do you think he's dangerous?"

"You never know," the guard said. "I've been tracking him since I first spotted him crawling under the fence in the north pasture."

Beth then advised the guard that using handcuffs wasn't in keeping with the Fourth Way, and that it might arouse anxiety among the students, most of whom were now watching this little drama. The Kid then explained that he was just there to look for Anna Asparagus.

"I won't put handcuffs on if you'll come with me quietly, without any fuss," Ishmael said.

"Where're we going?" The Kid said.

"Not far," Ishmael said. "We want to talk to you."

The Kid considered making a run for it, but wasn't sure which direction to head. And if he did and was caught it would simply compound his guilt in the eyes of the Fourth Way. Or maybe the guard in his zeal to do his duty would shoot him in the back. Either way, it was too chancy.

The Kid was now being escorted down a gravel path, Ishmael just behind him pointing the way poking him in the back with something hard. They were out of sight of the gathering now.

The Kid turned around to see that Ishmael had drawn his gun. He asked the guard what that was for and was told to keep his mouth shut.

As they walked, for the first time since his arrival, the Kid was aware of the pungent smells a working farm offered, from cow manure to the sweet aroma of honeysuckle, along with the sound of pigs squealing in the distance.

The destination turned out to be a white, mud splattered pickup truck. It was parked near the barn. Ishmael indicated with his gun for the Kid to climb in. He got in thinking the guard was going to drive him to the front gate and tell him to move on down the road and not come back. Instead the guard holstered his gun and drove down a narrow dirt road.

"Where're we going?" The Kid said.

"You'll see soon enough...Wichita Kid."

The guard chuckled to himself. A couple of minutes later they pulled up in front of a long gray trailer home. It was propped up on blocks in the middle of a field south of the compound. A sign above the door in large red and black letters said: Fourth Way Police Headquarters. Ishmael turned off the engine, pulled out his gun, and motioned for the Kid to get out. Once out, he ordered him to go up the stairs into the trailer. This was not the scenario he had pictured for the Wichita Kid, hero of the plains.

Inside the door was a small vestibule area with a built in Formica table that served as a check-in desk. A second security man was sitting behind the desk reading a girlie magazine, a can of Coors beer in front of him. "This Betty Page is something else," he said to himself. Now he looked up, clearly annoyed that he was being interrupted. His bulky frame and flat nose made the Kid think he was an ex prizefighter.

"What've we got here, Ishmael?"

"How you doin', Bull?" Ishmael said as he holstered his gun. "Caught this intruder here sneaking around the farm. You ask me, I think he's up to no goddamned good."

Bull nodded.

"I never seen him around before, I can tell you that," the guard called Bull said.

A third security man came out of a tiny bathroom just behind the check-in desk, zipping up his pants. He was tall and thin with a long severe face burnished by the sun, and bald. Ishmael tipped his hat. "Hey boss." Bull nodded toward the Kid.

"Barney," Ishmael said to the third guard, "looks like we got us an intruder. Caught him myself. What do you want to do?"

Barney looked the Kid up and down.

"Suppose he could be a spy or one of them provocateurs come to disrupt the harmony of these sacred grounds." He chuckled." Process him in, the works, and then put him in the interrogation room," he said. "I got some business to attend to. I'll be back in a little while."

Barney put on a wide-brimmed felt hat which he snatched off of a nearby coat rack. Next he went into a drawer of the desk and pulled out a holstered gun which he slipped onto this belt, then stepped passed the Kid and went out.

"Some business," Bull said to Ishmael. "He's going to meet that girl whose been hanging around him, knock off a piece behind the barn. Shit, she can't be more'n seventeen. I guess the gun is to impress her."

Ishmael wiped the sweat from his brow.

"I wouldn't mind getting some of that myself," he said.

The so-called interrogation room was a darkish cubby hole in the back of the trailer with a couple of chairs and small table. A portrait of Zoltan hung over the single bed that was up against the wall. A small window above was the only light. The room reeked of stale cigarette smoke and was oppressively hot and airless. After taking a couple of mug shots and fingerprinting him, Bull took his wallet. The Kid thought he was done for when Bull started to pat him down. But he didn't detect the gun in his boot, at least not at first. When the Kid was ordered to sit down his pant leg hiked up and revealed a strange bulge. Bull reached down and felt his ankle, then reached up under the pant leg and yanked the taped gun out. He examined it then put it in his belt.

"You got lots to talk about soon as Barney gets back," Bull said, "I knew you was dangerous," he added as he left and closed the door behind him, followed by the click of a lock.

"Can I get some water?" The Kid yelled after him.

It was over an hour before the door reopened and Barney stood there looking in. He looked gaunt, like he had not had a good meal in ages. He smacked his lips as if the Kid looked like a broiled steak. Barney took off his sunglasses. The Kid, now sweating profusely looked away. He figured Zoltan's little army of security guards didn't have much to do day in and day out.

Barney sat down in the chair opposite the Kid. He set down a glass of water in front of him and offered up a cigarette. The Kid took it. Barney lit it for him and sat back lighting his own cigarette. The Kid gulped down the water as Barney watched.

"Ishmael says you call yourself Wichita," he said. "I seen your out-of-state driver's license, though. It don't say Wichita. It says your name is Charles A. Kendall.

At that moment I retreated from my persona as the Wichita Kid back to myself.

"Most folks call me Tuckie,"

"Tuckie, eh?" Barney said. "Sounds like a pussy name."

Then we just stared at each other.

Chapter 32

Barney started to say something but was interrupted when Bull stepped in and handed him a can of beer and stepped back out again. He took a swig and set the can down in front of him, smacking his lips.

"So, what are you doing snooping around this private farm?" Barney said. "Signs say 'No Trespassing,' am I right?"

"I'm looking for a woman," I said.

"Yep," he said and laughed. But what's the real reason? Why the gun?"

I told him I was looking for Anna Asparagus. He leaned forward and said, "Bullshit! Who'd you want to kill?"

Barney bored into me, his narrow dark eyes ablaze. He sat back, reached into his breast pocket and pulled out a piece of paper.

"Found this in your wallet," he said. "It says Jimmy Oliver slash Zoltan. Now what does that mean?"

I hesitated, trying to think of a story. After a couple of moments I told him that Jimmy Oliver was a friend from Los Angeles and that he told me about the teachings of Zoltan. "And so I decided to come up and join the group here. I'm trying to find myself."

Barney just stared at me. He took another drag on his cigarette and pushed some drops of sweat off the tip of his nose. "I tell you, you got some shit coming out of your mouth like...say one of them provocateurs? Come here to disturb the tranquility of the Fourth Way Farm? Happened once before, some crazed psychopath came here to denounce Zoltan saying he was God's messenger."

"What happened to him?"

Barney grinned, spittle forming at the corner of his mouth. His eyes rolled up.

"Just disappeared," he said. "Never heard from again." Barney leaned forward as if to tell me something in confidence. "This is sacred land, my friend. It's like a tiny country all unto itself with its own laws and its own justice. Since we don't have a prison there is only one punishment. And you are an alien. Get my drift?"

Barney took another drag on his smoke. We just stared at each other for a time, no one saying anything. Barney broke the silence.

"You could be a spy for some rival group, or maybe a cop. Zoltan has enemies out there beyond our borders here. You're a long way from home, Charles. You know what I think. I think you're an assassin."

Just then the door flew open.

"You want me to relieve you, boss?" Bull said.

"No," Barney said, turning to his underling. "But stay here. I need you to do something." He then raised his arms to stretch, exposing his sweat drenched underarms. He turned back to me and asked why I was out here on the coast. I explained about the contest and all. Barney turned back to his deputy.

"Man's gonna make a movie," he said.

"Maybe he'll put us in it," Bull said without any sense of irony. "I wouldn't mind being in a movie."

Barney rolled his eyes.

"Shut up, Bull!" He snapped. "What's the matter with you? Man's laying one on us."

"Hey, Barney," Bull wined in a low audible voice. "Don't talk to me like that in front of a stranger. God, you can be a real prick sometimes."

Barney ignored Bull. He was giving me a hard look now as if something just occurred to him. He pulled out a little notebook he said Ishmael gave him which contained his report. Barney scanned a couple of pages, then looked up again at me.

"Real interesting," he said. "Says here you looked to be snooping around the hot houses, that you disappeared very close to where they're located. You want to tell me about that, Charles?"

He then motioned for Bull to lean down. He whispered something in his ear and handed him the piece of paper from my wallet. Bull nodded and left. Barney, whose eyes never left me now squinted.

I shrugged.

"I don't know what you're talking about," I said.

Barney stood up and left the room, leaving a trail of body odor. He closed the door behind him. I looked at my watch. Three hours had passed since they had put me in that room. It hit me that Chick was going to be real pissed if I didn't make it to work. And Mark would be looking to meet up with me soon. A little while later Barney returned and went over the same questions again. I told him I had to get back to the city for my job. He just stared at me and lit a cigarette and blew smoke in my face.

After about a half hour the door opened and a man in dark sunglasses wearing a blue shirt and faded jeans poked his head in and winced. "Stinks in here," he said and then told Barney to bring the intruder to the main house. Barney protested, saying he hadn't finished interviewing me. The man repeated his order and this time with a sharp edge to his tone. He was clearly someone in authority. Barney shrugged and nodded.

Before leaving the trailer I was allowed to splash some cool water on my face from a sink near the front desk. Barney had bull escort me to the main house. The man in the dark glasses had gone ahead. Along the way, Bull asked me about the movie. I said it was in the works. He said he would really love to be in a movie because it would make his girlfriend proud of him. I told Bull I thought he'd be good in one of the parts. His face lit up. Just then I saw Beth coming toward us.

"Hi, Wichita," she said. "Is everything okay?"

"No talking to the prisoner," Bull said and pushed me forward.

"Names really Charles..er..Tuckie," I said. "That's what most folks call me."

Beth looked perplexed as she gave me a little wave.

The office was toward the back of the main house. It had a separate entrance. Bull and I were instructed by the man in the dark glasses to wait in the anteroom which was furnished with two couches and a coffee table. A large oil color painting of Zoltan hung on the wall. He looked younger, more like the Jim Oliver I remembered although the expression was stern and the eyes suggested great wisdom, as if they had seen the wonders of the ages and understood the mysteries of the universe. I noticed Bull staring at the portrait with reverence.

Fifteen minutes later, a dark-skinned man in a sparkling clean white jacket and slacks appeared through double doors. I figured he represented the next level in the hierarchy of the Fourth Way farm.

"Mr. Kendall, my name is Harbhajan," the man said, his accent slight. "I am Zoltan's deputy. He wishes to speak to you personally. This is very rare. Please follow me."

Bull, who looked stunned stood up with me. Harbhajan put up his hand when he eyed Bull.

"You stay here and wait," he said.

"Yes, sir," Bull said. He eased himself back down, looking dejected.

I followed Harbhajan through his office which was very large through another set of doors into the main office. It was a giant room with a great oak desk and leather chairs and couches. The walls were wood paneled. Pictures of Zoltan with various celebrities and public officials lined the walls, including one of the governor. A slot machine sat on a table against the opposite wall. Harbharjan instructed me to wait. I walked over to look at the slot machine. There were some quarters in an attached tray. I put one in and pulled the handle, just missing a payoff by one bell.

Just as I was about to try again a voice behind me said it was an antique and almost never paid off. "It teases you into thinking it will, sort of like a woman in a bar who wants a free drink." I turned around. Zoltan was sitting down at his desk. He gestured for me to come and take a seat in front of the desk. I sat in one of the leather chairs. Up close I could see that Jimmy Oliver had aged, and yet there was still something boyish in his face. His thin sandy hair had turned white and his face was a little heavier. But otherwise he had not changed all that much in eighteen years.

He opened a silver box on his desk, pulled out a stogie and fired it up. He offered me one. I shook my head. After taking a puff, he looked at me for what seemed like an interminable moment. It made me squirm.

"So," Zoltan began, "when I received a report an intruder had snuck into the Fourth Way Farm, my assistant and I assumed it was just someone wanting to join the Work, to enjoy the fruits of enlightenment and was embarrassed to go through the front door, so to speak."

I didn't say anything.

"It's true that some people have a hard time facing their wants and desires and so they back into things, back into their lives. We encourage potential students of the Fourth Way to seek their true nature, throw away the masks. And once they do that, they can begin to take control of their destiny. Don't you agree?"

"Yep," I said. "Couldn't agree more."

I glanced down at my watch. It was getting late and Mark would be looking for me soon, I thought.

"But, of course, we know that was not your real reason for coming here," Zoltan said.

"I'm looking for a woman named Anna Asparagus. Do you know her?"

Zoltan stood and paced back and forth, pulling on his stogie. He turned to me.

"Mr. Kendall, I'm informed by my police investigators that you had a gun on you. Would you like to talk about that?"

"I...I had it for protection," I said. "It's a dangerous world out there."

Zoltan grinned. He sat back down and took the piece of paper taken from my wallet out of the middle drawer of his desk and held it up so that I could see it.

"Jimmy Oliver," he said. "That's a name I haven't heard in a long time." He eyed me. "So, you're Adele's kid, all grown up and then some."

I nodded, surprised he remembered me.

"How's Adele?"

"What?" I blurted.

"How's your mother? Did she finally leave your father? You know that she was a very unhappy woman. Even at your age back then…what were you eleven or twelve…you must have sensed it."

Either this guy was a damn good actor or he…I thought.

"You know how she is," I said.

Zoltan looked puzzled.

"I don't know what you mean. I haven't had contact with her in all these years."

"Adele is gone," I said. "Dead. Her remains were found last year about five miles from our house. She was murdered. Does that refresh your memory?"

Zoltan shook his head.

"I'm so sorry to hear that," he said. "You know she was going to leave your father and come to California with me. We were going to rendezvous at midnight. I waited two hours but she never came. I thought she had changed her mind, so I went on. She was such a vibrant and beautiful woman. It's hard to believe anyone would harm her. The last thing she said to me was she had to take care of something before meeting me. She didn't say what." He folded his hands together in front of him on his desk and looked straight at me. "Do the authorities know who was responsible?"

I just sat there staring at him, feeling a little dumfounded.

"Oh, I see," Zoltan said. "You thought I killed her, is that it? Of course. And so you came here seeking justice."

"All these years I thought she was out here in California living the life," I said, waiting for her to send for me. I even got a postcard from her once. It was postmarked Los Angeles."

Zoltan furrowed his brow.

"That's very strange," he said.

Nothing was said for several moments. Zoltan then said he remembered that I had a nick name Adele had told him about that my father would not allow to be used in the house and that she had laughed at the telling.

"Tuckie," I said. "Royce hated that name. I think he hated me, still does."

"Very sad," Zoltan said.

He stubbed out his stogie, stood up and walked over to a large picture window and looked out at the land east of the house. I watched, trying to figure out what he said about Adele not showing up to meet him. It struck me as real, that he was telling the truth. If so, then what happened to her? And who sent that postcard?"

Zoltan looked pensive.

"What now?" I said.

Zoltan turned around and came back to his desk.

"You must stay here, at least for awhile," he said.

"Am I a prisoner?"

"A guest," Zoltan said. "Who knows, maybe you'll become a disciple of the Fourth Way."

"What if I want to leave?"

"The woman you were looking for, Anna, left the Work. As far as the Fourth Way Farm is concerned she passed away."

"She's dead?" I said.

He didn't respond.

273

Chapter 33

———

Zoltan offered me a stogie. I stared at it for a moment and wondered if taking it would compromise my prisoner of war status. You only gave rank, name and serial number according to the movies. But this wasn't really war so I took the stogie. Zoltan lit it for me with a small silver cigarette lighter. He placed it between us on the table where we were sitting. I glanced at it and noticed it had an inscription, but I didn't pay any heed to it. He asked me how I happened to come west besides to track him down. I explained the whole story. Zoltan nodded without comment. We were silent for several uncomfortable moments, me puffing on the stogie and looking around, but feeling Zoltan's eyes fixed on me, as if trying to see inside my head.

"I had you brought here because I wanted to tell you a little about your mother," he said. "Adele was a very complex woman, filled with conflicting emotions. You know, of course, she married your father – Royce – when she was still a teenager. It was primarily for security. But in time it all wore very thin for her, particularly since he treated her badly, even hit her sometimes." He paused, as if wondering if he should go on. He took another sip of his coffee. "She told me you saw us once in the cornfield. She was devastated. I don't know how you felt about it, but it was one of the reasons Adele decided it was time to make her escape. But more than that, she wanted to expand her horizons, to grow, and realize some potential she thought she had and I encouraged her to begin the journey. She was still very young, not even thirty. The hardest thing for her of course was to leave you. She hoped that some day you'd forgive her and come and join her."

"Did you love her?" I said.

Zoltan peered at me and nodded and pushed the cigarette lighter toward me. I picked it up and eyed the inscription: To "Jimmy from Adele."

"Yes. I loved her and I believe she loved me. Adele may be the only woman I have ever truly loved, and believe me I have been with many beautiful and brilliant women over the years."

Silence again for a few moments.

"This may shock you, but she told me she had had another lover outside of her marriage before me."

I was not really taken aback by this revelation. Even at age ten or eleven I had suspected something, like a sixth sense. She would disappear for periods of time without explanation. I heard Royce interrogate her sometimes, and heard him slap her when she told him it was none of his business.

"Did she tell you who it was?" I said.

Zoltan shook his head.

I was pretty sure I knew who it was.

"How long are you going to keep me here?" I said.

Zoltan stood up and paced the floor, still holding onto his stogie.

"I had hoped you would become one of us," he said. "Lady Beth has been speaking on your behalf. She has taken a liking to you and wants to be your mentor here."

"She's pretty," I said.

"Sexy, wouldn't you say, in a spiritual way." He sucked on the stogie. "We have a game. It's called the Fourth Way Encounter. People openly explore their deepest fears and secrets."

"Sounds real scary," I said.

"It's like lancing a painful boil," Zoltan said. "All the poison oozes out. Once they have let go, the Fourth Way, the Work as it's called, gives them a path to find their way back to themselves, their true selves cleansed of their defenses, their masks discarded, a redemption."

I nodded as if I understood.

"Oh, yeah," I murmured.

The phone rang. Zoltan went over and picked it up and listened for a moment. He said yes, and hung up.

"Tell me, Charles...Tuckie, what do you know of this place so far?"

"I don't know what you mean?" I said. "It's a farm. I seen lots of farms."

"But not quite like this one, eh?" Zoltan said. "I mean, what kinds of things do you think we grow here?"

I shrugged.

"You've got cows and pigs and you grow vegetables and stuff."

He looked at me and his mouth took on a strange twisted grin. It was almost like he was suddenly two different people.

"I think you know what I'm talking about," he said. "You were spotted snooping around the hot houses. My security people believe you are some kind of undercover government agent."

I laughed.

"The question is do you know what's inside them?"

"Nope," I said. "All I know is I looked in through a window and saw some strange-looking plants I'd never seen before. So, what are they?"

He stopped pacing and returned to his chair. He smiled at me, but it was like the smile of one of those mad men you see in horror movies. I felt a chill run up my back.

"We're doing someexciting things here, Tuckie," Zoltan said. "Things that some day could have far reaching effects, but in some quarters could be...misunderstood. If you get my meaning!" He tapped his fingers on the table. "How did you get here? I'm told you had no car. The other day someone came to the front gate and asked about you. Who was that? Who knows you're here?"

I shrugged.

"You're lying, Tuckie," he said. "Don't lie to me. I'm your friend. Who brought you and what are they up to?"

I stuck to my story about hitching a ride with some man who was coming through that way. Zoltan sat there for a long moment staring at me, his eyes flat, as if they were not really seeing me. Then his eyes focused and he smiled.

"I don't know what you know, but if you keep anything you learn about this place to yourself, as if national security depended on it, I might consider investing in this movie of yours. What do you say to that?"

I smiled back and tried to make Zoltan think that I knew what he was talking about.

"Good," he said. "I'm sure it will be a fine movie. Adele would have been proud."

I stood up, sensing that our meeting was coming to a close.

"On the other hand," Zoltan went on, "I again would encourage you to become one of us here at the Fourth Way. We are like a small country, fully self-contained."

"When can I leave here?" I said.

"Maybe tomorrow, maybe the next day. We'll see."

I knew then there was no way they were ever going to let me leave. Again, I wondered about Mark Horgan.

Later that evening I was taken by two deputies I hadn't seen before up the hill about a hundred yards passed the main house to a moon-washed encampment in a meadow. Small tents were scattered in a circle around a dying campfire. The glow from the embers looked somber, creating an aura of darkening red and orange. The sound of a guitar being strummed could be heard from one of the distant tents. The smell of kerosene lamps, which glowed from inside many of the tents, as well as a few that were hung outside, filled the air. It reminded me of one of those early Californian or Alaskan gold rush camps I'd seen in movies, like Call of the Wild. A few people meandered about.

I was taken to a tent at the far end. The bigger one told me to go inside and that they would not be far away. I just stood there. The smaller deputy gave me a little shove toward the entrance. I pulled back the cover flap and went in. This tent was much larger than the others, though it was old and had rips here and there. I could stand up in it. A Coleman lantern turned low sat on a half barrel in the middle.

Sitting cross-legged like a queen on a large gold and red pillow, guitar in hand, was Lady Beth, as Zoltan referred to her. She looked up and gave me a winsome, dreamy kind of smile. Her hazel eyes seemed to sparkle in the subdued light from the lamp. She stopped plucking at the strings and put the guitar aside, then gestured with her open arms to come and join her.

"I've been waiting for you," she said. "I've been waiting for you a long time."

I just stood there looking at her, feeling incredulous about the whole scene. She shook her head.

"Well, I don't mean literally," she said. "I mean…well you know…in the abstract."

"Right," I said.

"Come over and sit by me," she said.

After a time, I did and nervously fired up a smoke.

"So," I said. "Is this where Fourth Way folks live when they're here?"

"Zoltan plans to eventually build housing on this site," she said. "He's like a father, brother, and lover to all of us."

"Cool," was about all I could get out.

She spent the next hour explaining to me what it meant to be in the Fourth Way, living and working there on the farm and striving through the Work to enlightenment and salvation. "There are forces in the outside world working to prevent our awakening," she said. Beth said the farm was like a Utopia. Then she talked about G.I. Gurdjieff who I'd never heard of before I heard Zoltan say that name on his broadcast, and that he developed the Fourth Way back in the 1920s and 1930s from studying the ancients and something called Hermetic Principles. Mostly I just listened and smoked. Beth's voice had become soft and seductive. She was close enough that I could feel and smell her breath, which was warm and sweet. After a while, she reached behind her where she had a plate of cookies on a small table. She handed me one.

'Try it," she said.

"What about you?"

"Oh…I've already taken some," she said.

Beads of sweat formed on my brow.

"It's hot in here," I said and took a bite of the cookie. It was sticky on top with honey and covered with a sprinkling of seeds. "What are these?"

Beth just smiled, picked up another cookie and pushed it at my mouth just as I finished the first one. I let her feed it to me.

"These are magic cookies," she said.

They tasted pretty good so I had a couple more. After awhile I began to feel very strange and I noticed the light from the lantern began to change colors and give off weird beams of light like shooting flames, constantly changing as if looking through a kaleidoscope and soon the whole inside of the tent was filled with blazing hot colors, swirling and evolving. When I looked at Beth, she looked like an angel with an aura that enveloped her. I could feel intense heat radiating through my body. Beth said something about the heat. She removed her shirt, revealing her very white breasts, and the full cotton skirt she wore. She did not have on underwear. Beth encouraged me with her eyes and hands to do the same. I stripped down to my shorts to cool off, but I was also overcome with a strange feeling of freedom I'd never felt before, kind of like spontaneous combustion of inhibitions. For a moment I heard Maggie's voice accusing me of lacking spontaneity. If only she could see me now, I thought.

Beth plucked her guitar. I suddenly stood up and danced around the tent, with total abandon, completely out of control until I felt real dizzy, began falling and landed on top of the pillow next to Beth. She put the guitar down and pulled me on top of her, fondling me until I was aroused enough that she was able to guide me inside of her. My vision blurred and the tent had turned into my father's mortuary. I could see the bodies of men and women, people I'd known growing up strewn around on gurneys like slabs of meat. And there was Royce presiding over the dead like a mad monarch, Zona standing by his side. At the same time, I could feel Beth's hands on my behind, pulling me deeper and deeper until I felt like I might disappear. I pulled away and off of her and went into a fetal position. Her hand touched my back.

"What is it?" She said. My head was very hazy but then I was aware of her asking me questions. "Who do you work for, Tuckie? Are you working secretly for Zoltan? I know he has spies amongst us. What are you really trying to find out?"

I did not answer. In the morning I opened my eyes. Beth, still naked came into focus. She was sitting up watching me, sipping something from a cup. My head ached.

"Tea," she said. "Would you like some? I can heat it on the Coleman stove."

I shook my head and pulled on my pants and climbed into my shirt. Beth grabbed a cold wet cloth she had ready and lightly bushed my face with it. It was soothing. The day was already hot.

"You were pretty wild last night," she said. "It was like a whole other you came out. I mean, wow, it was something."

"What happened to me?"

"I probably shouldn't tell you this," she said, "those cookies you ate had seeds on them that we've been experimenting with. In their pure form they can be dangerous. But we've developed a hybrid that is hallucinogenic. It's called Moon Flower. Zoltan believes its powers will one day change the world."

Just then we heard a commotion outside Beth's tent. Someone was yelling. A moment later the flap to the tent flew open and Deputy Ishmael, out of breath and sweating hard stuck his head in and looked at me.

"Come down to the house immediately," he said.

Beth quickly pulled on her shirt and skirt, not embarrassed at all by the intrusion.

"What is it?" She said.

"It's a raid. Police and Sheriff's men and FBI agents are swarming all over the place, demanding that we produce this young man. Television cameras and reporters are here too. It's crazy."

Chapter 34

————

It was pure bedlam out in front of the main house. More than a dozen police and sheriff's cars were lined up along the dirt road from the front gate. The entire encampment had been alerted, many of the residents ran to see what was going on. Ishmael was practically pulling me along with him. Beth right behind us. We began making our way through the gathering crowd. Beth was suddenly beside me. She leaned in close and said in my ear that I should tell what happened to me, that I was a prisoner of the Fourth Way. I just looked at her, certain I had not heard right.

Several Sheriff's deputies were keeping the crowd, television cameras and reporters at bay. One of the deputies with a bull horn ordered the crowd to move back. Harbhajan appeared in the crowd. He spotted us, came over and guided me toward the front porch of the main house. Beth stayed behind. Television cameras began swinging toward me, but it was clear that the reporters were uncertain as to who I was or whether or not they should bother.

"What's happening?" I said to Harbhajan.

He said there have been erroneous news stories that you had been kidnapped by the Fourth Way and held prisoner here. "This is very bad," he said. He went on to say the authorities had a warrant and are planning to search the entire place. "There are police officers inside the house now tearing through files and papers. It violates the sanctity of the farm."

Zoltan was standing on the porch. He was talking to two men in brown suits. Harbhajan said they were FBI agents. Also on the porch was a high ranking uniformed police officer. Next to him was the county sheriff. There was a lot of yelling and booing as the crowd swelled. Folks began chanting: "Fourth Way, Fourth Way is the way."

"What are you going to tell the authorities?" Harbhajan said as we reached the steps.

I did not answer. He looked very nervous and was swallowed up by the surging devotees. I started up the steps. The large familiar figure of Mark Horgan became visible. He'd been standing in the background talking to one of the sheriff's deputies. He did not see me. Mark then pointed a finger at Zoltan and screamed out, "What have you done with Charles Kendall?"

I stepped onto the porch next to Zoltan and yelled that I was there, raising my voice a few notches to be heard. The news people moved in closer, cameras flashing, TV cameras on tripods were quickly set up and trained on me. I scanned the crowd and saw Beth, her face a strange questioning expression. She began moving around the crowd and disappeared. I turned around and nodded at Mark who looked stunned to see me standing there. He came over.

"I thought you were probably dead!" He yelled.

The sheriff joined us.

"You Charles Kendall?" He said.

"Yes."

"Have you been held here against your will?"

I looked at Zoltan who was stoic. But I could see in his eyes that he hoped my answer would be the right one. Suddenly members of the press began shouting questions at me. "Were you kidnapped? What kind of secret society is this? Are you okay?" A beautiful young woman reporter in a blue suit I'd seen before on television said it was her understanding that the so called Fourth Way was actually a sex cult. She wanted to know what kind of orgies were conducted there at the farm? "Could you comment?"

I whispered to Zoltan that it would be good if he invested in my movie. He nodded.

"I don't know what you're talking about," I said.

"Sure you do," she yelled back. "Kinky group sex, Pagan rituals, the whole bit."

An older male reporter nearby her said, "What's the matter honey, you feel you're missing out?" She ignored him.

One reporter, a young man with gobs of yellow hair insisted that the Fourth Way was really a sanctuary for space aliens dropped off by flying saucers. Laughter rippled through the crowd. The reporter was dead serious and said that it was well known that UFOs had been sighted in the area.

Behind the crowd, Barney, Bull, Ishmael, and a few other Fourth Way Farm deputies stood looking scared, surrounded by police officers. The Sheriff asked me again if I'd been kidnapped or held there against my will. I asked if I could borrow a bullhorn for a moment, that there was something I wanted to say. The Sheriff was reluctant but then said okay and one of his deputies handed me the bullhorn. I turned to the gaggle of news people and the Fourth Way devotees. A hush came over everyone. I put the bullhorn up to my mouth and pressed the trigger.

"My time here at the Fourth Way Farm has been the greatest experience of my life," I said.

The crowd broke into cheers and thunderous clapping. I looked for Beth, but she was nowhere to be seen. I handed the bullhorn back to the deputy. The Sheriff looked completely taken aback. Zoltan gave me an almost imperceptible approving nod.

"Mr. Kendall, you're telling me...and the police who came here to rescue you and the news media present that you were not kidnapped and have not been held here against your will?"

"Yes, sir," I said. "That's what I'm saying."

"You're associate Mr. Horgan says otherwise, that you were supposed to meet him a few days ago and didn't show up and he was not allowed entry and even told there was no such person as Charles Kendall on the premises."

I shrugged.

"A real misunderstanding," I said. "Besides, I called myself the Wichita Kid."

I was then taken into a room in the house and questioned by the two FBI men who seemed to have taken charge. They both carried very stern expressions affixed on their thin faces. One had a thin mustache. The other one had no chin to speak of. They did not believe my story.

"Do you consider yourself a good American, son?" No-chin said.

I nodded and was told to say yes or no into the microphone they had placed in front of me.

"Yes," I said.

The one with the mustache walked around behind me and leaned down, his mouth only inches from my right ear.

"Have they threatened you?" He said. "Threatened your family? Is that why you said what you said out there…great experience. Huh? You don't have to be afraid. We'll protect you, Mr. Kendall. Frankly, we've been investigating this guy…Zoltan and his followers for some time now. You've given us the break we were looking for, the warrants to come in and clean house."

"Fucking A," No-chin muttered.

Mustache straightened up. He offered me a cigarette and lit one up for himself. No-chin began pacing around. He looked like he was trying to think of something. He whirled to me.

"We think this might be a front for a Communist cell," he said. "You ever been to those red countries?"

I didn't answer, just took a drag off my cigarette. After a while the door opened and to my shock Beth walked in. Only now she was a completely new person, not the Beth I had spent the night with in a shabby tent, stoned on strange cookies. This Beth was dressed in black slacks and a white blouse, a holstered gun on her belt and probably wearing underwear.

"Meet Special Agent, Dorothy Stoner," No-chin said.

Beth...err... Dorothy nodded at me as if she'd seen me for the first time and said something in private to Mustache. He nodded and she turned to me and said it was nice meeting me. She then left. Mustache told No-chin about the hot houses which Beth apparently had led them to, recommending that what was being grown there be confiscated and analyzed. That something called Moon Flowers was a cover for cannabis plants, possibly worth millions.

Mustache told me that Beth told him that I lied about not being a prisoner there. I did not change my story. They kept at the questioning for another two hours before letting me go. Outside I found Mark. We heard that Zoltan and Harbhajan had been taken into custody. One of the Fourth Way followers yelled out that Zoltan was God. Barney was also arrested for outstanding warrants. Mark and I started for his car which was parked in the grass on the side of the entrance drive. We were suddenly surrounded by reporters and television crews all throwing questions at me at once. Mark tried to run interference, but it was no use. I spent the next forty five minutes telling my entire story, about the contest, my movie script and Starburst/Meade Productions, and how I had come there to the Fourth Way Farm to find this woman Anna Asparagus. I even talked about Chick's Hamburger Palace and how I worked there to make ends meet.

"This is truly an American story." A male reporter for a national newspaper said. "Our readers will love it."

A woman reporter who, like the earlier male reporter harped on the outer space theme. According to her name tag, she wrote for a publication called "Flying Saucers Are Here." She asked if I believed rumors that Zoltan was an alien from some nameless planet who had disguised himself as a human. This also brought laughter from the other reporters which did not seem to faze the flying saucer reporter. "We know they kidnap humans," she yelled. "Humans are disappearing everyday." More laughter.

On the way back to Hollywood, we stopped at a café on Ventura Boulevard and ordered cheeseburgers and coffee. Mark asked me if I had found Anna Asparagus. I told him that I heard she might have died. He then left the table and returned a minute later with a newspaper which he threw down in front of me. It took me a moment to comprehend what I was looking at. There was a two column head shot of me. The Caption read: Alleged Victim, Charles Kendall. Next to the picture along the top right hand side of the front page was a three column bold headline.

MISSING WRITER MAY BE CULT VICTIM
Los Angeles, Calif…Police and Federal agents are
Investigating the reports that missing Hollywood
Writer, Charles "Tuckie" Kendall, is being held
captive by a secret cult located north of Los Angeles.
Authorities would neither confirm nor deny the reports.
But sources close to the investigation who wish to remain
anonymous said a breakthrough in the case was imminent.

When I finished reading the whole story which jumped to the back page I put the paper down and looked up. Mark was grinning at me like that Cheshire cat in Alice in Wonderland. All I could see was his mouth in a huge crescent.

"Wow!" I said. "How'd they get this story?"

Mark shook his head.

"You know the press, man."

"Where'd they get my picture?"

Mark took the paper and looked at the photo. He turned it around so I could see it.

"Check the credit."

"Margaret Langston," I said aloud. "Maggie?"

Mark told me he got the picture from Maggie after a final interview during which he told her he would not include her in his report on Margo Benson. He then gave it to the paper.

"I've never had my picture in the paper before," I said. "You shouldn't have done it. I don't like it."

"You don't like it?" Mark said. "You kidding, man? That picture and story has been in every newspaper in this country, and in Europe as well. I mean speculation was that you were dead, murdered by some fiendish satanic cult. I tell you, Tuckie this whole thing is a great opportunity. Don't you see that?! And it's just the first act."

"First act?"

"This is juicy stuff. You been out of the sticks long enough to figure that out, haven't you. This is the kind of publicity that sticks to the ribs."

"But it's not real," I said. "At least all that stuff they're saying which I reckon you told them."

"What's that got to do with anything?" Mark said. "The point is, this could be good for your career, and maybe mine too. Listen, out here perception is nine tenths of the truth."

I fired up a smoke and sipped my coffee.

"How's this going to help my career?" I said.

"Just knowing how things work," Mark said. "It's like you jumped on a bucking bronco and now you got to ride it for all it's worth. So, ride it. Ride it hard, man."

"I don't know if I can do that," I said.

I told Mark about Zoltan and how his real name was Jimmy Oliver and that he and my mother were once lovers and that I had thought he murdered her.

"Jesus!" was about all Mark could muster.

I borrowed some change and called my answering service. There was an angry message from Chick, and a hysterical message from Jenny. I called Chick to tell him I'd be by to pick up my stuff, certain I'd been fired. One of the waitresses answered. She said they'd just heard me being interviewed on radio. She sounded breathless as she told me everyone in the place listened.

"You're a celebrity," she said.

Chapter 35

When I came into the Hamburger Palace, I was met with cheers from the two waitresses, both of whom kissed me, and a new fry cook who came around from behind the counter and shook my hand. Customers clapped. What I didn't realize at first was that Chick had organized the greeting committee. I was relieved. They even hung a banner up behind the counter that said: "Welcome Back Tuckie." I felt my face turn hot with embarrassment. Chick stuck out his hand and pulled me in for a quick hug.

I noticed that there were clips from every newspaper in Los Angeles posted on the walls, some with my picture. Every mention of the Hamburger Palace was underlined in red. In one paper Chick was quoted as saying I was like a son to him. He came up behind me.

"You like my quote?" Chick said and put a hand on my shoulder. "I was worried about you, man."

Chick's quote was followed by a quote from Royce Kendall, identified as my father, who'd been contacted in my home town. "Communists are everywhere, godless heathens," he said "I'm sure they're trying to get to me through my son, Charles, because Royce Kendal never minced words about the Reds."

"How'd they ever find my father?" I said.

"They got their ways," Chick said laughing.

Chick closed early and set up the TV out front where everyone including a few favorite customers could sit and watch the evening news.

"Hollywood Writer Found" was the top story. There was film at the scene. It was black and white and a little grainy. The first clip was that of the woman reporter who asked me if I'd been forced into joining sex orgies. The waitresses giggled and the men howled with laughter. "You should be so lucky," one of the male customers who stayed said. Next they showed the woman who asked about Aliens from outer-space. There were shots of Zoltan being led away by plain clothes officers, his followers screaming insults at them as they passed, some even throwing handfuls of dirt. A male reporter for the channel we were watching then came on and said Mr. Kendall was a happy man today after several days of alleged captivity. He will return to working on a movie he called The Prairie Wolves. "Watch for that one," he said and signed off.

"We got us a goddamned celebrity," Chick said and slapped me on the back. "There are some messages for you."

He handed me a small pile of torn pieces of brown paper with notes scratched on them. I stuffed them in my pocket and had a bowl of stew for dinner. Later that night I sat on the cot in back and went through the messages. There was an urgent call from Sherry Woo, a call from Jenny Gifford, one from Moe Miller, and one from an Italian film producer who wanted to talk to me about The Prairie Wolves. The call came all the way from Italy.

A hard driving rain moved in early the next morning. It woke me at four a.m. I got up, made some coffee and called Jenny. With the time difference I was sure she'd be up. After several rings, Jenny's mother answered.

"Hello, Mrs. Gifford," I said.

"Who's this?" She said sleepily, with a touch of anger in her voice.

"Hope I didn't wake you," I said. "It's Tuckie."

"Tuckie?" She said. "Tuckie Kendall what on earth are you doing? When are you going to get some sense and come home where you belong! We saw you on the TV last night. You looked like a bum."

I heard Jenny's voice in the background. She picked up an extension, her voice sounding raspy and told her mother to get off.

"You okay, Tuck?" She said.

Jenny then went into an almost hysterical rambling about how it had been reported that I might be dead and how she was being asked out on dates but turning them down because she was waiting for me and not getting any younger and why weren't we engaged, and she wanted children and she was sure Royce would give me my old job back in the funeral home if I came home, but if I was still bent on trying to get my movie made she had a plan which she would not divulge. "You should call Zona," she said. "Your father's not well."

"I have to go," I said and hung up, thinking Jenny was getting stranger and stranger. And what did she mean she had a plan?

I shaved and washed up in the basin. It was still raining when the lunch crowd emptied out with just a few scattered customers left. I made myself a grilled cheese sandwich and was about to take a bite when Sherry Woo came in. She spotted me behind the counter and came over. Water dripped off her hat as she sat down on a stool. She looked desolate. I gave her some coffee. She lit a cigarette.

"Can you believe this weather?" She said and eyed me for a moment. "I'm glad to see you're okay. The whole thing sounded very weird."

I nodded.

"Have you seen the morning papers?"

I shook my head and took a bite of my sandwich.

"It's really crazy," Sherry said.

"It's mostly crap," I said with my mouth half full. "I mean I can imagine."

Sherry took a sip of her coffee and then a long drag on her cigarette.

"I just came by to tell you I was fired."

"What?" I said.

"Yeah," she sighed. "A few days ago."

"Why?"

"Fucking bitch Jocelyn. Just walked in and cold as ice told me to get my things, no warning, nothing. I thought maybe she'd found out about

293

our little enterprise to try and get Frank to producer your script. But now I think it was something else. Anyway, they owe me for a week. I'll probably never get it."

"Did Frank Meade come back?"

Sherry nodded.

"Something's going on there, but I don't know what it is," she said. "He may even be planning to fold the place. It's depressing."

Sherry told me she tried to get another job as a production assistant or anything, but according to her there was nothing. "It's dead as a whore's dream out there," she said and then giggled at her own words. "My uncle who was a cosmetic salesman used to say that after a day of no sales." She looked out toward the street. "Looks like it's letting up a little."

Sherry said she had decided to go back up to San Francisco, stay with her family for a while and try to find something. "Like it's always a quest, isn't it," she said, more to herself than to me.

"Back home my friend Marco always liked to say, 'must be down the road apiece,' and then he'd laugh and add that it could be love or a cold beer on a scorching hot day."

Sherry laughed, but I sensed a deep sadness in her. She gave me a phone number where she'd be staying and said to call her if I ever got up that way. I came around the counter. She stood and there was a moment where I thought we would hug. But the moment passed and she left.

Over the next several days the news about my rescue was splashed across the front pages of all the local newspapers. The coverage ranged from straight forward to the bizarre. One of the tabloids had a picture of me surrounded by alien-looking creatures that had been drawn in by an artist. The headline read: Writer Meets Space Aliens. I was quoted as saying, "They want our souls."

I was amazed at the unending stream of calls that came in from all over the country. One woman from South Carolina got through to me at the Palace and asked if by any chance I had come into contact with her husband who had disappeared six months before and that she knew he had been abducted by creatures from outer space. He had always told her that one day it would happen. She began crying, explaining that they had forgotten to take her and she was terribly lonely. I tried to explain that it was all a lie about this space stuff. She screamed at me that my mind was poisoned and that I was in their power. I hung up.

There were messages on my answering service from Herman Zeppelin who had some news; Moe Miller who said it was important and call him as soon as possible; Iris Madigan wanting to get together; Jocelyn Bukowski who said Mr. Meade would like to talk to me; and one from Frank Meade himself saying I should come to Starburst/Meade Productions. I figured it was a trap and the police would be waiting for me.

I told Chick about the calls and he got after me for not answering them. It didn't matter because I was going home, getting out of Dodge as they say.

"Man, this is your time," Chick said. "You can't be running away now."

"I've done a heap of thinking on it," I said. "It just don't seem right," I said. "All this stuff about my being kidnapped…"

"A heap of what?" Chick said. "Jesus, ain't you learned nothing since you came out here? I mean fate has dealt you a hand and it's got some aces in it and you should play 'em that's all I'm saying, man."

Later, I packed my meager belongings in my old suitcase. Chick drove me to the Greyhound bus terminal. On the way, Chick kept going on about how this country was built on grit and bullshit and that that was reality. I paid no mind.

"I'm going to miss you, man," Chick said as I got out. "When you get your head straight come back. I'm going to need a good manager for the new place."

We shook hands. Inside the terminal I purchased my bus ticket. I thought about Royce and decided that there was probably nothing really wrong with him or I would have heard from Zona. I picked up a copy of Variety. A woman and her daughter who looked to be about eight were sitting close by on the bench. I could feel the woman was staring at me. After a moment I looked at her and smiled.

"You look very familiar to me," the woman said. "Are you in television or something?"

I shook my head and began going through Variety. I turned the page and then suddenly flipped it back. On the front page, which I almost missed, was a bold headline and one paragraph item that sent an electric shock through me. It was an announcement:

STARBURST/MEADE TO FILM NEW PIX

Veteran low-budget indi producer, Frank Meade, today announced his company will produce The Prairie Wolves, the company's first production in years. Meade said he is very excited about the script penned by new scribe, Charles Kendall. This is the same Charles Kendall who has been in the news as a reported kidnapped victim by an alleged dangerous cult.

Details of the production schedule to be released later.

Boyd Imwald, out of retirement, has been signed to the helm.

"Jesus," I said aloud. "This is crazy!"

"Oh my god," the woman with the young daughter screamed. "It's you. You're the guy, the one who was kidnapped by aliens and taken to another planet or Russia or something. I've seen your picture. You're clean shaven now, but I recognize you, I know it's you."

It was as if she had just met Cary Gant or Tyrone Power. She tugged at her daughter who was reading a comic book. Other folks in the terminal were looking at me.

"He's the one sweetie pie," she said. "He's the one who's been in the papers and on television and everything. You've seen him."

The little girl put down her comic book, looked at me, her face filled with skepticism, and then annoyance. She made a face and went back to her comic book.

Chapter 36

————

Long after the woman and her daughter left to catch their bus, I was still sitting on that hard wooden bench in the depot. It was like being in a dream where I couldn't move. My own bus had left without me, my ticket still clutched in my hand. It would be 24 hours before the next bus. I kept wondering if the item in Variety was part of a trap to lure me into revealing the blackmail plot and turning me over to the police. Part of me wanted to go back home. I missed the seasons and the smell of freshly tilled earth. And then there was Jenny. I felt there was something strange going on with her that I didn't understand. On the other hand I had to find out if the Variety story was really true. Or was it part of the trap?

After a cup of coffee from a stand in the terminal and a smoke, I decided to test the situation. I went to a phone booth and called Starburst/Meade. Jocelyn answered in her usual unfriendly tone. But when I told her it was me she immediately went into reverse and acted like she was my best friend. Even her voice seemed to change. She told me Mr. Meade was there and very anxious to talk to me. Frank Meade came on the phone.

"Charles…I guess it's Tuckie, right? I'm glad to finally hear from you. How the hell you doing? How'd those kidnappers treat you? Sonofabitch, that must have been a scary scene. Huh? Yeah. Am I right? Listen, we have to talk. Where are you? I have good news. Why don't you come to the studio right now and we'll put this whole thing together, just the two of us. We don't need that little fucker Fat Eyes. He'll just screw up the works. We are going to make a goddamned movie from your script. Right? I've got a contract all drawn up, ready to be signed."

"Huh?" I said. "A contract?"

"Yeah, you know. One of those pieces of paper says we're doing business."

I put my hand over the mouth piece for a moment, trying figure what Frank Mead was saying. Were they going to arrest me the minute I stepped into the studio? Was that it?

"I...I don't know," I said. "I mean, is this a joke?"

"Shit no!" Frank said."

I was silent, taking deep breaths.

"You there?" Frank said. "What's going on? What do you say?"

I could feel sweat forming on my brow and trickle down along my nose.

"I don't know," I blurted out. "I was about to go back home and forget the whole thing."

"Why the hell would you do that?" Frank said.

I fired up another smoke and took a drag.

"I mean how come you're suddenly producing my story and I don't know anything about it. What right do you have to do that?"

I could tell that Frank put his hand over the phone, then muffled voices saying something. It sounded like he referred to me as a nut case.

"Listen," he said, "I don't have time for this bullshit. You want to see your script as a flick or not. Isn't that why you came out here from wherever you came from after winning our contest? If not I'll hang up the fucking phone now. I got other scripts."

"I'm just trying to figure it out," I said. "Can I ask a question?"

"Make it quick!"

"I was wondering, why do you want to produce The Prairie Wolves now? Is it because of that film of you?"

A long silence followed.

"What film?"

"You know, Mr. Meade...err Frank," I said. "The one I gave you when I saw you that time."

"I don't know what you're talking about," Frank said. Without bothering to cover the phone this time he said to Jocelyn, "This asshole says he gave me some film. You know about any film?" He came back on. "Don't know about any film."

I figured maybe it wasn't a trap after all and decided to risk meeting with Frank Meade.

"Good," Frank said. "We'll do the contract and I'll throw in the five hundred to seal the deal. I tell you, Tuckie. I think that story of yours has hair on it. You know what I mean!"

I called Chick and told him I was staying after all. He told me to stay put and someone would pick me up.

"And listen," he said. "I'm glad you came to your senses, kid. My old mamma used to say, you can never really leave unfinished business. It follows you forever."

I was pacing back and forth in front of the bus terminal having a conversation with the Wichita Kid when a dark figure, silhouetted against the afternoon sun appeared out of the corner of my eye. I sensed the figure was coming toward me on the sidewalk. I could tell it was a woman. I turned to see Maggie. She was smiling and looked beautiful, like the all American girl in a white blouse and pleated gray skirt with her dark hair falling around her shoulders, and heels. I'd never seen her in heels before.

"What're you dong here?" I said.

She told me she had stopped by the Hamburger Palace to see how I was and was about to leave when Chick stopped her and told her where I was and needed a ride.

"Is that okay?" She said, her blue eyes searching mine, as if trying to see inside my head.

"Yeah," I said. "It's okay."

We sat in Maggie's car for a time. She told me she had seen me on TV and wanted to know all about what happened. I told her the story, but left out the part about Beth. She thought it was really some form of weird fate that Zoltan had been involved with my mother when he was Jimmy Oliver so many years before. "I've seen him on his Sunday TV show spouting esoteric crap," Maggie said. It turned out, according to news reports that the Fourth Way Farm, which was suspected by the FBI of being a Communist Cell was actually a cover for a multi-million dollar operation growing some exotic hallucinogenic plant. Zoltan's attorney claimed his client was secretly growing the plant for experimentation by an unnamed branch of the government.

Maggie told me she would take me back to the Palace if that's what I wanted. I shrugged and nodded.

"Actually," she said, "I...I would really like it if you came back to my place with me. You know, and stay there again. I've missed you. I promise I won't go crazy on you."

"I don't know," I said.

She started the car and began driving.

"You never came back or even tried to talk to me," she said. "I know I was going through some bad stuff. Even though you don't talk much, it was nice with you there. Not so lonely. I guess I didn't realize it until you weren't there anymore. It's really stupid I know, but..."

"I talk," I said.

Maggie laughed.

"Right," she said. "Well, there's talk and then there's communication, you know."

I was beginning to feel tight as I often did around Maggie. What was it about here? She must have sensed it.

"Sorry," she said. "I didn't mean to make you nervous."

We didn't say anything for a while. Maggie broke the silence and told me the terrible news about Grover Marcuse. He was dead. He had committed suicide a few days before, hanged himself in his studio. It was Maggie who'd discovered him.

"That must have been horrible," I said.

"He just went silently into oblivion, no indication that he was even thinking of such a thing. I cried for two days. Luckily there was a crypt already paid for, next to his father."

"You're still living there?" I said. "Who owns the house now?"

"That's the thing," Maggie said. "He had no family, no relatives. He once told me after a few drinks that he was going to leave the house and whatever else he had to me. I just laughed it off. I don't know if he made a will. He told me the house was free and clear, no mortgage, no leans."

Maggie drove directly to the house. I guess it was sort of unsaid that I was okay with it. She gave me a tour of the old place. I thought it was spooky, like something out of a real grizzly horror movie. The floors creaked and the windows looked like they had not been washed in a hundred years. We walked along upstairs hallways that were dark and musty and peered into dusty rooms that looked mummified, made ready for guests that never arrived. Silk canopies shrouded giant beds like great cobwebs. Pictures of Grover's father, Francis Wallace Marcuse, the silent screen star, hung on many of the walls as if to watch over his domain. In some of the photos he stood next to other stars of the period.

"Cool place, eh?" Maggie said.

When we got to the master bedroom Maggie told me she had moved into it.

"Look at that monster bed," she said. "I'll bet a lot of sex took place on it. Grover never would come into this room. He told me there were too many ghosts. Doesn't bother me though."

Maggie suddenly ran and bounced on the bed, then stood up and jumped up and down like it was a trampoline. Later she showed me a makeshift darkroom down in a basement room underneath the kitchen. There was an enlarger and several pans with chemicals that had a strange smell. There were prints hanging by clothespins from a line strung across the room. I recognized some of them which had been taken at the lunch Grover Marcuse had arranged with Fat Eyes. There was a close-up of Bambi leaning into Fat Eyes, and another of Grover looking morose. It was eerie. There was one of me looking pensive.

"I've decided that I'm a photographer," she said.

Before meeting with Frank Meade I called Fat Eyes at Maggie's urging. She thought I should have someone helping me and reminded me that Herman Zeppelin had a reputation for being savvy about these things. Fat Eyes was aware that a deal was in the works and said he would be happy to represent me. We agreed to meet at Barney's Beanery. The plan was for Frank Meade to join us later. I wore my gray second hand suit complete with shirt and bow tie. It looked rumpled after having been stuffed in my suitcase.

"You look like one of those early century Ellis Island immigrants just off the boat," Maggie said.

Maggie drove. The Beanery was crowded. Fat Eyes' blonde girl-friend was there, fondling him under the table with one hand and sipping beer with the other. She interrupted the conversation several times demanding to know what her role was going to be and how many lines she would have.

"Let's not get ahead of ourselves," Fat Eyes said. "First we have to put together a deal. Then we'll see what follows."

"What follows better be good for me, sweetie, or mama's gonna cut you off at the pass if you know what I mean. We're talking my career. That's your number one priority."

"And it is," he said, clearly keeping his impatience in check. "Just you wait, baby."

We talked for almost an hour, mostly about what I should expect and what I should demand. It was decided that Fat Eyes would do all the talking. He noted Frank Meade was pissed that he had called to set up the meeting. When Frank Meade joined us at the Beanery he brought Jocelyn with him. She carried a well-worn leather satchel briefcase. She set it down and pulled out the contract Meade had drawn up. She then lit up a fat cigar and leaned back like she was about to watch a favorite show.

The highlights of the contract called for Charles Kendall, that's me, herein called "Writer" to do whatever rewrites necessary as determined by Frank Meade, herein called "Producer" and Boyd Imwald, herein called

"Director." All principal's compensation was to be deferred until said movie, herein called "Project" with the title "Cobra Woman Versus The Prairie Wolves in the Vortex of the Valley of Darkness" had paid back its negative cost at which time Writer would begin to receive royalties based on two net points. Further, all first and secondary rights to said script and title will become property of Starburst/Meade Productions Inc. Upon signing, "Writer" will receive a $500 advance.

I was kind of stunned. "What?" I said. "Where'd that title come from? I mean it was just The Prairie Wolves."

"Kid," Meade said, "It's not about the weekend marauders you called The Prairie Wolves. It's about revenge and justice by a venomous woman and what could be more venomous than a cobra? Right? It will sell."

Fat Eyes began going over the contract. Frank Meade looked at me and began talking excitedly about the project and how he wanted to get some name actors. "We'll do it right, pay 'em scale of course." he said. "I think it will be my best film. Of course we'll have to do some work on the script, tweak it here and there. Standard stuff."

"I'm gonna be in it," Bambi said, now on her fourth beer.

I saw Maggie wince out of the corner of my eye. Frank looked at me and narrowed his eyes.

"Who the fuck says?"

"Herman!" Bambi said.

Frank Meade shifted his eyes to target her.

"Yeah, well when Herman makes a goddamned film he can put your ass in it along with chimpanzees and bush-baby freaks as far as I'm concerned."

A sly grin crossed Jocelyn's narrow slit of a mouth as she blew smoke across the table at Bambi.

"What?" Bambi said. "Did you hear that Herman?" She screamed and looked like she was about to toss her beer at Frank. "You cocksucking has-been pig! Herman says you haven't done squat in the last ten years. So go fuck yourself."

303

Other customers began looking our way. I slid down in my seat. Maggie shook her head. Fat Eyes ignored the scene. When he finished looking over the contract he held it up in front of Frank Meade's face and tore it in half, and then in pieces and tossed them on the table.

"What the hell are you doing?" Frank Meade said.

"I wouldn't insult my ass by wiping it with that toilet paper you call a contract. "When you're ready to talk seriously let us know. Come on Tuckie. You've got a marketable script here. I know another producer who'll be interested."

Jocelyn perked up and leaned forward.

"Your ass," she said. "What other producer, your blonde tootsie here?"

Bambi glared at Jocelyn.

"Why don't you take that tank you use for a body and find a big male dog that will stick it to you. Make sure it's blind."

Jocelyn started to come out of her seat but Frank Meade put his hand on her shoulder and kept her in check. Fat Eyes and Bambi stood and motioned for me to come with them. Maggie also stood.

"Don't do it, Tuckie!" Frank Meade said. "Don't let this ugly little twerp fuck things up for you. You want to make a movie or not? You go with them now and I'm out. This is your one dance with me."

His eyes were burning into me. After a long tense moment I stood and walked out with Fat Eyes. Meade yelled after me. Outside I demanded to know what was going on. Maggie tried to interject but Fat Eyes told her to stay out of it. I could see that it hurt her, but she backed off.

"It's nothing more than process," he said. "This is just the first round. Now, you either trust me or you don't. If you don't, go back in there and make your own deal. But I can tell you he will fuck you every which way he can, and then some."

I nodded.

"You really don't get it, do you," Fat Eyes said. "You're hot right now. All that shit about your being kidnapped and held prisoner has made you into a kind of folk hero. That means you're a marketable commodity. Frank Meade knows this."

"But he said..."

"Forget what he said," Fat Eyes said sharply and leaned in toward me, looking conspiratorial. "Everyone has a parallel language. It's an unspoken language between the lines, and you read it like you read the small print."

"What do we do now?" I said.

"Nothing," he said. "We wait. There is one more thing which will spur Frank to come around. Word on the street is he has a promised investor. No one knows who it is, but without a signed contract the investor vanishes. Capiche?"

A week went by with no word. I couldn't stand the wait any loner and called Fat Eyes and left a message on his answering service that I could be reached at Maggie's number. I had forgotten that I had discontinued my own answering service. He finally called back and yelled that I had screwed things up because they couldn't get a hold of me. Fat Eyes then calmed down and said he'd been out in his rose garden.

"You like roses?" He said.

"What about the..." I started.

"They're like angels, so delicate, and as exquisitely beautiful as their fragrance is sweet. Sometimes we have to stop and think about the roses."

He paused.

"We have a deal."

Chapter 37

———

It was 8:00 o'clock in the evening when Maggie and I got to the hotel. It was on Wilshire Boulevard near Doheny Drive. It was a big relic of a place, about twenty stories. It looked dark and monolithic against the night sky. Its one claim to elegance, at least on the outside, was a forest green canapé that covered the entryway.

I didn't know why Frank Meade wanted me to be there, only that it was important. He'd left a message on my restored answering service. When I called back, Jocelyn answered and was cryptic, saying only that I was to be there at eight and to look professional, whatever that meant. It was strange because several months had gone by without a word after signing the contract. In the meantime I had gone back to work at the Hamburger Palace.

One day Mark Horgan came in and ordered a cheeseburger and chocolate milkshake. With his mouth full, he told me how he was practicing his singing for his role in The Prairie Wolves. He was also taking acting lessons.

"I'm counting on that part," Mark had said, with a hint of a threatening tone. "My mother expects to see me in it. You don't want to disappoint my mother."

"Right," I had said. "I'm sure she'll be proud."

Mark gave me the evil eye.

"Seems like it's taking a long time to get The Prairie Wolves into gear," he said and stood up. "I'll be hearing from you."

I told him the new title.

"Jesus," was all he could get out.

Inside the hotel far surpassed the dim promise of the outside. It was vintage opulence. I watched Maggie as she strode across the lobby floor ahead of me. She looked real good in a low cut, black evening gown, heels, and her hair swept up in a bun. The only thing marring the sparkling new Maggie was the stained P-coat which she had draped over her shoulders. She said it was a matter of balancing images, which I didn't get. As for me, I wore the gray suit I had bought at the Salvation Army store which Maggie had tried to iron. It had been wrinkled from being stuffed in the suitcase.

The suite was on the 15th floor at the end of a long hallway. A blond-haired young woman in a maid's uniform with a short bob-tail skirt answered the door. She asked who we were. I told her Mr. Meade was expecting me. She gestured for us to come in, looking me up and down.

Beyond a short entry hall was a front area larger than most home's living rooms. A couple of rows of folding chairs were set up in the middle of the room. Against the far wall was a maroon couch. There was a bar with a middle-aged bartender behind it setting up glasses. He paid no attention to us. We looked around. Down the hall was a large tiled bathroom complete with a claw foot tub like the one back home, only bigger. There was a huge bedroom and two other rooms off the hallway. One was another bedroom. The other room was locked. I could hear someone talking on the other side.

"What do you think is going on here?" Maggie whispered to me as the bartender mixed us each a drink.

I shrugged, fired up a smoke and noticed posters of Frank Meade's old movies, placed on the floor leaning against the back wall. There were also boards with publicity pictures of some of his stars, most of whom I'd never heard of, except Iris Madigan. An illustration of her was featured on one of the posters. She was being carried off, almost naked by the Gorilla Man. The movie was called Revenge of the Gorilla Man. An actress named Virgie Lowe was featured as the heroine in all the other posters which included Space Alien, Swamp Monster, and Attack of the Sea Scorpion.

Frank Meade suddenly appeared. He had come out of the locked room down the hallway and immediately went to the bar. The bartender, who had yet to say a word, poured him a drink. He took a gulp, turned around and looked at Maggie and me as if he didn't know who we were.

"Mr. Meade," I said. "It's me, Tuckie Kendall."

He nodded.

"Right," he said.

"Just wondering what we're doing?" I said.

"Talk to Jocelyn when she gets here," Frank said and eyed Maggie. "Who's the chick?"

"This is Maggie," I said. "You remember her, she was …"

Frank put up his hand, sat on one of the barstools and took another gulp from his drink.

"You his chick?" He said to her.

"I'm nobody's chick," Maggie shot back.

Frank laughed.

"Spunky broad, eh!? Well, as long as she's not a freak, she can stay for this little shindig. I don't like freaky broads, you know."

"I'm with you, Frank," I said.

He looked incredulous, turned with drink in hand and went back down the hallway and disappeared back into the locked room.

"Asshole," Maggie said.

A few minutes later Jocelyn rushed in carrying a stack of folders. She placed one on each seat of the folding chairs. Still a little out of breath she told us that the purpose of all this was to hold "an investors soiree."

"Soiree?" I said. "What's a soiree?"

"It's a party, dumb fuck," Jocelyn said, "In this case an Angel party." Then she grinned at me showing her uneven stained teeth. "You got a few things to learn, boy."

Frank soon emerged once more from the back room. He explained to me that he was trying to line up investors for Cobra Woman vs. Prairie Wolves. "You have to give them something that promotes confidence that you can deliver a marketable product, and that it will make a profit. No guarantees. The folders contain a prospectus and a disclaimer in the unlikely case the project goes into the dumpster. He had Jocelyn read off the list of invitees from a clipboard.

"You think they'll all come?" Jocelyn said, eyeing the list over Frank's shoulder.

"They know Frank Meade always has an extra surprise for them. Moe Miller will bring some of those bottom feeders he hangs out with and I got a few others used to throw a few bucks into my earlier films."

"Moe Miller's coming?" I said.

Frank nodded.

"You know him?"

It was about 8:30 before anyone showed up. The first potential investor to arrive was the owner of a used car lot named Nick Yeager. He was followed by Moe Miller, his unlit cigar hanging out of his mouth, then a doctor named Ron who owned a couple of clinics, a burlesque house owner named Tiny, who of course was big as a house, a developer named Howard, and a mysterious weasel of a man named Beanie who sold jewelry, mostly out of the trunk of his car, according to Moe who knew him and asked him when he was going to get a real store.

"I like the overhead, Moe," Beanie said.

Before long, the room was filled with 18 potential investors. They all seemed to know each other as they began chatting. Fat Eyes soon arrived with Bambi. Moe nodded at Fat Eyes and they shook hands. The last to arrive was a tall skinny man with shaggy gray hair, balding in front, wearing faded jeans, stained white shirt open at the collar and blue blazer. His black horn-rimmed glasses magnified steely bloodshot eyes. When everyone was settled in with drinks and hors d'oeuvres Jocelyn handed out a ticket with a number on it. She said the tickets were for a very special drawing at the end of the presentation. The prize was a secret.

310

Maggie and I sat on the couch against the wall near the bar. The skinny man in the blazer took the club chair across the room by himself. He didn't seem to belong to the investor group.

During a lull, Moe spotted me, got up and came over.

"Hi, Mr. Miller…Moe," I stood and stuck out my hand. He ignored it. I then introduced Maggie. He nodded at her.

"You were a friend of my niece's right? You were at the funeral, gave that cockamamie eulogy or whatever you want to call it."

I nodded and reminded him that I had been to his store and that we had met at the Farmer's Market. Moe looked me up and down and took the cigar out of his mouth.

"You were in the news about being held prisoner by some cult or some goddamned thing," Moe said.

I nodded.

"You some kind of a screwball?" Moe said. "Trying to fit in, but don't quite make it, if you know what I mean?" He looked me up and down again. "Screwball. Maybe that's a good thing."

Moe went back to his seat, shaking his head.

"What do you think he meant?" I said.

"I can't imagine," Maggie said, clearly trying hard to keep from laughing as her mouth quivered.

Frank began his presentation by first introducing the skinny man in the blazer as his long time director, Boyd Imwald, whom he considered a genius. Boyd Imwald gave a quick waive of his hand and fired a smoke. Frank then went through the prospectus, page by page. He ended by saying The Prairie Wolves, re-titled "Cobra Woman versus the Prairie Wolves in the Vortex of the Valley of Darkness" cried out to be filmed and is almost guaranteed to make money…or" he chuckled, "be a good tax right-off. It needs one more word in the title but haven't figured it yet."

Frank then did something astounding. He acted out the story, even going so far as to get into costume, from business man to weekend roustabout in a black leather jacket and a bandana around his forehead. Jocelyn helped with the transition. He turned his back on the audience and she pasted a heavy moustache on him at which time he whirled back around and spurted out some dialogue. By this time the room was filled with the acrid smell of cigar and cigarette smoke. When Frank finished there was dead silence as the group just stared blankly at him. He took a bow and got a less than enthusiastic round of applause.

"Okay," Frank said. "You jackoffs don't know a performance when you see one. Cobra Woman/Prairie Wolves is going to kick ass and take names."

"It sounds like it's got some traction," Nick Yeager the used car dealer said. "Love the title."

"I always knew you were a ham, Frank," Moe yelled out.

This got a laugh. Frank then introduced me as the young genius who authored the script. He motioned for me to stand. I did and nodded at the investors.

"He don't look like any genius to me," someone yelled from the back.

Frank asked if anybody had a question for me.

"Yeah," Tiny, the burlesque house owner said. "Anybody get laid in this turkey?"

Frank laughed and clapped his hands.

"Everybody gets laid, Tiny."

"I don't get the title," said the man called Beanie who sold jewelry and who I learned later was tied in with the west coast mob and off-shore gambling. "It's a mouthful."

I nervously stared at Frank.

"What the fuck, Beanie," Frank said. "It's self explanatory, poses conflict." Beanie nodded.

Next, Jocelyn set up a sixteen millimeter projector and Frank showed clips from some of his films. Virgie Lowe was featured in all of them as the beautiful innocent ingénue. One scene showed her running through the jungle in a skimpy leopard skin costume. It was an outtake because the top fell off revealing her breasts. This got cheers from the group. Virgie looked down to see what had happened then turned to the camera and thrust out her middle finger.

"Turn that cocksucker off while I get my tits back in hiding," she said.

In the final clip a brief pornographic scene of a couple having sex on a table had been inserted as if part of the movie. This got a big hand. Maggie was laughing so hard tears were running down her face.

Frank ended his presentation by telling the group the budget he was looking at and that it would be the biggest budgeted film of his career. He also noted that Boyd Imwald had consented to come out of retirement and direct. Moe Miller stood and said he had heard that Frank had a secret investor from out of the area who has already come through with a chunk of money.

"Where did you hear that?" Frank said.

"I have sources," Moe said. "Just wondering that's all."

Frank nodded and then spoke to the group in general.

"I'm going to try and get Virgie Lowe for the starring role," he said. "She's been making pasta westerns in Europe these days."

He whispered something to Jocelyn who quickly made her way down the hall to the locked room and went in. The bartender followed.

"Now for the icing on the cake," Frank said. "And I do mean cake."

A hush came over the investors as a sense of anticipation filled the air. The door to the locked room opened and Jocelyn came out marching to the sound of a kazoo she had in her mouth. She was followed by a cart with a giant cake sitting on top. A streamer with "Cobra Woman" in large letters was stretched around the top layer. The bartender pushed the cart to the front and center of the room. Jocelyn then went over to the bar and picked up the bowl where she'd put the stubs for the door prize tickets. Frank asked Maggie to pull the winning ticket out of the bowl. She hesitated, then shrugged, got up, went over to the bowl.

"What do we get if we win?" Ron the doctor said.

"The lucky winner will get this cake," Frank said.

"What're we gonna do with a goddamned cake?" Tiny said.

Frank laughed.

"You can't always tell a cake by its frosting," he said.

Jocelyn gave what could be considered a drum roll on her kazoo. Maggie looked around at the anxious faces and then pulled the stub with a number on it out of the bowl. Jocelyn hit a high note which turned out to be a cue for what happened next.

Suddenly the top of the cake erupted and out popped a naked woman, with bits of confetti on her shoulders and hair and a painted green cobra baring fangs circling her breasts and stretching to her navel. Everyone clapped and cheered. Frank told Maggie to hand the slip of paper to the woman in the cake. She reached out and when the woman turned her head to take it, my mouth dropped open. It was Silky, looking a little fleshier than the last time I saw her. She was wearing a long black wig like the one she had used dancing at that Hollywood bar. A few freckles still showed through her make-up.

"Jesus!" I said under my breath

Silky looked at me and I could see the surprise in her face and then a pleading in her eyes not to let on that I knew her. She turned and called out the number on the slip. It was number twelve. Nick Yeager, the used car man waived his ticket excitedly. "So, what do I win?"

"What you win," Frank said, "is one full night of fun and frolic with this young lady and this hotel suite. That is if you can handle it, Nick."

Without thinking, I grabbed Silky by the arm, just as the Wichita Kid would have, and pulled at her.

"Come on," I said "lets get out of here."

"Hey, get your hands off me," she screamed and reached back into the cake and pulled out a kimono which she wrapped around her.

"What the hell's the matter with you?" Frank said to me. "You want to queer this deal? Get your chick and get out of here."

"It's not right to give her away like a turkey at a raffle," I said. "I mean she's a girl…"

Frank glared at me. All eyes in the room were on us.

"The fuck," Frank said. "Listen, I paid plenty for her, punk. "It's good business."

Silky whispered something to Frank, then climbed out of the cake and scooted back down the hall and disappeared. I looked over at Maggie who had a puzzled expression on her face. I noticed Frank was distracted in conversation with Moe and a couple of the others. I raced back down the hall, checked two rooms and then the master bedroom. I went in and locked the door behind me. Silky was on the toilet with the bathroom door half open. She spotted me through the opening.

"Can't a girl take a pee without being harassed?" She said.

"Sorry," I said and went and sat on the bed.

"Oh, for Christ sake," she said. "What the hell did you follow me back here for anyway? Does that hick brain of yours want to save me from this terrible life I'm leading?"

I heard the toilet flush and Silky emerged adjusting her kimono.

"You still dancing at that club?" I said.

Silky sighed, grabbed a drink that had been sitting on the dresser, put a cigarette in her mouth and sat down next to me. For a brief moment her energy seemed to collapse and she became sullen. I fired up a smoke for her and one for myself.

"He canned my ass," she said after taking a drag. "He was a fat pig who never took a bath and he wanted to get into my pants. One night after work he pushed me down on the floor in the back, smelling sour and the sweat gushing out of him. Somehow I squirmed out from under him and hit him with a nearby bottle. Anyway, as I ran out, he screamed at me not to come back.

There was a heavy knock at the door.

"Hey, baby you in there? It's, Nick, the guy with the winning ticket. Everyone's leaving. I'm going back to get my drink and be right back."

"Okay, sweetie," Silky yelled. "I'll be waiting." She turned to me. "You better get out of here."

She suddenly began laughing, almost in tears.

"What's so funny?" I said.

"I didn't know what this was all about when Frank Meade hired me. But don't you think it's a gas that I end up, in my small way, helping you with your stupid career?"

"Why don't you come with me?" I said.

Silky stood up, walked to the dresser and wrote something down on a piece of paper, then gave it to me.

"My phone number where you can reach me if you ever have need of my services. I do it all. The price is extra for sixty nine. Now get lost, okay."

I shook my head and stuffed the paper into my pocket. I went back to the front and found Maggie sitting on the couch talking to Beanie who had his arm draped across her shoulder.

"Where have you been?" She said jumping up, leaving a disappointed looking Beanie.

I didn't answer.

"You know that woman?"

Fat Eyes came over with Bambi.

"Congratulations, kid," he said.""Don't forget, I own ten percent of you."

Bambi peaked around from behind Fat Eyes.

"And don't forget to write in some real good dialogue for me," she said.

Chapter 38

H e had a hacking cough that telegraphed his presence from the outer entrance hall. It was a deep unsettling hack that Boyd Imwald squeezed in between drags on the cigarette that dangled out of the side of his mouth. Frank Meade was thumbing through some notes. He was sitting on the famous couch in Sherry Woo's little film. He looked up when he heard the coughing getting closer and glanced at his watch.

"It's the great director himself," Frank said. "We've been waiting."

Boyd Imwald ignored him. Frank got off the couch and took his place at the head of a make-shift table Jocelyn had set up for a reading of my script. It was an eight foot piece of thick raw plywood resting on two sawhorses. Boyd stood looking at us as if he thought we might be imposters. He squinted at the actress Virgie Lowe, who was sitting directly across the table from me, and belched.

Virgie looked up at the bony figure of Boyd Imwald and sneered.

"Disgusting," she said.

Miss Lowe wore a blazing red, tight fitting dress as if she were attending a cocktail party. She sipped coffee from her personal mug and smoked a cigarette from a long cigarette holder and eyed the director. The script was spread out in front of her. When Virgie first walked in, Jocelyn remarked, "The cunt's wearing her fucking power dress."

To me, she looked too hard and too old to play the young wife of my story. Frank Meade thought she was box office.

I fired up a smoke and watched. The tension was thick as molasses, you ask me. Boyd Imwald, his lean frame stooped, eased himself down into the chair at the opposite end of the table from Frank Meade. I thought he looked a little like the actor John Carradine. His pale blue eyes were sunk deep in the hollows of a very gaunt face, making him look like he'd just been released from a concentration camp.

"Now that our scrawny-assed director has joined us, can we get on with it?!" Virgie Lowe said.

Others at the table were the Assistant Director, Bruce Richmond, who sat next to me, cinematographer, Lazlo Munkacse, who was said to be a Hungarian refugee and former freedom fighter. He sat next to Boyd Imwald. Sitting at Frank Meade's right was Jocelyn. On Frank's left was Bonnie Robertson. I was told she was brought in to be script coordinator, whatever that meant. I sat on the other side of Bonnie. Next to Bruce Richmond was Fat Eyes with a petulant Bambi at his side. Frank put up his hands to halt the chit-chat going on. Silence as all eyes were on Frank.

"We've been fortunate enough to sign Virgie Lowe for the lead in…" He stopped as if he forgot the title and looked down at the cover page and read, "Err… Cobra Woman versus The Prairie Wolves in the Vortex…of the Valley of Darkness. As the cobra woman heroine, Virgie will carry the film. Let's have a little hand for Miss Lowe."

"Vortex?" I said after no one clapped. "What's that exactly?"

"Puts extra hair on it," Frank said.

"It's a long fucker," Virgie said.

Frank began clapping. Jocelyn, Bruce Richmond, Bonnie and I followed, weakly. Virgie Lowe also clapped and nodded. She was attractive, I thought, blondish brown hair and a heart-shaped face. But you could tell she was no spring chicken. I figured she had to be almost twice the age of the heroine in the story, maybe more. In any case, there was something hard about her, particularly her eyes that looked like they'd seen it all.

Virgie Lowe then announced that she was used to more lavish productions than this appeared to be.

"Jesus, Frank," she added, "Can't you afford a goddamn table. I mean in the old days we at least had a real table for pre-production readings."

Frank rolled his eyes. Jocelyn sent a cloud of smoke from her cigar toward Virgie.

"Sweet, baby," she said. "You mean we're not up to your standards?"

Virgie gave Jocelyn a sardonic grin and stuck up her middle finger.

"Let's knock off the nonsense. I want to see every cent on the screen," Frank said and looked at Virgie. "Movie goers don't give a shit about a table."

Virgie, ignoring Frank, looking bored and checking her fingernails said, "Charming as always, Jocelyn. "Why don't you shove that nasty cigar you keep sucking on up your fat ass, or better yet, up that thing you call a twat. Probably the closest thing to a cock you've had in a decade or two."

Jocelyn started across the table at her but stopped when Frank hit the table with his fist and this time yelled at the two of them to knock it off. Bruce Richmond leaned over to me and whispered that bad blood between Jocelyn and Virgie went way back. Suddenly Boyd stood, looking a little wobbly. He puffed on his cigarette and looked down the table at Frank.

"What're you doing, Boyd?" Frank said. "Sit down."

"I'm not sitting down," Boyd said in a raspy voice, "until you assure me that there's money. I heard you didn't have the bankroll to make this flick. I ain't wasting my time."

"Money's on tap," Fat Eyes said. "I can vouch for that. A secret investor has filled the gap. Am I right, Frank? Two hundred big ones."

Frank nodded. Boyd seemed to think this over and then sat back down. Bonnie Robertson who'd heard about the anonymous investor whispered to me she'd heard it was mob money.

I listened as the conversation got around to casting. Who would play Star-Dancer, the avenger for hire? Should he be an unknown or an established actor?

"I would think an unknown, someone hungry who can give a good imitation of an actor," Boyd Imwald said. "Cost less."

"Half the parking lot attendants in this town could fit that bill," Virgie Lowe said. "I wonder if there's somewhere in the script where he could throw a spear. I mean, he uses a cross-bow. A spear would be cool, don't you think?"

There was no hint of a joke in her tone or demeanor. Everyone looked at her as if they thought she had derailed. Boyd looked up at her.

"You got a thing for spears?" He said.

Virgie Lowe looked at Boyd with contempt, then grinned.

"Here's your spear, Boyd," Virgie Lowe said and thrust up her middle finger.

"You're a class act," Boyd said. "Now can we start going through the script?"

A couple of nights later, I had a very strange conversation with Jenny. I called her just to say hello and tell her the progress and the new title of the story. She did not sound like herself. At first she said she was glad and that to her it meant I would soon come back home. I said it might be some time yet. She then accused me of never wanting to come back to her and that I sounded different. Her voice turned dreamy at that point and she talked about moving to Africa and become a bush pilot. Then with a burst of excitement she told me about an older man from Chicago who wanted to take her to the Caribbean. "It was nice talking to you, Tuckie," she said and hung up.

I called home. Zona answered. She told me she had not talked to Jenny but had heard that Jenny was telling people she had a secret plan for getting me back home. Zona also reported that Royce had had a bout with pneumonia but was okay now, and that the sheriff had been around a couple of times to ask more questions about Adele.

"I think he just wanted to show us that he was still working the case," Zona said. "I don't think they're getting anywhere."

The next time we met at Starburst/Meade, Boyd Imwald looked around the table, sipped his coffee, which he spiked with Old Kentucky, lit a cigarette, and eyeballed everyone then decreed that while he was director he was to be considered God. "Anyone not get that concept?"

Everyone stared. Virgie Lowe said under her breath, "He's in his petty tyrant mode."

Boyd looked at her.

"You say something, Virgie?"

"Not me, Boyd. Heavens no!"

Fat Eyes cleared his throat.

"Does this mean we have to genuflect when we come to the table?" He asked.

Boyd took a deep breath, which for him was a struggle. You could hear the gurgling in his chest.

"Frank, what the hell is this sawed-off weasel and the floozy doing here anyway?" He said.

Frank put up his hands in a gesture of surrender and explained that Mr. Zeppelin had a stake in the project. Boyd made no secret of his displeasure with that explanation.

After everyone got their coffee, we sat silently staring at the pages of the script which Jocelyn had mimeographed. Suddenly, Boyd Imwald threw his script down on the table in front of him.

"Now tell me again who wrote this piece of shit?" he said as he went from face to face at the table, stopping at me.

"You wrote this garbage. Right?"

"Yes, sir," I said.

"He's hot," Frank interjected and quickly explained that I was the one who recently made the headlines after being kidnapped by some "crazy assed cult."

"You're shitting me," Boyd Imwald said. "Well, all right, then, we're gonna make some new words, page by page. We'll wade through the muck to the end and god knows what we'll find waiting there for us. Bonnie, you got your blue pencil ready?"

Bonnie nodded. Virgie then said she'd like to see her character fleshed out more and that the rape scene needed work. Boyd just glowered at her and ignored Bambi when she asked about her part. Over the next week the script must have been rewritten about thirty times. I lost count. Everyone had an idea even the janitor, a young black man named Roger who came in once a week to sweep up. He said he was an aspiring screen writer and asked if he could say something, confessing that he had read a copy of the script he'd found in the trash. His suggestion was that the heroine be trained by the half-breed Indian Star Dancer to become the avenger herself, infiltrating the lives of her attackers and taking them down one by one.

"Best idea I've heard yet," Boyd said. "She transforms from an innocent young bride who is raped after her husband is murdered to the Cobra Woman, an angel of death. Good stuff."

It was hard for me to believe, but I spent the next two weeks at Boyd Imwald's side at his invitation. "From now on you call me Boyd," he said. I think he liked that I asked him how he got started. He told me he began as a carpenter and grip back around 1910 when he was nineteen years old. He eventually became an assistant director of westerns at the old Republic Studio. "We had three to six day shooting schedules in those days," he said. "The trick is to create your own signature, your own stamp," he told me and grinned. "Mine's low, but it's mine. Once you've got that no one can take that away from you." He also taught me that movies are never, or rarely, shot in sequence. That sometimes the last scene is shot first, that it's all budget, logistics and scheduling.

I watched as Boyd worked out scenes on a sketch pad, drawing action frames and noting the kinds of shots and angles that best dramatized each individual scene, a master shot (MS), wide shot (WS), point of view shot (POV), and MOS shots, etc.

"What's MOS?" I said.

"Mit Out Sound," Boyd said. When I looked puzzled he explained that a famous German director could never pronounce the W in with. It always came out M and thus, part of the language.

Open auditions were announced in the trades and actors, men and women of all sizes and shapes came in droves. Some camped out in front of the door in the early morning hours, and by noon there was a line around the block. They came from far and wide carrying their resumes and photos. One male actor even came from Mexico City, where he was visiting. Mark Horgan showed up. I told Boyd he was someone I knew and had promised a part. Boyd told me not to talk to actors. "They're sycophants, bugs that want to get under your skin, looking for a line of dialogue as if it were the fucking Holy Grail. However, as it turned out, he thought Mark had the right look and cast him as one of the attackers. I didn't say anything about his singing.

Around three in the afternoon on the second day Bull showed up. No longer in his uniform he looked shrunken, defeated. He had no picture, nor even a resume. Only that his girlfriend thought he should try out. I was able to talk Boyd into casting him in some very small part. Bull almost cried when I told him he was in. He told me Zoltan was no longer in custody and back at the Fourth Way Farm, a martyr to his followers. Bull also said the authorities still weren't sure what plants were in the hot-houses. "Zoltan said only that they were very special, exotic hybrids that would someday change the world."

For four days the actors filed in and presented themselves. Some of them had experience, some had just finished acting school. They would say a few words about themselves, whether or not they were represented, and if they belonged to the Screen Actors Guild or the Screen Extra's Guild. All of them agreed they would work for scale. I didn't know what that was. Boyd explained it to me. The last one to arrive was Iris Madigan. Boyd was happy to see her, apparently an old friend. He immediately signed her up to play one of the wives of the attackers. It was about this time, with everyone standing around, that we heard from Gertrude.

"Frank fucks frogs," the mynah bird said.

After a few giggles a hush came over the room as if waiting for another declaration from Gertrude. It didn't' come.

I was still working evenings at the Hamburger Palace. A few nights later, the woman FBI agent who'd called herself Beth showed up. She sat by herself in a booth and ordered a steak. I watched her from behind the counter. After she finished eating, she ordered coffee and motioned for me to join her with a nod of her head. I did not want to have anything to do with her, but my curiosity got the better of me. I took my break. She smiled at me from across the table, a very warm smile as if we were old friends meeting for the first time in years.

"Hello, Wichita Kid," she said.

"What's your name again?" I said. "Your real name."

She lit a cigarette and sipped on her coffee, eyeing me over the rim of her cup.

"Dorothy," she said. "Dorothy Stoner."

I nodded and fired a smoke.

"How you doing, Tuckie?" She asked.

"What do you want?"

She looked out the window as if thinking about what she wanted to say. She looked back at me and gave a short laugh.

"Can you believe that Zoltan was under a contract with the...well it hasn't been disclosed yet but we in the Bureau think the CIA. They do a lot of covert experimentation using contractors. I worked undercover for close to six months at the Fourth Way Farm, based on a tip that he was operating a communist cell. I mean, Jesus."

"What would the CIA want with hallucinogenic stuff?"

Dorothy shook her head and rolled her eyes heavenward.

"I read that he was released with no charges," I said.

She put out her cigarette.

"You doing anything later?" She said. "I'd like to see you, maybe go have a drink."

I looked over to see Chick eyeing me from the kitchen doorway. It was his way of saying, don't take too long.

"Why?" I said.

"I heard you're going to make a movie," she said. "Anyway I just thought it would be nice to clean things up a little. When we, you know, slept together in that tent I...I wasn't faking it."

I shrugged and then told her that someone was picking me up. She said she understood.

After we were silent for a few moments, Dorothy told me she was being reassigned to another city and wanted to warn me about Frank Meade. She stood to go, turned to me and said, "He's mixed up with some very bad people. Be careful."

Chapter 39

———

Boyd Imwald was shrewd, I'll give him that. All the actors hired were given a copy of the shooting script and ordered in a shrill voice, like a knife cutting through the room, to memorize their lines before going on location. Boyd sounded more like a dictator ready to order executions than a film director. One of the actors in the back of the room began laughing loudly.

"Oh, sure, yes sir," the actor said mockingly, snickering and saluting. He was a young man in his twenties. All eyes were on him. "I mean God has spoken."

"You back there, smart ass!" Boyd barked. "Get your face out of here. You don't work here any more."

The actor protested weakly saying he was just kidding and sorry and really needed the job because he had a family to feed. Boyd was unimpressed. The young man left in tears. Later, when I mentioned to Boyd that the actor might really have needed the job Boyd did something he almost never did, he laughed.

"One thing you have to learn about actors, besides what I already told you about their low status in the hierarchy of homo-sapiens. Like dogs you have to condition them right from the start or you won't have control later."

I must have looked puzzled. Boyd motioned me closer.

"That young man I fired?" Boyd whispered. "If truth be told, he's my sister's nephew and was working for me when he shot off his mouth. A little show for the troops. Now that's between us. Consider it part of your education."

I just stared at Boyd for a long moment.

"Right" I said.

Virgie Lowe brought a young man with her who looked very young, no more than eighteen. She introduced him as her personal assistant. His name was Harlan. He didn't say much but grinned a lot and looked very pretty. When Virgie wanted a glass of water or a cup of tea he hopped-to like his life depended on it. Everyone watched with interest.

"Where'd you find that one?" Boyd said. "Last I heard, statutory rape is still a crime."

Virgie glared at him, her eyes narrowed into two dark slashes so that you couldn't see them through the mascara.

"Why don't you fuck off, you flea-bitten old bastard," she said. "Without me you don't have shit for a movie."

Boyd ignored her and went back to marking up the last version of the script. Suddenly Mark Horgan, who'd been standing off to the side with some of the other actors stepped forward, script in hand and asked where in the story was he going to sing.

"This ain't no musical," Jocelyn said, which got a laugh from the crowd.

Mark glanced at her, his heavy face getting a little red.

"I studied opera," he said, his tone very serious. "I was told I could sing, My mother expects me to sing.."

"Your mother? Jesus. Who told you that?" Jocelyn said.

Boyd started hacking at that moment and left the room. Mark then looked at me. I shrugged. When Boyd returned, he told Jocelyn to give everyone the shooting schedule.

At that point I couldn't begin to figure the devils we'd encounter during the filming of Cobra Woman/Prairie Wolves, nor the unforeseen turn of events that would change everything.

Filming began in a small borrowed house in the San Fernando Valley. It took most of the day. There was a short dialogue scene between

Virgie's character and an actor named Ralph who was playing her husband. He was supposed to look a few years older, but in fact looked many years younger, a difference that leaped off the screen at daily rushes. Virgie wanted to fire the makeup girl. Boyd said he thought she was performing miracles as it was. Virgie threw up her hands and excused herself to go to the ladies room.

"Miss Lowe needs her personal makeup person," Harlan said. "She's a star."

Boyd looked at him.

"Son, are you fucking that old lady?" He said. "Or is she just blowing you?"

"Sir?"

"Keep your mouth shut," Boyd said.

Harlan went and stood guard outside the bathroom door.

The next day we moved out to an area near Victorville in the Mohave Desert. The night before, Bruce Richmond said the photographer hired to take publicity stills had called to say he was sick. A replacement was needed immediately. I told them about Maggie. Bruce and Boyd shrugged. She was put on the payroll at $25 a day as the production photographer. I'd never seen Maggie so excited. She grabbed me and kissed me like there was no tomorrow. And she didn't mind taking her car for the sixty-five mile drive from the Marcuse house.

It was cold out on the desert in those early morning hours. The air was crisp and smelled newborn with the thin scent of sage. Bruce Richmond made sure hot coffee and pastries awaited the cast and crew upon arrival to kick-start the day's work. The location was off a dirt road a few miles from the highway. By mid-morning everyone was sweating as equipment was set up. By late afternoon our faces were burnished by an unforgiving sun. Some of the crew had stripped down to just wearing shorts and broad-brimmed safari hats. A set designer was hired for the day to create a camp site where the rape and murder scene was to take place. Shooting didn't begin until dusk when the sun had sunk below the mountains and shadows created the illusion of night. A portable generator powered the lights. By midnight the cold had returned just as filming was completed. Harlan was quick to wrap a blanket around Virgie who had complained all evening about having to be out in this godforsaken wilderness half naked.

Boyd told me to write a new scene to be shot the next day at an ancient inn out on Old Mojave Road. It was called the Kit Carson Trail House which had been built around the turn of the century as a stopover for travelers and traders heading west. The road was not much more than a wide dirt path surrounded by cactus and desert willows. The Trail House was in a remote location about ten miles from where the camp scene was shot. This is where the newlyweds first encounter the four men who later attack them. Rather than drive back to the city, Maggie and I slept in her car. The next morning we drove to the Trail House. I got some coffee and went into the rented trailer which served as the production office and began working on the new scene on lined yellow paper. Boyd wanted something that would foreshadow trouble ahead. I wasn't sure if I could even do it. I closed my eyes and in the theater behind them, I raced back to recapture the movies I'd seen growing up and remembered specific scenes that I tried to emulate. Meanwhile Boyd was shooting a scene of Virgie and the male actor playing her husband in their station wagon. It was the opening scene. Later that day I gave two pages I'd written to Boyd.

"Good, you're getting the feel for this shit," Boyd said after reading the pages. "You've plugged some tension into this fucker."

Boyd told me Virgie was demanding script changes, soft-focus lenses, and new camera angles that would be more flattering. Lazlo, the director of photography was exasperated with the numerous holdups she was causing and threatened to quit. She blew up at Maggie for taking a candid picture of her before her make-up and wig were on. "Get out of here you little cunt!" She screamed. Maggie shrugged and backed away.

That night Frank showed up. I overheard Boyd tell him that Virgie's constant outbursts and demands, which had already cost the company in lost time and money, were in danger of bankrupting the production.

Frank's response was, "Don't worry about it." He then sat down with Jocelyn in the trailer and signed checks.

One day after, a disastrous day of shooting, I wondered aloud why Boyd put up with Virgie. Bonnie Robertson overheard me and told me Virgie and Boyd had once been lovers and the rumor was she was holding something over him. It was a dark secret whispered about in cafes around the lower depths of the movie colony for years. Bonnie said the story was that Boyd had killed a man one night who he caught in a motel with Virgie. The room was under the man's name and no one saw either Virgie or Boyd go into or out of the room. It was chalked up as a robbery. No charges were ever brought.

"This of course is strictly entre nous," Bonnie said, grinning. She added "between us."

As days wore on, the cast and crew looked to me bedraggled and anxious for the whole thing to be over soon. At night a lot of beer was consumed. An antique 35 millimeter projector had been set up in the bar of the hotel we were staying in. We all sat and watched rushes that usually arrived back from L.A. by eight. Watching the raw scenes filmed that day made me squirm as some of the hardened crew members gave cat calls. I would nervously fire up a cigarette and grimace. This one night Boyd was sitting next to me. He said out of the corner of his mouth: "I'm beginning to feel like Sisyphus."

"Who?" I said.

He just glanced at me and shook his head.

During the day there was no let-up of the blistering heat. The catered food was barely edible and toilet facilities were primitive.

Maggie, in jeans and light checkered shirt was buoyant, constantly snapping pictures. At the end of the day, she raced back to the Marcuse house and her darkroom. After developing the film and making prints with her enlarger she would race back to the location with her days output. Even Mark was impressed with her work and the pictures she'd taken of him.

"I'm beginning to like that girl," he said over a beer with me. "She makes me look like a heavy, which I am in this little story of yours. But, I like the look. My mother probably won't approve."

Two weeks into filming The Prairie Wolves, Boyd's hacking cough went silent. Boyd died in the middle of filming the final desert scene in the Kit Carson Trail House.

Here's what happened. During a lunch break Boyd carried his shabby-looking three-ring binder with the shooting script and his notes and disappeared into the trailer. After lunch everyone gathered in the main room of the Trail House to begin setting up for shooting the scene which Boyd had blocked out earlier. He'd had Bruce, the assistant director chalk the marks on the wooden floor where the actors would stand. Lazlo took light readings while his assistant loaded the camera and then measured the distance between the camera lens and the marks. Windows had been covered outside. It was to be a "day for night" scene.

When Boyd had not shown after a half hour into the schedule, Bruce went and knocked on the trailer door. No answer. The door was locked. He thought maybe Boyd had fallen asleep. Bruce and the gaffer got a crowbar and pried the door open. They found Boyd stretched out on the bed in the back. His eyes were open. I went in and after them and knelt down by the bed and closed Boyd's eyes. I calculated that he'd been gone for half an hour to forty minutes, explaining that I had worked in my father's mortuary.

"He just turned sixty six," Bruce said, a tear rolling down his cheek. "He was a great man."

Frank arrived with Fat Eyes just as an ambulance was taking Boyd's body away. The medics said it looked like a massive heart attack. The county coroner would make the determination.

"Sheeee-it," Frank screamed when he heard the news. "This is costing money, all these people standing around with their thumbs up their asses."

Frank asked Bruce to take over temporarily until a new director could be found.

"How about a little respect for the dead," Bonnie said. "Want to say a few words?"

"Fuck the dead," Frank said, "the living are still stuck with the goddamn bills. So, who's going to direct this cocksucker?"

"I'm strictly an AD," Bruce said. "I don't want to direct."

"Jesus," Frank said. "I thought all AD's wanted to be directors when they grew up."

Bruce shrugged.

"Guess I haven't grown up," he said.

Frank threw up his hands.

"I have to get back to L.A. and then I'll be out of town for a few days."

Bruce cleared his throat.

"If I could say something," he began as Frank stared at him with suspicion. "Boyd told me he'd taught Tuckie here a lot in the last few weeks and said he'd probably be good director some day, a natural."

Frank scoffed and looked over at me.

"Yeah, in about a hundred years," he said.

Bonnie Robertson remarked that what Bruce suggested made sense. "No one knows this movie better than Tuckie."

Frank scanned the room.

"Say, where's that cunt, Virgie?"

"She's upstairs taking a nap with her assistant...Harlan," Bruce said. "I was supposed to call her when Boyd was ready."

Frank was silent for a few tense moments then motioned for me and Lazlo to follow him. We went into the trailer and closed the door. It stank of beer and stale cigarettes and body odor. Frank lit a cigarette and wiped the sweat from his brow with his handkerchief. He sat down at the tiny Formica table and seemed to be pondering the options. He looked at Lazlo.

"I don't think we can get a director on such short notice, particularly one who'd work for deferred compensation and maybe a couple of points."

Lazlo grunted his agreement. Frank outlined the choices: say a prayer for Boyd and shut down the production, cut the company's losses and return what's left to investors, or…" he stopped and looked at me. "Or go with a new director. Are you that director, Tuckie? Can you handle it?"

"I…I don't know," I stammered.

Frank looked around and shook his head. He put out his cigarette.

"What a shit hole," he said aloud more to himself than to us. "Lazlo, can you help with the setups and technical shit?" Lazlo nodded. Frank said to me, "What it will take is you taking charge, like you're the goddamned King, or as Boyd put it, God himself."

I pushed my hat back on my forehead and fired up a smoke, trying to go through in my head what I'd learned as if flipping through filing cards, each with a notation. Then for a split moment, I was the Wichita Kid, gun in hand riding across the plains.

"I'm your director," I said in the strongest voice I could muster to mask my terror.

Lazlo patted me on the back and grinned. Frank looked at me with a surprised expression.

"Good," he said. "Bone up. "You've got half an hour to prepare. Every minute costs mucho bucks. Don't forget that. One take a shot. That's the goal."

"Don't worry," Lazlo said to me in his thick accent. "We'll make it work. We'll make a good picture."

Chapter 40

———

Back inside the Kit Carson Trail House, Frank grabbed a bullhorn and announced the decision that from that moment on, Mr. Charles Kendall would be the director of Cobra Woman/Prairie Wolves. I felt a strange kind of tingling sensation course through me. As a symbol of support, Lazlo hung Boyd's View Finder around my neck. Everyone just stood there in stunned silence. I could just imagine folks asking each other if this was a joke. Bonnie Robertson began clapping. After a moment everyone else joined in and wished me luck. Frank put down the bullhorn, shook my hand and left. Fat Eyes, who'd been standing off to the side. came up to me and whispered in my ear that he hoped I knew what the fuck I was doing.

"Or at least act like you do," he said. "Power is as power assumed."

Fat Eyes followed Frank out. It was the first time I'd ever...no the second time I'd ever seen him without Bambi trailing. The first time was in that bar my first night in L.A. which seemed like a thousand years ago. As I watched them leave I had a terrible sinking feeling, the trepidation that I now had the weight of the production on me. I looked around the room. Everyone was staring at me, watching, judging, waiting, waiting for something to happen, for me to stumble.

It was late afternoon. I told Bruce to continue the break. I then went back to the trailer, which in a way felt a little ghoulish as I went through Boyd's notes for the next scene. Several of the working script pages were dog-eared, coffee stained and filled with chicken-scratch notes in the margins, almost impossible to decipher. The only piece of luck was that it was Friday and there would be a break during the weekend. The next scene called for Virgie's character to be asked to dance by one of the scary men, played by Mark Horgan, who later attacks her and her husband at their campsite. A jukebox would provide the background music. I didn't need Boyd's notes. I knew this scene.

Before leaving the trailer and rejoining the production, I stood in front of a full length mirror attached to the door of the tiny head. I took my hat off and pushed some sweat-drenched strands of hair back from my forehead. As I stood there I thought I saw something different, a look, a nuance of expression staring back at me, eyes a little narrower, a slight change in the curve of my mouth that suggested…what? The terror I had felt earlier had ebbed. A new Tuckie had moved in to take over with a steely sense of purpose. "Power is as power assumed," I said aloud. Then I practiced saying "Action!" for a few seconds.

I stepped out of the trailer into the blazing desert heat. It was late afternoon and still had to be over a hundred degrees. I walked to the Trail House. Inside everyone was milling about. Some members of the crew were playing cards and drinking beer. I nodded to Bruce who picked up his bullhorn and yelled for everyone that it was time to go to work. He told actors to find their marks. He sent Jake, the one they called the "Best Boy," to go and fetch Virgie who apparently had locked herself in an upstairs room to sleep off a hangover from some heavy drinking the night before. Jake came down and threw up his hands. It was another half hour before Virgie came down the stairs, blurry-eyed and disheveled. Harlan followed like a puppy dog licking at her heels.

Virgie looked around and spotted me with Boyd's viewfinder hanging around my neck. I was looking at her, but talking to Lazlo out of the corner of my mouth.

"What's going on?" Virgie said. "Where's Boyd?"

A hush came over the room. Maggie, who'd been taking random shots of the set stopped and looked at me. I eased myself down in the director's chair.

"Well, what's happening here?" Virgie demanded, looking around the room at blank faces. "Harlan, get me an iced coffee."

Harlan scurried to a room in back where supplies were being kept. Lazlo approached Virgie and put an arm around her shoulder. Virgie looked at him. "What the hell are you doing?"

"I'm afraid there's bad news," he said. "Boyd's no longer with us."

"What?" Virgie said, pushing Lazlo away. "What do you mean?"

Lazlo explained that Boyd had died a few hours before and has been taken away. Virgie just stared at him in disbelief.

"I don't believe this," she said, then looked at me.

"What's he doing wearing Boyd's viewfinder?"

Harlan returned with the iced coffee and handed it to Virgie. She took a sip, continuing to eye me over the rim of the glass.

"Tuckie's our new director," Lazlo said.

Virgie laughed and began pacing around the open space of the room, taking short sips of her drink.

"Now, let me get this straight," she began. "You mean Boyd croaks and you put this corn-fed hayseed in charge? In a pig's ass."

"That's the story, sweet stuff," Jocelyn said. "Frank's orders."

"This is really beautiful," Virgie said, then screamed at the top of her lungs, "bullshit!"

I got up and moved out in front near where the camera was positioned.

"We're set up to shoot the scene, Miss Lowe," I said trying to sound respectful but business-like. "It's getting late. We've already lost a lot of time. Could you get made up and then stand on your mark?"

Virgie shook her head and laughed which sounded almost maniacal.

"I'm not shooting any goddamned scene until we get a director I can work with. No offense...what's your name...Tuckie. I don't work with amateurs. I don't know what got into Frank." She looked around at the crew, as if looking for confirmation. "He must have been drunk."

All eyes were on me. I repeated what I'd said in the exact same tone and added that we have other setups to complete.

"We can sit here until the fuckin' world freezes over and pigs fly as far as I'm concerned," Virgie said.

I looked at my watch and stepped forward. I noticed Mark sitting on a stool at the bar grinning at me as if to say, "What are you going to do now?"

"Is that it, Miss Lowe?" I said.

"You understand English?" she snapped. "Yeah."

I nodded and wiped beads of sweat off my brow with the back of my hand. It was clearly my move. I could try and reason with her I thought, but in the end it wasn't going to work. In the back of my head I also thought this might be an opportunity. I turned to Bruce Richardson and told him to shut it down and we would reschedule the scene for Tuesday.

Virgie who was whispering to Harlan looked at me with hard eyes.

"I don't think you understand, Mister," she said. "This production doesn't do shit on Tuesday or any other day until I get someone here who knows what they're doing. Got that, Buster?"

I smiled at Virgie. She rolled her eyes.

"You don't have to be here," I said. "Like you said, that's it."

At that moment silence filled the room and no one moved as the tension had reached a crescendo. Like an angel on my shoulder I could almost hear the Wichita Kid whispering in my ear that this was the moment of truth. In as strong a voice as I could muster I told Virgie, whom Fat Eyes called the queen of low budget movies, that she was no longer needed or wanted. As of that moment she was terminated. Out of the corner of my eye I could see Jocelyn grinning at me and giving a thumbs-up. As for Virgie, the dark circles under her eyes and the lines in her face had suddenly magnified. Color had drained from her cheeks, giving her an ashen look, accentuated, I thought, by her ruby red lipstick.

"Are you saying I'm fired?" Virgie said. "You pipsqueak, without me there is no picture. Investors will head for the nearest exit when they hear about this. So, fuck off!"

She threw the mug of what was left of her iced coffee across the room, just missing Bonnie Robertson. The glass shattered and what was left of the coffee sprayed against the wall. Her one person entourage, Harlan, followed her as she stomped out to her 1950 Lincoln Continental. With Harlan at the wheel and Virgie sitting in the back, the car peeled out in a cloud of dust.

Later when the crew was packing up the equipment Lazlo told me he thought getting rid of Virgie was good, and showed that I was in charge, but added that she could be trouble. "She felt humiliated, so I'm certain we have not heard the last of her," he said, "and what about a replacement?" He suggested a couple of young actresses he knew but wasn't sure of their availability. I did not say it but I thought by firing her she might turn around, come back and be a little more cooperative. She did not. At this point I felt like I was sinking into quicksand with no branch to hang onto. For a moment I watched Maggie in her sweat-stained T-shirt and jeans, still snapping pictures.

Mark and I sat at a table in the back of the Trail House with a couple of Cokes. He told me he overheard some of the actors and crew members taking bets on whether or not Cobra Woman/ Prairie Wolves would ever see the light of day. He quoted one of the male extras who said: "This is a stiff if I've ever seen one." Mark asked me what I was going to do. I confessed that I did not know. But there was something, an idea in a dark corner of my mind that I couldn't quite grasp. Mark then brought up the subject of his singing and wondered where in the story he could perform? He also grumbled that he had to play a heavy and wondered if a bad guy would sing. I told him I thought the singing would balance his character. In opera bad guys sang didn't they? I'd find a spot. Meanwhile, Jocelyn, acting as paymaster set up a table and handed out checks for the week's work, telling everyone to report back on Tuesday.

I rode back to the city with Maggie. It was a cool, clear evening, a welcome relief after the Mojave. We stopped at the Hamburger Palace and took the only booth left. Chick came over and sat with us. I gave him a brief rundown of the day's events.

"Sounds like you better find yourself a heroine before Tuesday," Chick said shaking his head sympathetically. He went back to work. We ordered cheeseburgers, fries and coffee.

"What do you think?" I said to Maggie.

She lit a cigarette and managed a very nice smoke ring which floated out toward the isle.

"Weird," she said. "Frankly I think it's a damn miracle that it's come this far. I mean when I first met you and you were spouting off about your career and all, I thought it was bullshit and would never come to anything. I mean, it's not big time or anything. In fact it's kind of the slums, but it's something. I don't know what you're going to do, but I have this feeling down in my crotch that you're going to pull it off somehow. I mean there's this something in you…"

"What?" I said.

"Like when you went to Margo Benson's funeral…crazy as shit, not something a normal person would have done. Yeah, it's because you're kind of…well….crazy I guess."

I just looked at Maggie with a blank face then feigned madness, raising my hands like talons ready to strike. She laughed and I grinned.

"Your crotch?" I said.

Maggie giggled.

"You got a better place?"

Back at the Marcuse house we slept in the master bedroom upstairs. Maggie said the bed was a classic four-poster. At least Maggie had cleared out the cobwebs. But it was still a dark shadowy house. It all seemed creepy to me. Somehow I managed to sleep. At about three in the morning I awakened from a dream, a very vivid dream. Awake, it was hard to pull the fragmented images together into a cohesive picture, like trying to see the patterns of a kaleidoscope.

I was driving along an unfamiliar country road and someone was with me. I remembered that I looked over and saw a girl's profile, but I didn't recognize her. There was something mysterious about the girl. Her

340

face was hard to see, as if there was a haziness separating us in the car. Drifting back into the gray liquid of the dream it hit me. It was a sign. I jumped out of bed and scrambled around in the dark looking for my pants which I found on the floor at the foot of the bed. My wallet. I pulled it out of my pants and went downstairs where I turned on a small lamp next to the phone. Inside the wallet, after some fumbling I found what I was looking for, a piece of paper with a phone number on it.

"Hot damn!" I said excitedly to myself. "Hot damn!"

I phoned Mark Horgan who sleepily answered after seven or eight rings.

"Jesus," Mark said. "What time is it?"

"I need you to do something," I said. "Get a pencil and write this phone number down."

"It's after three in the goddamned morning," he said.

"What difference does that make?" I said. "It's for the cause."

Silence for a long beat.

"Oh?" Mark said. "What's the cause?"

"Your mother getting to see you sing in a movie," I said. "That cause. All those lessons paying off at last."

Mark coughed into the phone. His mother apparently awakened by the phone came into his room and asked who it was. He put his hand over the phone. Muffled I hear him tell her it was okay. Then back to me.

"I'm coming to know you, Kendall, and the signs are not good," Mark said. "Okay what's the number and whose is it?"

I gave Mark Silky's phone number and asked him if he could find an address. Mark sighed heavily into the phone and said he'd call me back when he had something. I fixed some coffee and began looking through the script for Cobra Woman versus the Prairie Wolves in the Vortex of the Valley of Darkness and made some notes of my own. After a time I put my head down on the table and closed my eyes.

As first light began to peak through the windows the phone rang. It startled me. After shaking some of the sleep from my head I picked up the receiver. It was Mark. Through his contacts at the LAPD he'd obtained an

341

address. I wanted to go right away and had to talk Mark into picking me up. It was almost nine before Mark got there, over an hour since I'd talked to him. He told me his mother insisted on him eating some breakfast before he left: two eggs, potatoes, toast and coffee. I made a face but didn't tell Mark what I was thinking.

The address turned out to be number 207 in a run-down apartment building near Echo Park off of Alvarado. This was pretty close to skid row. Mark said it was one of those places where the toilets are always backed up and the cockroaches are as big as mice. When we were a block away, we stopped and I called the number from a phone booth. After several rings a woman answered, her voice thick and scratchy like she had sand in her throat. She said something undecipherable and the phone went dead. I could not tell for sure if the voice belonged to Silky.

In the entry hall of the building the 207 mailbox had the name M. Jones on it. The second floor hallway smelled of mildew combined with the unmistakable odor of something that had died.

Number 207 was at the far end of the hallway toward the back of the building. I put my ear to the door and listened while Mark stood to one side. A radio was playing inside. I knocked. No response. I knocked again, much harder this time. Muffled sounds came from inside, movement and voices. Finally a male voice from the other side of the door demanded to know who was there. I started to ask if Silky was there but remembered she was using another name.

"Is...is Delilah there?" I said.

Long silence.

"Who wants to know?"

"A friend," I said.

"She ain't got no friends," said the male voice. "Beat it."

I looked at Mark who raised his eyebrows. Mark leaned closer and whispered, "Talk money."

I nodded and said there was money owed to her. After a few moments the door opened a crack and a grizzled man with foul breath and bloodshot eyes peered out, a cigarette dangling out of the corner of his mouth. He looked to be about fifty. I tried to see around him. The man who was only wearing boxer shorts moved the door to close the gap.

"What the fuck do you want?" He said.

"I want to see Delilah," I said. "I have some money for her."

"Oh yeah! Give it to me. I'll see she gets it."

I shook my head.

"My boss says I have to give it to her in person."

"Boss?" The man said. "Who's your boss?"

"I can't tell you that," I said. "I'll just take the money back."

I started to turn away. The man shut the door, took the chain off and opened it again to let me in. The stench of the apartment almost made me puke. Mark moved in behind me from around the corner.

"It's like an oven in here," Mark said.

"What the hell is this?" The man said. "You the heat?"

Mark gently pushed the man aside and followed me over to a Murphy bed where a woman wearing only panties was sprawled face down across a stained mattress. Her very white body glistened with beads of sweat. Gobs of red hair fanned out, completely hiding her face. I didn't have to see her face. I knew that hair. I reached down and shook her by her shoulder. Silky moaned softly, lifted her head and tried to look around.

"What the... Jesus..." She mumbled and went into a fetal position.

"Hey," the man yelled. "That's my ole lady. If you ain't cops, give her the money and get out."

Mark turned and eyed the man with an ice cold stare. The man shrank back. I looked around, found a man's blue work shirt on the floor and put it over Silky. I pulled her up to a sitting position. She smelled like three-day old garbage, yet still held onto that angelic face of hers. The dissipation had not yet taken its toll. Mark found a pair of dirty tennis shoes that he slipped onto Silky's feet. As we guided her out, the man began screaming that his ole lady was being kidnapped. Suddenly the man produced a knife. He started to run at my back, the knife held high. Luckily Mark caught what was happening out of the corner of his eyes and shot a meaty fist into the man's side. The man doubled over in pain and was knocked half way across the room. He slumped down on the floor and began crying that we were taking his ole lady.

Down at the car Mark stopped me as I started to get Silky into the car.

"What the hell is this?" He said. "I mean what do you want with this piece of shit? She's totally out of it."

I ignored him and pushed Silky into the back seat.

"Isn't she the stripper from that club off Hollywood Boulevard?"

I nodded.

"I don't like having trash like that in my car," he said. "She's gonna stink it up."

We drove back to the Marcuse house in silence. Mark helped me get Silky to the door. I said I would take it from there. Mark gave me a hard look, turned and left. I yelled after him that I'd see him on Tuesday. He waived me off. Inside Maggie was sitting at the table in the kitchen having coffee and a cigarette. The radio was playing Patty Page singing the Tennessee Waltz.

"Who's the chick?" Maggie said eyeing a sad-looking Silky.

Silky raised her head up and squinting slowly eyeballed the room.

"Where am I?" She said and then her eyes closed and she collapsed in my arm.

Maggie stubbed out her cigarette.

"What's her story?" She said. "Why'd you bring her here?"

I tried to prop Silky up.

"Could you help me get her to the shower," I said.

Maggie held her nose and then reluctantly grabbed Silky on one side and we guided her to the nearest shower. Maggie took it from there. I went back to the kitchen and poured myself a cup of coffee. Maggie came back, got her camera and snapped off a few shots of the naked girl sitting on a stool in the tub, the water streaming down over her. Maggie said later the girl just sat there, eyes closed looking like she was in a dark place. Couldn't be more than nineteen or twenty. Maggie told me the girl looked familiar, certain that she had seen her before.

"The investor party," I said. "She jumped out of a cake."

Maggie just looked at me, a strange expression on her face.

Chapter 41

––––––––

S ilky slept in an adjoining bedroom. I sat in the room for a while to
keep an eye on her, smoking and reading Confidential magazine.
Maggie went out to get groceries. After a while I went back to the
master bedroom and took a nap. When I woke up, I checked in on Silky.
She was gone. I began running from room to room and finally found her
sitting on the floor in the middle of Grover Marcuse's studio. Silky, wearing a pair of shorts Maggie gave her and a T-shirt was looking around at
the various paintings, sketches and poster-sized photographs, some of
Maggie that filled every inch of wall space. By now the works were covered with dust.

She turned around and glanced at me, apparently sensing my presence.

"This is some shit," she said. "What is this place, a museum?"

I gave her a brief history of the house as told to me by Maggie, and
about Grover's father being a silent movie star, and about Grover's suicide.

"So, whose house is this now?"

I shrugged. Silky got to her feet and looked me up and down.

"You've gone through some changes since we first met at…what was
that place…?"

"The Sanitary Café," I said.

"Right," she said, "in the middle of nowhere."

I pulled out a smoke and fired it up, handed it to Silky, and then
fired up one for myself. She started to wander around and without looking

at me noted that my hair was longer and I didn't have that "just fell off the turnip truck" look she remembered. Silky began running a finger along some of Grover's pieces leaving a clean line in the dust. There were several oils of Maggie, nude in different poses. Some looked soft and winsome and others, pouty, and still others, hard and even angry looking. I kind of thought Grover had captured Maggie's many selves.

"That the girl who helped me in the shower?"

"Maggie," I said. "Yeah, she modeled for Grover."

"Got a body that won't quit," Silky said. "If I were butch I could go for her." She suddenly whirled on me. "So why'd you pull me out of that little hell hole? I have a vague memory of being with some loser there. I don't think I knew his name. He wanted to be my pimp. God, I must have been really stoned."

I sat on the corner of one of Grover's work tables and took a drag on my smoke while I considered how to answer.

"I want you to be in "Cobra Women versus the Prairie Wolves in the Vortex of the Valley of Darkness," I said.

"The what?" She said.

"My movie. It used to be called The Prairie Wolves, but the producer change it. You don't remember? You were there for the investor's meeting. You jumped out of a cake."

A long moment passed. Silky flicked some ashes from her cigarette on the floor and nodded.

"Oh, that," she said, pushing that thick red hair of hers back along her shoulders. "I had to fuck some old guy. Wait, you mean you want me to act in it?"

"Yeah."

"Act in a flick?" She said. "I never acted before, well if you don't count porn loops."

"No matter."

"Would I get paid?"

I nodded. She pursed her lips.

"So who do I have to blow?"

348

I just looked at her and shook my head.

"Okay," she said. "It can't be worse than turning tricks for fifteen bucks a throw... twenty for round the world."

Later I gave Silky a script to read with her part underlined in thick black ink. She sat in the kitchen with a strong cup of coffee Maggie had made, and began her journey through the pages. Sometimes she would look up and make a face like she was being tortured.

"Wow, this is a mucho role," she said. "I thought you were talking about some bit part, man."

"Just be natural," I said. "You're the star. You are seeking revenge for being raped by four men who also kill your husband while on a camping trip in the desert. You meet a mysterious man, kind of a wizard, named Star Dancer to help you. He, and this is new from my original story, through magic gives you the power to turn into a cobra at will to take your revenge."

"What kind of shit is that?" Silky said.

Tuesday morning we got up real early to head out to the desert and the Kit Carson Trail Inn to reshoot the scenes that had formerly been shot with Virgie. I put on my rumpled gray suit from the Salvation Army, white shirt and bow tie, and cowboy hat. Both Maggie and Silky screamed with laughter when they saw me. "I think the suit helps establish authority, don't you think?" I said. With that, Maggie got her camera and snapped off a few shots. I just stood there like some kind of ogre.

"You are crazy," she said. "It's the goddamned desert!"

Maggie drove. Silky sat in the back seat and mumbled her lines to herself. Once on the site, the wardrobe and makeup woman spent an hour transforming Silky. She brushed Silky's hair until it looked like strawberry blond silk, and then dressed her in a full cotton skirt and pink blouse. Silky was hardly recognizable. She looked like the all American girl. Meanwhile, after a few snickers about my outfit we set up for the first shot of the day.

I sensed skepticism among the cast and crew about Silky. When a couple of the actors on the set asked her what films she'd been in before, she blithely told them she had stared in such films as Beaver Heaven, Hot lips In The Valley, and her all time favorite, Kiss of the Cocksucker. The two male actors just stared at her. It was clear they were not sure if she was putting them on or not. Silky kept a straight face. Later one of the two actors came over and asked to speak to me privately just before the camera was ready to roll for the first shot of the day.

"Mr. Kendall, I'm kind of concerned about being in a movie with…" He started and looked over at Silky who was on her mark. "You know, a porno queen. I mean it could hurt my career."

"Can't say as I blame you," I said. "But, you got to start somewhere."

The actor just looked disgusted and walked away. Later Lazlo whispered to me that he wasn't sure how Silky would come off, noting that she was not a professional actress. On the other hand, he had to admit the camera liked her, she had the right look. We did not know what that meant until we saw the rushes the following night, our last night in the Trail House. Everyone was invited to watch. Hamburgers, baked beans, potato salad and a keg of beer were catered by Chick's Hamburger Palace. Chick himself delivered the goods in a pickup truck.

We sat and watched the rushes in stunned silence. The camera was more than okay with Silky, it was head over heals in love with her, according to Lazlo who was assessing every frame. Silky, who was sitting at the bar nursing a beer, would on occasion, squeal when she saw herself on the makeshift screen. "Who's that chick?"

After the showing, everyone spontaneously clapped. Lazlo and Bruce Richmond agreed that on screen, Silky projected a certain beauty combined with a shining innocence and freshness, and yet at the same time oozing sensuality, like a young Clara Bow. More importantly she was a natural actress. Even Bonnie Robertson noted that she thought Silky was wonderful, a great discovery.

"This girl has something," she said to me, "She's incandescent. Where did you ever find her?"

"Oh, just around," I said.

Two days later after re-shooting the campsite scenes we located to a house back in the San Fernando Valley. Just as equipment was being set up in front of the house, Virgie Lowe drove up in her Lincoln Continental, Harlan driving. There was someone else in the car also, a dark figure. Virgie waived as if she were acknowledging a group of fans, got out and asked everyone to stop what they were doing and gather around her. Everyone stopped and looked quizzically at each other and then at me. I had just come from the trailer and was standing behind some of the crew. Harlan stood a few feet behind his mistress. The other person in the car got out on the other side, came around and stood next to Virgie. He was a short heavyset man in his fifties. Virgie shook a few hands and announced that she was back to resume her role and that she had good news.

"This is George Evans," she said, putting a hand on the stocky man's shoulder. "Some of you may know him or of him. He will be the new director for the..." she turned around and motioned for Harlan to step closer. "What's the name of this thing?"

"I believe it's called Cobra Woman versus Wolves, or something like that," he said in a low voice.

"Right," she said, and named several low budget films George Evans had directed.

Virgie looked around, holding her smile, lots of teeth showing. No one moved.

"Well, come on people," she said. "Let's welcome George and get to work. I know you'll all love working with him."

At that point, Jocelyn stepped forward and took the always present cigar out of her mouth and spit a wad of tobacco juice at Virgie's feet.

"Does Frank know about this?" Jocelyn said.

"Of course," Virgie said. "He approved my choice. George has his full support to take over this little epic. Where's that fellow, what's his name, who was filling in? George will need the director's shooting script and production notes."

Jocelyn moved a step closer and told Virgie she thought it was bullshit and demanded to see something in writing from Frank. George Evans stared at the ground, his embarrassment obvious. I pushed my way to the front and asked Lazlo if we were ready to shoot the first scene. He nodded. Jocelyn moved back to where she had been standing before. I turned to Virgie.

"Would you mind moving across the street, Miss Lowe," I said. "We're trying to work here."

"I'm not going anywhere," Virgie said. "If anyone is taking a hike, it's you sweetie."

Virgie reached into her handbag and produced a folded piece of plain white paper. She unfolded it. It looked like it was hand-written from where I was standing. She began to read:

"Dear Company, I am pleased to announce that Miss Virgie Lowe and a new director, Mr. George Evans have agreed to return to complete the filming of 'Cobra Women versus the Prairie Wolves in the vortex of the Valley of Darkness' Please welcome them and give them your full cooperation. Miss Lowe is to resume her role in the film, thus reassuring our investors. Sincerely, Frank Meade, Executive Producer."

Jocelyn rolled her eyes as a murmur rippled through the crew. She marched up to Virgie.

"Let me see that," she said, snatched the memo from Virgie and silently read it.

"You see," Virgie said. "No Virgie, no movie. Right in the crapper."

"Right," Jocelyn said. "You have a nice way of putting things."

Bambi, who'd been in the house practicing her one line, came out just in time to hear the last of the memo being read. She said to no one in particular that she thought I was doing okay.

Virgie tried to snatch the note back, but Jocelyn held it out of reach.

"As Frank's right hand and assistant producer it's your responsibility to make all this go smoothly. I think George is ready to go to work now."

"Of course, Virgie," Jocelyn said. "Give me a moment. I need to do something."

All eyes were on Jocelyn as she made her way around the side of the house. A minute later she returned at a gallop carrying a garden hose which she pointed at Virgie and George Evans. Everyone quickly moved back, giving her a wide berth. Jocelyn opened fire with a heavy blast soaking Virgie and George Evans before they had a chance to react. They both turned and ran back to Virgie's car with Harlan trailing. Virgie jumped into the driver's seat.

"You fucking bitch," Virgie screamed out the window. "Your ass has had it!"

"Beat it, motherfuckers," Jocelyn yelled as she turned off the nozzle.

We all watched as Virgie drove down to the end of the street, did a u-turn and came back full speed and drove up on the lawn missing Jocelyn by a few inches. The Lincoln Continental careened into one of the large reflectors that had been set up, knocking it about fifteen feet. Virgie then tore down the street and disappeared around the next corner. The neighbors who had lined up along the sidewalk across the street began clapping.

"Jesus," Bonnie Robertson said. "They think it was all part of the movie."

Lazlo shook his head.

"She'll be back with reinforcements," he said. "She has a copy of the location schedule."

I looked at Lazlo and nodded.

"I've got an idea," I said.

Chapter 42

———

I t was simple. In front of everybody, I dramatically tore up the schedule and announced that we would tell everyone the new location the night before, and who would be needed.

"That should keep Miss Lowe guessing," Lazlo said. Jocelyn nodded and silently clapped.

"Do you think she has any spies who might keep her posted?" I said. Both Lazlo and Jocelyn shook their heads.

"Everyone hates her," Jocelyn said.

Bruce Richardson, on the other hand, was furious that anyone, particularly some "novice punk director" like me would dare tear up his well thought out and efficient schedule. He threatened to quit.

Bonnie Robertson, who was standing close by noted out of the side of her mouth that Bruce was a good AD but inflexible when dealing with bumps in the road. "He's also a classic anal retentive," she said to me. I wasn't sure what that meant but pretended I did. "Maybe you could sweeten the pot for him a little," she added.

Lazlo suggested I offer him an extra incentive. So, I told Bruce the production needed him and promised him a bonus when production wrapped, also that he was the only one who could solve the problem of rescheduling. Bruce scoffed at any notion that a bonus was possible, but agreed to stay on.

"No question that Virgie's a fruitcake," Bruce said. "But it's kinda like we're being held hostage."

The script called for one scene to take place in a roadside nightclub. Bruce found the perfect place in the valley. It was a small dingy club called "Lenny's Hot Spot." It was like an old time saloon with a bar that ran the length of the place and seated about sixty people at tables. There was a stage at the far end. Perfect. We began setting up in the afternoon. The owner, a burly man in his sixties named Jake was excited that a movie was going to be shot in his club and that he would get a hundred dollar location fee. But he refused to close the place down to his regular customers, most of whom show up just about every night.

The scene called for the four men, who had killed the heroine's husband and raped her, to bring their wives to dinner at the nightclub. Iris Madigan playing one of the wives looked glum. She cheered up when I told her I'd work in a line for her. While enjoying a carefree evening they are being watched from a table in the shadows by the heroine and her hired enforcer, Star Dancer. Everyone agreed that Silky made her character's transition from the innocent young bride to a woman seeking revenge and justice very believable. "The girl has talent," Lazlo remarked. Her quarries were unaware of being stalked by this young woman they left for dead two years before. Star Dancer has introduced her to the cult of the cobra, she is now Cobra Woman.

Mark Horgan playing one of the killers was continually after me to find a way to let him sing. In the old westerns bad guys didn't sing, only the heroes in the white hats, though the Wichita Kid never sang. I told Bonnie we needed a way to let Mark sing. She went and got a cup of coffee, then came back and told me she had an idea.

"Create an amateur talent night as part of the scene," she said. "It will be an added cost, but should be able to squeeze it in. See what Jocelyn says."

Jocelyn scowled when I told her the idea.

"Who gives a rats ass if this guy sings or not?" She said, but after some edgy discussion she finally threw up her hands and agreed to the extra setups. "I gotta tell ya, there's not much wiggle room here."

This would be Mark Horgan's big scene, as I had promised. Mark was happy now. His mother would see him sing. By the time we were ready to shoot the first scene, the club was full of Jake's regular customers, some of them on the rowdy side. Jake told folks as they came in that a movie was being shot and asked that they keep down the chatter. Bruce didn't like it that we didn't have full control over the place. Carlo the sound man said he was going to have trouble blocking ambient chatter during dialogue scenes. Lazlo shrugged it off and said we should consider Jake's regulars as extras. Jocelyn handed out release forms to everyone in the place and paid each one dollar. One chunky guy absolutely refused to sign a release and threatened a law suit if he ever saw his face on a screen. He and his girlfriend were guided by the owner to a table in the shadows. The girlfriend complained that she thought they were being treated like lepers and demanded that she be in the movie. The chunky boyfriend grabbed her by the arm and dragged her out of Lenny's Hot Spot. Jake followed them apologizing as they left.

By eight o'clock some of the customers were well on their way to drunken oblivion. Meanwhile a large bearded man with rolled up sleeves revealing tattoos of tigers on each arm accused Bruce of giving his ole lady the eye and demanded that he step outside. Bruce shook his head while the woman screamed at the bearded man that he was the biggest jerk-off she'd ever gone out with. Fat Eyes showed up with Bambi to be extras. Bambi had already had her one line in the film back at the Kit Carson Trail House.

There was a battered piano on the small stage. The owner's daughter agreed to accompany Mark when they were ready to shoot his singing scene. She said her father was Leonard Bartholomew and that Jake managed the place for him. She also said the clubs guitarist and base player would join in. Mark thought to bring his own sheet music.

"When I became a cop, my mother practically disowned me and told me I was a bad son," Mark said. "I told her I had to make a living. I had a wife and kid to support. Made no difference to mom. Why couldn't

I be like Mario Lanza, she would say. That could be me kissing Kathryn Grayson, she would say."

At around eleven o'clock Mark followed a woman from the audience who had volunteered to be one of the amateur performers. She was booed off stage half way through her song by the drunks. Mark then went on the stage and sang the drinking song from the Student Prince. His voice filled the room. Some of the crowd snickered. Mark had to sing the piece all the way through several times. Finally a grizzled man in a green T-shirt sitting up front began making loud noises and banging an empty bottle on the table.

"I didn't come here to listen to this opera shit," he said. "Let's get some country up there."

Mark stopped and looked at the man. Everyone was sure he was going to come down off the stage and smack the guy. But oddly enough some of the other hard-case customers told him to keep his trap shut. He sunk down in his chair and didn't make another sound. When Mark finished there was a smattering of applause. He took a bow.

Silky disappeared. One morning the following week I went to get her out of bed for the days shooting and discovered she was gone. We had only a few more days of filming her scenes which were crucial. Maggie, acting like the proprietress of an Inn had assigned Silky her old basement room. A search in every corner of the house proved fruitless.

"Girl's gone," Maggie said. "I guess we should have kept her on a shorter leash."

"Maybe she went for a walk," I said. "She'll come back."

Maggie laughed.

"You kidding?" She said. "She's gone, Tuck. I've seen her kind before, white trash without a lick of sense. Don't care about anything least of all herself. I will admit though, she looks good on screen. So what now? You can't finish the flick without her."

With Maggie driving we spent the next hour and a half searching the streets, back alleys, a few bars down the hill that were already open, and later the apartment near downtown where Mark and I had found her. No one answered. We showed people hanging around on the street out front an eight by ten glossy of Silky that Maggie had shot. Most just shook their heads. One guy said he remembered her from months back, if it was the same girl. I went to the nearest phone booth and called Jocelyn to delay production until the afternoon. I called Mark and told him about Silky. We met at the Hamburger Palace. Maggie, who was still a little leery of Mark, gave him a few prints of Silky. Mark gave them to his contacts at the LAPD and the county sheriff's office and asked that they be on the lookout for her.

Over the next few days we shot everything we could around scenes with Silky. Lazlo, Bruce and some of the others had other film jobs to go to with fast approaching start dates. It was a Thursday evening when we finished what we could. I had Jocelyn tell the cast and crew to take Friday off and report back on Monday. I noticed the actor playing Star Dancer taking swigs from a silver flask he carried around. It was clear he was feeling no pain when he stood up and yelled at everyone to pay attention.

"I heard some talk that our so-called star Silky has taken a hike," he said and looked at me. "True?"

"You're drunk," Jocelyn said. "Be here Monday, sober."

I was hoping that Silky would turn up over the next three days. But by Sunday night with no word from her or about her, it looked bad. Maggie just looked at me, fired up a smoke and shook her head.

"I hate to say it," she said, "but without your star Silky, Cobra/ Prairie Wolves is DOA."

It was one of those L.A. nights shrouded in a cold heavy mist that had suddenly rolled in from the north like a bad omen. To take my mind off the impending disaster I worked the counter at the Hamburger Palace, breathing in the smell of onions and burgers on the grill. It made me nostalgic for MARCO's back home. Chick yelled at me to move faster, commenting that this movie stuff had slowed me down.

Around two Monday morning my sleep was shattered by the harsh sound of the phone. I was afraid to answer and let it ring several times.

Finally I jumped up and staggered across the room and picked up the receiver.

"Who's this?" I said.

"Mark. I think they found that crazy-assed Silky."

I could feel my heart racing.

"Where?"

"She was arrested by a vice cop for soliciting," Mark said. "Down near Watts. Luckily one of the officers was someone I know. His partner had seen the picture of Silky and thought there was a resemblance. Anyway, the one I know told his sidekick to hold off on booking the woman until he was able to get a hold of me. So, we're meeting at an all night diner on South Vermont and we'll see. I figure you'll want to come."

"Yeah," I said.

I got dressed and went downstairs. As I passed the darkroom I heard a noise and knocked on the door. Maggie opened it. A red light was on inside.

"I couldn't sleep so I came down here to make some prints," she said. "Why are you up?"

I explained about Mark's call and that the police found someone who might be Silky.

"Great," Maggie said without much enthusiasm. "Maybe your flick is still alive after all."

"What's the matter?" I said.

Maggie rolled her eyes and started to close the door. I put my foot in the way. She looked at me with searching eyes.

"You in love with that chick or what?" She said.

"Where'd that come from?"

Maggie shrugged.

"I don't care. It's just that you seem awfully taken with her," she said. "I've seen how you look at her when you're directing her in a scene."

I shook my head.

"You want to go?"

"No," Maggie yelled. "I don't want to go."

I figured Maggie was going through one of her strange times which seem to come over her every so often. Marco used to say that when women got strange it usually meant they were on the rag. I was a teenager before I knew what that meant.

Outside it was almost pitch black. The early morning air smelled fresh and crisp. I walked down to the bottom of the driveway of the Marcuse house. Mark picked me up fifteen minutes later. He handed me a Styrofoam cup of hot coffee which tasted good, just the way I like it with cream and sugar. We were silent for the first few minutes driving. I fired up a smoke. Mark told me to open the window and blow the smoke out. He reminded me he didn't like cigarettes stinking up his car.

"What happens if it's her?" I said.

"We negotiate a deal with the officers."

"What kind of deal?" I said.

"Don't know," Mark said. "Guess we'll find out if it turns out to be Silky."

Just before getting to the all-night diner Mark told me the woman they picked up had been turning tricks for ten bucks a pop at some flop house down on Jefferson near Vermont. They got an anonymous tip from some woman that she was working the area. One of the officers in plain clothes spotted her and approached in an unmarked car. She pitched her services and they nabbed her.

"My friend told me they think one of the other working girls in the neighborhood turned her in. Silky, if it is her was probably undercutting their standard rates. But I gotta tell ya if this is your girl I'm dumbfounded. It makes no sense, you know. I mean why does a beautiful girl like that...like Silky put herself on the street. She has this opportunity to be in your film. It's like some Buddhist monk setting himself on fire."

I shrugged.

I don't know," I said. "I guess she's crazy."

Mark turned on the radio to a top forty station. The disc jockey was reading a commercial for Clyde Wallach's Music City. He then played "Singing the Blues" by Guy Mitchell. I sat back and closed my eyes letting my mind drift into the music and imagined myself sitting on Jenny's front porch on a warm evening drinking lemonade and counting fireflies in the distance. It made me feel strangely sad. Like a waking dream, the scene changed to the prairie and I could make out a dark figure on a horse in the distance. It was the Wichita Kid silhouetted against the moon. He waived and rode off. But there was something about his appearance I couldn't quite get, like he was trying to warn me about something, something bad.

When I opened my eyes we were pulling up in front of the diner. A sign in the window said Open All Night. The place was designed to look like a railroad dining car.

"Let me do the talking," Mark said.

Inside we found the two officers sitting in a booth toward the back. Other than an old man behind the counter there wasn't another soul in the place. Mark introduced me and then we ordered coffee and donuts. The officers, Pete and Tommy, both in plain clothes, seemed a little nervous at my being there. Mark explained that I was directing a picture the woman was in, "if in fact she is our girl," he was quick to add. This seemed to pique their interest. Suddenly they both eyed me, nodded and smiled as if this were their seal of approval.

For the next few minutes Mark and the officers made small talk about the department, the chief, and the flourishing "meat market." I learned this was code for prostitutes' primary territory.

"There must be a convention in town," Pete, the younger of the two officers said. "Girls are coming in by the bus loads, mostly we think from up north."

"Some of them don't look more than fourteen or fifteen," Tommy, the older officer said.

"Yeah," Mark said. "Some sad cases out there. So, where's the girl?"

"She's a wild one," Tommy said. "She bit me on the arm and tried to kick Pete here in the balls."

"Cute, though," Pete said. "Got to admit that."

"Yeah," Tommy said. "And if she hadn't missed with that kick you'd be singing a different tune, and probably a few octaves higher."

The officers and I laughed. Mark was stoic. He took a bite of his donut, a sip of his coffee and eyed the officers.

"Let's cut the chitchat," he said. "Where's the girl?"

"We got her in the back of a van out back in the alley," Tommy reported.

Mark shook his head and rolled his eyes.

"What're you two, crazy," he said. "If she's still there it'll be a miracle."

I watched Pete and Tommy look at each other. Tommy gulped the last of his coffee and stood up.

"Don't get your panties in an uproar, Mark." He said looking down at him. "She's handcuffed and kind of out of it. Must be on something."

"What do you guys want for turning her over to us if it's our girl?"

Tommy, who was on the outside stepped out onto the aisle. He leaned down and whispered something in Pete's ear then stood straight again.

"How about your friend here put us in his movie," Tommy said. "Nothing big, just so's we can be seen, so's our friends could recognize us."

Mark looked at me. I nodded.

"Let's have a look," he said.

Tommy and Pete led the way out back to the alley where a white van was parked. Tommy unlocked the back and swung open the two doors. He handed Mark a flashlight. Mark crawled in. The girl was lying on her back with a white sheet covering her as if she were a cadaver. Mark lifted the sheet. Her face was covered by her hair. He pushed it aside, then turned and looked back at me.

"Looks like her, but I'm not absolutely sure."

I crawled in beside Mark and looked. No question. It was Silky. She moaned and opened her eyes just a sliver.

"Chick's pretty messed up, you ask me," Tommy said. "That your girl or not?"

"Yep," Mark said. "That's our star."

"So, we got a deal?" Tommy said.

I crawled back out of the van and told the two cops I would give Mark a schedule to give to them on when and where to show up. We put Silky in the back seat of Mark's car. On the way back to the Marcuse house, Mark began laughing aloud.

"Can you figure those two officers Tommy and Pete just want to be in a movie as if it was the most important thing in their lives. What is it? I tell you people will sell their souls to be on celluloid. Maybe…maybe it's a way to sort of like finding immortality or something."

Silky made grunting noises from the back seat. She kicked off the sheet which was still covering her. All she had on was a flimsy black skirt, torn along one side, a dirty blue shirt, and one shoe with a broken heel. Her legs were bare. She suddenly screamed that two men fucked her in the back of some van and didn't give her squat.

"Can you describe the two men?" Mark said.

"Huh?" Silky said. "Who are you?"

"I said can you describe the two men in the van?"

She seemed to think this over.

"They must of worn masks or something," she said.

Back at the Marcuse house Maggie spent the day getting Silky back into some kind of shape. By night she was her old self, more or less. Good enough to continue working on the picture. Later Maggie asked her why she took off. Silky said she didn't know, only that when she saw herself on the screen and it wasn't really her but someone else, someone she would like to be, but could never be in a million years she got scared. Maggie wasn't buying it but pretended she understood.

Over the next few days production took place on the streets, often using only a hand-held camera. The equipment was being carried around in an old milk truck followed by a rented station wagon pulling the trailer. Permits had not been bothered with. On one occasion the police showed up when a crowd gathered to watch and were about to move us along when Tommy and Pete who happened to be there that day intervened. The officers left us alone on the condition we would not take too long.

A major blow to the production came that Friday. I realized that my seeing the Wichita Kid when Mark and I were going to pick up Silky must have been a premonition, a foreboding of something dark waiting down the road apiece.

Chapter 43

———

It was Friday. We were just getting ready to begin the day's work. I was in the trailer, sipping coffee and going over the schedule board when Jocelyn came crashing through the door. She was out of breath and pouring sweat. Her face was crimson and contorted. She looked like some kind of a human mutation. She stopped to catch her breath and eased herself down in a chair across the little table from me. She swallowed hard and took one last deep breath. I fired up a smoke and waited. I thought maybe Virgie Lowe was back. Then, like a dam bursting she began gushing it out of her that there was no money, that she had discovered the money in the separate account she had set up for the production of Cobra Woman/Prairie Wolves was gone, cleaned out, and so was all the money in the Starburst/Meade account, gone. She wasn't even sure if last week's checks would clear. But she hadn't heard from anyone so maybe they had.

"In any case there will be no checks today," she said.

I just stared at her for a time.

"What?" I said.

"You deaf?" she said. "There's no m-o-n-e-y!"

"I thought we had enough to finish," I said, thinking there must be some mistake.

Tears began to roll down Jocelyn's cheeks and she put her head in her hands for a moment then looked up.

"Frank must have taken the money," she said. "The Bank told me the accounts were cleared out and closed."

"Have you talked to him?"

She shook her head.

"He's gone," she said. "Split, vanished. No one knows where he is, not even his wife. I talked to her last night."

"So what do we do?" I asked.

Jocelyn said she didn't know and noted that the crew lives paycheck to paycheck when they're getting one.

"I don't see anyone sticking around when they find out," she said. "And there's the rental equipment, camera, sound, lights. Jesus. We were supposed to get them a check a couple of days ago. They were already threatening to pick everything up if they didn't get paid soon."

I took a drag on my smoke and closed my eyes for a moment.

"Maybe Frank will come back and straighten things out," I said.

Jocelyn looked pained. She met my eyes and then slowly shook her head.

"He's in some kind of big trouble," she said. "He owes on gambling debts. I'm afraid he's into the pinky ring boys from Vegas for big bucks. He told me this one night after a few drinks. Fact is, I don't think he ever intended to do this film."

I just shook my head. It figured, I thought. Why else would he let a nobody from nowhere direct a movie he was producing.

"His wife thinks he might have fled the country," Jocelyn said.

"Guess we have to do something," I said and looked at my watch.

"How bout shaking Fat Eyes," Jocelyn said. "He has money, doesn't he?"

I liked that idea. I called Fat Eyes from a pay phone a few blocks away. After explaining the situation, some of which he had already heard about through the Hollywood underground, I bluntly told him he needed to put up the money to finish the film and keep Bambi happy. He growled at my mention of Bambi and told me that was none of my business. Then he started laughing as if he'd suddenly thought of an old joke.

"As for putting up money," Fat Eyes said. "I don't got squat, kid, tapped out. Lost much of what I had on the ponies. Fuckers had lead in their legs."

"What should we do?" I said.

There was a long silence. Fat Eyes then said, "Offer more points. Everyone takes deferred compensation in return. The investors have points, Frank Meade has points, I have points, so give out some more points. What the hell, give out Frank's points."

"What are points exactly?" I asked.

"Shit, don't you know anything?

He explained how points represented a value of the product, like having stock in a company."

I came back to the trailer and told Jocelyn about Fat Eyes' idea. She told me it wasn't legal because all the points had been assigned, that The Prairie Wolves production was like an independent company. She asked me if I had another cigarette. I gave her one and fired one up for myself. She went and opened the trailer door, looked out at the crew setting up for the first shot of the day, closed it and turned to me. "On the other hand we might keep everyone working with points," she said. "They'd have a feeling of ownership."

"How many investors are there?" I said.

"Ten put up $20,000 each and one anonymous investor kicked in $200,000. Only Frank knows who that was. I asked him if it was mob money, but he was emphatic that it wasn't. Frankly I can't imagine where it came from."

Jocelyn agreed to take points from Frank's bank and spread them around. She would have to call a temp from the agency she used to help out for the week. At the end of the day Jocelyn gathered everyone around. She announced that as Frank Meade's representative the production was out of money. You could feel the anger ripple through the company. After a few moments, a quiet came over everyone as Jocelyn raised her hands. She then told the cast and crew that she was authorized to offer points to everyone if they stay and help complete the picture. "Or," she said, "I could issue undated checks to be held until new money can be found."

There was a lot of grumbling but in the end, everyone agreed except Bonnie Robertson.

"I'm a professional," she said privately to Jocelyn, Bruce and I in the trailer. "I don't take points, particularly when they aren't worth the paper they're written on."

Bruce tried to dissuade her. She was doing double duty as the script girl as well as handling the slate board.

"Good riddance!" Jocelyn said, "One less mouth to feed at the trough."

"We'll need a new script girl," Bruce said.

"The temp from the agency will be here Monday," Jocelyn said. "She can fill in. I've used her before. She knows how to time scenes."

Bruce looked at me.

"Where are we going to get more cash?"

I shrugged and explained that I had tried Fat Eyes, but there was one other possibility that I could think of.

I called Moe. He wouldn't take the call. I got Maggie to take me to his store. Silky went with us. She sat in the back seat humming to herself. When we pulled up in front, Silky leaned forward.

"Tell Moe I'll give him the best blow job he's ever had if he'll spring for some money."

Maggie laughed, turned around, and gave Silky a thumbs up. I left them in the car. Inside, Iris Madigan spotted me and came over. She told me she was angry with me because I had not considered her for a larger part. I told her Boyd Imwald had cast the film and that I just picked up the pieces after he died, and reminded her I did give her an extra line.

"I'm a journeyman actress," she said. "You could have put a little more meat on the part."

"Is Moe here?"

She indicated the mezzanine with her head.

"He's in the office," she said.

I quickly explained the situation and told her if Moe came through I would write in more dialogue for her. For a moment Iris beamed and then shrugged as I turned and headed up the stairs. I flew past Moe's secretary, who tried to stop me, into his inner sanctum. Moe looked up from some papers on his desk. He looked startled. I explained what had happened.

"I knew we shouldn't have trusted that bastard Frank," Moe said. "Anyway, I'm not throwing good money after bad. You think I'm nuts?"

"If we don't finish the film nobody will get any money," I said.

Moe leaned back, laughed and lit a cigar.

"Kid, do you think anybody gives a rat's ass. It's a fucking right-off. Now get out of here before I call one of my security guys."

I just stood there feeling stunned and embarrassed.

"Thanks, Moe," I said. "And fuck you too!"

Moe jumped up from his seat.

"I said get out of here you cocksucker and don't come back!"

As I left, heads were poking out of a couple of doorways to see who the object of Moe's wrath was. I could feel Iris's eyes on me as I made my way out.

Chick turned out to be our savior. Over the weekend I borrowed $2500 from him. He reluctantly accepted my signed note. He was more interested in extracting a promise that he would get a credit as Associate Producer. Said he had a daughter that would be very proud if his name was on a film. I took the money and put it in my personal account where I had been depositing my pay check from the production which had been enough to make ends meet with a little left over I paid some money to the equipment rental company and the lab where the film was being processed, producing a work print, sound print for syncing up, and a negative.

Monday morning, a woman I hadn't seen before approached me by the trailer. She looked to be fifty-ish, attractive with long graying hair and a smooth round face and deep green eyes. She looked a little like Adele might have looked so many years later if she were still alive.

"Hi," she said. "I'm Anna. I'm from the agency. You're Charles Kendall, right?"

I nodded, trying to concentrate on the day's schedule which I had on a clip board.

"I know about you," she said, sounding a little mysterious. "I mean I read about you being up at the Fourth Way Farm. I was once a devotee of Zoltan's and the Fourth Way, but, well, I left in the middle of the night and never went back."

I put the clipboard down and stared at her.

"Are you the one they called Anna Asparagus?"

Her eyes lit up.

"Wow, yeah, that was me," she said. "That was my Fourth Way name, because of my eyes. Someone thought they were the color of asparagus. It's actually Anna Martin. Why would you have guessed that? I mean that's really bizarre."

"Zoltan told me you were dead," I said.

"I was dead to him, once I left the compound without permission," Anna said. "Some of the games they were playing were getting too scary. I heard they actually had a burial ceremony for me. But why would you have been talking to Zoltan about me?"

I told her I had gone there looking for her. Anna Martin was totally taken aback and asked why? I dug into my pocket where I still kept the congratulatory letter from Starburst/Meade. It was now falling apart at the folds. I showed it to Anna and asked her if she had written the note at the bottom and signed it Frank Meade?"

She examined it carefully and shook her head.

"I was working for Starburst/Meade at the time helping to handle the contest responses but I never wrote that. I'm sure Frank Meade didn't either. Does it matter?"

I laughed and shook my head.

"No," I said. "Not now. But it did kinda change my life. It's a mystery. No one knows who wrote it."

I put the note back and gave Anna a copy of the script and a stopwatch to time the takes.

At first I barely noticed the two men in black suits hanging around during the last three days of shooting. Both of them were thick, one about six feet, the other about five ten and both had dark hair slicked straight back from their foreheads. They were both very tan and both wore the same style black glasses. They never spoke to anyone as near as I could tell. Some of the crew members began to notice them also since they showed up at our three last location sites. The thing that stood out, aside from their fastidious dress, was real severe demeanors. The hard expressions seemed pasted on their faces. During a break on the last day of shooting, the two cops, Pete and Tommy, now in plain clothes, sidled up to Mark while I was talking to him. Both had also noticed the strangers. At the moment, they were standing on the periphery of the production. Pete remarked that they looked like mismatched bookends.

"Mark, you ever see them guys before?" Tommy asked.

Mark looked over and caught the eye of the larger of the two strangers.

"No," Mark said. "Look like a couple of enforcers."

The bigger of the two strangers looked away and said something to his partner. They both then looked over toward us, expressionless.

"I got a hunch they're packing," Tommy said. "I think I'm gonna check 'em out when we're finished here."

Later I told Mark what Jocelyn said about a couple of guys coming to Starburst/Meade the other evening looking for Frank. I told Maggie to see if she could get a shot of the two strangers without them knowing it. She nodded.

We were shooting the last scene in Santa Monica in front of an auto repair shop. For some reason getting equipment set up was moving along slowly, clouds were darkening and rain was not far behind. It was already eleven in the morning.

"Can't we get things moving faster?!" I snapped at Bruce and Lazlo.

Bruce pretended he didn't hear me. Lazlo, who was adjusting the camera, slowly turned to me.

"No we can't," he shot back. "We do what we can do. That's it. That's what we can do."

"I've seen corn grow faster than these guys move," I said. "Do you see the sky?"

Lazlo was now glaring at me, his dark eyes bulging. No question, everyone's nerves were frayed. But this was a critical scene and we only had this one chance to get it on film. I knew that we could not hold anyone past the end of the day.

"You got a hair up your ass or what?" Lazlo said. "I tell you I hear anymore of this shit, I walk away. That's it." He stepped over to me his face in mine."You ask what I see. I see that you have become possessed by this piece of celluloid shit we are calling...what is it? Oh yeah, The Fucking 'Cobra Woman versus the Prairie Wolves in the Vortex of the Valley of Darkness.' Don't worry. We will finish it."

Bonnie Robertson came stumbling back declaring that she wanted to be in at the finish.

"She's drunk," Bruce said to me as Bonnie sat down in one of the director's chairs and began making frantic notes on the script.

The lead villain in the film, whom I called Marcus, owns the Auto Repair Shop in the story. A few nights before, Silky's character, called April, meets Marcus in a bar with Star Dancer nearby. She lets him think she is attracted to him. Though he is married with two young children, he figures a fling with this pretty young woman would be a nice diversion. He tells her about his garage business. Meanwhile we know she is plotting his demise by her Cobra persona. In a follow-up to pursuing a clandestine relationship with Marcus she brings her car to his auto shop on the pretext that something needs to be checked. They make a date, but now that he sees her in the light of day he feels he has seen her somewhere before. Something familiar, but can't quite place her. He tells her he believes he has met her before. She denies this. Marcus also knows that something has befallen two of his friends who were his accomplices to murder and rape on that fateful desert trip. But he does not yet make the connection.

"The audience must feel her mission of seeking justice is threatened by Marcus' suspicions," Bonnie said.

Meanwhile, Silky's character has already made contact with the fourth member of the group, Hank, played by Mark. He is the only one not married and she finds she is attracted to him, creating an inner conflict she has not yet resolved. What she doesn't know, but the audience does, is that Hank has followed her to Marcus' Auto shop and is now suspicious of her himself as he watches her with his friend. Later in the story, which was shot the week before, Hank and Marcus meet and figure it out. This ultimately leads to an obligatory scene of violent confrontation and denouement where Mark is the only one left and April leaves him unharmed and walks away.

Bonnie, her voice slightly slurred suggested a close up of Hank in a point of view shot, watching April to heighten suspense. Bruce agreed. Next, a trucking shot of Silky walking back to her car.

Bruce announced that it was a wrap. Everyone clapped, even some bystanders who'd stopped to watch. At about that time it began to sprinkle. Silky came over and grabbed me by the shirtsleeve. She pointed in the direction of the two strangers who were still watching from the edge of the scene.

"Who are those guys?" She said.

I shrugged.

"The men in black suits?" I said. "I don't know."

"No," Silky said. "I don't mean them."

She nodded toward Tommy and Pete who were only a few feet from the two heavies.

"Just a couple of extras," I said.

"Oh, yeah," Silky said. "I know them from somewhere and I don't get a good feeling about it."

She walked over to the trailer, sat on the stoop, lit a cigarette and continued to eye Tommy and Pete. She got up and came back over to me.

"I think they're cops and they're after me," she said.

I ignored what she said and told her there was going to be a wrap party at Star/Burst Meade that night.

"I guess it's kind of a tradition," I said.

Silky walked away and I knew we would not see her again.

Chapter 44

The wrap party at Starburst/Meade turned into a drunken scramble. Two fights broke out. Bottles were broken, trashcans turned over and a table was smashed up when a stunt man picked it up to see how far he could throw it. Luckily it didn't hit anyone while in flight. I had a few beers and mostly watched the goings on from the sidelines with Mark who did not stay long. Maggie took pictures as if gathering evidence for some future insurance claims. She asked me where Silky was and I just shook my head. Finally Jocelyn got up on a chair with a bullhorn and screamed at the crowd of partiers to cool it or she was going to turn the fire hose on them. "This is a place of business," she said.

There was a trickle of laughter, but you knew the rowdies figured she was serious and a quiet came over the room. It was now well into the early morning hours and folks began to leave. What nobody was saying, but everybody knew, was that the place, the home of Starburst/Meade Productions, was in fact doomed. Meanwhile, the stereo was playing Heartbreak Hotel by some new rock star named Elvis Presley.

Later, after most of the crowd had left, Bruce Richmond reported that when he delivered the last of the film to the lab, he'd been told that they were going to hold the negative and work print until their bill was paid in full.

"How much?" I asked.

"Seven thousand bucks," Bruce said.

I felt my heart sink. I looked at Jocelyn. She just shook her head and waived her cigar in the air.

"Damn," was about all I could get out.

Jocelyn said some money had come in from the last contest but that it was just enough to keep the place open temporarily. We all stood there silent for a time.

"There has to be a way," I said aloud, but more to myself than the others, and looked over at Maggie who was sitting on a stool by the bar looking sympathetic. We went back to the Marcuse house. Since Maggie was feeling no pain, I drove. The rain was coming down hard and I could barely see the road going up the hill and almost went off the embankment. Maggie screamed and I hit the brakes just in time. Inside the house, we crashed on the monster bed. It was almost three in the morning. Before drifting off Maggie said she thought Silky was amazing in the film but in real life a lost soul, angry at the world like a caged wild animal.

The next day, the Los Angeles News had a front page headline:

PRODUCER DISAPPEARS.

Well-known producer of low budget films, Frank R. Meade is reported missing, according to police sources who said an investigation is underway. Meade's wife, Pamela Andrews, a prominent real estate broker, filed a missing persons report. According to the report, she last saw her husband about two and a half weeks ago. He told her he was going to meet someone on a business deal and never returned. In her statement to the police it was not unusual for him to be away for long stretches of time, but not without some word. Meade, 57 is well known for making low-budget science fiction, horror and crime films.

A gossip columnist in the same paper recounted a story from a guest at a recent "soiree" thrown by Pamela Andrews, wife of well known producer, Frank Meade. "A feature of the party was to have been a travel film that Mrs. Meade planned to show to invitees, about 30 women, according to the source who wanted to remain anonymous. After she started the projector, she left her guests to tend to something in the kitchen. She soon heard screams followed by squeals and uncontrollable laughter. She returned to the room where the film was running to find her guests enjoying a little sex film staring her husband and an unknown blonde. Mr. Meade was naked and painted up like an aborigine tribesman, according to my source. While some of the guests were shocked and walked out, others were highly amused by the scene. Reportedly, Mrs. Meade was not amused and quickly shut the projector down. Meanwhile, Mr. Meade has reportedly vanished. And no wonder."

I almost choked on my coffee.

Police detectives visited Starburst/Meade Productions and questioned Jocelyn about her long-time boss' whereabouts. Later they showed up at the Hamburger Palace where they found me in one of the booths munching on a sandwich. All I could tell them was I hadn't seen Frank Meade in more than a month. They took notes, thanked me, and left. Chick, who'd listened in from the next booth joined me, bringing a cup of coffee with him.

"How you doin', kid?" He said.

"If it's about the money…" I started.

Chick reached across the table and put a hand on my shoulder.

"Don't worry about it," he said. "You'll either work it off or find some way to pay me one way or the other, I'm sure. I read about that producer…Meade. Strange business, you ask me."

I just grunted and told him there may not be a movie and that the lab was holding all the film.

"Don't matter," Chick said. "You done what you came out here to do, ain't that right, I mean when you think about."

I just stared into my coffee cup.

"I should call Jenny," I said absently. "My girl back home."

"What about Maggie?" Chick said. "Anything going there?"

I shook my head.

"She got eyes for you, kid, that girl does," he said with a wink. "I seen her watching you when you weren't looking. I know the look."

I gave a forced laugh.

"We're kind of more like roommates." I said.

Just as Chick stood up, Mark came lumbering into the place, water dripping from his hat and raincoat. He spotted me, came over and sat down across the table where Chick had been sitting. One of the waitresses immediately brought over a cup of hot coffee and set it down in front of Mark. I fired up a smoke. Mark took a sip of his coffee.,

"Nothing better on a night like this," he said. "This rain is depressing."

We were silent for a time. I was thinking of home, about how the earth smelled when it rained, the sweet fragrance of the rich low country soil. "I wonder what the Wichita Kid would do?" I said aloud without realizing it.

"What?" Mark said. "Who?"

"What are you doing here?" I asked.

He gave me a strange look and then said someone called and asked that he come and get me to meet with Jocelyn what's-her-name over at Starburst/Meade's, that something had come up. It was important.

"Who called?" I said.

"My mother took the message. Said she thought it was a woman, but hard to tell for sure. Mother was reluctant to give me the message, said she didn't like the sound of it."

"I wonder what it is?" I said.

On the way, Mark again said he suspected Maggie of being involved in the drug scene. I told him that was crazy.

"Maybe," he said. "But how does she support that big house you guys camp in?"

I told him she has been taking in borders, mostly people she knows who've left home and need a pad, or know someone she doesn't know who needs a place to stay, that they chip in to help pay expenses.

"Maggie's working on her photography," I added. "She's actually had a couple of photos in magazines."

"Good for her, but maybe she should be careful about who camps out there," Mark said.

Rain was still coming down hard. Mark was driving at a snail's pace on Santa Monica Boulevard. Neither of us spoke for a time.

"You ever been married?" He said suddenly.

I shook my head.

"But you've got a girl, right?"

"Back home," I said. "Jenny. Jenny Gifford. She's an officer in a bank. Her father is the president of the bank. We talked about marriage once. What about you? You have a girl?"

Mark gave a sour expression.

"I don't get much in the way of opportunities to meet women. Sometimes I try to pick up a stray at a bar now and then, but I'm not much good at it, you know. I mean, women don't get too excited about me. I always start to sweat. Even my ex gave me the heave-ho. Mother was happy about that. Never liked my ex and made no bones about it."

He added that on two occasions he had slept with a hooker he knew. But afterward he was always depressed. A brief silence followed and then he said, "When...if Cobra Woman/Prairie Wolves ever hits the theaters and there I am on the screen, bigger than life, I might have better luck. It's weird when you think about it, I mean, being in a movie kind of gives you a feeling of importance, like your image lives on long after your gone."

"Yeah," I said. "I never thought of it like that."

"So what happens to the film now?"

"Post production," I said. "That's what they call it."

All I knew was it would have to be strung together, sound synced up and everything, maybe add some music. But first, I had to find some way to get it from the lab. Luckily the shadow of a cobra had been shot on a wall early on by Boyd Imwald.

"Don't forget to put my name in the credits," Mark said.

381

As we pulled up in front of Starburst/Meade Mark said the message was for me to come alone. Mark said he would wait in the car and give me a ride back to the Marcuse house when I was finished. He added that he was curious about what was going on.

The front door was unlocked. Inside, there didn't seem to be a soul around. The air was permeated with the acrid smell of booze and cigarettes lingering from the night before. I called out Jocelyn's name. After a few moments Anna appeared in the doorway of Frank's office in back. She looked pale and frightened. I just stood there in the middle of the main room watching her. Finally she approached.

"I was working late to finish up some bookwork for Jocelyn when these two men barged in. They want to see you. It's the two men in the black suits who were hanging around the last few days."

"Where are they?"

Anna turned her head around toward the office and then in a low voice said they were in Mr. Meade's office.

"I don't like them," she whispered. "They were going through Mr. Meade's desk and papers. I told them they shouldn't be doing that. They told me to shut up and mind my own business."

"Where's Jocelyn?"

"She went to visit a sick friend or something."

I nodded and fired up a cigarette.

"Guess I should go see what they want."

I started toward the office, then turned back and told Anna that if I didn't come out in a few minutes she should go tell the man sitting in a car out front that I might be in trouble. She nodded vigorously, looking very anxious as she watched me turn and head on back. Frank's office door was closed. I stopped, took a deep drag on my smoke and opened it. The two men stopped rummaging and turned to me.

"Hey," the smaller of the two said, smiling pleasantly. "Just the man we want to see."

I stepped in and scanned the room. It looked like a wrecking ball had hit it. Files overturned, papers scattered everywhere, desk askew and the phone ripped out of the wall.

"Why do you want to see me?"

The larger man slowly maneuvered around behind me.

"Cause you're the man," the smaller one said. "We figured that if anyone knew where Frank Meade was it would be you."

I shook my head and stamped out my cigarette on the floor before it burned my fingers.

"I don't know," I said. "I told the police that."

"Yeah, we know," the larger man said behind me. "But that doesn't mean shit, does it? We think maybe you're protecting him. I mean we just want to talk to him."

"That is the people we work for want to talk to him," the smaller man said. "That's all, nice and friendly."

I moved to my left so that I could see the larger man out of the corner of my eye. This whole scene reminded me of an old black and white movie with Humphrey Bogart dealing with a couple of goons working for some gangster.

"What do they want him for?" I asked.

The smaller man stuck some chewing gum in his mouth, went and sat behind Frank's desk, leaned way back and swung his feet up on top. He grinned, showing even teeth that looked like they had been scrubbed until they shined, and dialed up a friendly looking wink.

"It's business," he said. "Just some business."

He suddenly jumped up, clearly impatient and came around the desk to face me. I figured he was about five ten and weighed in at around two hundred pounds. He stood in front of me, his heavy face only a couple of inches from mine. His breath smelled sweet from the gum.

"As I said, I haven't seen him in weeks. Can I go now?"

The bigger man moved back behind me again.

"We ain't finished," the smaller one said, his eyes boring into mine as if searching for some hint that I was lying.

He stepped back and took a folded piece of paper out of the inside pocket of his coat and opened it up. "This is a copy of a promissory note signed by one Frank Meade. It was notarized here in California. It says he owes the people we work for a certain amount of money. As collateral he put up this movie called Cobra Woman versus the Prairie Wolves in the Vortex of Valley of Darkness." He looked at me. "What the fuck kind of title is that? Anyway, you get the idea?"

He handed the note to me. I gave it a quick look.

"I don't know anything about this," I said and handed it back.

"The point is," the smaller man said, "no Frank Meade to make good on his debt, we got to take possession of the film."

I just looked blankly at the bull of a man standing in front of me.

"So, where's the film," the man behind me said in my ear. "We can do this nice and quiet. We just load it up and take it with us now. No fuss."

I told them it wasn't there and that it had to be edited. I felt the bigger man's hand come down on my shoulder and grip it hard, then wrap around the front of my neck, squeezing the air out of me. For a moment I couldn't breathe. He released his grip. I stepped away so that I could look at both of them.

"It's at the lab," I said.

"So, go get it," the larger man said.

I explained the situation and that there was no money to pay what was owed. The two men looked at each other. The smaller one grabbed my arm, his earlier friendly tone gone.

"Don't jack us around, Kendall. We aim to get that film and hold it until Meade comes through. Got it?"

The door to the office flew open and Mark Horgan's large frame filled the doorway. He stood for a moment taking in the scene, looking over the two men.

"Tuckie, he said. "I can't wait any longer. Let's go, man."

"Beat it," the larger man growled. "We're busy here."

Mark just stood there and grinned.

"What's the matter?" The smaller man said. "You don't hear so good?"

Mark looked at me.

"I got to take a piss," Mark said and took a couple of steps in.

"Does this look like the can to you?" The smaller man said.

With sudden lightening speed Mark grabbed the smaller man by the lapels and threw him half way across the room.

"I was thinking I'd piss on you," Mark said.

The larger man started to reach inside his coat pocket. But when he looked up Mark had his forty five out and pointing at the man's chest. Mark stepped over and pulled back the lapel of the larger man's coat to reveal and a gun in a shoulder holster. The bigger man let his arms dangle at his sides and seemed to relax. Mark gently pulled the gun out of its holster and held it up.

"You got a permit for this piece?" Mark said.

"Who's asking?" The man said. "You a cop? I thought you were one of the actors."

"Use to be on the force. I'm a PI now…and an actor. But I still got lots of friends on the force I can count on when I need a favor. Capiche? You still haven't answered my question."

"I don't remember," he said and started to make a move toward Mark. Mark just nodded as if inviting the challenge. The smaller man had gotten to his feet by this time and stepped in between his partner and Mark. It was a tense moment.

"Okay, we got the message," the smaller man said. "But we still got a job to do here and that's to protect our employer's interest. We ain't going away, so what do you want to do here? Seems like what we got is a stand-off, you know. Our people expect results. That's what they pay us for. We're professionals. So even if we went away, others would come."

He handed the note to Mark who quickly looked it over and handed it back.

"So Meade's into the boys for $200,000. Assuming that's his signature."

"No question," the smaller man said.

Even though things had calmed down a little and I was still feeling the adrenaline racing through me an idea hit. I cleared my throat. Everyone looked at me.

"Well," I started, "you could get the film from the lab. You'll have to pay what's owed, $7,000. Then you'd have possession."

Mark looked alarmed. He pulled me aside.

"You can't do that," he whispered. "It'll never get finished."

I shrugged.

"Maybe," I said and turned to the two thugs. "What do you think?"

The smaller man rubbed his chin and said he'd have to check with his people.

"We'll be in touch."

As the two men left, the larger one held out his hand. Mark took the bullets out of his gun and handed it to him. I saw the man give Mark a very hard look as he holstered it, as if to say I won't forget you. He followed his smaller partner out of the office door. We watched after them until they disappeared out through the front entrance. There was no sign of Anna.

"So what the hell are you doing?" Mark said.

I fired up a smoke and sat on Frank's desk.

"Real simple," I said. "Once they get the film out of the lab, if their people okay it, we'll steal it from them."

Mark rolled his eyes.

"You mean you want to hijack the film? Are you out of your mind! These guys don't mess around. Even if you were to pull it off, these guys would come after you like a pack of hungry wolves. They will hunt you down and they won't be nearly as accommodating as they just were."

My plan came to me like one of those cartoon lightening bolts, fully formed. I laid it out in detail for Mark who listened, shook his head from time to time and then nodded when I had finished. Mark said that he could see how my plan might work but noted that the weakness lay in having to count on the behavior of the men.

"Pretty shaky," he said.

"You in or not?" I said.

Mark sighed.

"I must be as crazy as you," he said.

Chapter 45

———

Two days later, the rain had moved on leaving the Los Angeles basin smog free, the air smelling fresh and crisp. The two men from Vegas met with me and Jocelyn at Starburst/Meade. The smaller one quietly announced that they had approval to go ahead and pay the lab fee and get the film into their possession. The cost would, of course, be added to what is already owed by Meade.

We sat at a folding Formica-top table. Jocelyn had dragged it out from the back to replace the broken coffee table. Jocelyn, cigar in mouth, went eyeball to eyeball with the smaller man while his larger partner stood off to the side. It struck me as a good performance on her part because I figured her nerves were raw and somewhere inside she was shaking like a twig in a breeze. The smaller man made it clear they wanted the negative and all prints.

"If we give you authorization to take Cobra Woman/Prairie Wolves from the processing lab, we want assurances that it will be kept safe," Jocelyn said. "There's a considerable investment in the film. A lot more than what is owed your boss."

The smaller man, looking impatient, nodded.

"On the head of my first born," he said with a sneer. "When Frank shows up with the money he owes, the film is yours or Meade's or whoever the fuck it belongs to."

The larger man fidgeted, which did not go unnoticed by his partner.

"What's the matter with you?" The smaller man said.

"You know," the larger man said.

"What?"

"The language," he said in a very low voice as if he thought no one but his partner could hear him. "I don't like us to use that kind of language in front of a woman. We've talked about that. You know I'm Catholic."

The smaller man shook his head and began laughing.

"You mean this?" He said pointing to Jocelyn. "This ain't no woman. I don't know what it is, but it can't be a woman."

Jocelyn glared at the smaller man and began absently stroking some hairs that were growing out of a mole on her chin.

"You wanna see my twat, asshole?" She said.

"Let's finish our business," he said.

Jocelyn, smiling to herself, then went to her desk and returned with a piece of paper, pushing it in front of the smaller man.

"What's this bullshit?" He said.

"It's a receipt for the film," Jocelyn said. "You need to sign it."

The smaller man looked shocked.

"You saying my word ain't good enough?" The smaller man said with a strong edge to his voice. "Fucking Godzilla."

The larger man poked his partner.

"What's the difference?" He said. "Sign the paper and let's get out of here."

"Your word is shit!" Came a screechy voice from behind the bar. "Fucking Godzilla."

We all swung around to see Gertrude, her small dark body perched on a tiny swing, staring off into space as if trying to look innocent. "Frank fucks frogs."

"What the hell is that?" The larger man said.

"Frank's Mynah bird," Jocelyn said. "She's not Catholic."

The smaller man shook his head and scribbled his signature on the bottom of the form. I then told them the name of the lab was Filmando's

Hideaway on the outskirts of Glendale. The larger man wrote down the directions. Jocelyn told them they would need a van.

"There'll be lots of big boxes with cans of reels."

"We can rent a van," the smaller man said.

"What about our car?" The larger man said.

The smaller man said he figured he would drive the car and his partner would drive the van.

"One more thing," Jocelyn said. "We need to let the lab know when you plan to pick up the film so they can have it ready. The exact time, please."

The two men turned their backs and conferred.

"Ten o'clock on the dot," the smaller man said.

As they started to leave, the larger man turned to me, made a face and told me to get a haircut and get rid of the bowtie.

"It ain't makin' it." He said.

When they were gone, we both grinned at the same time.

"Those creepy fuckers scare me,' she said excitedly, "but if we can pull this off...Damn."

Mark Horgan emerged from the shadows in the back where he'd been watching.

"Like I said, it's a crazy scheme," he said and he came over to us. "When they catch on, and I think they will catch on at some time or other they will come after you. Make no mistake about that. And as I've said, they won't be too friendly."

Jocelyn opened the folder with the receipt.

"He signed it Zito," Jocelyn said. "No last name. What kind of name is Zito?"

Mark shrugged. I fired up a smoke.

"Maybe he's Greek," I said.

"Zito," Mark repeated, and his expression bunched up as if an icy chill had suddenly zipped up his back. "I think I've heard of his guy. A guy that goes by one name." He glanced at me. "If it's the guy I'm think-

391

ing of, he's very dangerous, a hit man from the Chicago mob. I'm going to check it out."

Jocelyn went to the storage room in the back, calling to me and Mark to follow. In the back, were large reel cans stacked on the floor. Jocelyn took a black marker out of her pocket and carefully printed "Cobra/Prairie Wolves" on the can of the first stack.

"Don't just stand there with your thumb up your asses we've got work to do. Every can has to be labeled."

"What's in them?" Mark asked.

"The first few cans contain the daily prints from the film," Jocelyn said. "The rest will contain outtakes from some of Frank's old movies."

"Salting the mine," Mark said.

"You got it big fella," she said.

We worked in silence for awhile which was finally broken when Jocelyn stopped and began laughing hysterically to herself. I'd never seen her laugh before, not like that. Both Mark and I stopped and looked at her.

"Jesus," she said. "Can you imagine that big guy worried about the kind of language his partner was using. Son of a bitch, that's a new one. And the thing is, he probably wouldn't think twice about shooting you."

That evening I outlined my plan to hijack Cobra Woman/The Prairie Wolves. We were joined by Maggie and a lean young man with a few days growth of beard who had been camping at the Marcuse house. His name was Arne Conklin. He said he was a free floater and had made his way down from Port Townsend, Washington. He'd heard about Maggie taking in borders from a friend. Arne was excited about being brought into the Cobra/Prairie Wolves caper. There was a good reason for bringing him in. He had a 1949 Volkswagen camper. It was a little beat up but ran well and I figured it would be just what we needed.

Another man who called himself Jason Mills joined us. He was a distant cousin of Jocelyn's who'd done time in San Quentin for armed robbery some years back. He was short and muscular with tattoos covering his arms. Jocelyn told everyone that Jason Mills was not his real name. He did not want his real name put on the street in case something went wrong. Jason also made it clear that he considered himself a professional and wasn't going to stand for any foolishness working with a bunch of amateurs. His helping was strictly a favor to Jocelyn.

"This ain't my kind of gig, man," he snorted and furtively checked around as if to make sure some unauthorized person was not within earshot.

Mark rolled his eyes.

"This is all you need," he whispered to me with unmistakable sarcasm.

"We can use the help," I said.

"Yeah, well you better keep an eye on him, that's all I can say." Mark said.

We gathered around the table to plan the abduction of the film. We slurped coffee, smoked, scribbled notes on eight-by-ten sheets of yellow paper and made diagrams of street intersections close to the Filmando's lab. There was a high level of excitement and energy in the room as everyone tried to insert ideas at once. Jason, who'd kept quiet while finishing off three beers, suddenly yelled that none of us knew what we were doing.

"First, you got to have disguises so's no one recognizes you. Then you got to look at the heist every which way from Sunday, turn it upside down and sideways so you know all the angles and all the things that can go wrong."

Jason took a swig from his fourth beer and went on waving his hands in the air like a conductor at a symphony. His dark eyes were dancing with intensity.

"Like, what if these guys who are picking up the film turn and go in the opposite direction? What do you do then?"

Jason directed the question to Mark who didn't react.

"So, what's your action, man?"

"Nothing," Mark said. "I don't plan to participate."

Jason squinted at Mark.

"So why are you here, man?" Arne jumped in. "Why are you even going?"

"He's riding shotgun," I said. "Just in case things get…"

Arne nodded. Jason was staring hard at Mark.

"You smell like a cop to me," he said.

Mark stood up, walked around the table to confront Jason.

"You're beginning to have an adverse affect on my disposition," he said.

Jason looked up at the hulking figure towering over him and nodded.

"Okay, pal." he said. "Forget it."

Mark continued to stand over Jason. Jocelyn said Jason didn't mean anything.

"Yeah, I didn't mean nothin'," he said.

"That's a double negative," Mark said and went back to his seat.

"Huh?"

Before anyone could say anymore I took control of the meeting and explained in great detail my plan. I had borrowed Maggie's car and gone out to the site of the film lab after the meeting with Zito and his partner and made a map of the streets with arrows to indicate directions. I had studied a California road map and figured the most practical route to be taken from the lab heading east for Nevada, to determine which way they would go. This would be an important detail. I also marked off assignment locations for each of the players working to pull off this job. Even Jason was impressed and told me privately he would be honored to work with me on a future job. After going over everything I felt a strange exhilaration come over me like I was out on the edge of the frame and into the hot zone.

"I like the disguise idea," I said. "Like a caper movie."

"We might have some old stuff in storage boxes out back," Jocelyn volunteered. "Wigs, beards, makeup and crap."

Mark remained stoic as the excited chatter continued and a sense of purpose filled the air. I was now envisioning the plot as a covert operation.

In my head I would now refer to everyone involved as operatives. I looked at my watch. It was now 10:40, less than twelve hours to go before operation Cobra/Prairie Wolves. I felt excited and scared as shit at the same time.

Chapter 46

———

The next morning, I got up early, made coffee and some toast, and then fired up a smoke. My heart was already racing as I thought about what was ahead. From the window I could see a sliver of the black water of the pacific shimmering in the morning sun. Outside I felt the hint of a breeze floating in from the northwest. The mood of the city felt good, even exuberant, which I interpreted as an omen for the work ahead.

All the players rendezvoused at Starburst/Meade at 8 a.m. A fresh pot of coffee and a tray of donuts were waiting for us, supplied by Anna at Jocelyn's request. We went over the plan one more time. Maggie would drive her car, accompanied by Jocelyn. Mark would drive alone. I would go with Arne and Jason in the VW Bus, which we loaded up with the newly marked cans of film. Earlier, while rummaging around through some boxes of props in back, Jocelyn found a set of walkie-talkies which actually worked. I gave one to Maggie who was to act as spotter and kept the other one.

Arne's VW Bus looked like a junkyard reject. It had a pock-marked, washed out green and white body, and chipped red doors. The doors looked like they'd been painted with house paint. The only windows were in front and one in the back. Despite its dilapidated exterior it seemed to run okay. Luckily, it had a pull-up door in back. A strange acrid smell permeated the interior.

"What is that smell?" I asked when we'd settled in for the drive out to Glendale. I sat in the front passenger seat, and Jason, who was behind me in a bucket seat, laughed.

"Smells like some good shit to me," he said. "Where did you say you were from, Arne?"

Arne at the wheel shook his head.

"Maybe some Turkish cigars I was smoking," he said. "They were old and pretty rank."

"Smells like hash to me, man," Jason said. "Some real kick-ass hash."

It took about a half hour to drive out to Filmando's Hideaway Lab. It was located in an old industrial area in the valley on the cusp of Glendale off of San Fernando Road. I had heard the general area had thrived during World War II producing munitions, small arms, airplane parts, parachutes and other items for the war effort. Now, most of the factories were either abandoned or producing household items. For the most part, it was a depressed location.

We were twenty minutes early. Maggie drove about a mile up the road and parked at an intersection near a public phone booth. A few minutes later I heard her voice crackling through the walkie-talkie.

"This is Maggie, the spy. Come in. Come in. Can you hear me? Over and out."

I picked up the set which I had put on the floor and pressed a couple of buttons before I could be heard on the other end.

"This is T. Are you in position?"

"Roger," Maggie said.

"Fuckin' A," Jocelyn was heard to yell in the background.

"Over and out," I said.

Jason reached over from behind me and patted me on the shoulder.

"Nice touch, man," he said and then put a dark wig over his butch haircut, and a pair of dark mirror glasses. "My own mother wouldn't recognize me."

I had Arne drop Jason off at the next cross street, about a half mile down the road beyond the film lab in the same direction Maggie and Jocelyn had gone. There was a stop sign which made it perfect for the operation. Jason would wait there to perform his task. I had Arne turn around, come back, and park the van about a half block down the road from Filmando's. Mark Horgan parked on the other side of the road. As we waited, I sipped coffee from a Styrofoam cup. Since this was an out of the way area there was little traffic.

My disguise consisted of a blonde wig and a dark red mustache. I wore a faded blue sweatshirt and camouflage pants I found at a war surplus store. Arne, who had five days growth of beard, simply wore a navy blue watch cap pulled down over his brow. We settled back to wait. My adrenalin was pumping. It was after ten and no sign of the two men from Vegas. I was beginning to think they had changed their minds. We continued to wait.

Finally, a blue Chevy van pulled up and parked directly in front of the lab. The larger of the two men was driving. He just sat there. It looked like he was talking to himself and waving his arms. He lit a cigarette and blew smoke out the window. A few minutes later, the one called Zito pulled up in a black Cadillac. They both got out and walked up the path and into the double glass doors, which were so dirty you could barely see through them. They were in there for almost twenty minutes before the larger man came out, got into the blue van and turned right into a drive and disappeared around the back of the building.

"Jesus, what's happening?" Arne said.

"I don't' know," I said. "Must be a loading dock behind the lab."

"What if he goes the other way when he comes back out," Arne said. "We're screwed, right?"

"Could be," I said.

Five minutes later, the walkie-talkie crackled again. Maggie wanted to know what was happening. I told her to sit tight, that they were probably loading the van. Another twenty minutes had passed when the smaller man, Zito, came out the front entrance, got into the Cadillac and sped off straight down the road in the direction of Maggie's post. I let out a deep sigh of relief. It meant the van would head in the same direction, the right direction. It also meant that Zito would be well ahead of his partner.

Several more minutes passed and no sign of the van. I figured it should have been loaded by then. After a few more minutes, I got out of Arne's VW and walked to the corner of the building and peaked around the side. The blue van was no where in sight. I just stood there staring at the deserted street trying to figure it out. As I turned to go back I spotted the van coming out of a driveway behind the lab and head toward the road we were on. I sprinted back to the VW and jumped in.

"The van's coming," I said, catching my breath. "Keep a good distance behind it."

The blue van turned right onto the main road off the side street as we had hoped and followed in the direction Zito had taken. Arne kept the VW about a block distance behind the blue van. When the blue van reached the intersection with the stop sign, it stopped just long enough for Jason to appear from behind a telephone pole, crouch down and run up to the back of the van and puncture the right rear tire with a very sharp ice pick, twice. We figured the tire had to go flat at least a quarter mile ahead of the phone booth and almost a half mile from the lab. I actually tested how long it would take a tire to deflate from the stop sign on, using Maggie's car. I figured the loaded van would take even less time.

The blue van actually made it a little farther than I had thought. This made me nervous because it meant we would not have as much time to make the switch as I had counted on. Maggie's job was to keep watch to see if the one called Zito came back looking for his partner and the van, also to report on when the larger partner finished using the phone to call for a tow operator to come and fix the tire.

After a couple of minutes sitting in the van the larger man climbed out cursing aloud at the sky as if he blamed the heavens for his problem. He went around to the back, bent down and inspected the tire, running his finger around the edge. Jason, who had followed the van, walking very fast ducked into an alcove of an empty building. The man from Vegas stood up, walked around and opened the back doors to the van.

"What if he decides to fix the tire himself?" Arne said.

"Mark said he's not the type," I said. "Besides he'd have to take all of the film out to get to the tire, jack and lug wrench."

The man smashed his right fist into the palm of his left hand and slammed the back doors to the Chevy and locked them. He suddenly looked back toward the VW. We ducked down. For a moment, it looked like he might walk back to where we were parked. Then he turned and looked down the road toward the phone booth. He could probably just make it out from his position. The big guy checked his watch and then began walking down the road at a leisurely pace. When he'd walked about a hundred yards Jason began to follow him. He caught up with the man from Vegas and said something. This was not in the script.

"What the hell," I said aloud. "What's he doing?"

Arne turned the VW around and backed up to within a few feet of the back of the van. We got out. Arne went to see if he could open the van doors. Mark pulled up behind the VW and parked.

"What're you guys doing?"

"The van's locked. Jason was supposed to pick the lock for us," I said.

Mark quickly produced a tiny set of tools he kept in his pocket and began working on the van's lock. In a moment he had the doors open. We did not waste time transferring the film to the VW through its side door and replacing the cans with the junk film. It was getting hot and we were all sweating. Mark took off his jacket and rolled up his sleeves. I stripped down to my T-shirt. Maggie called on the walkie-talkie and, sounding panicked, reported that the Man from Vegas had finished using the phone and was heading back to the van at a fast pace. We began working faster to complete the exchange. I peaked around the back of the van to see if I could see him. What I saw kind of startled me. Jason came out of nowhere and jumped in front of the big man. It looked like they might be arguing. The man then pushed Jason out of the way and continued coming closer.

Finally, the last can was in the VW. Both Arne and I closed the double doors of the van and Mark got it locked again. We jumped into the VW and pulled away, heading back toward the lab. Mark had hurried back to his car, did a u-turn and followed us. I looked out the back window. The man from Vegas had been distracted and apparently had not noticed us speeding away. Once we were about half a mile up the road we turned around and came back, passing the man from Vegas. He was leaning up against the van smoking. He glanced at us as we flew by but gave no hint of recognition or suspicion. Jason, who was about fifty or sixty yards down the road from the van, stuck out his thumb as if hitchhiking. Arne went passed him and then rolled to a stop. Jason ran and jumped in the van. I picked up the walkie-talkie.

"Calling Maggie."

After some crackling static.

"Maggie the spy here."

"Operation Cobra Woman/Prairie Wolves has been carried out," I said.

I could hear her say something to Jocelyn and then both let out a whoop.

"That was cool, man," Jason said.

I turned around and looked at him.

"What were you doing?" I said. "You were supposed to come back and unlock the van."

Jason shrugged.

"I forgot about that," he said. "I figured I'd slow the man down, asked him questions, like where Hollywood Boulevard was, and could he lend me some money. At one point I thought he was going to slug me."

"Hey," Arne said to me, "why don't you buy this buggy off me. Then you won't have to move this stuff."

"I don't have the money," I said.

"Nothing at all?" Arne said sounding surprised. "You can have it for three bills. She may not look like much but she runs like a sonofabitch."

I stared out the window at the passing scenery and fired up a smoke.

"What do you say?" Arne persisted. "I got the pink slip for this baby right here."

I shut my eyes and felt my head drifting into a kind of waking dream, a momentary murky nether place, a dark room with Cobra Woman/ Prairie Wolves nothing but a pile of celluloid in the middle of the floor, a figure standing on the other side soundlessly laughing. It looked like Jimmy Oliver as I first saw him, and the figure of a woman beyond him in the shadows, silent and mysterious and somehow familiar. Adele.

Arne's shrill voice brought me back.

"What do you say, man?"

"I'll think about it," I said.

"Cool," he said. "I think you should have this baby. Besides, I need the bread."

We were silent the rest of the way back. Just before Vine and Sunset Boulevard Arne pulled over, jumped out and told me to take the buggy, saying he'd catch up later. He said the pink slip was in the glove compartment. I dropped Jason off at Starburst/Meade and began driving absently toward the beach. My problem now was what to do with the film since there was no money for post production. I drove around for an hour until I found myself in front of Bonnie Robertson's apartment in Venice. I figured she might know something. There was a note on her door for a delivery man saying she'd gone to the beach. I drove to the beach. Before leaving the VW, I spread newspapers over the piles of cans. I found Bonnie's towel and umbrella in the same spot I'd found her before. Bonnie, looking trim in a one piece bathing suit was heading up the beach. She stopped short when she saw me, then eased herself down on her towel and began putting suntan oil on her shoulders.

"Don't want to get too burned," she said and pushed the bottle at me. "Here, put some on my back."

I did and then stretched out next to her and put on my dark glasses.

"So what are you doing here?" She said.

I told her I had the film and no place to go with it. Bonnie didn't question it. She told me she knew some freelance editors but there was no way any of them would cut film on the come. Bonnie was not very encouraging. That evening I was in a booth at Chick's, sipping coffee and going through my notebook. Inside, I found the scribbled phone number for Sherry Woo in San Francisco. I'd forgotten about her and wondered if she might know someone who could cut the film together. While I had not talked to her since she left, she had called Jocelyn a while back about where to send her W-2 form. Sherry told her she was working in the film scene in San Francisco and Marin County.

Chick came over from behind the counter and sat opposite me in the booth.

"That big feller, Mark, called here for you a couple of times," Chick said. "Says it's important that he talk to you right away."

"What for?"

"Didn't say," Chick said. "Said if you showed your face you were to stay here."

I shrugged.

"Can you lend me three hundred?" I said.

Chick straightened and shook his head.

"Big movie mogul needs to borrow more money." He said. "What about that twenty five hundred I already lent you? Am I ever going to see that?"

I told him I needed it to buy this van.

"Tell you what," I said. "I'll give you a producer credit as I promised and a point – a share of the movie."

Chick slapped the table and started laughing.

"That's about as good as a turd on a log," he said.

He got up, disappeared out back and returned a few minutes later and plunked down a small stack of bills.

"Use it wisely," he said and went back to work.

"Thanks," I said.

A short while later, Maggie showed up wearing bib overalls over a white T-shirt. I thought she looked sexy. She had a quick cup of coffee and told me she was heading back up to the house because there was going to be a party which Arne was organizing for her transient guests and wanted to let me know. "After all, we should celebrate the great film caper." She leaned across the table and whispered that one of the guys was supplying a kilo of Acapulco gold.

Later, I was almost out the door when the phone behind the counter began ringing. One of the waitresses picked it up and yelled that it was for me. I went behind the counter and took the receiver. It was Mark sounding excited.

"Don't go back to the house," he said.

"Why not?"

"That guy Arne's a narc," he said.

"What?"

I was incredulous.

"Listen to me. He's a federal narcotic's officer. No question. What's more, there's a raid planned for that house tonight in conjunction with the LAPD. Anybody who's there will get caught up in the net."

"You sure?" I said.

"It's for real," Mark said.

"I've got to warn Maggie," I said. "She just left."

"Forget Maggie," he said. "There's something else. My report was sent out to the client."

"What report?" I said. "What're you talking about?"

"My investigation into the death of Margo Benson. I was holding off but mother found the report in a sealed envelope, addressed and stamped. So she just went ahead and mailed it. I didn't know it until I heard from my client when I got back this afternoon."

"So what?" I said. "I mean that whole thing with Margo Benson was over a year ago."

Mark was silent on the other end as if trying to gather his thoughts. I could hear his breathing into the phone. It sounded heavy and labored.

"Does the name Jack mean anything to you?"

"Jack?" I said.

"Jack Wallace. He rents a little place behind another house in West Hollywood. Someone had a party at his house when he was away and according to him, you and Maggie were there and found Margo's body behind a couch the next morning. He said you and Maggie decided, against his advice to call the police, and instead took the body and dumped it in the hills. He signed an affidavit to that effect which I included in my report."

"Jesus," I blurted out. "It was Jack's idea because..."

"The point is my client is actually Moe Miller. He does not want to get the police involved. For starters, though, he wants to confiscate the film."

I held the receiver away from me and gulped air.

"You there?" Mark said.

"Yeah," I said after a time.

"I told Moe the film was at Starburst/Meade and he couldn't get it until tomorrow." Mark went on. "So he'll be sending some people. Get my meaning?"

"I think so," I said.

"This is the last favor I do for you," Mark said, lowering his voice. "Something about you that's just plain trouble."

Chapter 47

————

Night had fallen. I started north, fighting traffic on Ventura Boulevard which was also Highway 101. But I kept thinking about Maggie walking into a trap. It was eating away at me. Finally, I turned back and headed for the Marcuse house, still finding it hard to believe about Arne. He seemed okay, so friendly and loose. And the VW. It was almost as if he wanted to give it to me. At the next stoplight I checked the glove compartment. The pink slip was there. I wondered if I could get to the Marcuse house in time.

As usual, the road leading up to the house was dark except for a sprinkling of lights from houses I passed along the way. I parked on a small side street down the hill a ways and made my way up on foot, staying inside the shadows. Once at the edge of the property, I stayed low and made my way up along the side as far as I could go without being seen. A tall hedge provided cover. Sure enough black and white squad cars were all around the front of the house, red and white lights flashing. There were some unmarked cars as well. A few television cameras were set up on what was once a lawn, trained on the front entrance as officers were leading some of Maggie's renters out. No sign of Arne, or Maggie. The house looked totally dark.

Maggie's car was nowhere in sight. I then moved around to the downhill side of the house near where Maggie's old room was and stayed behind some bushes while my eyes adjusted to the blackness. This was a nerve racking business, I thought, as I gulped air. After a few moments I got down on all fours like a soldier infiltrating an enemy camp and crawled down around the back side of the house, then stood half way up to a crouch and took a step. At that moment, I stumbled over a body lying prone in the brush.

"What the...?" I blurted out.

"Shuuuu!"

It was Maggie. I lowered myself down next to her just off the path.

"What the hell's happening?" She said. "The Fuzz is all over the place."

"Your pal Arne," I said.

"Arne? Are they busting him?"

I stifled a laugh.

"No," I whispered, "he's the buster. Arne's an undercover federal narcotics agent or something like that."

Maggie rolled over on her side so that we were face to face. She was close enough that I could feel the warmth of her breath.

"Bullshit!" she said. "Who told you that?"

"Let's get out of here before they come down here," I said.

"I've got to get something in my darkroom," she said and then began crawling ahead. "Come on and help me."

I crawled up along side of her.

"You're crazy," I said

Maggie ignored me and began crawling again toward the basement where she had her darkroom. I didn't move, figuring I should scramble back down the hill to make my escape. Instead, I followed her. For some reason it momentarily brought back the memory of that time so many years before when I led Tony Billings and his Prairie Wolf gang through the cornfields on that warm summer day, only to discover my young mother Adele and Jimmy Oliver naked on a blanket, the white flesh of their glistening bodies almost glaring in the afternoon sun. I knew what they were doing and yet I was secretly glad for Adele because even at the age of twelve I could see joy in her face, something I rarely saw at home.

I caught up with Maggie.

"We're gonna get caught," I whispered.

"Maybe, maybe not," she said. "We got one thing going for us. There are no lights. The utility company shut off the power this afternoon."

We crawled silently on all fours like commandos passed Maggie's old room to the little door on the far side which led to the utility room. It was absolutely pitch black. Once inside, we slowly fumbled our way toward the makeshift darkroom. We could hear muffled voices and movement above.

"Bastards," Maggie said in a low voice.

I bumped into a laundry table which moved making a scraping sound along the floor. We froze and held our breaths. The door at the top of the stairs opened and someone with a flashlight began sweeping the area in front of us, missing us by a couple of inches.

"What's down there?" A male voice said to someone. "I thought I heard something."

"Nothing much," a familiar voice answered. "Rats maybe. It's a laundry room and storage area. We can check it out later. Let's start at the top and work our way down."

The door shut.

"Arne," Maggie said. "I can't believe it."

Inside her darkroom, Maggie managed to find a flashlight in a drawer under her work bench. It was dim but provided just enough light. She handed it to me while she filled a box with unexposed film, some prints and negatives, her camera, and light meter. She had a second hand enlarger, but it was too big to take.

Halfway down the hill she told me her car had broken down and she would have to put her stuff in the VW next to the boxes of cans with the film. The minute she climbed into the passenger seat she shook her head and looked around, as if inspecting the back.

"What's that smell?" She said.

I shrugged. Fifteen minutes later we were heading north.

"Where are we going?" Maggie said when she realized the direction we were taking.

"San Francisco," I said.

"What?"

"I'm going to try and find someone who might know someone who can cut the film," I said. "If you don't want to go I'll drop you off."

Maggie stared out the window and didn't say anything for several minutes.

"I have no place to go," she said finally. "Do you have any money?"

I nodded.

"Some," I said, realizing I still had the three hundred Chick had lent me, plus a little I had before. We were leaving with just the clothes on our backs.

Maggie fired up a smoke and said she was going to miss the old Marcuse house.

"County will probably take it over for back taxes," she said.

She finished her cigarette and after awhile she leaned back and dozed off. I turned on the radio to a music station. I stopped for gas just off 101 outside a place called Oxnard, and picked up a pack of cigarettes and some candy bars from a store next to the gas station. Maggie slept for another half hour. She moaned and opened her eyes.

"Where are we?"

"Almost to Ventura," I said.

"What about Arne's van here?" Maggie said.

I explained the situation and that I was going to buy it but…"

"He wanted to sell it to me real bad for some reason," I said.

"Yeah, he couldn't stand the smell," Maggie said.

When we reached Ventura, there was a news-flash on the radio about a big Hollywood drug bust. According to the report several young men and a couple of teenager girls, believed to be runaways were taken into custody for drug possession and trafficking. A large cache of hashish, marijuana, and heroin were found hidden behind a false wall in the house once owned by silent movie star Francis Walker Marcuse. Some of the suspects also had drugs on their person, according to federal agents on the scene. It was a joint effort with the Los Angeles Police Department. The radio newscaster ended by reporting that authorities were also looking for a 1949 Volkswagen van, described as having red doors, and a suspect who may be transporting drugs. "The suspect is: Charles Alvin Kendall, who also goes by the nickname name Tuckie. He may be traveling with a young woman, Margaret Allison Langston. The suspect may be armed and dangerous."

"God, I can't believe it," Maggie said. "Those fucking assholes bringing all that shit into the house."

"Forget that," I said. "You heard what he said about the van. Arne must have told them that."

Ten miles up the road it hit both Maggie and I at the same time. It was a setup. I pulled over to a rest stop and got out where the air was fresh, in contrast to the van. We began searching the van, every tiny nook and cranny for a possible hiding place, though we weren't sure what wewere looking for. We took the cardboard boxes containing the cans of film and stacking them on a nearby picnic bench. Maggie took a break and went into a crumbling stone restroom. She immediately ran out and declared she'd rather go in the field beyond the parking area. When she came back I was examining the engine compartment in the back. Maggie stuck her head in the door and said she thought the weird smell had gotten much stronger since leaving L.A.

"Like something died," she said.

Using her flashlight she scanned the inside, nothing except some old cigar butts. She scooped them up with some paper, wadded it up and tossed it out. Under a thin carpet was a floorboard which I was able to take off with a Swiss Army Knife screw driver. We pried it up and found the source of the smell. It was a dead cat that somehow got up onto a shallow well underneath the frame. It had white all over its mouth. I picked it up and wrapped it in a greasy towel I'd found. Next to the cat was a paper bag with the corner chewed off. Inside the bag was about three cups of a white powder in a chewed up plastic bag. The cat must have eaten some of the powder. Maggie wasn't sure, but she thought it might be heroin. "Arne must have stashed it there so it would be found, sonofabitch," Maggie muttered. "Probably worth a lot."

I took the bag and the cat and buried them in a shallow hole I dug with my hands in the field.

We repacked the van and continued north. We got into San Francisco about five in the morning and somehow ended up down near the marina. I parked on a side street and we both slept for a few hours. Outside, I took in the pungent smell of the bay waters and screeching of seagulls. We had breakfast at a café up on Lombard, scrambled eggs and toast for Maggie, a short stack for me, coffee for both of us and smokes.

"This is a great town," Maggie said. "When I was going to Stanford, some classmates and I would come up here sometimes on weekends and hit the bars. We all had fake I.Ds."

"We've got to do something about the van," I said absently. "How many vans around with red doors that don't match the rest of it?"

We decided we needed some clothes. At Woolworths Maggie picked up two pairs of panties and a brassier. Later we found a second hand store. Maggie bought a used pair of shorts, blouse, sweater, and jeans plus a small canvas carrying bag. I picked up a pair of faded Levis, a couple of T-shirts, a sweater, an army air corps flight jacket, leather with a fur collar, two army blankets and two pillows. We lived in the van for a couple of days, parking on slanted streets and slept in the back. It was tight with the boxes of film which we pushed close to one side. On the second night the fog rolled in thick and close to the ground and you could hear the mournful cry of a distant foghorn. Maggie was desperate for a shower so on the third day we checked into a sleazy hotel down on Mission. It was cheap enough so we stayed for two nights.

It took five days to track down Sherry Woo. I had started by calling her family. A woman who didn't identify herself and who barely spoke English always answered.

"Not here," she would say and hang up.

It was as though she was angry with me for even asking for Sherry. I called every day after our first day in the city. Finally on the fourth day, a man answered who turned out to be Sherry's brother, Tommy. After taking a meticulous history of my relationship with Sherry he offered to give her a message if and when he saw her or she called. His tone was not friendly, simply matter of fact.

"Can she call you somewhere?" He said.

"Can't you tell me where she is?" I said.

"No," Tommy said.

I told him I would just have to keep calling.

"I hope your mother or whoever the woman is who answered before isn't mad because I keep calling."

"Forget it," Tommy said. "She's angry because she has lost control of her daughter. Sherry's a wild child."

That night we stopped at a gas station in what Maggie called the Tenderloin and took sponge baths in the restrooms. Later we stumbled on a scene where two police officers were arresting a prostitute at the mouth of an alley. Maggie jumped out of the van before I knew it and began snapping pictures from about fifteen feet from the action. As the prostitute was being pushed into the back of a patrol car she spotted Maggie and stuck her tongue out. Maggie winked at her. The prostitute, who could not have been more that twenty, laughed. The two officers, who had not noticed Maggie, got in and drove off.

"Did you see that?" Maggie said excitedly. "Her expression was fabulous. I hope that shot comes out."

"That was nuts," I said. "Those cops could've decided to check us out."

I was becoming more and more nervous about the van. I wondered if the local cops had picked up the bulletin. Whenever I saw a police car I'd turn and go the opposite direction.

Over coffee in a little out-of-the-way joint, I told Maggie about my other fear.

413

"Those gangster guys will be looking for us…for me and the film as soon as they catch on to what they have."

"How could they possibly know where we are?"

I just shrugged. Later, I called Sherry Woo's home again and this time, Tommy told me he had talked to Sherry and that she was staying with a friend on a houseboat in an old shipyard north in Sausalito. He gave me directions and described the houseboat as a large green structure with a sign above the door that said: The Hallowed Ark.

"Sherry told me to tell you, you'll find her there after four o'clock in the afternoon." Tommy said. "She sounded very excited about your visit."

We drove across the Golden Gate Bridge and then down a narrow winding road into Sausalito, a small quaint little town right on the bay water. It seemed to consist primarily of small shops and seafood restaurants. I continued north about two miles to a dirt road along the waters edge. It was after five by the time Maggie and I found "The Hallowed Ark" after missing it a couple of times. The legend above the door in large purple letters had faded to almost invisibility. The ark was sitting on mud and listed slightly. Sherry Woo opened the door and immediately gave me a hug and nodded at Maggie. I hardly recognized Sherry. She was thin and her hair was cut very short. She looked more like a twelve year old boy than a young woman in her late twenties.

"When my brother told me you called, I couldn't believe it," she said and waived her arm around. "This is where I'm living at present, Richardson Bay. If my mother saw this she'd scream or have a heart attack. She hates the fact that I'm not home."

I looked around. The place was dank and dark and smelled of mildew. It was one large open room with a small kitchen in the middle, which Sherry referred to as a galley, a double bed toward the back, a couch, some chairs and a glass door leading to a small deck over where the water should be. Sherry got some paper cups and a bottle of wine and we went out to the deck and sat. I fired up a smoke and noticed that water was beginning to creep toward us.

"Tides coming in," Sherry said. "Before long we'll be floating."

414

"What a cool place," Maggie said, and asked if she could take some pictures. Sherry shrugged and Maggie, who had her camera strapped over her shoulder, began snapping away, mostly of Sherry and I, and inside the Ark.

We spent the next hour catching up, me telling her about finally making The Prairie Wolves, which was now called: 'Cobra Woman versus the Prairie Wolves in the Vortex of the Valley of Darkness,' and about Frank Meade disappearing, which she knew about because the local press had carried the story.

"Who came up with that title, Frank?" Sherry said, laughing,.

"The investors agreed with it, said it was more marketable." I said.

 She then told me she was a member of an underground film cooperative, that she and some others rent space in a World War II industrial building not far from the Ark. We were soon joined by a lean young man with shaggy hair and a few days growth of beard. His name was Ben. Sherry introduced him as her roommate. Ben just nodded and looked sullen. Sherry poured some wine for him. He pushed it away.

"What's the matter with you?" She said, and then sighed.

Without waiting for an answer Sherry turned to me and said Ben was a documentary film-maker working on a film about the waterfront life.

"I think it has potential," she said.

"It's shit," Ben said. He turned to me. "What's your scene, man?"

"I'm...I'm a fugitive," I said.

"He made a movie," Sherry injected. "It needs to be edited. It's a full length feature."

Ben perked up.

"That right," he said. "Is it existential? What's it called?"

I told him and explained some of the plot. Ben just laughed and said it sounded like something you scrape off your shoes. I just stared at him impassively.

"Don't be an ass, Ben!" Sherry said and then turned to me. "Ben's really an editor. He's a genius at cutting film. He has his own thirty five millimeter Movieolla."

Ben grunted, got up and left. Around dusk, Sherry said she had to go pick up some money from a friend who owed her. I offered to drive her. The three of us piled in the van and drove north along the frontage road about a couple of miles. Along the way, Maggie noticed an area that looked to be the size of a city block mostly hidden by trees and tall brush. A scruffy-looking man perched on a concrete block at what looked like an entrance to the place, watched us with binoculars as we passed by.

"What's that?" Maggie asked.

"It's called Rubble City," Sherry said. "It's an encampment. Don't ever go in there. It's dangerous. There are a lot of crazy people in there. They say there are over a thousand people living there, mostly hobos, gypsies, down and outers and other misbegotten souls. Nobody bothers them. Even the sheriff won't go in there."

Sherry added that during the war, there were warehouses and factories stretching along the property. After the war, the buildings were torn down to make way for development that never happened. All that was left are some partial structures and foundations.

When we got back, one of Sherry's neighbors, a woman named Roberta, offered to let Maggie and I stay in a back room she had on a houseboat just down the road. We slept on a mattress on the floor. Before drifting off, we heard the sound of tiny feet running around the room. We flipped on the light and there staring at us as if we had invaded his home was the largest rat I'd ever seen. Maggie screamed. The rat turned and disappeared through a hole in the wall. Roberta came running in.

"What's the matter?" She said.

"There was a rat in here," Maggie said.

Roberta laughed.

"Must have been Jasper," she said. "He's a squatter here from time to time. That's life on the water."

Chapter 48

T he next morning I went to a local hardware store and bought two gallons of flat gray house paint and two brushes. I parked the van in the grassy area just off the dirt road across from the Hallowed Ark. Maggie and I then set about painting it from one end to the other. It took about two hours including smoke breaks. The directions said it would take about four hours to dry. Afterward Maggie took some pictures of me standing next to the van, paint brush in hand. I took some shots of her with her camera in the same pose.

"It looks like hell," Maggie said. "But no one will ever recognize it."

Around noon Sherry guided us to a little waterfront place down the road apiece called The Top Deck Galley. It was close enough to walk. As we went in I noticed a sign in the window: Fry Cook Wanted. The place looked like it had been built out of planks from an old sailing ship. Inside the motif was ancient mariner. There was sawdust on the wooden floor, a few bronze portholes, an ancient ship's wooden steering wheel on a stand with a polished compass, and large pictures and paintings of square rigger sailing ships from the 1800s on the walls. It was a little smaller than Chick's Hamburger Palace. The smell of sizzling bacon and onions hung in the air. After a fifteen minute wait we were seated at a table next to a large picture window which looked out at a Marina.

We all ordered eggs with hash-browns, toast and coffee. After finishing we fired up smokes and sat silently staring out the window. Sherry looked pensive, even a little sad.

I could see Maggie eyeing Sherry with interest.

"Where's your friend Ben?" She said.

"He's sleeping in," Sherry said.

"What's the matter with him? Maggie went on. He's so unfriendly."

Sherry took a drag on her cigarette and pursed her lips, as if giving Maggie's comment some thought.

"He's depressed," she said. "He can't seem to get going on his waterfront film. Sometimes he's like a lost soul. It makes me want to cry sometimes because he's very talented."

A couple of evenings later I was coming back from applying for the fry cook job at the Top Deck Galley. I spotted a figure staggering up the road just ahead of me. It was Ben. He stopped, stared at me in the dim light of dusk and then fell flat on the dirt road, mumbling to himself. I went over and started to help him up, but Ben rolled away from me.

"I don't need your help," Ben said, slurring his words. "And that van of yours looks like an abortion."

I stood there looking down at Ben.

"What the hell you looking at?" Ben yelled and pushed himself up to a sitting position. "I don't get it. How come some hick like you has a film under his belt and I don't have shit. No sense. I mean I been to film school. I apprenticed with a top editor. I got credentials. What've you got! Ole Sherry, though, she parades you around and says we should take care of this guy. Fuck that, man! You're bad karma, that's what I say."

When I didn't say anything Ben went on gathering momentum as words tumbled out of him, most not making any sense.

"I know the goddamn plot here," Ben snarled. "You're hanging around waiting for me to cut your film, right? Huh? Why don't you just come out and say it motherfucker?"

Finally Ben hauled himself up to his feet, staggering and weaving his way in a circle around me as if sizing me up like I was some kind of prey. I started to walk on to the Ark where Maggie and I were camping.

"Don't worry," Ben yelled after me. "I'll cut your film. Wanna know why? Cause I ain't got nothing else to do." He laughed as though this were some great irony. "Bring your shit to the old Industrial Building Warehouse tomorrow. Bring a work print, your negative, the optical sound print, and a copy of the shooting script. Also bring a list of credits which we'll have to shoot and tack on."

I turned and watched him stumble off, skeptical about his ability. That night, Maggie, Sherry and I had a drink at a small bar in Sausalito. Sherry told us Ben had come from money and was trying to make it on his own. She said he gets manic some times, but added that it was no wonder. He was gong through a really bad time. His younger brother had been killed in an auto accident a few weeks before and his mother had committed suicide six months earlier. His father was a wealthy lumber broker and sent just enough money for Ben to live on every month.

"He must be hard to live with," Maggie said.

Sherry shrugged.

"He...he has his moments," she said. "But one thing I know, he can cut your film."

"You really think so?" I said.

Sherry nodded and added that she hoped I could pay him something.

Jocelyn had made up a credit list which she had given to me. I found it in a greasy envelope stuffed into the glove compartment of the van and added Chick Hanover as an Associate Producer with a pen.

In the months that followed Ben set to work editing Cobra Woman/ Prairie Wolves. He worked in a back room of the old warehouse which was about a half-mile south of the Hallowed Ark. He did not want me coming around. Sherry said he was putting in as many as twelve and even eighteen hour days, as if he'd become obsessed with the film. Sherry said Ben was like a ghost slipping in and out of the Ark at all hours.

I got the job as fry cook at the Top Deck Galley. At first, the woman who owned the place, a tough Greek woman in her fifties named Damali Megalos gave the job to a young man who claimed all kinds of experience. One of the requirements of the job was to put on a little show for the customers. The show involved flipping an egg by tossing it almost to the ceiling and have it drop back down into the pan unscathed and ready to serve. Maggie and I were there for breakfast the morning the new fry cook started. A customer sitting at the counter ordered two eggs over easy. The fry cook broke the eggs in a small pan and when they were cooked enough on one side he tossed them in the air. But when they came down he missed them with the pan and they splattered on the floor. After he cleaned up the floor he was immediately relegated to peeling potatoes out back. Mrs. Megalos was furious and embarrassed. Without her permission or saying anything I stepped behind the counter and demonstrated how to flip eggs, tossing them up to the ceiling and making a soft landing in the pan, sunny-side up. I got a hand and a few whoops from the customers. Mrs. Megalos was impressed and hired me on the spot.

"Where did you learn to do that?" She said.

"Back home at my friend Marco's diner," I said. "I worked there after school and during the summers, and at Chick's Hamburger Palace in Hollywood where I perfected it. When do I start?"

Mrs. Megalos looked at her watch.

"You're already ten minutes late," she said.

My new job paid me fifty dollars a week for five and a half days, Tuesday through Sunday noon. The Top Deck Galley was closed on Mondays. It was a busy place. I enjoyed watching the waterfront characters that came in, some of whom worked on boats or were fishermen. On my breaks I made notes and even attempted sketches of some of the more interesting faces. After a few weeks, Mrs. Megalos let me open up on my own at six in the morning to catch the early breakfast crowd.

One early morning, a large disheveled looking man was standing outside peering in the window. It was still dark out, but I could see him. There were no customers in the place yet. The man came in. He was grizzled with a florid face, full graying beard, red eyes and a bulbous nose. A tattered gray overcoat hung loosely from his shoulders. After looking around as if to make sure no one else was there he took a seat at the counter. Without asking I put a fresh cup of coffee in front of him. The man, who smelled pretty ripe, nodded, took a sip of the coffee and asked if he could have something to eat, noting right away that he did not have money to pay. I was about to tell the man I could not do that, but something in the man's eyes stopped me. While he looked like a man who'd gotten old before his time, there was something iron tough in his face. After he removed his hat, his large head looked even larger with its crown of thick yellow-white hair. He told me he sometimes came by to see if there were any edible scraps in the garbage bin out back.

"What would you like?" I said.

Without waiting for an answer I served the man a plate of scrambled eggs, hash browns, sausages and biscuits. When he was finished he asked if he could come back. I looked at him for a long moment and then nodded, telling him to make it early before other customers got there. After that, the man began coming around every morning right before opening. Sometimes he was already there waiting for me. He never said much. On a couple of occasions he dug into the pockets of his coat and pulled out a few coins which he offered. I refused any payment. One morning I asked the man where he lived.

"Must be close," I said.

The old man pointed in a northerly direction.

"A couple miles from here," he said. "Folks call it Rubble City. We call it Freedom Haven."

I told him I'd heard of it, actually passed it a while back.

"I'm the mayor," he said. "Duly elected. Name's Milo. Come on by sometime, but when you enter, be sure to tell anyone you meet there you're my friend. Some of the folks there get real nasty with strangers. Don't trust outsiders. You can't blame them. Society and life has not been too kind to the Rubble City population. What's your name?"

"Charles," I said. "Folks call me Tuckie."

Milo just nodded. He stopped coming around after that and I wondered if something had happened to him. I realized I had become fond of the old man. He was kind of a philosopher, which I knew little about, but enjoyed listening to him just the same once he opened up. He said that Rubble City was like an island for the misbegotten.

During that time, Maggie moved in with a sixty-four year old man named Jean Luc Badour who lived on an old ferry boat nearby. He was an artist, a sculptor who occasionally got commissions for public buildings. Maggie said she adored him. I guess I felt the pangs of jealousy, which surprised me. I realized I had probably been taking her for granted. I had tried to act casual, but in the end asked her to stay. She had just looked at me with tears in her eyes and told me it was too late. I shrugged and later got drunk at a local bar. I knew I would miss her warm body next to me at night.

In the meantime, Maggie's fortunes had been changing in other ways. She sold the picture of the prostitute sticking her tongue out while being arrested to a local magazine. Then she happened on a burning car one day and began snapping pictures of a young mother struggling to rescue her baby from the flames, risking her own life as firemen tried to intervene. But the heart-stopper showed the mother's clothes on fire as she lifted the baby out of the back and high above her head to keep it safe. A fireman took the baby and another threw her to the ground and flapped his jacked over her until the flames were out.

Maggie sold that picture to a local weekly newspaper. It was picked up by a daily and later a national magazine which captioned it: "A Mother's Heroism, a Moment of Truth." Photo by Margaret Allison Langston, with a picture of Maggie inset next to it. To Maggie's amazement the photo was submitted for a Pulitzer Prize. Not long after Maggie came into the Top Deck and told me she was now working as a stringer photographer for a daily newspaper.

"They'll give me photo credits," she said. "Not to mention pay me. Grover would have been proud of me. Poor Grover. Well, it's a long way from dancing naked for my room."

I nodded.

"How's what's his name…Jean Luc?"

Maggie gave me a Cheshire grin.

"Good," She said. "Real good. He loves me."

"Isn't he a little old for you?" I said.

Maggie leaned in close and whispered.

"He's like a sex machine," she giggled. "He knows how to make a woman happy."

One night Jean Luc threw a party on his boat in celebration of Maggie's picture being published. He invited Sherry, Roberta, several members of the houseboat and waterfront community and me. We drank wine and Jean Luc entertained us playing French gypsy songs on his guitar. When Jean Luc, switched to Flamenco, Maggie, drunk by this time, got up and began dancing, stripping as she moved around until she was naked. She then ran out and down the dock and back whooping and hollering. Neighboring houseboat dwellers came out on their decks to see what the racket was all about and clapped as Maggie passed by.

A couple of weeks later, on a Wednesday, Sherry told me Ben was almost finished with editing my movie. He would show the finished film at the warehouse Friday night. A close friend who was night manager at a lab over in South San Francisco had agreed to run a release print using old stock. Sherry said Ben had also added some canned music.

I was excited. But then the next morning while having coffee I happened on two very crazy news stories which gave me heart palpitations. The headline in a couple of the morning Bay Area daily newspapers which were sold at the Top Deck read:

PRODUCER FOUND DEAD
The remains found in a shallow grave earlier this week
in the Nevada desert have been positively identified as that
of Frank L. Meade, well known Hollywood producer of
low budget films. A yellow Thunderbird belonging to the
producer was found abandoned in Paradise, Nevada.
Meade's wife Pamela Andrews Meade had reported him
missing several months ago and that he had been in the middle
of producing a new movie when he disappeared. In a related
story the film in question, entitled 'Cobra Woman versus
the Prairie Wolves in the Vortex of the Valley of Darkness,'

has disappeared. According to sources who wish to remain
anonymous, it is believed that the film's writer, Charles
Kendall has gone into hiding with the film in the San Francisco
Bay Area. Kendall, some may remember, made national news
last year when it was reported that he had been kidnapped
and held hostage by a mysterious cult. At the time some
tabloids had suggested he may even have been taken by
aliens. Meanwhile, a source close to the investigation said that
Meade had had large gambling debts and may have been the
victim of a mob hit.

"Jesus," I said, wondering how anyone could know where I was.
Where could the paper have gotten that information?"

It was late afternoon. I got off work and headed for the barge. All I
wanted to do was go sit in my room in the back alone, reread the story
and think about what I should do. As I entered the barge, Roberta
stopped me. She looked pale and nervous.

"Two men came here looking for you," she said. "Said they were
friends of yours, but if you ask me they were pretty scary types. Big guys
in dark suits."

"Where'd they go?"

"They waited in your room for a while," Roberta said. "I didn't
want to let them in but they were insistent. After awhile they left and said
they would catch up with you later. I did tell them you might be at the Industrial Warehouse where Ben is finishing your movie."

"Oh, shit," I said.

"Should I not have told them that?"

I shook my head. I remembered Sherry told me Ben was going to be
in San Francisco over night with some friends from his home town. So the
warehouse studio would be locked up. I made a dash to my room. It
looked like a cyclone had come through. What little clothes I had were
strewn around, the mattress was now turned on its side and leaning
against the wall, my notebooks had been tossed across the room, some

pages torn out and left scattered on the floor. I threw my things into an olive drab canvas duffle bag another purchase from a war surplus store. I started out toward the front through the ark when I heard male voices coming from the front room. Roberta was trying to keep them at bay. My heart instantly went into racing mode. I turned and scampered out through the back door to the deck, made my way along the narrow cat-walk on the side to the road. Sure enough there was the dreaded black Cadillac parked on the road in front. No question that car symbolized the presence of something evil, of death come a calling. I figured they had caught up with Frank Meade and now it was my turn.

I hopped into the VW and headed up the dirt road, trying to think like the Wichita Kid. What would he do in a situation like this? I started to pass Rubble City, stopped, backed up and tried to peer through the trees and tall brush that together acted like a rampart protecting this mys-terious encampment, hiding its secrets from the outside world. I drove through the entrance, basically just a wide path, and slowly made my way deeper and deeper into the inner sanctum of this strange place. It was anything but the Land of Oz, more like an invisible colony.

At first there wasn't much to see. The VW felt like it was going to shake apart as it bounced over ruts and bumps. The path ended at the edge of the city. I got out and began to gingerly make my way through the bones of buildings that had once stood there. It looked like something from old newsreel footage of bombed out European cities after World War II. Except for a breeze that swept through from the bay, it was eerily silent. I could feel eyes watching me from every direction.

Rubble City was a dizzying maze of giant concrete foundations jut-ting up from the ground, deep basements and subterranean compart-ments. For a moment I considered turning back, sensing danger with each step I took into this dark, foreboding frontier. But I continued forging ahead, step by step. Just ahead of me sitting on top of a large concrete block was the hulk of an old Packard sedan with no wheels, rusting. It looked like it had long ago given up as a vehicle for transportation and transformed into a shelter, a home. Three pairs of eyes were peering at me from inside, children's eyes.

"I know Milo," I yelled into the air. "I've come to see Milo. He's my friend."

I soon came to an open depressed area which was surrounded by broken walls and old timbers with moss growing on them. It was a kind of village. There were men and women milling about, both old and young, and children playing amidst tents, make-shift hovels, lean-tos, and a wooden boat turned upside down and propped up by rough timbers. I could see there was a sleeping bag underneath. There were several small open fires where people were cooking something or boiling water. Everyone stopped what they were doing. All eyes were on me, eyes that said I was an intruder, I was danger. I approached, holding up my hands.

A bearded man suddenly jumped in front of me from out of nowhere. Before I knew it he had a knife at my throat. He had crazy eyes and his shirt smelled of cheap wine. Other men began to appear and soon formed a circle around me. Before seconds had passed there were maybe fifty men, all pressing me.

"What do you want here? The man with the beard said, in a strong guttural voice. He had large yellow teeth and his breath was foul.

"I came to see Milo," I said.

The man pushed his knife a little harder against my throat.

"No one by that name here," the man said. "Now get out."

I met the man's eyes, which were dark and intense. He gave me a push and I almost fell backward. Just then a booming voice from behind me seemed to roar out of the depths.

"I know this man. Back away!"

The man with the beard nodded at me and immediately moved back several steps and returned his knife to its sheath. I felt a wave of relief as I turned around and saw Milo coming up to the edge of the clearing, two large men at his side. Milo had the presence of a King entering his court. Then I couldn't believe what I was seeing. A black man I'd seen before appeared behind Milo. I could almost see a spark of recognition in

426

his eyes as he looked at me. It was the man I had encountered on a bench on Santa Monica Boulevard the year before who said he'd fought in World War I. His medal hung from his tattered jacket. He limped a little as he moved closer to me. I was not sure if he actually recognized me, but he nodded at me as if he did. One thing was different. He had a glow about him that was not there before.

Milo beckoned me to follow him.

Chapter 49

———

Milo sat like a potentate on a block of concrete, his legs dangling over the side. He packed some tobacco from a pouch into a pipe and lit it. The smoke drifted gently east with the breeze. I had followed him through the squalor of the encampment, passing micro hamlets along the way, clusters of inhabitants living in structures made from packing crates, reclaimed timbers, sheets of corrugated metal, and pieces of canvas. It looked like one of those African townships you see in National Geographic. Folks waved to Milo as he passed by along the jutting remnants of what must have been great buildings that had once stood there. As I trailed behind, I got cold hard stares. Then down some moss covered steps to a flat area and a small garden adorned with a metal arch and some folding chairs.

This was Milo's private domain. His home was a basement with steps leading down from the garden. He invited me to take the tour. Inside was like a cave, dark and musty. There was a double mattress covered with army blankets, a small wooden table, an oil lamp and books lined up on a board resting on two cinder blocks. In one corner close to the entrance was a Franklin stove with the flu going up and running along the ceiling to the outside. On a cardboard box by the entrance sat a portable windup record player. There was also a working faucet just outside the entrance. Milo told me it had been disconnected long ago but he had tapped into a water main near the road. Rubble City folks brought buckets and filled up when they needed water. Set back along side of Milo's home was a tattered tent. Above the entrance was a scrawled sign that said: PRIVY. Next to the tent was a bathtub sitting out in the open with a makeshift canopy.

Milo told the two men who acted like secret service types, disguised in rags, to leave us. They did. He made a pot of coffee by pouring the grounds into a battered-looking coffee pot filled with water and set it right in the middle of a small camp fire. While we waited for the coffee to boil he put a 78 record on the record player. It was Stan Getz playing "There's a Small Hotel" on his saxophone. It sounded mellow and for the first time since entering Rubble City I began to relax.

"We're not totally uncivilized here in the sovereign state of Rubble City," Milo said. He grinned through his full beard as he handed me coffee in a tin cup.

I took a sip. It was real strong, bitter and hot.

"How long have you lived here?" I said.

He put his pipe down and sipped his coffee.

"Let's see, it is now 1957 and I came here in 49 not long after the buildings here were demolished. They'd been put up as part of the war effort. I was the first to arrive but soon, others started coming when they heard about me and this place. It was like we were settlers on an unclaimed island, folks without homes or means to buy or even rent a home. County tried to kick us out a few times. Posted cease and desist notices. But here we are. Most of the men here are vets, came back after World War II and Korea all messed up in their heads, couldn't find jobs, society not happy with their behavior. Here they survive with some dignity, even contentment. Some work at menial jobs to feed their families and generally get by, others collect junk which they sell. Lots of ways to make a buck."

Milo sighed. For a moment he seemed pensive, far away.

"Were you in the service?" I asked.

Milo nodded.

"I fought in the pacific theatre," he said. "Came home, found my wife had left me for another man, and my old job as a factory foreman no longer existed. I worked at odd jobs for a time."

I fired up a smoke and took another sip of my coffee and asked him about the black man I'd seen. I told him about my encounter with him in Los Angeles. Milo laughed and said he just showed up one day. "It's his home now," he said. "He consults on security."

"I tried to enlist in the army," I said, "but was turned down because they said I had a heart murmur. I didn't, but that's what they said."

"I fear our way of life here is doomed," Milo said as if he hadn't heard me. "Some day Big Money in the name of progress will push us out to make way for prime development. It's the way of things. And we'll be like refugees from another world."

I just shrugged.

"I saw some young women when I came into Rubble City," I said. "Hobo girls?"

Milo laughed.

"Most come with their men, some are runaways, and I don't mean teenage kids. Grown women, some in their twenties, some a little older escaping from a bad marriage or some trouble or other. We have a few night girls here...you know, like the old west at prospector camps. They service some of the single men in return for protection and some loose change if available."

Milo asked me if I had family somewhere. I told him about Royce and Zona back home and Jenny and about Adele.

"No suspects?"

I shook my head.

We were silent for a time, enjoying the coffee and the music and the sound of seagulls scouting the shoreline. The dusk sun was casting dark shadows like tentacles across Rubble City. I fired up another smoke, sensing that Milo was watching me as if trying to figure something.

"Who's after you, son?" He said at last. "Police? Someone?"

"How'd you know?"

"I got a sense for these things." He said.

I explained about the two men from Vegas, about the film and about Frank Meade and the authorities finding his remains. Milo was attentive.

431

"I guess you'd like to be rid of them," he said after relighting his pipe.

He suggested I stay there for the night. I didn't argue. He gave me an old sleeping bag to crawl into. As night moved in, it got cold. We went inside his hovel. Milo lit a fire in the Franklin and it gave off a glow that made the place toasty and actually cozy. He also lit his oil lamp which gave off plenty of light. Without saying anything, Milo opened a can of chili con carne, poured it into a saucepan and set it on the top of the Franklin and served it on tin plates. It tasted good and for a moment I imagined myself camping out on the prairie after a hard day herding cattle.

Later Milo told me he'd been thinking and laid out a plan he'd conceived for me to follow if the men from Vegas came after me.

"Do you know their names?"

"I remember one of them is called Zito," I said.

"Good," Milo said. "That's good."

Before turning in I slipped out under the cover of a very black night and found a phone booth at a gas station near town. I called Mark Horgan collect. His mother answered and wouldn't take the call. Luckily Mark grabbed the phone when he heard my name.

"Where the hell are you?" Mark hollered into the phone. "Our friends from Vegas are looking for you. They figured out they got snookered. I've been looking for you too. You better pray I find you first."

I told him where I was and that the two henchmen had found me, suddenly feeling like I had been thrown into the middle of a grainy black and white B movie plot.

"They came to the place where I was staying," I said. "How did they find me?"

"There are spies everywhere," Mark said. "They have good sources, including inside the police department. Are you driving the VW van that Arne was driving?"

"Yeah," I said. "They spotted it."

Mark told me to get rid of it and lay low until he got there which would be in a couple of days. I had already been looking at a 1940 Ford station wagon with wooden side panels and doors, a couple of days before. I'd spotted it parked in front of a side street up the hill from town with a for sale sign in the window. The wood was badly weathered, raw in some places, but the motor sounded okay when the owner started it up for me. The man wanted $300 for the car. I told him I could only afford $150 and that was the end of the discussion.

I agreed to meet Mark at the Palace of Fine Arts in San Francisco. He told me he would have to confiscate the film. He was still working for Moe Miller and his friends who had invested in it. I didn't say anything. I went back to Rubble City and after taking a few wrong paths, found my way back to Milo's. Luckily I had the flashlight which was in the glove compartment of the van. The black veteran suddenly appeared in front of me like a ghost and said I should not worry, that battle plans were being made. He then disappeared into the darkness.

The next morning I awoke shivering just before first light and tried to shake the sudden foreboding that hit me as I struggled toward consciousness. Outside as the sun was just beginning to peak above the horizon I threw cold water from Milo's faucet in my face. I peed in Milo's privy which looked like fly city and left.

On my way to the Top Deck Galley, I stopped at the Hallowed Ark. Sherry, still half asleep told me Ben would not be back until early evening. I told her I needed a phone number for him.

"The screening is tonight. I'm very excited." She looked at me closely, rubbing her eyes. "What's the matter? You look like you've seen a ghost or something."

"If you see two men in dark suits lurking about, or they come to your door, don't answer."

"Huh?" Sherry said.

She jotted down a phone number for me and closed the door. I looked furtively in all directions and then continued on to the Top Deck to start my shift, leaving the van down the road a piece in the opposite direction. There was no sign of the black Caddy. I worked through the day, fearing the two henchmen would come through the door at any moment. Around lunch time, Milo showed up. It was the first time he'd ever come in when other customers were there. It looked like he'd cleaned up for the occasion. He wore a frayed tan corduroy jacket over a black turtle neck sweater and a floppy hat. He ordered a steak and eggs with a beer. I wondered if he could pay for it. He did and even left a small tip.

"I'll be coming back to Rubble City tonight," I said in a low voice leaning over the counter. "If those men I told you about spot me they'll follow."

Milo nodded.

"Make sure they do spot you," he said. "You know what to do. Leave the rest to me."

Milo tipped his hat and left.

I worked an extra half shift, picked up my pay and my share of the tips and gave notice to Mrs. Megalos. She was not happy, but I think sensed I was in trouble. "Such is life," she sighed.

What I remembered that morning was the page that had been torn out of my notebook by the two men had a note scribbled on it that there would be a showing of the film at nine o'clock on Friday evening, second floor of the Industrial Building Warehouse. And it was now eight. I went to a phone booth and called the number Sherry had given me for Ben at the warehouse building. No answer. I tried again and let it ring for a long time. Still no answer. I was certain he was there, figuring he might be in the head.

I walked back along the dirt road, staying in the shadows until I got to the van, got in and drove to the Industrial Warehouse. Inside, I climbed the stairs to the Film Cooperative Studio. The door stood open. It was dark inside the studio's outer room. I found a light switch that turned on a single low hanging ceiling light under a factory style green lampshade.

The place seemed deserted. But then I heard a voice and music coming from a radio in the back room where Ben had worked on the film. I moved quietly to the door which was closed and put my ear to it. I

434

knocked. No answer. I took a deep breath and slowly turned the knob and pushed open the door. The workroom was pitch-black inside. I was suddenly filled with a sense of dread as I tried to see with what little light was coming in behind me from the other room.

There was no wall switch in this room. I stumbled around until I found a table lamp which offered enough illumination to take in most of the room.

Like my room back at the Ark, it had been ransacked. Everything was topsy-turvy. Metal film reels were strewn about, raw sixteen millimeter film racing across the floor like streamers, shelves pulled own, boxes over turned. Ben's Moviola appeared to have been sledge hammered beyond recognition. It was then that I heard the sounds of moaning coming from a far corner behind wooden crates. There was a trail of blood on the floor. I cautiously moved around behind the pile of crates. There was Ben sprawled on the floor face down. I bent down and turned him over. His face was a mass of raw, swollen flesh, caked with blood. His left eye was completely shut and black, and his jaw looked broken. I went into an adjoining bathroom, soaked some paper towels and gently patted Ben's face.

"I don't know anything about a film called Cobra Woman versus the what?" he whispered.

His right eye cracked open and tried to focus on my face.

"Oh, it's you," he said. "I knew you were bad karma, man," and weakly tried to push my hand away. I asked him if the people who did this to him took the film. But Ben fell back into unconsciousness. I called an ambulance and gave a phony name. I then hurriedly searched the studio. The film wasn't there. I tried to revive Ben without success. Soon the screaming of a siren was closing in.

I got into the van and sat for a moment. I figured the gangsters had the film and were heading back to Nevada or wherever they came from. In the morning I would head back home. It had been awhile since I had talked to Jenny or Zona. For the moment nothing much seemed to matter. I went to the house where the old Ford station wagon was still for sale. I offered the owner $200, we settled on $250 and the van. We exchanged pink slips. As I pulled away I looked in my rearview mirror. Bogies at six o'clock I said aloud to myself. The black Caddy was about fifty feet behind me. Son of a bitch they must have followed me from the Industrial Warehouse, I thought. But why? I wondered. Did they want to punish me for switching the film on them? The only other possibility I reasoned was they did not get the film. And if they didn't have it, who did? My heart started pounding with renewed excitement and spirit. I figured they wanted me to lead them to the film.

I drove slowly, heading back to the waterfront road. After a couple of blocks I checked the rearview mirror again just to make sure they were following. The Caddy was there maintaining about a half a block distance behind me.

Once on the dirt road that ran along the shoreline, I sped up a little and a few minutes later turned into Rubble City. I did not know what would happen if the two men from Vegas followed me into that no-man's land, but I knew Milo had something in mind if they did. The Caddy followed. I drove as far as I could and stopped. As Milo had instructed I honked three times, alternating with flashing the headlights. The horn sounded like the last gasp scream of a prehistoric monster. It had to have carried across the encampment. I turned off the car and lights. The night was black.

I got out of the Ford and saw the Caddy pull up about twenty feet behind me. The two men got out leaving the headlights on. In front of the car they looked like two giant shapes silhouetted against the headlights. It looked like the smaller of the two men, the one called Zito, had a flashlight. A thin fog had settled in over Rubble City, having drifted in from the bay. It gave the place an eeriness that reminded me of a Frankenstein movie.

As I began to make my way along a path Milo had worked out for me, the crunch of gravel under my feet telegraphed my position.

"Hey, Charles Kendall," the one called Zito called out to me. "We just want to talk to you. Have a friendly chat, you know. If you make us follow you it won't be so friendly."

"What is this place?" I heard the bigger one say.

As I moved deeper into Rubble City I felt there were eyes on me from every dark alcove, every pit and behind walls. The two henchmen followed, cursing as they struggled to negotiate the treacherous jungle and tangle of concrete and rebar I was leading them into. At one point my two pursuers stopped. I had the feeling they sensed something was amiss. But then they continued until they reached a small clearing. On the other side there was a glow from a fire in an oil drum coming out of the mist. Suddenly, from the darkness a voice whispered, almost ghost-like the name "Zito." It sent a shiver down my spine. Then another voice and another saying the same thing until his name became a chant. Both men stopped and looked around.

"What the hell?" Zito said. He pulled out his gun and whipped around a hundred and eighty degrees, shining his flashlight into the night. "Who's there? Who are you?"

While both men were trying to see where the voices were coming from, a chunk of concrete came flying through the air and hit Zito on the shoulder. He whirled around and fired a wild shot into the darkness. Another missile from another direction struck Zito on the head. The larger man was hit on the leg. Then a volley of concrete chunks, all sizes and shapes coming from every direction, found their marks. The two men were completely surrounded by an invisible army of Milo's Rubble City soldiers. One large piece of concrete hit Zito in the temple. He staggered onto his hands and knees, apparently stunned, dropping his gun. His partner was hit in the back of the head with a good sized rock. He went down. I watched from the other side of the clearing as Milo's band of troops became visible in the glow of the fire. Bandanas covered their faces. Some also wore goggles making them look like creatures from outer space. They moved in close and with certain finality hurled a barrage of stones and pieces of concrete at the two henchmen who lay helpless on the ground. As Zito tried to lift his head one of the soldiers stepped forward and hit him on the back of his skull with a club. There was a crushing sound. Pools of blood were forming around the bodies and I realized that the two men from Vegas would never leave Rubble City.

Milo appeared. He beckoned for me to follow him out of the clearing for about fifteen feet or so back into the shadows. We stood silent for a moment. He lit his pipe and looked toward the clearing.

"Those guys won't forget this night," I said nervously.

"I told my people they're emissaries of evil, come to take away their homes here. The people of the Republic of Rubble City saw them as symbols of all that's wrong and threatening."

"What will happen to them now?" I said.

Milo put a hand on my shoulder, like a father about to admonish a son.

"You should go now, my friend," Milo said. "And you should never talk about this night or even mention that you were ever here to anyone, ever."

I drove the Ford back to the Hallowed Ark to say goodbye to Sherry. No one was there. I went to a payphone and called Sherry's mother's home. Her brother answered. He told me she'd gone to Marin General Hospital to visit a friend. I started to hang up but he stopped me and told me Sherry said that I should go see someone named Maggie.

"Did she say why?"

"No. Just that it was important."

I drove the couple of miles back to the ferry boat where Maggie lived with Jean Luc. I walked up the narrow gangway and knocked at the door. After several knocks a porch light went on and Maggie looked out the window and then opened the door. She stood there in a black T-shirt, black panties and unlaced combat boots holding a beer, a cigarette dangling out of the corner of her mouth. It reminded me of the first time I saw her at Jack's place the morning after the party. It seemed like a century ago.

"You look like ten bags of shit," she said. "And don't smell much better."

"Guess I could use a shower," I said.

438

Maggie stepped aside.

"Towel's on the rack," she said.

"Where's John Luc?" I said.

"Out with some gypsy friends," she said, then gave me a look. "Don't even think about it."

From inside the bathroom I called out through the door as I stripped down that Sherry had left a message to come here.

"She left something here for you," Maggie said.

The shower felt incredibly good. I lingered in the warmth of the steam. Maggie handed me a beer when I came out wrapped in a towel. She led me back to a storage area and pointed to several boxes stacked in a corner. My heart started racing as I bent down and opened one of the boxes. There were large 35 millimeter real cans inside with the title: "Cobra/Wolves." Run time 94 minutes was scrawled underneath with a black marker. I jumped up, letting my towel drop to the floor and kissed Maggie hard on the mouth.

"I love you," I said.

After I put my clothes back on I carried the boxes out to the station wagon.

"Where are you going?" Maggie said.

"To find a theater somewhere in America," I said. "I think I know of one."

"Maybe I'll see your movie one day," she said. "One of the boxes has all the eight-by-ten stills I took during the shooting. You may need them.

"Yeah," I said. "Great!"

"It's been weird," Maggie said, and kissed me. "Real weird."

I got into the car and drove away. In the rear view mirror I could see Maggie watching after me. And then she was gone.

Chapter 50

——————

Zona came into the kitchen. Slogging her way through morning grogginess, she was at the moment concentrating on tying her tattered pink robe. Pushing loose strands of damp hair away from her face, she shuffled across the floor to the stove and put on a pot of coffee. She switched on the radio and sighed as a male voice said it would be overcast that day with possible rain by late afternoon. Country music followed. She turned it low.

I sat silently at the kitchen table watching Zona from across the room as if behind an invisible screen. Her body movements struck me as tired, defeated, yet somehow she was still a very attractive woman, even with no makeup and her hair pretty much a mess. And it made me wonder how, or why, she had devoted the prime of her life to making Royce happy. It never made sense to me. Zona and Adele were never very close, but then they were years apart in age and had probably lived in different worlds growing up. I knew something we never spoke of in our house, that Zona had been adopted by Adele's parents when she was a baby. Her real parents had died in a fire and there was no other family. How did I know this? I snooped a lot when I was a kid.

Zona went to the refrigerator and poured a small glass of orange juice which she threw down like a shot of Wild Turkey. One more which she held up, drank and then dropped the glass as she turned and momentarily looked wide-eyed and terror-struck to see this strange-looking man making himself at home in the kitchen. The glass bounced.

"What the…?" She spat out. "What in the world?"

Zona looked closely at me, squinting as if the light had dimmed. I could see the threat of my presence was beginning to wane as recognition phased in. Zona slowly walked around me, inspecting me from all angles. I had several days growth of beard, very shaggy hair hanging down from under a floppy hat, and tired eyes. I would have fit in at Rubble City.

Before Zona had come downstairs I had noticed a piece of paper on the kitchen counter. It was an unfinished letter response she had hand written to someone who had written her some time before. I found myself staring at the letter for several moments without comprehending the words so much as the cursive style of her pen. What was it?

"I can't believe it," Zona said. "Charles?"

I twisted around and looked at her full on. Her blue eyes looked a little hazy.

"How you doing, Zona?" I said.

She just kept shaking her head.

"I declare you scared me half to death," she said. "I…I didn't know you. The way you look and all. I thought you were a burglar or something." She laughed. "I mean how did you even get into this town without being arrested? You know how folks are around here. God, you've changed."

"Where's the old man?" I said.

"He's asleep," she said.

"Good."

"We haven't heard from you in some time now so you don't know," she said, now pouring two cups of coffee. She put cream in mine and added a little sugar, brought the cups over and sat down opposite me. I fired up a smoke and took a sip of the coffee.

"Know what?" I said.

"Royce had a heart attack and then a stroke about a month ago. He barely lived through it, but it took its toll."

I pondered this for a moment.

"Guess I should go see him," I said.

Zona looked me up and down.

"Good heavens, not like that," she said. "Probably finish him off." She put her hand over her mouth to stifle laughing. "Yeah, he'd be a goner for sure."

I found myself laughing with her.

"You're right," I said. "I'll clean up first. What else? Sheriff Crowley still looking into my mother's murder?"

Zona took a swallow of her coffee and shook her head.

"Haven't heard much," she said. "I ran into him in town a few months back. He said the trail was just too cold, but they would keep the case open."

As I pushed myself up from the chair, Zona leaned over and kissed me on the cheek.

"Welcome home, Charles," she said holding my face. "You look thin."

Our eyes met for a long unsettling moment.

"I'll wait to see him. Right now I need to get some sleep."

Zona nodded.

I went up to my old room which had not been fiddled with one iota since I last saw it. I fell across the bed and was out.

In the early evening, just as the sun was casting its last ray of orange glow over the land, I opened my eyes and stared at the ceiling. And for an instant I wondered if it had all been a dream. But then the parade of faces I had encountered over the last two years passed on the screen behind my eyes, beginning with Silky. Where was she now, that urchin with the angelic face, star of "Cobra Woman versus the Prairie Wolves in the Vortex of the Valley of Darkness"? No question, I had felt a strange fascination for her, for her wild, spontaneous spirit. Real different than my feelings about Maggie. And then there was Jenny for whom I was also not able to get a clean fix. Then, I remembered Mark Horgan would be looking for me in San Francisco and feel betrayed. Couldn't be helped.

I would have to go see Jenny first thing. After a long hot shower I shaved, brushed my teeth, trimmed my own hair, and dressed in some jeans and blue and white checkered shirt I'd found in my dresser. They were a little loose. I went downstairs and found Zona helping Royce eat some soup out on the front porch. It was warm and pleasant. The air had that incredibly sweet earthy smell I loved. The porch planks creaked as I walked around to face Royce. The old man was in a wheel chair. He raised his head slightly and struggled to nod at me, the whole left side of his face drooped like melted wax.

"Communists, here," he managed to get out, each word coming slowly from the right side of his twisted mouth. Despite his infirmity his hooded eyes blazed.

Zona made a face.

"He believes communists have infiltrated our community," Zona said. "God knows what they would want with it. He thinks they want our land to either build missile sites or grow food to send back to Russia. Some folks around here are even building bomb shelters."

I sat down on the wicker settee.

"Who's running the mortuary?" I said.

"I am," Zona said. "With the help of Zeke."

"Who's Zeke?"

"New man your father hired. He's been there a year now. Knows his stuff. Business has been slow though. Folks not dying like they used to. Anyway, I want to hear all about California and what's happened with your movie."

"I'll tell you later," I said. "I have to go now."

I was halfway down the path when Zona called to me, telling me to wait that she had something she needed to tell me. I waved her off and climbed into the Ford.

It was probably the saddest sight I'd ever seen. The WOLF looked like it had died a painful death. I got out of the car and stood in front the old theater, looking up at the once proud marquee. Two large plastic letters were on one side, hanging askew, remnants I figured of the last feature that played there. Sheets of plywood had been nailed over the box office and glass poster panels. If someone had boarded up the home where I grew up, it would not have hit me half as hard as this. But, then I guess the WOLF was my real home.

The lights were on at Henry and Cora Zickwolf's house. Cora answered the door and when she saw me she just shook her head.

"Land sakes, Tuckie. What a surprise. Seems like you've been gone forever."

She invited me in and fixed some tea for both of us which she served in their tiny living room. Cora then told me Henry had passed away six months before. She could no longer operate the theater.

"It just wore me out," she said. "And besides, the customers had dwindled to less than a trickle, even on weekends."

"I'm sorry," I said. "Sorry about your husband and the theater."

I told her about my movie and the one thing in the world I had wanted was for Henry to see it and now Cora Zickwolf was my last chance to get it seen.

"What are you saying?" She said.

"Would you open the theater and let me show my movie?"

Cora stood up, still holding her cup of tea and wandered around the room as if pondering the question. She turned to me and shook her head.

"I'm afraid not," she said.

"Why?" I asked.

"Lot's of reasons," she said. "Too much involved. Even the power is shut off."

"Please, Mrs. Zickwolf,"

"I think it's time for you to go, Tuckie." She said. "I'm sorry about your father. I hope he's getting on all right."

As I began walking back to my car, Cora Zickwolf called out to me from her door.

"Don't you understand?" She said. "That theater killed my Henry. He spent over thirty years worrying about that damn place."

She shut the door and I thought I heard the muffled sound of a sob. As I pulled away from in front of her house I wondered if Cora Zickwolf had always felt that way about the WOLF. I knew or felt that she had al-

445

ways been an unhappy person, but had probably never let on the depth of her despair. Now I was beginning to think that no one including myself would ever see Cobra Woman/Prairie Wolves. Only Ben, someone I had barely known had seen it finished.

Time to go see Jenny. My desire to see her was suddenly very strong and I tried to imagine the expression on her face when I showed up at her door. I wanted to hold her and kiss her and take her down to the lake where we could be alone in the dark. In that moment I realized I had missed her more than I realized. As I drove back through town I noticed there was virtually no life, no activity along Main Street. It had once thrived at night, folks going to the café, the ice cream parlor, the park and gazebo where local musicians sometimes gathered for an impromptu set, to the WOLF Theater to see a double feature. Now a handful of locals were milling about in front of the drugstore. A woman came out that I recognized. It was Vera Fouts. She saw me, waived and came running over and stuck her head in the car window.

"Charles, you're back," she said excitedly. "I heard you were in Los Angeles."

"Hi, Vera," I said.

"How'd you like it out on the coast?" Vera went on. "I was there once. Lots of palm trees. Did you see Marco's sister while you were there? She lives in Gardena. Well, great to see you." Vera turned and was off.

Jenny's house was dark. At first I thought everyone had turned in early. But even in the dim light I had a sense that something was not right. I got out of the car with a flashlight and walked up to the porch. I shined the light in through the front window. The place looked hollow. There was no furniture, and a blanket of dust covered the hardwood floor. I walked around and checked other rooms. The house was empty.

Later at home Zona made us some hot chocolate. She had put on a pink cotton dress and fixed her hair as if she were going out on a date. Royce was in the living room watching television. We sat out on the porch.

"It's a lovely night," Zona said, looking up at the stars.

"What happened to the Giffords?" I said. "I went to see Jenny and..."

"I wasn't sure if you knew," Zona said. "I started to tell you before, but you left in a hurry."

I took a sip of my hot chocolate and looked questioningly at her.

"There was a scandal," she said. "It began to come out when Jenny had a breakdown. She disappeared one day and they found her the next day down by the lake in nothing but her underwear, rocking back and forth, making strange animal noises. Her clothes in a pile nearby. As the story goes she was like a wild animal fighting with authorities and acting like she was mute. The sheriff's deputies had to drag her out of there. Her parents had her committed to an institution upstate. And that's where she is."

I put my cup down, fired up a smoke and tried to figure what Zona was saying.

"I can't believe it," I said.

"Anyway, Mr. Gifford resigned from the bank and he and his missus just up and left. Folks were saying they moved to Milwaukee. That's what folks were saying."

We sat silent for a time just staring out at the dark night.

"She did sound strange the last time I talked with her on the phone," I said, "but I didn't think much of it."

"Rumor has it that it all had to do with the bank audit," Zona said.

"What audit?"

"The bank was audited and it was discovered a big chunk of money was missing. Like $200,000 or something like that and it was under Jenny's control. It was in the newspapers."

I stood up and paced around the porch.

"How's that possible?" I said. "Jenny's the most honest person I ever knew. She wouldn't steal a nickel from anyone."

Zona shrugged.

"Just telling you what I heard," she said. "I think it's still under investigation."

"Was Jenny accused of anything?"

"Not that I know of," she said. "But when that audit came out that's when Jenny fell off the earth, so to speak."

Zona looked over at me, reached out and touched my hand.

"You've been away a long time, Charles. People change. Things change."

I finished my chocolate and set my cup down.

"I've got to see her," I said. "Where is she?"

"A place called Woodridge Sanitarium. It's a couple hours drive from here."

In the morning, I drove to Woodridge. It took almost two and a half hours. A receptionist, a gray haired woman in her late forties or early fifties was pleasant and officious.

"Who was it you wanted to see?" She said.

"Jenny Gifford," I said.

"Are you family?"

"We were kind of engaged," I said. "I've been away."

"I see," the receptionist said. "I'll have to check with the Doctor."

I sat in the waiting room thumbing through LIFE magazine. It was another half hour before an older man in a white coat came out and identified himself as Dr. Elmer Weiss the attending psychiatrist. He told me he had checked with Jenny's mother who had said it was alright for me to visit with her.

"I told Mrs. Gifford it might be good," Dr. Weiss said. "Seeing you might spark something."

I asked him what was wrong with her. He told me Jenny was completely withdrawn to some unreachable place deep within her.

"She's what we call catatonic," he said. "It's a form of schizophrenia. Something traumatic more than likely triggered it. We have not been able to get through to her."

Dr. Weiss escorted me through two heavy doors, down a long white corridor to a room that was barren except for one chair. The room was painted a pale blue and had a mirror almost running the length of one wall. He told me he would be observing from behind the mirror in another room. He left, closing the door behind him. A few moments later another door opened and an attendant wheeled Jenny in. I was taken aback at the sight of her. She looked thin and sallow, her eyes dark and sunken as if she'd been in a concentration camp. Even her once honey blonde hair looked dirty and unkempt. The set of her face looked lifeless like a mannequin in a department store window. Her head tilted to one side. She did not look at me.

"There you are Jenny," the attendant said. "You have a visitor."

The attendant looked at me, shrugged and left the room. I stood up and walked around Jenny, looking for any sign of recognition. None came. I sat in the chair opposite her and began talking to her. I told her about some of my experiences on the west coast, about making the movie from my script. Then I reminisced about how we used to sit on her front porch and eat her mother's apple pie. After almost an hour there was not one flicker of response.

On my way back, I stopped at MARCO'S. I sat at the counter. A new waitress who looked like she was just out of high school brought me coffee. I ordered a grilled cheese sandwich.

"Haven't seen you around here before," the young waitress said. "You from around here?"

"Marco here?" I said and eyed her nametag. "Peggy."

She giggled.

"He should be back soon," she said.

While munching on my sandwich I twisted around on the stool and scanned the place to see if there was anyone I knew. It wasn't exactly packed, but several of the booths were filled with locals, some of whom were vaguely familiar. The face of one lone man did catch my eye, a face that was looking at me and grinning. He waived, then got up and came over. It was Tony Billings, once leader of the dreaded Prairie Wolves. I hadn't seen him in years and almost didn't recognize him. Last I'd heard, Tony had enlisted in the army. I nodded at him as he approached. He stuck his hand out and we shook hands. I marveled at the fact that Tony was much shorter than me and looked a little paunchy around the face which was accentuated by his butch haircut.

"Hey, Tuckie," Tony said. "How are you, man?" Long time, eh? You know. Shit!"

He was grinning from ear to ear as if he'd just found his best friend.

"It's been awhile," I said. "You back here now?"

"I got a month leave. I'm still in the service, a twenty year man. You know. Retire, have a little money coming in from Uncle Sam. How about you? I heard you went out west to work on a movie or something. That right? You gone Hollywood and all that shit? Fuck any of them starlets, man? Eh?" Tony landed a playful blow on my shoulder. He lit a cigarette and offered me one. I took it. "So what's the movie called?"

"Don't laugh. It's called Cobra Woman versus the Prairie Wolves in the Vortex of the Valley of Darkness," I said.

He began laughing.

"You're shitting me," Tony said. "Cobra Woman…the Prairie Wolves. Just like that bunch when we were kids. Hey you remember that time we saw those two humping in the corn field? Wow! So when can I see the movie?" When's it going to be in theaters?"

I shrugged.

"I don't know. Maybe never."

Suddenly a heavy arm came swooping around my back.

"Son of a bitch,!" a voice behind me said.

Of course I recognized the voice. I turned around to stare into the broad, sweating face of Marco.

"I got to go," Tony said. "Hey, lets get together some night and hoist a couple."

I nodded. Tony left.

"I need to talk to you," I said to Marco.

Marco looked askance at me.

"Sounds serious," he said. "Anyway, I want to hear all about what happened out there in California."

450

Chapter 51

─────

I followed Marco to an empty booth. He told Peggy to bring us a couple of beers.

"So, you finally come home," Marco said "I thought maybe you forgot about us country folks."

The beers arrived and we clinked bottles in celebration of my return. We drank directly from the bottles. I wiped my mouth with the back of my hand. Marco was watching me, as if looking for some sign of something in my face.

"How's your old man doing?" He asked.

"Holding on," I said. "Zona takes care of him."

I then gave Marco the highlights of my time out west, the strange characters I met, the Frank Meade story, the henchmen from Vegas, and the making of the movie. I also mentioned that Cora Zickwolf would not reopen the WOLF.

Marco shook his head.

"I heard she's had it rough since Henry passed," he said. "I...guess you heard about Jenny,"

I nodded and told Marco about my visiting her at the sanitarium and that it was like she didn't know who I was. That she didn't even look at me. We compared notes on what happened and his version was pretty much the same as Zona's account.

"Jenny came in here once a few months back," Marco said. "Asked if I had heard from you. I told her..." Marco suddenly jumped up and slapped his forehead. "Son of a bitch, I almost forgot. She left a letter for you."

Marco ran out to the back and returned with a yellow envelope. It was sealed with Scotch Tape and addressed in very neat print to Mr. Charles Alvin Kendall.

"It's no joke, this business with Jenny, eh?"

"No joke," I said.

"You gonna open it?"

I slippped the envelope into my jacket pocket. Then I eyed Marco as if seeing him for the first time, sizing him up so to speak. He must have sensed this.

"So, was there something else, kid?" He said as he finished off his beer. "What was it you needed to talk to me about? Come on, I'm busy."

I looked out the window, wondering if this was the time to get at what was gnawing at me. There would be no good time, I thought, but something had to be said. I told him about my encounter with Jimmy Oliver the transient painter Adele was supposed to have run off with.

"He calls himself Zoltan now and leads a cult or something on a farm north of Los Angeles. He was under investigation by the FBI and was briefly arrested when it was thought he and his followers had kid-napped me or had falsely imprisoned me which I said didn't happen. Also that he and his followers were growing marijuana which turned out not to be true."

"I heard about that," Marco said. "It made the national news. Folks around here were talking about it for some time. But I thought he was the one killed your mom. Have you told Sheriff Crowley?"

I told Marco that I had not, but that I planned to let the sheriff know that I had met Jim Oliver and where he is.

"I don't think he did it," I added.

"Why do you think that?"

"I...I don't know. I confronted him and he seemed genuinely shocked to hear that Adele was dead. He told me he was supposed to meet her but she never showed and he figured she had changed her mind and so he went on without her."

"You believe that shit?" Marco said.

"Yeah, I do," I said.

"Well, I don't buy it," Marco said. "But let's say he was telling the truth, if he didn't' do it, who the hell did?"

I shrugged.

"You got any ideas?" I asked.

Marco gave me a strange look.

"Why should I have any ideas?" He said. "Maybe some hobo passing through."

"You want to know what I think?" I said. "I think it was someone local, someone she knew, someone she wanted to see before she ran off with Jimmy Oliver. On the other hand I did get a postcard from Los Angeles, didn't I?"

Marco looked at me for a long moment, absently rolling the empty beer bottle between his hands.

"I knew about you and Adele," I said. "I've known since I was eight or nine years old that you were lovers. Of course in the beginning I didn't know all what that meant, what went on between a man and woman. But I figured it was something special, you know. Royce knew. I heard him confront her one night when she came home late from working here. But I didn't care. In a way you were more of a father to me than Royce ever was. So, it seemed like it was kind of natural."

Marco continued to stare at me. He lit a cigarette.

"You've changed, kid," he said. "You got some bark on you now. Yeah, I don't know this new Tuckie." He stood up. "I got to get back to work. Good luck with your movie."

I waived him off and watched him disappear into the back. Later I drove down to the lake and made myself comfortable under the shade of a tree overhanging the bank. For a while I threw pebbles into the water and watched the ripples. It was a place Jenny and I had come to often and I wondered if it was where they found her.

I got out my pocket knife and slit open the letter from Jenny and carefully unfolded it. It was written in perfect cursive and dated four months earlier.

Dear Charles,

I'm writing you this letter because I have not heard from you in some time and I wanted to tell you that strange things are happening to me which I can't explain and I wanted to write you before I could not write anymore in this world and I had to tell you something because you are not here to talk to and I really need to talk to you because I am now afraid of demons that have taken me over and are slowly but surely taking me to another place. I wanted you to be successful and accomplish what you wanted to accomplish and that you would then hurry back to me. I did something terribly wrong, at least I think I did because I see myself doing it over and over again in my dreams and I feel like I'm turning inside out, walls are closing in to crush me and I am hoping you will get this because I did talk to a person who shall remain nameless and he assured me that your movie would make a lot of money and everything would be good and you would come back only you haven't come back and I'm beginning to think you may never come back. You seem to have gone underground. I hope you get this letter some day which I'm giving to Marco for safe keeping because I don't know where to send it.

Yours Truly,

Jennifer Gifford

I read the signature line aloud wondering why she had been so formal. I dropped the letter next to me and fired up a smoke and tried to think about the meaning of the letter. I remembered Jocelyn Bukowski saying something about an anonymous investor. I would not believe Jenny embezzled money from the bank to help finance my film. It was a real absurd notion. I did not want to think about it, but at the same time I had to know.

I went to see Jenny a few more times over the next few weeks. I decided not to say anything about her letter. Instead, I talked to her for an hour or so, mostly about my father's health and Zona taking over the mortuary, the WOLF Theater being closed, and running into Tony Billings who had tormented me when I was a kid. Again, no response. She sat in the wheel chair and stared blankly ahead of her like a corpse with its eyes open. The doctor told me that sometimes in cases like this you can find a way in just talking to the patient about mundane things. He added that some never come out of it. I tried to reach her parents in Milwaukee. Whoever answered the phone would immediately hang up as soon as he or she heard my voice.

One afternoon I waited outside the bank for a woman friend of Jenny's, Earlene Bentley who had worked there for several years. I stopped her when she came out at closing.

"Tuckie Kendall," she said. "I declare. I hadn't heard you were back."

"Can I buy you a cup of coffee? I asked. "I need to talk to you."

"Bout Jenny?" She said.

I nodded.

"Can't say too much," Earlene said.

We went into the café, which was a few doors down from the bank, and took a table that was out of earshot of other customers.

"It's a real sad story, Tuckie," Earlene said. "It makes you want to cry. She was my friend. I mean it's so hard to believe Jenny could have stolen two hundred thousand dollars from her own father's bank. Mr. Gifford took it real hard. Had to resign of course."

I was thinking about Jenny's letter. Earlene sipped her coffee.

"I hate to say it but there really isn't any question. The money was traced to an account in Los Angeles, but the money apparently didn't stay there long enough for the authorities to catch up with it. Some folks thought at first that she sent it to you." She paused. "I wonder how the poor girl is doing?"

I told Earlene I'd been to see Jenny and that she was still in her shell.

"You two were supposed to get hitched, weren't you?" she asked.

"We…we'd talked about it," I said.

Over the next few weeks I worked at the Kendall Mortuary. Zeke did not turn out to be one of my favorite people. I found him to be arrogant and make stupid jokes, undertaker humor. But he knew how to embalm and was a wiz at cosmetics.

"You, of course, are the heir to the business," Zona said one night after dinner. "When your father became incapacitated I felt I had to do something to keep it going. Do you think you'd want to take over one day?"

"I don't know," I said.

"Guess you got to think on it," she said.

Later, Sheriff Crowley came by with an FBI agent and questioned me about what I knew about Jenny's alleged embezzlement from the bank. Did I know why she would have sent the money to someone in Los Angeles? I told them I knew nothing and that I was shocked when I learned what had happened. The FBI agent took some notes but seemed satisfied that I was in no way connected with what happened at the bank. I had already burned Jenny's letter. Before they left, Sheriff Crowley noted that he was keeping Adele's case open. I decided to wait before telling him about Jimmy Oliver.

One evening, a few weeks later, Cora Zickwolf showed up at the house unannounced. Zona answered the door and invited her in. I was upstairs in my bedroom. Earlier, I had put the old folded letter from Starburst/Meade Productions on my bedside table to study it. It was falling apart at the folds and part of it was dappled with droplets of coffee stains. For the zillionth time, it seemed, I examined the mysterious hand-written note at the bottom. It made me laugh to look at it. I decided to frame it.

Zona called me from the downstairs hall. I was lying on my bed staring at the ceiling and thinking about Adele, wondering if she would have stayed with Jimmy Oliver and be part of his transformation into Zoltan and the Fourth Way, whatever that was. I did not believe she ever really loved Marco. I figured he was a diversion, but his rough edges would not have attracted a beautiful sensitive woman like Adele for the long haul. Adele was an enigma, even to me as a kid, though at the time I could not have put a name to it. She must have had an inner life that no one saw or had any inkling of all those years ago, except maybe Jimmy Oliver.

"Charles," Zona called again.

Lost in my reverie I didn't answer.

"Charles, you have a visitor."

With some effort I pushed myself off the bed, slipped on my shoes and went downstairs, wondering who could possibly be visiting me. As I entered the living room Mrs. Zickwolf, who had been sitting on the couch stood up and stuck out her hand. I took it.

"Good evening, Tuckie," she said.

"Mrs. Zickwolf," I said and gestured for her to sit back down.

I sat on the old wing chair opposite the couch. Cora Zickwolf looked thin, and tired. Her gray hair hung down in wisps, as if she hadn't brushed it in some time. She cleared her throat.

"You probably think I'm a mean-spirited old woman who doesn't care about anything anymore. And I guess if you're thinking that way, you wouldn't be too far off."

"I never thought any such thing," I said.

Zona brought in a tray of coffee and biscuits which she set down on the coffee table in front of the couch.

"Please help yourself," Zona said.

Cora thanked Zona and shook her head. Zona left the room. I fixed myself a coffee and sat back.

"I've come here because I've been thinking about what you asked me...and well Henry came to me in a dream a few nights ago. It was so powerful it was as if he were in the room with me, sitting on the edge of the bed and telling me things about our time together. Even his musk seemed to fill the room."

I took a sip of my coffee and noticed a tear running down Cora Zickwolf's cheek. She wiped it away with her fingers.

"Henry said I should open the theater and let you show your movie. So, I've been thinking about it all day and that's what I'm going to do. If you still want to show your movie you can use the WOLF. That's what I came to say."

I had held my breath as I heard the words come out of her.

"That's really…are you sure?" I said.

Cora Zickwolf laughed.

"I don't want Henry hanging around haunting me. And I fear that's what's going to happen if I don't let you do it. But, mind you, you'll have to get the old place ready yourself, clean it up. I'll see that the power is turned back on and all."

"Leave it to me," I said. "I'll get it into shape."

"Good," she said and handed me a set of keys. "The projectors are there and everything you'll probably need. Frankly though, I don't know who you're going to get to come and see this movie or yours."

I walked Cora Zickwolf to the door and thanked her.

"You won't regret this, I promise you."

As I watched her walk out to the car, I unconsciously gripped the keys in my hand so hard they left deep creases in the skin. It struck me that Cora Zickwolf was happy for the first time in a long time.

Chapter 52

—————

It was eerie walking through the WOLF. The power had not been
turned on yet. The only light was from an old Boy Scout flashlight I
carried. The place creaked and moaned as a strong breeze from
across the prairie swept through town. I wandered down one isle of the
theater to the stage and then up the second isle. The folding wooden seats
were shrouded in dust and there were cobwebs everywhere. The floor was
littered with the skeletal remains of popcorn, wadded up pieces of paper
and shards of broken glass. In the lobby, white sheets covered the glass
candy counter. Lobby posters from "Invasion of the Body Snatchers" were
still in their frames.

I went back into the theater and sat in one of the 400 seats, switched
off the flashlight and stared into pitch blackness. I tried to conjure the
ghosts of the WOLF and listened for sounds, sounds from another time,
another era. And soon I began to hear the faint sound of music from The
Desert Song staring Dennis Morgan and Irene Manning, and I could see
the Riffs singing their battle cry as they charged on horseback across the
great white dunes of the Moroccan desert. Then I saw the western plains
and the lone dark figure galloping toward me, silhouetted against the purple sun, and I knew it was the Wichita Kid come to tell me who killed
Adele. Then, I tried to imagine Cobra Woman /Prairie Wolves up on the
screen.

"Hey, Tuckie," someone shouted which quickly brought me back. "You
in here? I know you're here somewhere."

I jumped up and switched on the flashlight and made my way back to the lobby. Tony Billings was standing there looking at one of the posters.

"Tony," I said. "What're you doing here?"

I went by your house. Your aunt told me you might be here. Said you were thinking of opening up the old place so I come over. Saw the front door was open so I came in. So, here I am." He laughed self consciously. "Say, that aunt of yours is a looker. Not that old either."

"Zona, yeah, I guess," I said. "I just want to show my movie. That's all I want to do."

"Great," Tony said. "I wanna see it. 'Course I'm kinda surprised old Cora Zickwolf is letting you do it cause I remember when she shut the place down she was quoted in the newspaper that as far as she was concerned she never wanted to see it open again."

I shrugged.

"I guess she blamed Henry's love of this old place for his death," I said.

"So, you want some help cleaning the joint up? I'm not doing anything. We'll get a couple of the guys from the old gang to help out. I mean the movie is called The Prairie Wolves, right?"

I took out my cigarettes, offered one to Tony who took it and we fired up our smokes. I took a deep drag and slowly blew the smoke out across the beam of the flashlight.

"I could use the help," I said. "But I don't have much money."

"Forget it," Tony said. "The guys will do it for nothing. Both of them work, but I know they'll pitch in when they're off. Hey is there any light around here?"

"Power's supposed to be turned on tomorrow," I said.

We stood there in awkward silence for a time, both puffing away on our smokes. I was suddenly feeling like I did not really want anyone to intrude, or share this time with me, but I figured I would need the help if I was ever going to get the WOLF fixed up enough to open.

"So," Tony said. "Is it going to be like one of them premiers?"

I nodded, even though I hadn't thought of it like that.

"Yeah," I said. "Like a premier, a world premier."

We both laughed. I then led the way up the stairs to the projection booth. It was also covered in dust and there was a trail of rat droppings that ran along the floor to a small hole in the wall behind a stack of empty reel cans. I scanned the room until my light landed on the two IPC Simplex projectors I had learned to operate so many years before. I had always thought they looked like giant ray guns trained on some unseen enemy through the small square holes. I checked them out. They were operable.

"Wow," Tony said."I've never been up here before. All the years I came to this theater and never knew what the projectors looked like. They're strange looking you ask me. What's that behind them?"

"Carbon arc lights, high intensity," I said.

"Motherfucker," Tony said, and stamped out his smoke. "You know about all this shit?"

I nodded.

"Old man Zickwolf taught me," I said. "This was like my second home."

We left and I locked up. Over the next two weeks Tony, the other two members of the Prairie Wolves that were still around, and I worked mostly at night. We cleaned the floors, scrubbed the woodwork, painted walls and repaired a few small rips in the screen. Also the curtains, which were caked with dust and grime and had become home to numerous spiders and other vermin, were taken down and washed. No easy task.

As the work continued, I noticed an awakening of the town. Nothing dramatic, but people were beginning to notice that something was going on at the WOLF. With the help of Zona, I made a hand-painted banner which we hung over the marquee. It said:

"COMING SOON TO THIS THEATER – WORLD PREMIERE"

461

The banner generated more curiosity from passersby. At one point I was out front cleaning the glass of the ticket booth when a couple strolled by. I overheard the man say it was the craziest thing he'd ever heard, this premiere or whatever it was.

"That Kendall kid never was playing with a full deck," the woman with him said. "I remember him from high school."

At the beginning of the third week when the theater was almost ready, The Courier, a county-wide newspaper had a mention of the premiere in a column. It said the wolf theater had been chosen for a world premiere of a new movie, never before seen. The writer of the column had heard this from a caller who wondered whether or not it was some kind of a joke. Since the columnist didn't know who to call to confirm the story, it was written as a piece of gossip from a reliable source.

One afternoon, shortly after the column appeared, a reporter stopped by the mortuary unannounced to interview me about this "so called" premiere.

"My name is Daren Erskine," the man said and showed me his press credential. "I'm from the National Wire Service." He laughed to himself. "I got to tell you I've been all over trying to track you down, Mr. Kendall, for days."

He was a slight young man who looked to be in his late twenties with receding brown hair and horn-rimmed glasses. Zeke and I were in the middle of preparing a deceased man for burial.

"I'm real busy," I said.

"I only want a few minutes of your time."

"What for?" I said.

"I want to write something about this…premiere. I'm told you're the one to talk to."

I turned away and shut my eyes for a moment, thinking this was not good. He went on.

"It struck me as unusual to have a world premier of a movie in this part of the country, intriguing actually."

"I'm busy," I said and started to walk away.

Daren Erskine cleared his throat.

"I don't get your attitude," he called after me. "Look, I can write the story with or without your help. Only then it might not come out the way you'd like it to come out. No guarantees of course."

I looked at Zeke who looked puzzled. I told him I would be gone for a while. I looked at my watch. It was almost one thirty. I suggested we drive over to MARCO's for lunch. The reporter happily agreed. On the way, I asked him how far the wire service reached. He told me it was national and international, but that this story would probably stay in the state. I felt relieved. We found an empty booth and both of us ordered hamburgers and fries. We also ordered strawberry milkshakes.

"Good day for shakes," the reporter said sucking on his straw. "The thing is, I don't know if this is a story or not. I'll have to pitch it to my boss. What do you think?"

I shrugged. The reporter grinned.

"I mean frankly it's a zany idea, you know," Daren Erskine said. "A quiet little hamlet in the middle of nowhere, let's say at the very heart of America, having a World Premiere of a movie. It's kind of crazy, really. But then that's the story."

I just looked at the reporter as I finished my milkshake, making strange gurgling sounds as the last of it came up through my straw.

"Okay," he said. "I guess what I'm interested in is how this all came about." He produced a small notebook and pencil. "So, begin at the beginning."

I told him the whole story except for the part about the Fourth Way episode and the two men from Vegas.

"So, let me get this straight," he said, writing furiously in his notebook. "It was the handwritten note on the letter informing you that you won a writing contest that...well basically changed your life...so to speak?"

I nodded.

"Yet everyone at..." he quickly glanced down at his notes... "at Starburst/Meade Productions denied writing it."

"Yep," I said and fired up a smoke. I offered him one, but he said he didn't smoke.

"So, did you ever find out who did write it?"

I looked at my watch and then shrugged.

"I have to get back to work."

I took the reporter back to the mortuary to get his car. Before he left I invited him to the premiere which was set to take place in one week – Saturday night.

To help publicize the event a crude flyer was made and run off on a mimeograph at the mortuary. In large bold print the flyer said:

Charles A. Kendall and the Wolf Theater present the world premiere of - COBRA WOMAN VERSUS THE PRAIRIE WOLVES IN THE VORTEX OF THE VALLEY OF DARKNESS. – an action packed new movie, never before seen. Adult admission, 50 cents, Kids under twelve, 25 cents.

With date and time on the bottom of the flyers they were tacked up on every telephone pole around the county, left on counters in restaurants and other business in town, on car windshields and on the doorstep of homes. Tony and his boys helped.

The local paper did a story on the upcoming premiere. The story quoted a few random locals who said they had heard about the event and were looking forward to it, and that it was particularly exciting to hear that WOLF would be open again. I was named as the local boy who brought the movie home, as if there were something heroic about it.

While preparing envelopes one evening to send flyers to businesses at the county seat, Zona said something very strange.

"I tell you I never thought Royce's little joke would come to this," she said, talking mainly to herself. But when she looked up and saw me staring at her, her face went flat and then she gave me a hurried smile, apparently in an attempt to have her comment dismissed. We were in the kitchen. Royce was in the living room watching television. I had been munching on a cheese sandwich which I put down and joined Zona at the kitchen table. I continued to stare at her.

"Gracious," she said without looking at me. "Whatever made me say that?"

"What did you mean by my father's little joke?" I asked.

"Oh, nothing," Zona said. "How about a cup of coffee? I'll make some."

I could tell she was nervous, her hands trembling as she ran her tongue along an envelope to seal it. I reached over and put my hand on her wrist as she started to pick up another envelope.

"What did you mean, Zona?"

She looked at me now.

"Okay, okay," she said. "You remember that hand-written note on that letter you got from California, about the contest you won?"

I nodded slowly and pulled the letter from my pocket, unfolded it and laid it out on the table in front of Zona. "You mean this one?"

Zona stared at it, took a deep breath and nodded.

"Well, it's all so silly," she said. "I mean who do you think wrote it?"

I continued to look at her without reacting.

"Well, it was Royce. At his insistence I steamed open the letter when it first arrived and...well...he read it and said we should write a note, like it's personal. Our little joke, he said. Well the truth is, I actually wrote it and he kind of dictated the message.

She looked at me with a forlorn expression as if she'd just lost her best friend.

I looked away and then back at her again.

"I mean, it was just a silly joke...only when you took it real seriously, well I was going to tell you, but Royce wouldn't let me. I know he pretended otherwise but he thought it would be good for you to...you know."

I felt stunned and thought what a stupid fool I'd been to think I was going to start my career writing movies. All a lie. And for a moment I considered scrapping the premier and burning the film. But, I figured it was too late for that. I had to go ahead with it now.

Zona started to say more, but I left the letter on the table and walked out. I went to the WOLF. It was almost eight o'clock. To my sur-

465

prise, Tony and his friends were there working, finishing up last minute details. We took down the banner and put the large red plastic letters up on the marquee, spelling out: World Premiere of the movie.

"You think anyone will come?" Tony said later when we were finished for the night.

"I don't know," I said. "I guess if there isn't much on the tube that night."

Chapter 53

The week slipped by fast and Saturday, the day of the premiere, was suddenly upon us. We were scrambling to get ready for the evening's event. Tony had called the high school earlier in the week and got the band to come and play in front of the WOLF. Meanwhile, the young waitress at MARCO's, who chewed gum faster than anyone I'd ever seen before, asked if any of the stars were going to show up for the Premiere.

"They always have stars of movies at their premieres you know," she said.

I told her they were all probably working on other films. She looked disappointed. I went home and put on a rented tuxedo. Zona helped me with the tie. Back at the theater I did one last check of everything including the projectors, which I had cleaned and tested. It was time to declare the WOLF Theater ready for action. Some of the women from a local sewing club made shirts with the legend, "Cobra Woman Versus The Prairie Wolves" with a crude picture of a cobra encircling the words for Tony and his helpers to wear during the event. The town was buzzing and there was a renewed sense of life in the air.

At about 5:30, sheriff Crowley showed up at the theater. He needed to talk to me right away, privately.

"You sound real serious, sheriff," I said.

"I'm afraid it's serious," he said, his voice subdued.

"Is it about my mother?"

The sheriff shook his head. I shrugged and led the way into the tiny office just off the lobby that once had been Henry and Cora Zickwolf's. I could feel my heart racing now as I went behind the desk and sat down. The sheriff's lined face looked very glum as if someone close had just died. My first thought was that maybe I needed a special permit or something. Sam Crowley just stood there for an awkward moment, his large frame and girth practically filling the tiny space. He sat down in the chair opposite the desk and bent his head down.

"Okay," I said. "What is it?"

"You know, Charles I've known you since you were a pup, known your whole family. They're part of this community. Even knew Adele since she was a young woman, god rest her soul. I don't always agree with Royce, but still always considered him a friend. Course, with the stroke and all don't see much of him these days."

I fired up a smoke, leaned back and watched the sheriff grapple with whatever it was he had come to say.

"And," he went on, "I admire the fact that you brought this movie of yours back to your home town so that in a way it is all of ours to share. That's why it pains me to have to do this."

"Do what?"

"Shut you down," he said.

I took a drag on my smoke and waited. The sheriff took his hat off and scratched his large florid face.

"Man came out here from California to stop you from showing your movie, Charles. I'm real sorry."

"How's that possible?" I said.

"Got a court order," the sheriff said. "Or, so I'm informed by the clerk at the court."

"Let's see it," I said.

"Don't have it yet. Man's gonna meet me here." The sheriff looked at his watch. "Anytime now."

We sat there silently for several long moments, avoiding eye contact. I shut my eyes and tried to think who could be behind this?

"Spent many an evening in this old theater," sheriff Crowley said absently. "Lots of memories. You too, I imagine."

"Can you tell me who's doing this?" I said.

The sheriff grimaced and shook his head.

"Me," a voice said just as the large shape of a man appeared in the doorway. He had on a light tan jacket, pink shirt open at the collar, a broad brimmed hat and dark glasses. He took off his hat and removed his sunglasses which he shoved into a breast pocket. My mouth fell open.

"How you doin' Tuckie?"

"You know this man?" Sheriff Crowley said.

I nodded. Mark Horgan introduced himself to the sheriff and handed him a large manila envelope. The sheriff opened it and looked over the papers.

"Yep, this is a legal order to cease and desist, Charles," The sheriff said. "Nothing I can do."

I found myself staring up at Mark Horgan, hardly listening to the sheriff.

"What're you doing here?" I said.

"Chasing after you. I shoulda figured you might come back to your home town. I looked all over San Francisco and the Sausalito waterfront for you, then back to L.A. Saw Maggie. She said she didn't know where you went. I even caught up with Silky who said she didn't know anything."

"Where did you find her?"

"Actually it was an accident. I saw her on the street one night hustling for tricks. She's now living with some old guy in a car up near Griffith Park."

I stubbed out my cigarette and shook my head as I tried to picture Silky in such circumstances. It just seemed like she was determined to go under.

"How'd you find me?" I said to Mark.

Mark laughed.

469

"Hell, it was in the newspaper. A story on the wire out of Chicago about a wacky world premiere in this flyspeck of a town, which ain't even on the map in the heart of America."

"Jesus," I said. "I wonder if those people from Vegas saw the story?"

Mark wiped his brow with his handkerchief.

"I wouldn't worry about it," Mark said. "Those two hoods that came around disappeared and their boss is now up on federal charges for racketeering. But, Moe Miller and his investors want the film and I've been sent here to collect it."

"One showing tonight?" I said.

Mark shook his head. I looked from him to the sheriff who just sat there staring at the floor.

"How can we cancel," I said. "Folks are coming from miles around."

Mark shrugged.

"Can't help that," he said and looked at the sheriff. "Sheriff, I can take it from here."

Sheriff Crowley stood up.

"Sorry, Charles," he said. "I'll be available."

He waived his hat and left. I had an idea and excused myself, telling Mark I'd be right back. I went to the rear of the theater behind the screen and found Tony in the storage room going through stills Maggie had shot during the making of the film. There were several action shots of Silky and the other actors including Mark. I told Tony to feature Mark's picture in the poster windows with his name printed underneath.

"Why his picture?" Tony asked. "Is he one of the stars?"

"Yeah, and he's here. Special appearance. Come all the way from Los Angeles."

"You shittin' me?" Tony said. "Wait till I tell folks when they come."

I looked at my watch. It was now 6:15.

"Spread the word that one of the stars would arrive at seven o'clock," I said.

I went back to the office and found Mark standing outside the door. I invited him to go to MARCO's with me for coffee. He looked at his watch.

"I don't know. I've got a rental car which I'm driving back to the airport tonight and it's a long drive. How far is this place?"

I told him it was just a few minutes away.

"I have some things I want to tell you about," I said.

Mark looked at me with wary eyes.

"Okay, but it will have to be quick."

We took Mark's car. At MARCO's we took a booth. The young waitress brought coffee for me and a coke for Mark. She glanced up at the clock on the wall behind the counter then back at me.

"You look real cute in your tuxedo," she said. "Aren't you supposed to be at the theater? When I get off I'm coming to see your movie. I'm real excited."

Mark watched after her as she went behind the counter to pick up an order.

"Too bad," he said.

"So, how's your mother?" I asked.

"Good," he said.

"Doing any singing?"

"I don't have time for this chit-chat," he said. "What was it you wanted to tell me?"

I sipped my coffee and fired up a smoke and eyed Mark over the rim of my cup. His demeanor was flat, no expression at all.

"You know," I said. "Moe will just put that movie in a warehouse somewhere and write it off. It will never be seen."

Mark was stoic.

"Yeah, probably," he said finally. "I mean Damn, why'd you get mixed up in that Margo Benson business anyway? I always thought Maggie had something to do with her death. But it eventually became clear that Margo had gotten mixed up with the wrong crowd. Makes no difference. Moe wants the film and he's my client."

471

I told Mark that if it hadn't been for the Margo Benson business I never would have met him and he would not have been in my movie. He just looked at me and said he appreciated the irony. I then leaned across the table and spoke in a high whisper.

"All your work for nothing," I said. "I mean you are one of the stars. This is your chance. Your mother would want this, for her son to be seen in a film acting and singing. All the training heading for the cesspool. I'll bet she'd be real proud knowing folks somewhere had seen her boy perform."

Mark looked away and let out a soft whistle.

"You can get real intense, can't you?" He said. "Can't do it." He glanced up at the clock behind the counter. "Shit, it's almost seven. Let's go."

I figured my little plan was not going to work and resigned myself to the fact that I would have to turn the film over to Mark and cancel the premiere. I felt sick to my stomach as we drove back to the theater.

The high school band was out in front of the theater playing. Two majorettes were performing routines to the music. A large crowd had gathered along the sidewalk, spilling out onto Main Street to the point of blocking half the street. We parked in a driveway next to the theater. As we approached the crowd, I scanned the faces, many of which I'd never seen before. It looked like folks had come from all over, from low country to the south, and small hamlets that made up the northern edge of the county. In the most recent newspaper article publicizing the event I was referred to as "The County's own Charles Kendall" in a caption under a picture of me they had taken the week before.

As the band played its own peculiar rendition of "Strike Up The Band," sheriff's deputies were busy trying to hand out notices that the event had been canceled. But it looked like people were too caught up in the excitement of the moment to pay any attention to the flyers, most of which were finding their way to the ground. It was a little after seven and the crowd was continuing to swell as more and more people showed up, many of them teenagers in pickup trucks, roadsters, and motorcycles. A

472

long line had formed at the box office where Tony had stationed himself to sell tickets.

People in the crowd turned to see who had arrived and began waving and shouting as I made my way through the crowd, with Mark close behind me. I had an idea and pointed to Mark, shouting that he was one of the stars of the movie. Suddenly Mark found himself swallowed up by his new instant fans, sucking him in like quicksand. A sea of hands reached out for him with pieces of paper to sign.

"What's this?" Mark yelled at me above the cheers.

I shook my head and put my hands over my ears. Sheriff Crowley was standing on the periphery of the crowd looking perplexed. I realized that the mass of folks could easily turn into an angry mob. It looked like the sheriff was trying to wade through, but kept getting pushed back. Some of the men standing on the street in bib overalls and T-shirts gestured angrily to the sheriff to stay out of it. He then moved around to the other side and signaled his deputies to stand back. A few minutes later, two radio station reporters were getting interviews along with a TV reporter and cameraman from a television station upstate.

Meanwhile Mark was being carried along by the first wave of the crowd into the theater. And before he realized it he was into the role of celebrity, completely caught up in the moment. I watched as he nodded at fans, shaking hands, smiling, and signing autographs. At one point he looked over at me and threw up his hands in surrender. The lobby was now packed and it was hard to move. I just grinned at Mark and waived. Then someone held up one of the notices and yelled at the top of his voice that the premiere had been canceled. And for a moment it was as if the world stopped and the voices in the lobby became hushed, faces suddenly looked angry. I quickly found a chair by the candy stand, got up on it and yelled that the notice was wrong and the premiere would go on as scheduled. Mark confirmed by nodding. You could feel a sigh of relief zip through the crowd and the noise level resumed.

I began greeting people as they streamed into the theater to get seats. Some recognized me, I guessed from the photo in the paper and asked me to pose with them, which I did. Others who knew me were congratulatory. It was all very exhilarating. This was my moment, I thought, the peak of my so called career.

Someone tapped my shoulder. I turned around to see Cora Zickwolf standing there smiling at me. She did not say anything, just reached up on the tip of her toes and kissed me lightly on the cheek. "Henry would have been so proud," she said in my ear. She then went into the theater. As the crowd thinned out in the lobby, I spotted Zona wheeling Royce in through the front doors. She saw me and came over.

"This is really something, Charles" she said. "All this excitement right here in our little town." She reached up and straightened my bow tie which had gone askew. "You're not mad about what I told you, are you?"

I shook my head.

"Just goes to show I never really did know my father very well."

I looked over at Royce. He looked a sad sight from the blustering robust person I remembered when I was growing up. Zona was watching me.

"I've been with Royce a long time now and I still don't know the man," Zona said. "I do know one thing though, deep down he loves you. He may not have always shown it, but I know it's a strong feeling in him."

Zona kissed me on the lips and went back to stand behind Royce's wheelchair. I watched after her, not really sure what to make of what she had just said. I could see Royce straining to look at me, his solemn face now betrayed by just the hint of a grin on his lopsided lips. Royce? Old Royce Kendall, that rabid anti-communist nut case. He engineered that note? It was still hard to fathom.

I went into the theater, down the aisle and climbed up on the stage and looked out at the filled seats. The place was packed. Standees lined up along the side walls and in back behind the last row of seats. Zona wheeled in Royce and down the aisle to a small cleared section. Marco came in the other door with Vera Fouts and stayed in the back.

I just stood there, frozen. Tony suddenly appeared on stage with me. He quieted the crowd and then introduced me.

474

"Hi," I said. "I'm Tuck...no...I'm Charles Kendall. For those of you who don't know me this is my home town, this is where I grew up. My father is Royce Kendall. He owns Kendall Mortuary."

There was spontaneous cheering and applause as if I'd said he was giving out free tickets to the circus or something. I looked down at Royce and saw a tear rolling down his cheek. I thanked people for coming and introduced Mark as one of the stars of the movie they were about to see.

"Came all the way from Los Angeles just to be with us here today," I said. "Stand up, Mark."

Mark who looked nervous had taken a seat near the front. He stood up and waived to the crowd. More clapping and cheering.

I cleared my throat. I thanked Cora Zickwolf for allowing Cobra Woman versus the Prairie Wolves to be shown in her theater. I also said I was dedicating the film to the memory of Henry Zickwolf who taught me how to run the projectors, Royce Kendall without whose...help this premiere probably wouldn't be happening, and finally Tony Billings and his gang who helped get the theater ready. There was another round of applause. Then a male voice from somewhere in the audience shouted: "We came here to see a movie!"

I made my way to the projection room and sat down in a chair next to projector number one and closed my eyes. In an instant the lone dark figure of the Wichita kid appeared on the horizon behind my eyes like an apparition. The kid waived to me and then disappeared over a ridge. I waived goodbye. Somehow I did not think I would see the Kid again, though I supposed if I ever needed him he would come.

The building suddenly started shaking as if there were an earthquake. Folks were stamping their feet and hollering, wondering why the movie hadn't started yet. I reached over to the rheostat and turned the lights down. The stomping of feet stopped and I could feel the anticipation of the crowd. I fired up the projector. It always took a few moments before the carbon light reached full power. The projector started rolling. Something I hadn't thought about or expected was music. Ben must have added it. I peered out at the screen through a small square peep window.

The film had started. It began with a black screen and an eerie sound, like from one of those weird musical instruments. Dissolve to the shadow of a woman moving stealthily along and suddenly the shadow is that of a giant cobra which strikes as the music screeches. Cut to:

A long aerial establishing shot of a station wagon driving along a narrow desert road. The title came up, crudely printed but readable: COBRA WOMAN VERSUS THE PRAIRIE WOLVES IN THE VORTEX OF THE VALLEY OF DARKNESS. More clapping and cheers from the audience mixed with laughter. Then the credits rolled. Ben had gotten everyone in there and made his own name bigger than anyone else's.

Cut to interior of the station wagon. Back of the heads of the supposed young newlyweds heading for a camping trip. But something was wrong. Close up of driver, the nice looking young actor who played the husband. It was then I realized I had not done this scene and a strange horrifying foreboding zipped over me. Cut to close angle on woman.

"Oh my god," I said aloud as I stared in total disbelief. There, big as life on the screen was Virgie Lowe looking overly made up, overly dressed, and pretending to examine a map. She turned to the man playing her husband, her face screwed up. Then she looked directly back into the camera. "So what the fuck is it we're supposed to be doing?" This was followed by a giant gasp from the audience. Off camera came the raspy voice of Boyd Imwald. "Cut this goddam motherfucker!"

I fired up a smoke, took a long drag, and screamed against the noise of the projector, then suddenly, uncontrollably laughed, laughed like I'd never laughed before.